DETROIT PUBLIC LIBRARY

3 5674 00736081 2

DETROIT PUBLIC LII

BL

D1216887

DATE DUE

BREAKFAST AT THE HERMITAGE

By *the* SAME AUTHOR:

DINNER AT BELMONT,
  A Novel of Captured Nashville

SUPPER AT THE MAXWELL HOUSE,
  A Novel of Recaptured Nashville

Breakfast at The Hermitage

A NOVEL OF
NASHVILLE REBUILDING

By ALFRED LELAND CRABB

THE BOBBS-MERRILL COMPANY
PUBLISHERS
INDIANAPOLIS   NEW YORK

COPYRIGHT, 1945, BY THE BOBBS-MERRILL COMPANY

PRINTED IN THE UNITED STATES

AUG 5 '75

628

To the

MEN AND WOMEN OF NASHVILLE

WHO HAVE HELPED TO PRESERVE ITS OLD BEAUTY,

TO CREATE ITS NEW

PART ONE: THE FIRST BREAKFAST

PART ONE

THE FIRST BREAKFAST

1

A TWO-HORSE wagon loaded with three human beings and an assortment of plunder wound its slow way along the Murfreesboro Pike. The horses were gaunt and tired, moving along with great effort and under compulsion. The man who drove was slender and wiry, and the wind and rain and sun had wrought their coloring in his face. A long sandy mustache, curving in a graceful sweep downward, gave depth but not variety to his complexion. There was the hint of a twinkle in his little sharp eyes and the hint of a smile upon his face, but fatigue was plainly in the background. He had driven from Huntland in Franklin County with only brief stops to permit refreshments for family and horses. But more than eighty hours of almost continuous driving had not disturbed his good humor. Mr. Courtney Justice's good humor was never disturbed. He had spent his life up to that moment being good-humored. He had hunted foxes in inevitable high humor. He had attended all the political speakings within his range with no abatement of good humor, even if a Republican spoke. Periodic droughts and untimely frosts had never touched the fountains of his good humor. Nothing had. In terms of worldly substance life had not yielded much to Mr. Justice—only those two indifferent horses, that wagon and the plunder therein. Mr. Justice was turning the pages of a new chapter in his life. He knew it, but the consciousness laid no heavy hand upon his native cheer.

"Never saw a purtier day," he observed in tones high-pitched and slightly roughened from much whooping on of hounds hot upon the scent, and from resounding endorsement of proclamations of political faith. His optimism as to the weather apparently went unmarked by either his wife or his son who sat with him on the wagon seat. "Yes sir, we couldn't have a purtier day to go to our new home on. Looks like a good sign to me."

"We haven't any home, Courtney," his wife reminded him.

"We'll get one. I ain't uneasy. Things'll work out. You'll see. I ain't done much by you two, but I aim to."

9

"We haven't complained, Courtney."

"You would have if you wasn't a couple o' angels." Mr. Court-ney's affirmation was made with a proper touch of self-abnegation. Neither his wife nor son replied. They had often been referred to as "angels" in lieu of something more substantial. "You'll see," he repeated, with abiding cheer. "I'm starting new. Did you ever see a new leaf turned over, like the feller said? I'm one. I ain't been the same man since I built that new barn for Mr. Moore."

His wife corrected him. "Helped build it, Courtney."

"Well, yes," admitted her husband. "I reckon you could call Buck Larkin the big boss, but that don't cut much ice. I hit two licks to his one."

"Mr. Larkin was the contractor, Papa," said the son who had a feeling for words.

"Seems like I did hear him called that," Mr. Justice admitted cheerfully. "Now what would you call me, Hunt?"

"You were a carpenter, Papa."

"I reckon that's it. Carpenter? Sounds good, doesn't it? They paid me purty good. Reckon I'll do still better up here."

His economic expectations went uncommented upon by his fam-ily. "Up here in Nashville I won't have so much to take my mind offen my work. Well sir, I'm still glad I give them houn's to Pink Mason for nothin' instid o' sellin' them to Gran Lipscomb for ten dollars. Pink'll treat 'em better."

"Maybe his children won't get as much to eat now."

"Dogs or children, Pink is a good provider. I'll miss them houn's though."

His wife and son knew that he would miss them but there seemed no need for a reply. Besides they were terribly tired. Huntland was a long way off and much of the road was rough. They had many times dropped off to sleep during the night but the shock of the wagon dropping into a pothole had rudely broken off each period of sleep. Mr. Courtney Justice had closed his eyes only briefly since they left Huntland, but for him that was no great ordeal. Often the chase had lasted through the night with no visible drain upon his strength, certainly none upon his good cheer. The horses, too, knew that Huntland lay far to the southward. Eight times they had been fed corn from the sacks in the rear of the wagon, but their harness had remained on them, and loss of sleep was more exhausting to them than to their owner. They were gaunt and weary and took each step with obvious effort.

"Look, Mama, look, Papa, isn't that a pretty house?" The boy pointed to the left. Happiness shone through the fatigue in his eyes. "Just look at it, Mama."

"It does look mighty fine," said his mother.

"What makes you all the time interested in houses, Hunt?" asked Courtney Justice. "I never saw such a boy." But Hunt did not reply. He was looking back at the home.

Presently Mr. Justice resumed his commentary. "Never had a notion of moving to Nashville when I started building Mr. Moore's barn." His wife opened her lips to remind him that he had merely assisted in the building but closed them before a word issued. She knew that Mr. Justice would at intervals throughout his days mention that he had built Mr. Moore's barn, that in time Buck Larkin would fade out of the barn's construction, leaving him its sole builder. Mrs. Justice knew her husband; at any rate she used to know him. Lately some qualities had entered into him that puzzled her greatly. She was never more surprised than when he sold the underprivileged little farm that yielded the family meager sustenance. That was followed hard upon by giving away the four hounds that had been his pride and joy. And that night he had announced that ere the month had lived out its days they would remove to Nashville, there to live permanently.

"Courtney!" His wife's voice was sharp. "What's the matter with you? What are you talking about?"

"Nothin' to get excited about," he said cheerfully. "Well, set down, both of you. I reckon I'd better tell you. I've turned over a new leaf, as the feller said. I've sawed and hammered a little all over this part of the country and never thought nothing about it. But I hadn't been buildin' Mr. Moore's barn more'n two days when I had a change. Yes sir, I had a change. Somehow, I liked that job fine. That's the first time I ever saw much to hammerin' and sawin'. It got so I just loved to see that barn go up. One day when I was quitting work, Mr. Moore said, 'Come here, Court, I want to talk with you.' For a minute I was right skeered he was a-goin' to give me my walkin' papers, but he wasn't. He bragged on my work, said I ort to have men workin' for me stid o' the way it was, said you was a fine woman and I ort to give you a better show, said Hunt ort to have a better chance'n he could get down here. He talked a right smart. He said we ort to move out o' Huntland; said it looked like I went fox huntin' just to give the saw briers a chance to grow in my cawn fiel', said mebbe I ort to move to Nashville; said he'd heard there was plenty of work for a feller there; said if I done as good as I had on his barn I could have fellers workin' for me inside a year. What was that word you said, Hunt?"

"Contractor." The boy's tired eyes were shining.

"That's it. Now, you watch. Inside a year I'll be one of them. You both know I am a changed man or I'd a-never give them houn's away."

"I knew you were something, Courtney," his wife said.

"I got a good price for the place. Mr. Looney is a-goin' to pay cash. You'll have to sign the deed, Lizzie."

That was only two short weeks ago and here they were nearing Nashville. The past lay behind them, its bridges overturned. There was fear in the woman's eyes, the fear of one facing the untried, the unknown, but there was the brightness of hope, too. The boy's eyes were bright and eager. There was no shift in the good cheer so clearly lined on Mr. Justice's face. It was a morning in late September. There was the dim vague feel of frost in the air, but the days were clinging tenaciously to their warmth. They would not yield to frost for yet a while. The corn was cut and placed in shocks that spaced the fields with a design proportioned and satisfying. The skies were softened by the fragile vestments of autumn and a faint mist touched the distant hills with lovely unreality. Above, a sprinkling of crows wheeled in their aimless courses, and their hoarse cries turned to music, finding its perfect part in the symphony of September.

The tired team toiled up the long hill. At its summit Mr. Justice motioned with his whip.

"There's Nashville," he said. "We're just about there."

They were then within plain view of the city. There towering was the University of Nashville, lately become Peabody College, and there was the lower bulk of the Howard School. In the background Fort Negley dominated the city's southern borders. The faint irregular grill of the streets was discernible. They dropped down the long grade of the town side of the ridge on past the junction with Chicken Pike and within a few moments they had crossed the boundaries of Nashville, and the wagon was moving along Lafayette Street. The fear in the woman's eyes had deepened. She touched her husband's arm.

"Courtney, what are we going to do?"

He looked at her. "Don't you worry, Lizzie," he said cheerfully, "it'll work out all right. You'll see if we don't sleep in our own house tonight." She did not reply and his eyes rested upon her very intently for a moment. "You're tired, honey. I'll tell you what; mebbe we ort to go stay at a hotel till tomorrer. We got some money."

"No," she said sharply. "Let's find a house like you said."

He looked at her again. "All right, but right now we a-goin' to rest them hosses and let 'em eat a bite. A snack wouldn't hurt us neither." He pulled the team into a street to the right. Presently they came to a vacant block, overgrown with young hackberry and Osage orange trees. He guided the team into a little cleared place. "Wait a minute. I want to look aroun' a speck." He was back in two minutes. "Now ain't we lucky? There's a spring back there with plenty o' water for the hosses. Looks good enough for folks. What you say, Lizzie, we start a fire and bile some o' them eggs in that bucket? No, I'll do it. I want you both to rest. Can't go to our new home all frazzled out." He assembled the unburned fragments of a previous fire and soon had a fire burning merrily. He lifted a bucket from the wagon bed and, carrying it in one hand, he led the horses toward the spring in the rear.

Nashville was booming then and Mr. Justice soon found that there were not many houses available for his new home. They would take a street, drive its length, then move over to the next one as one progresses who plows corn. Two or three times they found vacant houses but they were in such wretched condition that the Justices didn't stop long.

"There'll be a nice one, you just wait. Everything'll be all right, Lizzie. It'll work out all right."

But the fear in his wife's eyes had deepened. "I wish we were back at home, Courtney." Her voice was scarcely above a whisper. They turned into Oak Street.

"Look there, Lizzie." Her husband pointed with his whip. It was a crude sign in the yard that had caught his alert eyes.

TO LET
See Owner Next Door

"Whoa," he said and the tired horses quickly obeyed. The three looked. "Purty, ain't it? I guess that's the one, Lizzie. What you say?"

"I guess so, Courtney." Mrs. Justice's voice was just above a whisper.

The boy's eyes were shining. "I like it, Papa. I think it's fine. We could have flowers."

"Hold the reins, Hunt. I guess I better go over there and see the feller."

"Be careful, Courtney. It might be too high."

"I like it, Papa," said Hunt Justice.

The "feller" proved to be a woman. She stood in the doorway and placed her large brown hands on ample hips while Mr. Justice mentioned a possible interest in the house to which he pointed. For a full minute she made no answer but when she removed her eyes, Courtney Justice had been explored in full detail physically, socially and economically. Mrs. Callie Elrod's eyes then came to a stop, focused upon the wagon and its occupants. She said:

"I won't rent to anyone I don't see beforehand. Bring 'em in here."

Mr. Justice returned to his family. "Get out, Lizzie. You, too, Hunt. She wants to see you."

The boy climbed down from the wagon seat. The woman sat looking at her husband uncomprehendingly.

"She don't want any onery people in her house. Mebbe she ain't so sure about me. She wants to see you."

They went up on the porch where Mrs. Elrod stood, hands on hips, awaiting them.

"Well, ma'am, here we are. My name's Courtney Justice. This lady's my wife and he's my boy."

"That's all?"

"They ain't no more, ma'am."

The woman's eyes surveyed Lizzie Justice in great detail. Then, they rested briefly upon the boy. She removed her hands from her hips and said, "I guess you want to see inside the house."

"Yes," said Lizzie Justice.

"I expect I'll rent it to you. Wait'll I get the key."

They walked across the yard to the vacant house. Mrs. Elrod did not look at them again. Her investigation had been completed. At the front porch she spoke to Courtney Justice.

"I reckon you'll want to see the barn. It isn't much but it'll keep your plugs dry. You go look at it while we look inside."

Twenty minutes later they stood out in the yard of the little house on Oak Street. It was much warmer and thin rifts of gray-blue September clouds drifted languidly across the sky, at intervals dimming but never concealing the sun. Now and then a leaf, its stem old and numb, lost its hold upon the bough and sank reluctantly to the ground as though feeling beyond its zest for life that it was time to go. The air was heavy with a soft, sleepy silkiness that one half expected to touch when he reached out his hand.

"It'll be raining tomorrer," said Courtney Justice with cheerful irrelevance.

Mrs. Elrod did not seem to hear him. She turned to Mrs. Justice. "You want to live here?"

"I like it," said Lizzie Justice, and her eyes were upon her son.

"We could have flowers there." He pointed to the margins of the yard. Again Mrs. Elrod's eyes rested speculatively upon the boy.

"Well, you can have it. Eight dollars a month. Man yesterday would have paid me ten. Didn't like him. Could get twelve if it wasn't for the graveyard."

"Graveyard!"

"It makes some people uneasy." The eyes of Lizzie Justice and her son followed Mrs. Elrod's gesture. They saw it then. Across the street, beyond a line of straggling shrubbery was a great sprinkling of gravestones, a few white with newness, most of them dull with the gray of age, most low and modest, a few towering as if death had not weakened the arrogance of life.

"I saw them before we stopped." Courtney Justice's sharp little eyes had had long whetting from searching the terrain for fleeing foxes.

"I don't think it will bother me," said Lizzie Justice.

"It oughtn't to," said Mrs. Elrod; "dead people are safer'n living ones. There's a lot o' stealin' now but none on this street. I say they ain't nothin' like a graveyard to keep scalawags off. They ain't many buryin's any more. Place's just about filled up."

For a long moment there was silence. "Better take it," continued Mrs. Elrod. "It's not that I'm in a hurry to rent it. I can do that any day. I think maybe you'd make respectable neighbors and I guess your boy'll want to go to school. The new academy ain't so far."

"We'll take it," said Lizzie Justice.

"I'm agreeable," said her husband. "I'm not skeered o' graveyards. I've slept in 'em."

"If Mr. Elrod had left fox huntin' alone, he might not be sleepin' in one now. What else you do?"

Courtney Justice's mouth opened in the center to reply. Then the opening traveled to the right until it came closest to his son who stood at his side almost hidden from Mrs. Elrod.

"What's that word?" The voice issued from the corner of his mouth, after the fashion of a ventriloquist.

"Contractor," said Hunt, catching his father's cue and speaking in low tones.

"I'm a contractor, ma'am."

Mrs. Elrod smiled frostily. She had not missed the play. "If you're that highfalutin' maybe I ought to charge you more. Well, it ain't for me to give advice but you better forget about fox hunting if you want to get along at . . . what was that word, son?"

The boy gulped. "Contractor," he said.

"You've done got your first job," said Mrs. Elrod. "I can use a contractor on my back paling fence, first rate. I guess what's the matter with it now was the man I got to put it up was just a carpenter."

A trace of pink grew into the background of Courtney Justice's browned face, but he said nothing.

"Don't bother about my fence. You can work on it any time you're not busy at your contracting." She turned to go. Then she faced them again. "I'm goin' to fix supper for all of you. You'll have all you can do to get that plunder in and set."

Lizzie Justice's protest was one of the conventions of the country people. "We don't want you to go to any trouble. . . ."

"Supper'll be ready just about sundown. You got work to do and you need sleep."

"It's mighty neighborly of you," said Courtney Justice.

Mrs. Elrod moved with decisive steps across the yard toward her home. Then she stopped and pivoted about. "I'm askin' eight dollars a month. Cash in advance. Save's misunderstanding."

Courtney Justice's right hand moved toward the pocket in which he kept his wallet.

His weather forecast went wrong. It did not rain the next day. The clouds had disappeared and a chill crispness had come into the clear air.

"Turned cold without rainin'. Hope it doesn't frost for a while yet. Catch a lot of late stuff back home."

"This is home now, Courtney," corrected his wife. "I guess you'll go looking for work today, won't you?"

"I aim to." But there was no enthusiasm in his affirmation. "I

guess I'll go try that man she told about." He pointed in the general
direction of the house next door.

"You ought to go early. You'd stand a better chance."

"All right, all right," he said, lifting his hat from the post of
the chair on which it hung. "If I don't get back don't wait dinner
for me. Maybe he'll want me to start right in. Hunt, you rastle
some stovewood for your ma, somehow. If you don't see me before
supper you'll see a hungry man then."

"Take Hunt with you." There was tension in the woman's voice.
Her husband looked at her curiously and a bit tenderly.

"I reckon you can trust me, Lizzie. You know I ain't no hand
with a bottle and I expect there ain't a fox houn' in the whole
town."

"Take him with you, Courtney. Let him see around. We going
to start him to a school and he won't get to see much after that.
Take him with you. If you got that stovepipe fixed I'll take care of
the stovewood."

"It's fixed, Lizzie. Going to start him to the school she told
about?" His head motioned again toward the Elrod home.

"I've been thinking about it. Leave your money here, Courtney.
It isn't safe carrying it about in your pocket. You won't be needing
it."

"I reckon I won't, but I'm right keerful." He handed his wallet
to her. She stood watching them as they went on out Oak Street.
Then she went back into the kitchen and began to put her kitchen
things on the shelves where they belonged.

2

Mr. Ed Crayton was so busily and profanely engaged in the dis-
charge of his helper from his further employ that he failed to
observe the approach of Courtney Justice and Hunt.

"And don't you ever let me set eyes on you again." Mr. Crayton
hurled the words at his erstwhile employee's retreating form. "You
ain't no more of a carpenter than I'm President Jeff Davis. If I
ever set eyes on you again I'll—I'll . . ." Unable to formulate ex-
plicitly his procedure in the event his helper returned to visibility,
he gasped and sat down on a timber, mopping his brow furiously.
Presently he looked up and saw Courtney Justice.

"What you want?" He roared with such explosiveness that
Courtney Justice temporarily forgot what he wanted. "I ought to
have killed him!" Mr. Crayton surveyed the situation and lowered

his voice. "You know which end of a hammer to hit a nail with? Next time I will kill him. You ever carpentered any?"

The question restored Court's aplomb. "I've just finished building Mr. Moore's barn."

"Oh, you did! Now ain't that grand! He ain't fit to live, no sir! Well, you're hired. Six bits a day and if you make a mess like that other feller done you better hide out, brother, 'cause I done used up all my kindness and forbearance on him. What you think he done? Well, I'll tell you. I was away not more'n two hours yestidy and it'll take twicet that long to fix up the botch he made. The minute I turned my back he cut loose and put in two-by-fours in that framing instid of two-by-sixes like the contract called for. Why? 'Cause they were stacked closer, and besides, he ain't got nothin' a-tall from the ears up. He got some of the sheathin' on, too. Now we got to tear it all out and start over. You just happen by, Mister?"

"Mrs. Elrod sent me."

"She did? You mean Callie Elrod?"

"Yes, sir. We rented her house. She lives on Oak Street."

"That's her. If she sent you I reckon I got to treat you right. Your pay'll be a dollar a day. I aim to treat Callie's friends right. But—" and his voice became threatening—"I'll take a leg off you if you ain't worth it. That your boy? Well, he's hired, too. Two bits a day. Got to get this litter cleaned up and this stuff straightened out. Can't tell where anything is. You two git to work right now."

"He's a-goin' to start in to school."

"Well, he ain't started yet. Won't hurt him to work till he does. What was it you said you been doin'?"

"I put up Mr. Moore's barn for him."

"Well, git it out o' your head this is a barn. It's a house and it's got to be put up like a house. It's got to look like a house. You, son, you look like you got sense. Pile this litter over there out of the way till we can haul it off. Straighten all this stuff out where a feller can get what he needs without hunting two weeks for it." He turned to Courtney. "You rip them two-by-fours out and then you put two-by-sixes in just like it says on the specifications. Sence you ain't got your tools with you I'll lend you some, but if you don't use 'em right it'll take more'n Callie Elrod to keep me from getting riled—and I'm dangerous when I do, brother! You get that stuff ripped out, and two-by-sixes put in. I ort-a killed him." He went on down the street.

Courtney Justice looked at his employer's retreating form a

moment. "That's getting hired right sudden-like," he said cheerfully. "I'm purty lucky, Hunt. We got the wrong size in Mr. Moore's barn once and I had to rip them out. I know prezackly what to do."

Late in the evening the man and the boy returned to the home on Oak Street. Lizzie Justice waited on the porch for them, though there was chill in the evening air.

"We're hired, Lizzie," her husband announced cheerfully, when he was halfway up the walk.

"I was getting a mite anxious. What you been doing, Hunt?"

"I've been working, too, Mama."

"You ort to have heard Mr. Crayton—he's the one Mrs. Elrod sent us to—brag on him. Said he was the best hand to clean up he ever had."

"He liked Papa's work, too, Mama."

"I found what I'm to do," said Courtney with cheerful pedantry. "I was well nigh certain when I worked on Mr. Moore's barn. I am certain now. Mr. Crayton's a right keerful man but I satisfied him. Dollar a day straight."

"I get a quarter, Mama."

"I'm glad your daddy's got work, but you're going to school. I wouldn't have come here if it hadn't been for that."

"I reckon he can work some. On Saturdays maybe. I told Mr. Crayton he might start to school before long."

"Before long! Courtney Justice, he's not going to wait till before long. I'm taking him tomorrow."

If Courtney Justice was a new man there were also signs that his wife was a new woman. He had never seen in her such a quality of determination.

"If it wasn't for him going to school I wouldn't-a moved up here," she repeated. Her husband's mouth popped open in sheer surprise but he quickly regained control.

"All right, Lizzie, all right. I expect you're right. Better get him started. Supper about ready, Lizzie?"

3

Principal Joseph Yeatman of the Academy regarded with disgust the record books before him.

"They expect me to keep books on the boys' immortal souls,"

he complained. But he was principal, and there were obligations that he could not evade. One was that he must know his boys—all phases of his boys. He was thinking of them then, studying them as they marched across the field of his inward vision. It was his belief that one stitch of considered observation might save nine of discipline. Bart Halloran for instance. Bart's mind was most pleasingly active. But so was his body, at times disturbingly active. He must give thought to Bart. His mind moved to Gordon Hicks, then to Ivo Burns. Ivo was the dandy of the Academy. Somewhat oddly, Ivo's companions by common consent assigned him special privilege. He could, with assurance, wear clothes and use words which essayed by any other boy in the Academy would have resulted unpleasantly. One day Ivo replied to a question asked him on the playground, "I'd *rother* not say." The boys filled the air with their derision. Their ridicule pleased them so much that they built it into an antiphonal chant, the use of which was their main recreation for two days. One group would in unison call out, "What did Ivo say?" And the other group would answer in full voice, "Ivo said he'd *rother* not say." And Ivo stood on the side lines and smiled with faint loftiness.

It was of Ivo that Mr. Yeatman was thinking, and a faint smile wreathed its way across his classic features. Just then a knock sounded imperatively. The principal hoped that it wasn't a matter of discipline. Such seemed to him no more than a necessary futility. But it was discipline. The door opened and Professor Clark stood there, a towering six feet two of him. A dangerous fire glowed in his eyes and his right hand gripped fiercely the shoulder of Bart Halloran, whom he was propelling across the threshold and into the office.

The principal spoke tentatively. "Ah, Professor Clark," he said.

Professor Clark came to a stop. "Sir, as I recall your instructions as to discipline, matters within the classroom belong to the instructors, but elsewhere to you, sir. May I inquire if that is correct?"

"Yes, Professor Clark, that is correct."

"Then he's your case." Professor Clark bent a baleful look upon Bart Halloran and continued. "Though I could wish it were otherwise. I could handle this myself—perfectly, I believe."

"But, Professor Clark, what . . ."

"As I came along the hall just now on the way to your office for a supply of chalk, I passed this—this young man and two of his fellows. This one pretended to slip and fall just in front of me. . . ."

"Ah," said Professor Yeatman, "something like what they call blocking in the sports."

"Precisely, sir, and most reprehensible. I am positive that it was intentional. It was most embarrassing, sir."

The principal's mild blue eyes rested upon the boy, still held in a viselike grasp.

"Very well, Bartley?" he said inquiringly.

"I didn't see him, Professor Yeatman. . . ." The boy's voice was hoarse and uneven. "We were walking in the hall and I slipped. I didn't see Smack Me Down at all."

"Smack Me Down!" said Professor Yeatman in his restrained, quiet voice, into which an arresting quality was introduced.

"Smack Me Down!" said Professor Clark in a loud and outraged voice. "What do you mean?"

"It's what all the boys call you," explained Bart, feeling perhaps that he'd just as well be hanged under one label as another. Then Bart's eyes warmed a bit under the influence of an effort in Irish diplomacy which he was about to undertake.

"I don't think they ought to do it. I don't think it's fair. I wish I hadn't said it. I reckon it just sort of slipped out."

"Smack Me Down?" Professor Yeatman said, still puzzled. Then that faint wisp of a smile retraced its way across his features. "Oh, I see. It's a penalty for those complicated initials of yours."

"Whose initials, sir? Oh, I see. Mine. S. M. D. Smack Me Down! So that's what the boys call me? So that's it!"

The principal was canny in the ways of his staff. He knew, for instance, how Professor Clark's sense of humor might follow hard upon his sense of outrage. He read the signs even then.

"Professor Clark, suppose you deal with Bart yourself. You have my consent." He bent his eyes upon the material on his desk.

"Very well. Thank you, sir." The brawny hand fell firmly upon Bart Halloran's shoulder, and the two withdrew from the office. Two minutes later Professor Clark was back, his face red with restrained mirth.

"Smack Me Down!" he chortled. "Well, I've granted that young jackanapes amnesty—temporarily, you understand. If he ever tries to trip me again I'll dismember him. Smack Me Down!" He chortled loudly. "By the way, Professor Yeatman, what do the boys call you?"

Again the faint wistful smile moved across the principal's face.

"I fear, alas, that my life has been too sheltered. I've never had a nickname."

When Professor Clark had gone, Joseph Yeatman sat in his office and let his boys march across the screen of his vision.

A knock—this time a timid knock—sounded. Professor Yeatman waited a moment, while his faculties reassembled, and then bade someone to come into his office. The door opened and a woman came upon the threshold and stopped there timidly, apologetically. Professor Yeatman's quick and searching glance revealed that she was tall and thin, and that her dress of melancholy black was clean and duly starched. Her face was dark and framed by a bonnet of dark gray gingham. Her regular features were set against a background of fatigue and of strain. A boy of eleven or twelve stood just behind her in the doorway.

"Won't you come in, madam?"

"Are you the professor?"

"I'm one of them. Won't you sit down, madam? And you, too." He placed chairs for both of them, but they remained standing; so did the principal. "Can I be of any service, madam?"

"I want to start him—" she made a slight gesture toward the boy standing just behind her—"I want to start him in your school."

"Sit down, madam. Please." Reluctantly she sat, holding herself stiffly erect.

The boy sat too, his eyes never leaving his mother's face.

Joseph Yeatman had worked indefatigably to increase the attendance of the Academy, but he was conscious of regret for the words he felt obliged to speak.

"I'm very sorry, madam, but the Academy's enrollment has reached the maximum—I mean it is filled," he added hurriedly.

"He won't take much room."

The principal sensed the resolution in the tired, slightly sad voice. "Our enrollment has been large this fall. In fact, I was advised last week by the trustees not to accept any more scholars. I'm very sorry . . ."

"He won't take any room hardly and he won't be no trouble at all." The quiet, tired voice bored into the silence of the office.

"Yes, madam, I know, but I have my orders."

"If it's the money, I have it here." She indicated a purse which she held tightly clenched in her hand.

"It isn't that, madam, I assure you." The principal was embarrassed. "It is merely that we are badly crowded and that I have instructions from my superiors."

"I wouldn't have moved to Nashville except to start him to school. We sold our place . . ."

There was a desperate sort of pleading in the tired, low voice. The principal sensed it and flinched inwardly. The boy felt it and instinctively he laid his hand very gently upon his mother's. For a full half minute the principal said no word. Then he spoke, and his voice was soft with kindness.

"It may very well be, madam, that your son is good enough to atone for my violation of an order. We shall arrange somehow to find a place for him."

"Thank you," she said simply. "I want you to have the money now."

"As you desire, madam. I assume the lad will enter his classes tomorrow."

"Not tomorrow," she said, sharply for the first time. "Now. He will stay now. He brought his dinner with him. Hunt will be a good boy."

"I do not doubt it, madam. Somehow, I feel that I am singularly honored by this meeting."

The strain had gone from the woman's face. She said, "Thank you," after which she whispered something in the boy's ear. Then she went out of the office and down the walk, and the years had fallen from her as an unfastened mantle drops from one's shoulders.

4

The driver of the Weaver Coles's carriage had completed an errand and was cutting across to the Murfreesboro Pike on his way back to Kingsley.

Suddenly from up Carroll Street came a great clatter of running feet, accompanied by the sounds of excited, boyish voices. The driver looked. A boy was running swiftly toward him, and in full chase close upon him were four others. The boy being pursued was obviously in a state of panic. The driver drew his team to a stop. "Whoa," he said to his team, "looks like our side's about to git whupped. Whoa. I expect Gin'ral Lee'd sort o' like for me to help out."

Just then the leader of the chase overtook his prey and, leaping upon him, bore him to the sidewalk. "So you got to go home." He spoke in a high-pitched, mocking voice. "So you got to go home and won't play with us!" He pushed the boy's face violently against the gravel of the street. "So you don't want to play with us." The other three boys stood about regarding the scene approvingly. The driver's dry, laconic voice cut through the confusion.

"I didn't know the Yankees was back; no sir, wasn't expectin' 'em," he said.

The boy loosened the grasp upon his victim. "What Yankees?"

"What Yankees? Ain't you all Yankees?"

The boy was standing. "We're not Yankees," he declared vehemently. The other three added vocal support to his denial.

"You ain't? Well, I declare. You ack jest like you was."

"We don't either. Don't you call us Yankees."

"Well, they's four of you an' they's jest one of him. Any time I see four fellers runnin' lickety-split after one I knows they's Yankees."

"Don't you say we're Yankees."

"I ain't sayin' you is. I'm a-sayin' you bin actin' like Yankees. You ever hear o' four Rebs chasin' one Yankee? Well, I ain't. One Reb'll chase two Yankees, but even Ol' Bed Forrest wouldn't take out after four. Nobody would 'ceptin' Ol' Jawn Hood. But ain't no four Rebs ever chased one Yankee. Shucks, we ain't that pore-mannered. I don't blame you, son, for retreatin'. That's what Gin'ral Lee done when four Yankees took after him."

"We weren't going to hurt him."

"That's jest what the Yankees told Gin'ral Lee; said they wasn't a-goin' to hurt him a-tall, but they didn' fool him none. Nosirree, he retreated!"

"We just wanted him to play with us," explained one of the boys.

The boy spoke for the first time. "I couldn't play. I had to go home. I told my mother I'd come home."

"Any time one Yankee comes at you give him a good whuppin'. If they's two you start retreatin'."

"We are not Yankees, I told you."

"Nosirree. Jest five nice Reb boys. And one o' you's got to go home now. Yessirree, and the rest o' you's a-goin' to walk with him part o' the way to see that no Yanks don't jump on him."

"We'll go," said the much-sobered Bart Halloran, the spokesman of the four. "We was just playing all the time. Where do you live?" he inquired of Hunt Justice.

5

On Saturday morning Mrs. Polk answered a knock which sounded at her side door. A workman stood at the door, holding in his hand a kit of carpenter's tools.

"Mornin', ma'am. Mr. Crayton sent me to fix your back porch."

"He promised all right but I had about given him out," Mrs. Polk said, a little grimly. She looked somewhat uncertainly at the man. "Mr. Crayton promised to repair it himself."

"Yes'm, that's right. He did." The man's voice was the very essence of good cheer. "He aimed to come but we startin' on a new house Monday and he had to get it staked off. We just finished one last night, after dark. Ter'ble lot of buildin' goin' on."

She saw then that a young boy was with him. The man explained, "That's my boy. He helps me some on Saturdays. I reckon, ma'am, the lumber for that repair work's done come."

"Two weeks ago. I'll show you where it is."

All day long the sounds of hammer and saw sounded from the back porch, and now and then Mrs. Polk could hear the cheerful sound of Courtney Justice's voice as he talked with his son. In the early afternoon Mrs. Polk was in the kitchen checking her pantry supplies. The outside door was a bit open and she overheard a conversation from the back porch.

"Papa, you haven't fixed that right. You've left it rough."

"It don't show," said the man's cheerful voice. "I'm in a hurry."

"But, Papa, this is a fine house."

There was a full half minute of silence. Although she could not see them, she could imagine father regarding son in wide-eyed surprise. Then the man spoke. "All right, Hunt, all right. I'll saw that off smooth."

"You must, Papa, you really must."

Mrs. Polk's head was cocked to one side in a characteristic pose and her eyes were shining. Her accidental eavesdropping had discovered a curious bit of dialogue. A young boy reproving his father for careless workmanship. A boy finding beauty in the chaste outlines of Polk Place. So she was not surprised when later in the afternoon she laid down the *Daily American* and, casting a casual glance out the front window, saw the boy standing down near the corner of the yard on Vine Street. And there was a rapt quality in the intentness with which he looked at the house. She put on a light coat and went out into the yard.

"Do you like my house?" she asked.

The boy had not seen her until she spoke. He flushed deeply but he replied in even tones, "I think it is the prettiest house I ever saw."

"Have you seen many fine houses?"

"Mr. Moore's house, but I like yours better."

"Mr. Moore's?"

"Yes'm. We used to live down there. Papa helped build his barn."

"Ah, yes," said Mrs. Polk, remembering that a barn might lend itself to crudities in construction. "Ah, yes. I'm glad you like my house. Wouldn't you like to see inside it?"

"Oh, yes, I would."

"I don't think your father will need you for a few minutes. Come inside."

They went into the house. The boy stood in the hall. To his right an arch of rich woodwork opened into the great parlor. He could catch glimpses of the furniture and furnishings, and the portraits on the wall softened by a dim light. To his left a hand-carved door of walnut opened into the library. He could see rising from the floor tier upon tier of books covered in leather or vellum or fine cloth. Before him the stairs rose gracefully to the rooms above. The boy said nothing but his eyes were warm.

"I love it, too," Mrs. Polk said. "It was built by Mr. Felix Grundy who knew how to plan beautiful things. I have lived here a long time and every year I love the place better. Would you tell me what your name is?"

"Hunt Justice. We haven't lived here long. We used to live at Huntland."

"Huntland? Oh yes, in Franklin County. I know the Moores there, and the Lipscombs. I am Mrs. Polk."

"Mrs. Polk! What Mrs. Polk? Not the—the—"

"Mrs. James K. Polk."

"He was President. . . ." The boy's face was tense with wonder. "We have been studying about him this week. He was a great man. Professor Garrett said he was."

"Then you go to the Academy. How fine!"

"I'm glad for Papa to work on your house. The one he has been building is ugly. I'd hate to live in it."

"May I give you a glass of milk?"

"Thank you, but Mama fixed our dinner for us."

"Yes, but it's been a long time since noon; besides, a boy needs plenty of milk. Come into the kitchen."

He was standing by the table drinking the glass of milk which Mrs. Polk poured when they heard the sounds of horses' hoofs and wheels crunching against the gravel of the driveway. Mrs. Polk moved over a few steps and looked out the window. "Why, it's the driver. I wonder what the Coles are sending me."

She met him at the door. "Come in, sir. It has been months since I saw you."

He came through the door carrying a sack in his hand. "Yes'm, don't git around much no more. I done settled down like a ree-formed fox hunter."

"Don't tell me it is sausage in that sack."

"Yes'm, that's what it is. Weaver Cole killed some hawgs yestidy."

"Bless the boy. He's . . ."

"No'm, he didn't send 'em. His wife said she et her first bite o' Weaver's sausidge at your house, said lots of girls didn't have much luck—all they got was husbands that was rich and good lookin', but that she had real good luck and got one that could make real good sausidge. Said she felt so grateful that you just had to have a sack. An' here I am with 'em, ma'am."

"Merrie makes a good speech," said Mrs. Polk. "What did Weaver say?"

"He jest grinned, ma'am, and fixed up the sausidge. Whereat you want it put, ma'am?"

"Bring it into the kitchen." The driver came into the kitchen. Hunt Justice stood there, an empty milk glass in his hand. The driver's eyes kindled with recognition.

"Hello, Reb. Any more Yanks been after you?"

"No, sir. They were playing. They didn't mean any harm."

"Well," said Mrs. Polk, "so you two know each other. What's this about Yanks?"

"I thought for a minute that they were at it again, but ever'thing turned out jest as friendly as a basket meetin'."

"How nice! A basket meeting sets a good pattern in friendliness. I'm glad you two are acquainted. Hunt thinks Polk Place is very pretty."

"Oh, I do," said the boy. He stopped as if conscious that he had said too much. "I must go now. Papa might need me."

"Where did you know that boy?" Mrs. Polk inquired when Hunt Justice had gone out the door and down the steps.

He told her of the episode out by the Academy.

"Very interesting," said Mrs. Polk, "indeed, very interesting. His father is repairing my back porch. This morning I overheard him reprove his father for some careless work. Later, he was out in the front looking at this house almost with awe in his eyes . . . and then I shall never forget the way he looked at things inside. . . .''

"He's purty young, ma'am, to notice sech things."

"That's why I am noticing him," said Mrs. Polk. "When a young boy notices such things, he's worth noticing. And I propose to notice that child a bit. Well, tell me how things are at Kingsley."

"You didn't make any mistake noticing Weaver Cole, ma'am. He's a born farmer, ma'am. When he looks at the groun' sumpin' starts a-growin'. I think things is mighty fine out there."

"Of course. Ellen and Weaver and Merrie Cole would make things fine anywhere. Does Merrie hear often from her father?"

"She had a letter yestidy. I hear them say he's a-comin' back next summer."

"To stay?" asked Mrs. Polk.

"No'm. He's back a-runnin' his old bizness. Said he thought he could manage to stay a month. Said the mill he used to have was jest about gone busted so he jest natchelly bought it back. Said it was doin' better already. Said he never did fit jest right down here."

"Looks to me as if he fitted pretty well. At any rate, his daughter fits well."

"Yes'm, that's what he said. Said it looked to him like he was sent down here jest to fetch her."

"I can't imagine a better reason. Is Ellen taking things more easily?"

"Not much. She works all the time. They all work. It ain't what I'd call a restin' fam'ly."

"The second time Weaver ever saw Merrie was in this kitchen," said Mrs. Polk with the flavor of satisfying reminiscence in her voice.

"Yes'm, she tol' me that. She's right friendly with me, ma'am."

"Friendly? Of course they're friendly. Even if they weren't, they'd have to be friendly to you. I suppose you're pleased out there."

"Me? I'm havin' a reg'lar picnic, ma'am; that is, exceptin' for the work."

"All you do is work with the horses, isn't it?"

"I work with 'em some, ma'am, but they's a sight mo' of work than that. You see, Mr. Lawrence made more show than he did crops. He put up a passel of fine fences but he got 'em set wrong. You couldn't do good farming with the fiel's like he fixed 'em. So

Weaver Cole's bin takin' up them fences and puttin' 'em down right. I bin helpin' him a right smart. I think I'm awful lucky, ma'am."

"We've had some hard times, all of us; but we've had our share of luck, too."

"I reckon I'd better be goin'. They's a lot o' feedin' to do out there."

"I wish I had something to send to the Coles." She stood for a moment, her finger to her brow. Then she brightened. "Wait a minute," she said. She returned presently with something wrapped in a newspaper.

"Give this to Merrie Cole. It's a picture of the White House with Mr. Polk and me standing on the portico. I'd like for her to have it."

She followed the driver to the door. "That boy—" she motioned toward the sounds from the back porch—"sticks in my mind. A small lad demanding better work of his father, looking spellbound at my home. I think I'll keep an eye on that boy. I tell you what I wish you'd do: Take him out to Kingsley sometime. If he likes houses, he ought to see that one."

"I'd be right pleased, ma'am."

"His name is Hunt Justice and he lives on Oak Street."

"Won't be no trouble to find him. I'll give him an invite some Sattiday. Lots o' times I make two trips then."

He drove around the circle and out into Vine Street singing merrily. When the Cole carriage had passed from view down Vine Street she turned and went out on the back porch.

"Jest finished," said Courtney Justice cheerfully. "I'd like for you to look it over, ma'am."

She looked it over very carefully. The work, though inexpert, was better done than she expected it to be. "It seems to be in very good order."

"I tried to fix it right, ma'am."

"I always look where it doesn't show. This seems all right."

A dull flush crept into his weather-beaten face. "Thanky, ma'am, thanky." He fastened his tool kit. Hunt Justice's bright eyes rested approvingly upon his father.

6

The members of the Old Table Club sat in the parlor at Myrtlewood. The host, Len Whitworth, passed cigars. A fire crackled cheerfully in the fireplace. For a while they talked of the day's current affairs.

The evening's program had for its subject "Our City's Current Pressing Needs." The Methodist preacher, Felix Hill, read a paper. It mentioned a great many needs, naturally the most prominent being the promotion of Nashville's church life. There were not enough buildings to provide places for all who wished to worship. Most were ill-equipped. The Sunday schools languished for competent instructors. The city's missionary impulses were ebbing in their vitality. . . .

When he finished his paper there was a general discussion in which most of those present engaged. It was the young lawyer, Mac Dickinson, who disclaimed the prior needs of the churches.

"I am a churchman," he said. "Every Sunday I sit in the First Presbyterian Church and hear Dr. Hoyt preach, and I consider him an able preacher, but I could worship just as devoutly walking in a country lane, or watching the lightning play about a summer cloud."

"You could, yes, but do you?" asked the minister.

"Yes. Sometimes I do. I have, I think, been nearest God when farthest from people."

"A hermit then would be the ideal worshiper?"

"Perhaps so, but that is not what I mean. He worships best who understands most. I'll not deny the need of some additional equipment for our churches, but the need is much greater for the cultural improvement of those who worship in those churches. I go about the city a great deal—as I am sure you do, sir—and I see a distressing amount of ignorance among our people—plain, stolid ignorance. Nashville's greatest need is for more schools and better teachers in them. It's too late to do much about this generation, but unless we do do something for the next it will be worse."

William Reese said that in his belief the city's greatest need was the interest of the best people in public affairs. "Do you want proof?" he inquired somewhat didactically. "Visit any voting place on election day. Whom do you find there? Not you gentlemen but our most indubitable and unmistakable human trash. Of course you don't walk down our alleys; your nostrils are too tender. Of course you don't visit our voting places; you do not care for the company you would be in. Of course you don't know that Titsy Harris announced for Building Inspector this afternoon. Of course it doesn't mean anything to you—to us—that he will very likely beat Ed Titus, an honest man, within his limits, by a landslide. What we need most is a revival in good citizenship."

"And that revival will best begin in the schools," said Mac Dickinson.

"I grant the schools some creative value in citizenship, but that is precisely where I place the church first," said the preacher. "We will not have clean alleys nor clean elections until we have clean hearts."

A slightly built young man who had been sitting quietly and listening intently spoke to his host in low tones. "May I say something, please?"

"Gentlemen," said Len Whitworth, "Eugene Lewis has something to say."

"I have," said the one addressed. He was small of stature but compactly built. He was chief engineer of one of the railroads. His friends called him "Major," a rank he had won in an eastern military academy. "Let me mention something which on the one hand is a pressing need and on the other a pressing menace. Some of the finest of America's early homes are within fifty miles of where I sit, and some of the best of those within five miles. You know them. Our Scotch-Irish forerunners loved fine homes and built them, and in them lived fine lives. If one built a fine home like Belle Meade, for instance, he would insist that life within it conformed to the home's dignity and grace. Or this home, sir." He bowed to his host. "It is an exquisite one. I have never missed an opportunity to observe a fine home, and this gallery is a new and refreshing experience."

"I never tire of it," said Len Whitworth.

"These homes," continued Lewis, "were built for complete living, for babies to be born in in dignity, to be used as altars for weddings, to die in with a sense of completeness. They were built to develop the best and most enduring in family life; in which to entertain friends; to serve food fit for kings; in which conversation should flow according to its highest canons. The silliness of fools is least becoming in them, and in them the sadness of bereavement, of tragedy may be framed in proper dignity." He paused. "We have always had poor and ugly homes. I suppose we always will. But in the early days we would build a hundred poor ones, and then one like Tulip Grove, or Kingsley, would go up and the blight of the hundred ugly ones would be taken off. But something has happened. A really great home hasn't been constructed in or about

Nashville in twenty years. Belmont and Burlington were the last. Some have been costly and pretentious but they have had neither beauty nor charm. What has happened to us?"

"The war . . ."

"No, Mac, the war won't explain our ugliness away. The Acklens moved into Belmont more than ten years before the war began. Besides, some very costly homes have been built since the war, but the glory of the old ones is not there. We have lost something, something very precious."

"We've lost it, indeed," said Mac Dickinson. "I rode along Base Street today."

"Precisely. That street is a monument to ugliness. Any house on it would in the end degrade any inmate."

"Home is where love is," said the preacher softly.

"But a hovel is where love dies," and there was the hint of sternness in the reply. "And that is what Base Street will be in a few years, a place of hovels, one-story hovels, two-story hovels with all sorts of tawdry curlicues and gimcracks. There isn't a good joining in any building on the street. The cracks will widen and widen and the weather will help the deformities to accumulate. Not a building on the street has even the hint of good taste in it. That wouldn't be so bad if it were confined to one street. A great many people have been coming to Nashville lately to live. So all over town we've been putting up ugly and desolate houses to sell them in their emergency. Every carpenter from a hundred miles around who can hit a nail two times out of three has been drawn into Nashville to help multiply these atrocities."

"They have just finished a hideous place not three squares from my home," said Dr. Briggs.

"They will come closer. Have the epidemics remained segregated? Did not one enter Polk Place and kill the President? This is no less an epidemic."

"Everything you've said plays into my argument," said William Reese. "You are willing to sit in a club and complain eloquently against our ills. It does not seem to occur to you in the slightest that the ballot box was devised as the proper way to check such evils. As a matter of fact, you lawyers know that we have already laws applying to the construction of buildings. Who enforces the application of those laws? The Building Commissioner, of course—only he doesn't. Most of you haven't the faintest idea who he is. Well, I had the honor to vote against him. He's a nincompoop who does exactly what he's told—by the wrong people. Who are the candidates in the coming election? I told you a few minutes ago, and the chances are you've forgotten by now. You'd rather complain and forget than remember and work. Titsy Harris is one candidate, and hovels in front of the fine homes your grandfathers built wouldn't bother Titsy in the least. That would probably be his program. Is there another candidate? There is. Ed Titus. Ed's a good, moral man and his name is about as old as Nashville, but that's practically a complete description of Ed. It's my opinion that Titsy's crowd maneuvered Ed's candidacy to forestall a more appealing candidate and incidentally to provide our aristocrats a chance to save their consciences."

"I imagine that you will vote for him." There was a faint flavor of irony in Mac Dickinson's comment.

"I suppose I shall. What else is there for me to do? But it will be the good people of Nashville who force that option upon me."

"Well, isn't it one of our most convenient platitudes that when matters get as bad as they can be they are just about ready to improve?"

"Oh, they can get worse yet. The office of Building Inspector is only one of the posts involved in this election. In the public mind it is perhaps considered a trivial one. But in every instance the candidates bear a strong resemblance to Ed and Titsy, one to get the votes of the inert aristocrats, the other to get the office. We wear the brand of the high and mighty, but we are being sold down the river, gentlemen."

It was then announced that refreshments were being served. The guests went into the dining room and sat at the table under the great, gleaming chandeliers.

Mac Dickinson's eyes moved about the table. "The aristocrats may be inert in politics but not in food."

"Thanks, Mac," said Len Whitworth. "Everything that you will be served tonight, except the coffee, was raised on this farm."

"Everything? Very interesting indeed."

"Well, I suppose we do use a little salt and some sugar. We couldn't raise the coffee, and we have made enough progress to make it pointless to give our time to the sugar and salt. However, my grandfather went to the salt spring and evaporated his own salt, and my father raised the sorghum which we used for sweetening. I have heard several of you mention a fondness for baked goose. The one before you was selected from our flock and specially nurtured for this evening. This bread and these cakes were from our own wheat fields, this butter and cream from our own cows. The corn from which the meal was made and the hens which laid the eggs that went into this spoon bread both grew on this farm. All the fruit that made these preserves and jellies grew at Myrtlewood. So did that watermelon." He pointed to a dish heaped with amber squares of sweet pickled watermelon rind. "Nature comes to a curious balance there. The melons that are best to eat never grow the best rinds for that." He turned to Mac Dickinson. "I confess that I never understood Jacob McGavock sending to New Orleans for the food he served at an important dinner. Myrtlewood could have supplied your grandfather, Mac, with food certainly as good even if not so fancy."

"May I withdraw the discussion from food, as delightful as it is?" It was William Reese, the club's secretary, who spoke. "There is one item of business. I have here a letter from Erwin Roane, who wishes to resign from the club. I suggest that it not be accepted."

"What reason does he give?" asked Felix Hill.

"Really none. Simply that it has become extremely inconvenient for him to attend the meetings, and that when he does come he is greatly humiliated by the disparity of his value to the club measured against that of the other members. It's not a very pleasant note, gentlemen."

"Perhaps I can explain," said the host. "I rode by Cherry Hill this morning. . . ."

"Cherry Hill, a lovely place! I beg your pardon, Len."

"Certainly, Eugene. It is lovely. Erwin was depressed, more so than I had ever seen him. He had just found out that those magnificent cherry trees on the slope this side of the house are about all dead. Nashville has had nothing more beautiful than those trees in bloom."

"I've heard them praised in Charleston," said William Reese.

"Those cherry trees were on his mind. He said it wasn't fair for them to die and him to live. They for a brief season each year gave rich experiences to those who loved beauty. He had never bloomed nor borne fruit."

"Neely Barrow," said Mac Dickinson.

"I reminded him of his granddaughter, and that left him a bit cheered but he said he couldn't come tonight. I must say, though, that that letter surprises me. This club is all the life away from Cherry Hill that Erwin still clings to, this and an occasional chess game with Colonel McGuire."

"That's all the more reason for us not to permit him to with-draw," said William Reese.

"How many could spare next Saturday morning for a labor of love?" inquired Eugene Lewis.

All could. Lewis outlined the labor he had in mind.

"I'll put a bug in Neely Barrow's ear," said Len Whitworth. "She'll do her part."

It was a nice bug, and Neely Barrow did her part. Len Whit-worth visited her surreptitiously the next day and when he talked with her her bright eyes grew much brighter.

It was Neely Barrow who maneuvered her grandfather into a trip to Mount Olivet Cemetery the following Saturday. They made such a trip every year in the early spring. But Neely Barrow explained that they probably wouldn't have such a fine day for the trip even if they waited for spring. Besides, it was likely to rain any day later on. In conclusion she wished to go then, not later. So together they set out on foot for Mt. Olivet three miles away. As they went out on the street and turned eastward hand in hand, Neely Barrow was buoyant and her grandfather was as free from the dead weight of the cold fingers of regret as he had been in a decade.

While they were away, the other members of the Old Table Club worked happily and diligently upon the premises of Cherry Hill. When they had finished, new cherry trees were set in precise order to replace those old and dying. Something would grow again at Cherry Hill, and again the cherry trees would bloom like heaven.

7

Spring again was in the land. The breath of it was in the lazy, random breezes which blew now gently, now determinedly, and now not at all from the Overton Hills. The fragrance of it was in the little wisps of odor from life bursting through the shell of win-ter, from life growing and blooming in the yards and fields and near-by thickets. The sight of it was in the fragile yellow-green lacework of the hackberry and willow trees. The sounds of it were in the voices of the birds who had endured the trials of winter merely to achieve the triumph of spring. They sang hopping about upon the ground, in flight in the air, or perched jauntily in trees, and their songs blended into the ecstasy of spring.

Hunt Justice and his mother were at work in the margins of their yard making ready for flower beds. The two had something in common with the birds.

"I've been thinking about this all winter, Mama," said the boy, a little breathlessly.

"Yes, Hunt, I thought of it, too."

"This is good ground, Mama."

His mother didn't respond to the comment, and the boy turned several forkfuls of soil before he spoke again. "I'm glad Papa sold the horses, Mama; we don't need them, and they eat a lot."

"It was Mrs. Elrod who sold them for him. She knew he didn't need them."

"I think it was nice of her. I think she's a very nice woman." He paused a moment. "What did he do with the money, Mama?"

"He put it in the bank. I went with him."

The boy went ahead with his forking. Then, "I wish, Mama, he'd build a pretty house sometime."

"Yes, Hunt, I wish he would, too, but I know Courtney Justice. He's a good man, but he won't ever build a pretty house. He wouldn't even know one if he saw it."

"Well, I would, Mama." For two or three minutes there was no sound except that of the fork tearing through the earth and the background of bird song that lessened in volume as the morning grew warmer. "That house of Mrs. Polk's, Mama, the one where Papa fixed the back porch—I liked it. She asked me to come back and see it sometime. Look, Mama, there's Papa. What you reckon he's coming back for?"

Mrs. Justice looked up from her work. Her husband was coming in at the gate. Fear tugged at her heart. Hunt saw the look on her face and fear tugged at his heart, too. Courtney Justice came up the walk, his tools under his arm. He read aright the concern on the faces of his wife and son.

"Don't you be worried," he said cheerfully. "Nothing's wrong with me a-tall. No sir, not a thing."

"Courtney, what made you stop working?"

"Got a holiday. Don't have to work any more all day, and I get reg'lar pay."

"What for, Papa?"

"To go to a speakin'. Ain't been to a speakin' sence we left Huntland. Yes sir, I was a-sawin' away at some two-by-fours when Ed Crayton come up and asked how I'd like to take the day off. He had me skeered for a minute. Then he went on to say that a friend o' his was a-runnin' for Buildin' Commissioner and that he was a-makin' a lot of speeches today and he wanted him to have a crowd. Seems like most ever' man in town who's a-puttin' up a house is goin' to send some o' his hands."

"All day, Courtney?"

"Yes, honey. This man's name's Titsy Harris and he's the man for the place. He makes a rousin' speech, so Ed says, and I'd sort of like to hear a good speech agin. He starts off at ten o'clock down at the boat landin', then at 'leven he makes another speech at the court-house, then at dinnertime somewhere over in Edgefield. We go along with him so's to make a show, but I'm purty glad to go. I'm hungry for some good speakin'."

"What time'll you get home, Courtney?"

"I don't rightly know, Lizzie. Sometime between sundown an' dark, I guess. Seems like he's makin' a lot o' speeches. I'll come soon as he's finished the last one."

"Courtney, I don't feel just right about you goin'."

"Don't you worry, honey. Git the same pay as if I was a-working. Don't you worry. Ed's a mighty fine man to work for. We mighty lucky, honey."

"Don't you get mixed up in anything, Courtney."

"I ain't a-goin' to, Lizzie. We just standin' up for our rights. Why, Ed says if Titsy ain't elected we'll have to quit bizness. The man who's a-runnin' agin him's a reg'lar big bug, an' if he's elected he ain't a-goin' to let anybody build a house less'n it's brick with stone pillars in front. Well, I got to fix up a bit an' git down to that boat landin'."

Courtney Justice fixed up a bit and left, his cheerful voice telling them not to worry and assuring them that everything was all right. His wife's eyes, still troubled, followed him along the street. "I wish he was back at work. That's where he is safest," she said, mainly to herself.

Again there was no sound except the fork digging into the ground and tearing away the clumps of soil.

"Look, Mama!" cried Hunt delightedly. He pointed to a robin which was making comic efforts to swallow a big worm which the fork had raised to the surface. Then the boy's quick eyes caught movement out in the street. "Look, Mama, there's somebody stopping. Do you reckon he's coming here?"

A man was getting out of a light spring wagon. He tied his lead horse to a sycamore tree by the street side.

"Oh, Mama, I know him," the boy said, speaking hurriedly. "It's the man I saw the first day I went to the Academy. You remember. That day about the boys, Mama? Yes, and when Papa and I were at Mrs. Polk's he was there, too. He's a nice man."

The man opened the lattice gate and came in. He lifted his hat. "Mornin', ma'am; mornin', son. You ricollèct me?"

"Oh, yes, sir. I told Mama about you."

"Thanky, son. You lookin' fine. Gin'ral Lee's done got the Yankee army licked, I reckon. Looks like you all fixin' to plant some truck."

"Flowers," said the boy. "We like flowers."

"I'm right thankful for the way you helped Hunt."

"Glad to speak a word for Gin'ral Lee," said the driver, winking broadly at Hunt Justice. He turned back to the woman. "Reckon, ma'am, you could spare your boy till sometime this evenin'? I'd like to take him a-visitin'." He turned back to the boy. "Miz Polk said for me to take you to see the house where I live. I think it's plumb purty. Reckon he can go, ma'am?"

"Where you live?" asked Lizzie Justice.

"Out at Kingsley on the Murfreesboro Pike, five or six miles. It's the Weaver Coles's house, ma'am. I live with them."

Lizzie Justice was no dull judge of people and their motives. Her inspection of the driver seemed to reassure her. "I reckon he can go. Can you bring him back?"

"Yes'm, tha's what I aim to do. I'm a-takin' some seed potatoes out now, an' I got to meet the six o'clock train. Mr. Lawrence—he's Miz Weaver Cole's daddy—is a-comin' on it. I'll take good care o' him, ma'am."

"Mama, I can't go. We've got to get this flower bed fixed, and I'm not going to leave you to do the work."

"Give me that fork," said the driver. "You go get primped up some. When I fixes groun' somethin' jest natchelly goin' to bust loose and grow."

Lizzie Justice and Hunt went into the house. When they came out the flower bed which they had marked off was not only forked but put in shape for planting. Lizzie Justice looked after them as they drove eastward on Oak Street. The birds had ceased singing. Suddenly an outbound freight train thrust its roar and clank upon the vernal quiet. The train skirted the cemetery, erupting volcanic smoke against the base of Negley Hill. It shrieked and clanged its way into the fields that lay against Nashville's southern border.

Then its clangor sank to a murmur, then to silence, and the serenity of spring again closed in upon Oak Street.

8

The driver turned from the Murfreesboro Pike into the entrance at Kingsley. Hunt Justice's bright eyes grew brighter as they envisioned the stately home standing not too near the highway to be defiled by it, not too far away to lose its common touch. "Oh!" the boy exclaimed. "Oh! Is this where you live? It's beautiful." Then unconsciously he clapped his hands. "I remember now. I saw this house the day we came to Nashville. I thought it was beautful then, but I was too tired to notice it much."

"I know," said the driver. "I like it, too. I think the whole road between here and town's right purty but when I come out I fin' myself kind o' waitin' till I git here so I can look at it real hard."

They drove around the house and into the barn lot beyond.

"All right, son, hustle for yo'self while I git these taters cut up for plantin'."

"I'll help you," said the boy shyly. "I always helped cut them."

"All right, son; we'll git these taters ready for plantin'. Then I'll show you aroun' some."

The day grew in its fullness and the sun poured its languid warmth upon the land. The driver wished to show many things about Kingsley to Hunt Justice, but the boy had eyes only for the house.

"Purty, ain't it? Well, son," he continued, with gentle impatience, "you stand right there and look at that house till you think you'll know it next time you see it. When you git through lookin', I'll be somewheres aroun'."

He saw Merrie Cole come out on the side porch, so he went across to her to explain the phenomenon of a young boy transfixed by the sight of her home.

"You remember, ma'am, me tellin' you an' Miz Cole about a lad that was at Miz Polk's? Well, I fetched him along in the spring waggin."

She saw Hunt then. "Why, that's nice."

"Looks like he's done took root, and liable to start growin' any minute. I brought him 'cause I knowed I was goin' back this evenin'. I told you, ma'am, about Miz Polk wantin' him to see Kingsley."

"Fine! You couldn't have chosen a better day."

Then Ellen Cole saw the driver and Merrie and came out where they were.

"I don't know how Weaver got the idea that the people of Nashville are going on an exclusive potato diet, but he seems to have it. He has decided to put the young orchard in potatoes, and he wants you to go back to town for five more bushels of seed."

"Now, ma'am?"

"That's what he said. He said he wanted to get them in the ground before it rains."

"All right, ma'am. You couldn't let that boy take your house back to town with him, could you? He's sure going to hate to leave it here."

Then she saw Hunt Justice standing by the hitching post, his eyes feasting hungrily upon Kingsley's classic lines. "Why, who is that child?"

"He's the one I told you about, the one that was at Miz Polk's that time. I brung him out, ma'am."

"Oh," she said, remembering vaguely.

"I aimed to take him back with me when I go after Mr. Lawrence, but I reckon he better go this time."

Mrs. Cole turned to go back into the house. The hand with which she held the door knob turned irresolutely. Then she came back to the porch. "Why not let him stay?" Then she remembered something else he had told her about the boy. "Didn't you tell me he was a scholar in the Academy?" He nodded. "Why, then, of course he must stay. This is Gordon Hicks' birthday. I asked his father to bring him out for a little party this afternoon. Gordon's in the Academy. That makes it fine. I'll go out and speak to him now."

She and Merrie went out into the yard. Hunt Justice withdrew his gaze from the house and looked timidly at them as they approached.

"This is my friend," said the driver with a touch of gallantry; "his name's Hunt Justice."

She extended her hand. The boy extended his timidly but not clumsily. "Good morning, Hunt. This gentleman has told me about you. Would you like for me to tell you about our house?"

"Oh yes, I would. . . ."

"It was built, of course, before I was born, but I've been told a great deal of its early history. Excuse me, please; this is Merrie, my son's wife." Hunt bowed, smiling faintly. He was aware that he was among friends.

"I've got to run around for a spell," said the driver. "You jest make yo'self at home, son. We'll be startin' back sometime about half after four."

"We don't like to hurry you, but I suppose you'd better take something with you and eat it as you drive along. Weaver said he'd have that orchard ground ready to plant by three o'clock."

"I'll be back, ma'am."

"Potatoes love to grow for Weaver, and he loves to grow them. He loves to grow everything. He is going to plant an acre in tomatoes, though what he'll do with them . . ."

"He'll do something," said Merrie Cole. "I never knew him to let anything waste yet."

"And I never knew who taught him thrift—no, nor industry either. I'll never forget the first potatoes Weaver ever planted. Nobody told him to; nobody knew he was planting them. The war was just over. One afternoon he came running into the house calling for me to come and see something. It was a patch of potatoes he had planted and I have never seen finer ones than came out of that patch. He was twelve then. A month later his father came home—came home to die. . . ." She turned quickly to Hunt. "Please excuse me. I fancy your mother likes to talk about you, too." Then a smile broke through the tears that stood in her eyes. "I think our dinner will be ready. We won't eat in much style but there'll be plenty. I'll show you the house afterwards."

They went into the house and sat at the small table in the pantry way. Weaver, who was husbanding his moments expertly for potato planting, had taken his food with him to the field.

"My son loves best to raise things, to plant them, to help them grow, and to harvest them. Is there something you want very much to do?"

"I think Hunt would like to build houses, Mother," said Merrie.

"Yes, yes, that's what I want to do most." The boy's voice was uneven in its eagerness. "Do you reckon I ever can?"

"We had to move away from here after—after the war. Weaver said we'd come back. I didn't see how he could ever do it. But right now he is planting potatoes here at Kingsley. If he could do that, Hunt, you can build houses."

"You haven't told Hunt about the party, Mother."

"Why, yes. It's so nice you could come to see us today. You know Gordon Hicks at the Academy, don't you, Hunt?"

"Gordon Hicks? He's in my class."

"Today is his birthday, and his father is bringing him and a few of his friends out. We are going to have some refreshments and play some games. We want you to join us."

Hunt fell back upon his mother's idiom. "I wouldn't be wanting to put you to any trouble."

"Then that's settled," said Merrie. "Excuse me, please. There are some things I have to do." She left the table.

"Merrie is happy today," said Mrs. Cole. "Her father is coming tonight. She hasn't seen him since she and Weaver were married. Let's go see the house."

She led Hunt up the fine stairs that rose from the back hall. A half hour later they came back down. The boy's eyes were bright from what he had seen and heard. "I have often carried visitors through Kingsley," Mrs. Cole told him, "but not one who has given me the pleasure you have." They went rather hurriedly through the parlors, for time was pressing Mrs. Cole. Then she went back to the kitchen and Hunt went out into the yard. The birds were not singing at all. The somnolence of midday had stilled their voices. Toward evening they would fill Kingsley with their testimony of the goodness of living. The sky was flecked with a faint, delicate lacework of spring clouds, outrunners of those bearing the rain against which Weaver Cole made haste. The film of haze against the distant woods had deepened. Someone was plowing in the field toward the asylum and the rituals he cried to his team seemed indeed a part of spring itself. In the field beyond the plowman numerous clumps of gray, drab grass moved aimlessly about the field, but a closer look revealed that those clumps were Weaver Cole's sheep nosing about for bits of the tonic greenstuff of early spring. In the front of the home the driveway inscribed its circle just in front of the giant boxwoods, then curved gracefully out to the Murfreesboro Pike. To its right stood the giant magnolia under which Merrie as a child had held court with the fairies. All of these things—the clouds in the sky, the sheep in the distant field, the plowman treading the dark green furrows and chanting the rituals of his craft, the great green magnolia tree—all of these seemed to form a circle of infinite fitness about the home.

Hunt Justice heard the sound of wheels grinding against the gravel of the driveway. He saw a carriage stop at the front and a gentleman alight, followed by two girls and two boys. Mrs. Cole and Merrie were hurrying out to meet them. Yes, one of the boys was Gordon Hicks, and the other James Parkes. He didn't know the girls. He couldn't be seen staring at them. Some innate timidity drew him to the rear of the house, out of sight. Presently, Mrs. Cole came out and asked him to come in to the birthday party. He followed her inside, wishing a bit vaguely that he didn't have to. One of the girls was Lena May Green and the other Neely Barrow Roane. He noticed the clothes they were wearing. He knew they had something his lacked but he was dimly aware of gratitude for his mother's insistence for him to wear his best. All of this was passing through his mind as he bowed somewhat stiffly while Mrs. Cole called each name.

"Hello, Hunt," said Gordon. He spoke cordially, but he was puzzled to find Hunt at Kingsley. "I thought you were going to plant flower seed today."

"I thought so, too," said Hunt, and let the matter drop there. The other children looked inquiringly at Gordon. "Hunt goes to the Academy," he explained; "he's the best scholar in our class."

"Why, he's blushing!" exclaimed Lena May Green, clapping her hands. "I used to know a quotation about somebody who blushes. I forget what it said, but it meant that anybody who blushes is always a good scholar."

"I got to try blushing, then," said Gordon. "How do you blush, Hunt?"

"It's dangerous," declared James Parkes, the acclaimed wag of Nashville's younger set. "Better not try it. I saw a man once who got to blushing and he couldn't stop. He got worse and worse. Finally he commenced blazing. They poured water on him but the more they poured the higher the blaze went. Made me nervous." He sighed deeply and relapsed into a most dramatic silence.

"Well, what happened?" demanded Gordon Hicks.

"I never did know," answered James, still sighing. "A three-legged rooster passed along and I got to watching it."

"Jim Parkes never told the truth in his whole life," said Lena May Green. "He'd drop dead if he ever tried to."

"You know what happens to people who tell the truth? Why, jails are full of them."

Mrs. Cole had arranged an out-of-door game for them to play.

She interrupted their badinage to invite them out to play it. They followed her and for an hour their voices sounded merrily among the trees. Sometime before four o'clock they all went into the dining room. On the dining table was a profusion of yellow daffodils. In the center of the table was a great cake with candles burning. A wish favorable to the future of Gordon Hicks was made by everyone present. Then Gordon with one gusty breath blew out the candles. When that ceremony was finished, they were seated and Mrs. Cole served each rich portions of cake and custard. Hunt Justice sat at the end of the dining room near the door that opened into the reception hall. In the chair next to him sat Neely Barrow Roane. Her cool eyes, black as jet, were studying Hunt as if some quality in him baffled her.

"You like houses, don't you?" she asked suddenly.

"Yes, I do." He said emphatically. Then he, too, was baffled. "What makes you think I do?"

"Well, that's all you've looked at. When we got here you were standing there just looking at the house. When Mrs. Cole went out on the porch to ask you to come in I went with her, not all the way but to the door. There you stood still looking at the house. Why, since we've been in here you haven't looked at me, or anybody—just at the ceiling, or windows or doors. I bet you didn't know yourself when you went and stood by that mantel and just looked at it. Now, did you?"

He asked a question instead of answering that one. "Do you like pretty houses?"

"I live in one. Do you?"

"No. We don't have any—much money."

"We don't have much money either, not enough to keep the house painted very well." She had the impulse to mention her grandfather's need for an overcoat but decided not to.

"We are going to raise some flowers. I worked in the flower bed some this morning."

"A house doesn't look right without some flowers. About a year from now we'll have some fine cherry blossoms. The old trees are about dead but we have some pretty new ones. My home is named Cherry Hill. There have always been cherry trees there."

"Cherry Hill! Isn't it a pretty name! Cherry Hill!" His tongue and lips moved as if he were tasting not only the beauty of the birthday cake but of Cherry Hill as well. "Sometime I'd like to see it."

"Oh, I would like for you to see it. So would Grandy—I mean Grandfather."

"My father helps build homes," he said gravely, "but they aren't pretty ones."

"Nobody's building any pretty houses. That's what Grandy says—and I think he's right. I don't think there's a pretty new house in Nashville." She pondered him a moment, her brows drawn into a quizzical pucker. "You're a funny boy. I never saw one before that cared a snap about houses."

"I want to build one someday, one like this one, or Mrs. Polk's, or—or Cherry Hill."

"Then you'd better come to see it. You couldn't build one like it if you'd never seen it, could you?"

Then they heard the knocker at the front door fall and Mrs. Cole went to answer it.

"Someday," Neely Barrow said gravely and deliberately, "I think you'll build a finer house than Cherry Hill. You ought to talk with Grandy. Only sometimes he's awfully sad."

Mrs. Cole came into the room with a gentleman. "We have a surprise guest for your birthday party, Gordon. Major Lewis has been calling on Mr. East, so he dropped in on his way back. Wasn't that nice of him?"

Eugene Lewis's eyes traveled over the group. "May all of your birthdays, Gordon, be spent in company so nice." He made the round, shaking hands with Gordon and each of the children. He came to Hunt last of all. "I'm sorry. I don't believe I have the pleasure of knowing you."

"He is Hunt Justice, Major Lewis. He's a scholar in the Academy."

"Thank you, Neely Barrow. A good scholar or I'm no judge of scholars." He shook hands with Hunt.

"He loves pretty houses," said Neely Barrow.

"Very interesting. So you like pretty houses?"

"Yes, sir."

"He's going to build one someday," said Neely Barrow.

"Is he? How delightful! I crave your better acquaintance, Hunt." He turned to Mrs. Cole whom he addressed with a flavor of formality. "How fine it is, madam, for the flower of our youth to gather in your lovely home. Oh, that I were young again to be one of them! Where, may I ask, is Weaver? Where is Merrie? I should by all means expect to pay them my regards."

"Merrie is upstairs. Her father is coming tonight, and she's getting ready to go meet him. Weaver is planting potatoes out in the young orchard."

"What's that you were saying about building a house, Neely Barrow?" Lena May Green asked the question as the caller left the room.

"I heard you say that Hunt is going to build houses," said Gordon Hicks. "Are you, Hunt?"

James Parkes sighed reminiscently. "When I was young I thought someday I'd build a house, but—" he sighed again—"I changed my mind."

"All right," said Gordon. "What are you going to build?"

"Who, me? Not going to build anything. I'm going to dig rivers."

Lena May squealed with delight. "Jim simply can't tell the truth," she said delightedly.

"Of course it's the truth. Got one river already planned. It's going to put this old Cumberland River clear out of business. Trouble with the Cumberland it simply wasn't dug right in the first place."

"I expect Mrs. Cole could lend you a shovel, Jim, if you are in a hurry," said Lena May.

At that moment Mrs. Cole came in to tell Hunt that Merrie and the driver were ready to start to town. The boy stood and bowed and asked the guests to excuse him. He was blushing again for no reason. Neely Barrow held out her hand to him and his blush deepened.

"You let me know when you build that house and I'll come to see it. Good-by, Hunt."

Mrs. Cole went with Hunt through the door into the hall out onto the porch.

"Hunt is the best scholar in our class," said Gordon, repeating what he had said earlier. "At least Professor Yeatman thinks he is."

"Professor Yeatman's a smart man," affirmed Neely Barrow.

"You must like him, Neely Barrow—I mean Hunt," quipped Lena May.

"I do," said Neely Barrow calmly.

"So he's going to build houses." Sarcasm dripped from James Parkes' tones.

"Yes, and he'll build them, too. He'll have a lot of them finished before you get your feet wet digging that old river."

Pardner and Robin Hood drew the carriage at a lively clip along the Murfreesboro Pike.

"Them's good hosses," said the driver with some irrelevance. "Robin Hood's twenty-five years past, and Pardner ain't much younger. That ain't young for a hoss. Gin'rally he's a daid hoss afore that. But jest look at 'em. You never see a spryer team o' hosses."

"Papa," said Merrie with more relevance. Her eyes were bright. "Papa's coming. Where do you suppose he is right now?"

"Right now," answered the driver pondering, "right now I'd say effn he's still on the train he's jest about Gallatin."

Merrie Cole wanted to talk, so she talked. "I haven't seen Papa since I was married. At first he didn't want us to marry, but after he saw Weaver he didn't have a single objection. How could he? Really, I'm sure he went back to Massachusetts so we could get married."

"That's a funny thing to do effn he didn't object."

"It's just like Papa. He's awfully proud. He had objected to us marrying, and that was the only way he could give in gracefully."

"I never rightly knowed Mr. Lawrence," observed the driver, "but I see him two or three times. Ain't no man in Nashville never he'ped out more'n he did the time we had the bank trouble. Yes sir, he shore made the evil doers repent, as the feller said."

"Papa's a grand man, and I'm so happy."

"Seein's he ain't been back afore this I reckon he'll be stayin' a right smart while."

"I doubt it. Papa's a Yankee. He never did understand these people. They kept him puzzled. I think they gave him a sort of helpless feeling, and Papa simply can't stand to feel helpless. He isn't that kind of man. I don't think he understood me very well either. I wish he'd stay all summer, but I look for him to get restless after two or three weeks and go back to the mill. He knows how to run it. He understands people back in Lowell. Nothing seems to puzzle Papa there. Where do you suppose he is by now?"

"Jest about a mile this side o' Gallatin."

"I wish it were an hour from now. He'd be here by then. I am so happy!" She paused a moment. "No, he never did fit down here. He knew mills and he knew Yankees, but he never knew these people. Papa couldn't farm either. I think he knew he wasn't doing his farming right, but I never knew it until I watched Weaver. No,

Papa didn't belong here, but I do." She laughed a merry laugh. "Wouldn't it have been terrible if we had never moved to Tennessee? I don't believe I could stand it." She turned to Hunt Justice. "We are neglecting you. I must be a little excited. Did you like the birthday party?"

"I thought it was nice. Your house is so pretty. I liked to look at it."

"Was that all you liked to look at?" she asked jestingly. "I should think you'd like to look at Neely Barrow, too."

The boy was blushing again. "Yes, yes. That's what we talked about—houses."

"She's the loveliest child in Nashville."

They relapsed into silence, broken presently by the driver's song.

> "I come to a river but I couldn't git across
> So I give five dollars for a old gray hoss."

The sun's rays were gilding the crown of Fort Negley as they drove into Oak Street. They let Hunt out in front of his home and drove on out toward Spruce Street. The first faint thickening of twilight gave a sort of holy softness and calm to the cemetery across the street. Mrs. Justice heard the gate click and came out on the porch. Hunt ran up the walk toward the house. He turned a sharp, quick look of inquiry upon the flower beds. It was as he had expected. They were planted. His mother had worked while he had been at the birthday party.

"Mama, you shouldn't have done that. I could have helped Monday after school."

"I didn't mind, Hunt. It wasn't hardly any trouble at all. You have a nice time?"

"Yes, Mama. It was mighty pretty where we went. And, Mama, they had a birthday party and invited me to it."

The pride in her eyes deepened. "Wasn't that fine! You went, didn't you, Hunt?"

"Yes, Mama. It didn't seem right not to when they asked me. It was Gordon Hicks's birthday. You know. I told you about him. He's in the Academy. Wasn't it funny for us both to be out there? They had the party for him. I wish you could have seen it, Mama. It was nice."

"I got the flower seed planted. Ground worked real well," she said absently. "Court hasn't come home yet. I wasn't going to start supper with both of you gone. Why, there's Mrs. Elrod."

Mrs. Callie Elrod came into the hall. In her hands she held something with a cloth wrapped about it. "I brought you a mess of wild greens. Picked 'em today. Brought some corn pone, too. Better eat it while it's hot."

"This is mighty neighborly of you. But Court isn't home yet and he's special fond of wild greens."

"I knowed he wasn't here, practically knowed it anyhow." She paused a moment, then proceeded to explain her awareness of Mr. Justice's absence. "Ain't Titsy Harris running for Building Commissioner, and ain't Ed Crayton scratchin' up the rows and tearin' out the middle for his election, and ain't Titsy speakin' in ever' wide place in the street today, and ain't Court Justice workin' for Ed, and ain't he hunted foxes anuff so that you could hear him yelling for a candidate three miles? Course he ain't home yet."

Mrs. Justice reeled a bit under the impact of this logic. Mrs. Elrod hastened to interpret for the benefit of a mind less versed in certain connections. "A politics meetin' without a crowd's just like a basket meetin' an' no baskets. All right. Titsy's got to have a crowd, ain't he? Ain't going to do Titsy no good for his feller citizens not to be there when he spreads the good word. And one good hollerer is worth a dozen with their mouth shet. Ed can't do any less'n provide a two-legged steamboat whistle for them meetin's. And I figgers that's just what he done."

"What's that got to do with he hasn't got home yet?"

"Ever'thing," said Mrs. Elrod very complacently. "When a man chases aroun' after politics meetin's all days, an' specially if he's a good hollerer, when night comes he gets drunk, or goes fox huntin', or both."

"Court doesn't drink a drop."

"Didn't think he did. He ain't got a drinkin' nose. His'n's too pale. But that man's got a fox huntin' look in his eye."

"He promised to quit fox huntin' when we moved here."

"Then he's backslid. I married a fox huntin' man. I know the breed. Mine's nose wasn't real red but it had a right smart pink in it. If he was at a wedding feast and heard a fox horn toot, he'd get right up and leave. He never oncet come straight home from a politics meetin'. He'd hear them houn's barkin' and he'd come by Mt. Juliet—or maybe Tyree Springs. Mostly he'd get in for brek-fust, and then agin . . ." She sighed. "That's all past an' gone. Eat your vittles before they get cold."

It was past two o'clock when Courtney Justice came home. His wife had not closed her eyes. Hunt had tried to stay awake with her. He had told her about the birthday party, and she had never taken her eyes from his face as he told the story. But at midnight his eyes began drooping so insistently that she would not permit him to remain out of bed longer. Within ten minutes he was sleeping soundly. In her room she sat grimly erect, rocking gently, aimlessly, staring straight at the burned-out embers in the fireplace. She heard the soft, clandestine click of the gate and went to the front door, carrying in her hand the flickering candle. Her husband came into the room.

"You oughtn't be up, Lizzie," he said, his voice cheerful but a bit roughened with anxiety.

"You oughtn't be out, Court," she said, and there were overtones of uneasiness in her voice.

"I know, Lizzie, I know. Maybe I done wrong but I ain't been fox huntin' sence we come here. Some of the men was going from the speakin' an' I guess I jest couldn't hold out."

"I am not thinking of you and I am not thinking of me. I just don't want this example of fox huntin' set before Hunt. I don't aim for him to make a fox hunter, Court."

"He won't. I promus you, Lizzie. I'll discourage him."

"I just as well tell you, Court. It isn't my mind for Hunt to turn out common. I been thinking all day. Hunt's a good boy. He belongs higher up than we've ever been. I won't complain against you. You've been pretty good to me, but I got to have your help for Hunt. I am not willing for him to turn out common." The woman's voice had risen and her chill, even tones had become almost shrill.

"Don't you worry, Lizzie. Right now I don't ever aim to go fox huntin' again. I wouldn't a-gone this time if tomorrer was a work day."

"It's a church day, and you're going, Court. We're all going. If you can fox hunt Saturday night you can go to preaching Sunday morning."

9

Visitors to the Academy always pleased Professor S. M. D. Clark. He ruled the boys in his classes with considerable austerity but he was proud of them. He had the rare quality of holding his approval at high value even though he awarded it generously. Professor Clark's very appearance somehow always thrilled the boys. He was tall, towering, very erect. He rarely smiled in the classroom. Once or twice each session, hardly oftener, a sudden thaw would soften the fixed formality of his features, and the room would be enveloped in the warmth of his fleeting smile. Almost immediately, however, the chill winds would blow across his features, and the freeze would close in. Among the boys the tradition persisted that once something had happened in the room that had completely torn down his resistance and that for a considerable period he had engaged in great hysterical peals of laughter. Entirely unsupported by factual details, it remained a vague though delightful tradition. If it happened once it might happen again.

"They say he shook the windows loose," affirmed Bart Halloran.

"It must have been *rother* amusing," said Ivo Burns, very loftily.

James Parkes paid Ivo very respectful regard. "You're a better man than I am, Ivo."

"Naturally," said Ivo.

"Yes sir, once when I was across the ocean in one of them faraway lands—I think it was Paris, England, maybe it was in Halifax, France, I forget—anyhow, I got to trying to talk like them foreigners. Well, it was too much for me, yes sir, it was too much." His long-drawn sigh suggested that whatever it was it was entirely too much. The boys stood looking at James.

When it became clear that he would not disclose the result of the excess without further priming, Gordon Hicks asked, "Well, what happened?"

James Parkes' face bore the solemnity of an owl. "I dropped dead," he said.

"That must have been *rother* amusing," said Ivo Burns.

The boys kept hoping for a second violent and sudden thaw to drive away the long accumulations of classroom ice. At infrequent intervals they were rewarded by a momentary warmth, but it would pass quickly and the ice age resume.

"Papa and Smack Me Down belong to the same club or something," said Gordon Hicks, "and Papa says Smack Me Down laughs as much as any of them."

"Wonder couldn't I go to that club?" asked Bart Halloran. "I'd like to hear Old SMD laugh once."

"May I *awsk* why?" inquired Ivo.

"Wait, men, wait." James Parkes held up an imploring hand. "Don't kill Ivo yet. Please don't. Give him another chance. I once knew a fellow that talked just like that and some boys started to kill him but I got 'em not to. And it was lucky I did, too. Yes sir, it really was lucky. Later he got cured and made a first-rate blacksmith."

10

One spring morning Professor Clark was much pleased to be visited in his classroom by Eugene Lewis. Two or three times each year he visited the Academy. Those visits were to him revealing experiences. They gave him insight into the generation which would succeed him.

When the boys came in from recess that morning, the visitor was sitting there in the room just to the left of Professor Clark. They sat, thought a moment, and took their Latin texts from the stack before them. Latin would come next. Hunt Justice turned quickly through the book to the page of the morning's assignment. But he overran it and came to a page which oddly enough he had not seen before. There was a picture and something about it caught and held his eyes. There was some printed material beneath the picture and it leaped out to grip his entire attention.

Professor Clark knew how to display a room to its best advantage for visitors. He knew the boys whose recitations would add less to the general credit of the room. Those might and generally did enjoy immunity when a visitor was present, but upon such he laid a heavy hand the following day. It was Professor Clark's plan to leave a visitor pleased with the performance of the Academy. He chose to call upon Hunt Justice first. "Hunt Justice, will you stand?"

His voice was clear and commanding, but it was rendered vague and diffuse by the time it had bored through to Hunt's consciousness. Hunt knew that someone was calling to him from a great distance. Why, that was Professor Clark's voice. He looked up. Why were his classmates staring at him? Then Professor Clark's voice came again. "Hunt Justice, will you stand, sir?"

The icy command threw some mechanism into gear and Hunt stood, his mind still held in thrall by the picture and the printed matter beneath.

"Will you tell the different endings of the genitive case."

Hunt knew that he was to tell something. Professor Clark was expecting it. The boys were watching him curiously.

"It is the most beautiful building in the world," he said, speaking rapidly, his voice high, edged with a thin metallic rasp. "It was built in the time of Peri—Peri—Pericles in 438 B. C. The builder was Phid—Phid . . ."

"Hunt Justice, are you rational, sir?"

Then Hunt remembered that the class was in Latin and he slumped heavily upon his seat and sat there, terrified by the enormity of his offense. Professor Clark hurried to cover the breach. "Gordon Hicks, will you stand, sir?"

The most beautiful building in the world had not placed its paralyzing touch upon Gordon. He knew a great deal about the genitive case. James Parkes might spin fantastic tales elsewhere but he was a realist in the classroom. He added his quota of facts concerning the genitive case. The lesson went forward smoothly, and ended on a rising and gratifying note. But the teacher was troubled. Could it be that the lad who had impressed him so favorably had turned a bit queer? He mustn't permit his dilemma to mar his visitor's appreciation of the Academy. It was his unvarying program to invite a guest to participate in the lesson he had witnessed. He addressed Eugene Lewis.

"You would add, sir, to the pleasure which your visit has already given us if you would question the young gentlemen upon the recitation they have just made. Have you questions, sir?"

"Yes," said Eugene Lewis, rising quickly and standing very erect. "I should like to ask the young gentlemen whom I have met before and most agreeably—" he gestured toward Hunt Justice— "what was the most beautiful building in the world? I am very much interested."

The pink flowed into Hunt's face which had been a dead white. He started to rise but checked himself. He turned his eyes inquiringly upon his teacher.

"Go ahead, sir. Answer the question."

Hunt rose quickly. "It is the Par-the-non, sir." He pronounced the word with equal accent upon each of the syllables.

"Oh," said Eugene Lewis, "oh, the Parthenon, of course. But tell me, please, how you happened to be thinking of the Parthenon."

"I'm sorry, sir." The boy's eyes were upon his teacher. "I'm sorry my mind got off the lesson, sir."

"Very remarkable," said the visitor, his eyes keenly upon the boy. "Very remarkable indeed. For five years I've been trying with feeling and diligence to interest the men of this city in better homes and buildings and yet the first actual affirmation I have heard on the subject is from a mere lad. Tell me," he addressed Hunt, "where did you get your fondness for beautiful houses?"

"I don't know, sir. I've thought about them as long as I can remember, though Mr. Moore's is the only very fine one I ever saw till we came here. Someday I want to try to build one myself."

The teacher dismissed the boys for recess then. Hunt Justice held back, lingering in the hall. Play seemed inappropriate at the moment. Out on the grounds one of the boys said with a display of fine sarcasm, "So-o-o Hunt is going to build a fine house."

Gordon Hicks faced the boy. "You try to be funny with Hunt, and I'll lick you."

"Oh, no, you won't," said Bart Halloran, "for that would be twice he'd be licked."

"I didn't mean any harm to Hunt," said the first boy. "I wouldn't mind helping him build his house." He paused a moment, and then as if reflection confirmed his shift in attitude, "Why, maybe Hunt's a ge-genius."

"Yes, and maybe I got two legs," said Bart Halloran.

Professor Clark felt the need of an apology to his visitor. "I apologize for the lad, sir. Ordinarily he is most prompt in his recitations. I cannot understand his confusion."

"A confusion," said Eugene Lewis, "which I pray may spread. Maybe it's an omen. That lad's preoccupation was pure relief. Maybe it was an omen," he repeated, "for I was thinking of him as I rode along. I had seen him once before and he is very rememberable. This visit has been most pleasing, sir."

How delightful would have been the report spread among the boys if there had been a witness to a brief scene in Professor Clark's office a few minutes later. He sat in his chair with the Latin book opened at the picture of the most beautiful building in the world. His face was red and there were crinkly lines about his eyes. "So Phidias took the endings of the genitive case and out of them made the most beautiful building in the world." At that he burst suddenly into great convulsions of merriment which did in some degree endanger the immobility of the rafters. He collected himself, gasped, and exploded again. "And Pericles got him to do it."

11

Weaver Cole was working in the fields. Weaver was always working. Good weather or bad, Weaver worked. Every fence at Kingsley was in prime condition. Not a gate dragged. The barn was a marvel of convenience and mechanical fitness. In the phrase of the driver, the fence corners were as clean as a hound's tooth.

Spring had settled down. No longer was the weather impulsive and uncertain, warm one day and chill the next, calm and serene in the morning, gusty in the afternoon. The redbud trees had carpeted the thickets and margins of the woods with their discarded bloom. The dogwood flowers had lost their chaste whiteness, and soon they, too, would follow their immemorial cycle to the ground which bore them. The japonicas were blooming in the gardens, and the more forward of the honeysuckle buds were opening along the old stone fences. The sun ran its daily course through skies soft and yielding, whose blueness was not yet rendered brittle by the heat of summer. Now and then a random cloud would briefly hide the sun, but there was no hint of rain in the shadow that fell across the fields.

Weaver Cole was plowing in the asylum field. Hour after hour the unplowed area dwindled steadily. The team moved with unhurried deliberateness. The horses seemed to know exactly what Weaver desired of them. He called no directions to them at the corners. The team shifted with precision and the furrow turned at right angles and ran steadily on. The cries of "Gee" and "Haw" and "Giddup" by men plowing in the adjoining fields were unending, but only the muffled tread of the horses, the clank of the harness, and the dull ripping sound of plow cutting through sod marked Weaver's progress.

In the afternoon Merrie Cole and her father went out to the field and watched Weaver plow. They sat on an outcropping stone near the gate and watched Weaver and talked. Mr. Lawrence's visit was drawing to a close, even sooner than Merrie had expected. That morning there had come to him a communication by telegraph wire from the manager of his textile mill. The mill had received a large and unexpected order. Mr. Lawrence knew that the mill needed him. It could move smoothly in its routine, but this was extra. Merrie knew her father well enough not to make an effort to dissuade him. She had watched him as he read the message, and for a moment she was very lonely. But just then Weaver came into the house and her loneliness passed. She belonged at Kingsley, and no place else in the world.

"I never belonged here," Dwight Lawrence was saying. "I thought I did at first, but I was creating nothing. I was making very little money and spending much. The net was a considerable loss. I didn't need the money, but I could never endure the sense of loss, of dwindling. When your mother died I knew I couldn't stay on. But even then I knew I'd never take you back with me."

"I know, Papa," said Merrie.

"I was very unhappy when I first went back. I missed your mother and you terribly, but the first day I worked there I had my first feeling of real peace in ten years."

"You didn't let the affairs of the bank dwindle, Papa. Weaver says if it hadn't been for you that day Nashville would have been set back five years."

A dull, reminiscent smile broke through his heavy features. "That was perhaps the closest I came to real happiness while I lived here. I love to do things to create something. I suppose I love to feel my own power. In my heart I have only contempt for a man who spends his life up to fifty or sixty making money and the rest spending it."

"I know, Papa."

"I hope never to be idle again. When I die may it be at work."

"I understand, Papa. I'm a Lawrence, too."

"It was for you, daughter, that we moved to Tennessee. I would not have had it otherwise."

Merrie's eyes drifted across the field to Weaver walking steadily in the furrow behind the plow. "You could never have made a farmer, Papa, but yonder's one."

"I suspected but never knew how little of a farmer I was until I watched Weaver. He makes it very clear."

"Isn't it funny, Papa, how we came all the way from Massachusetts just for me to find Weaver? I think it is the strangest thing I ever heard of and the loveliest, Papa."

The afternoon waned. Gold fused into the silver of the May sun. Weaver Cole, tall and quiet and indomitable, walked in the furrow that ran unerringly on toward the harvest.

12

That same afternoon Ellen Cole asked the driver to take her in to town to call on Mrs. Polk. It had been a demanding spring and she felt the need of the morale which the mistress of Polk Place always created within her. Mrs. Polk was at home and very pleased by the visit.

"You came, Ellen, when I needed you most. I'm famished for conversation. It's been a long winter."

"I've been looking forward to this visit a long time, Mrs. Polk."

"Keep in mind, Ellen, that I have no handsome son and charming daughter. I am more in need of visits than you are. Come in, dear."

"It's perfect outside, Mrs. Polk. Would you like to drive about the city awhile?"

"Ellen Cole, you're an inspired woman. I can be ready in exactly one minute."

The driver in his most courtly manner assisted the two ladies into the back seat of the carriage. Then he climbed into the front seat and waited for orders. Mrs. Cole looked expectantly at Mrs. Polk, who said that anywhere would suit her perfectly just so it was four or five blocks from home. They drove down Union to College, then turned south. They crossed Broad Street and a moment later the driver brought Robin Hood and Pardner to a stop.

"Mind, ladies, effn I stop a minit? Ol' College Grove's drivin' that streetcar an' I'm afeard he's jest about run out o' good advice. Him and me fit the war together."

"Fortunate indeed is the man whose counsel is replenished so opportunely," spoke Mrs. Polk in the voice of an oracle.

"Yes'm, I aim to help him out the best I can," said the driver with a becoming display of modesty.

The wheels of the streetcar protested quite audibly the sudden application of brakes. The driver of the streetcar eyed the approach of his visitor with all the malice of a suspicious nature. "Well," he said, "so you done got all mired up in trouble and tribulation and need a helpin' hand."

"That ain't the way it is a-tall," explained the driver patiently. "The streetcar comp'ny's jest about stood all it's a-goin' to. Some people think starvin' would be mighty onpleasant for a man o' your hankerin' for vittles."

"Oh, ho, my eyes done bin opened. Yes sir, they done bin opened. I orta knowed you ain't the man to hold a job with the big bugs. But, pardner, I'm a-warnin' you. Don't you go to tryin' to trigger me outa the position I'm a-renderin' such satisfaction in."

"I see my time's plumb wasted. I tried to warn you an' my

words done fell on deef ears an' the desert air, as the feller says. Well, when you ain't tetched vittles sence the Baptists done fell from grace jest ricollect I tried to warn you. Well, adoo, as the sayin' is."

He started back to the carriage but College Grove hailed him. "Wait a minit. Effn we got ever'thin' else all settled, I'd like to ask a special favor. Titsy Harris's a-runnin' for Buildin' Commissioner an' they ain't bin a nobler man run for office sence Andy Jackson. Yes sir, as one man to another who fit with Jawn Hood I'm a-askin' you to render him suppo't an' assistance."

"Which side of a jailhouse door's he a-livin' on?"

"You shouldn't make such references an' him a lot sanctifieder than you'll ever be. Pardner, I'm a-dependin' on you votin' for Titsy." He looked at his watch. "Three minits late!" he exploded. "Lucky I ain't haulin' nobody. You vote like I said, pardner. You got a chancet to clear yourself of a lot of misdeeds and oneriness." He drove away in a trot.

The driver looked after him reflectively. "He's a-disimprovin' right fast," he said. "He ain't got the sense to know I don't vote in town."

His eyes were bright when he climbed into the carriage. Badinage with College Grove had always left him refreshed. He had been missing it of late. "I'm mighty thankful, ladies, but he's a frien' an' it's bin a right smart spell sence I see him."

"You first met him in the army, I believe," observed Mrs. Polk.

"Yes'm. My first helper got killed at Chickamaugy, an' I got him then."

They drove out College for a few squares and then kept bending to the left and edging up the hill. Mrs. Polk looked up from a stretch of intense conversation with Mrs. Cole.

"Why, there's Cherry Hill! Of all the lovely places! 'I will lift up mine eyes unto the hills.' Stop for a moment. I want to see the cherry trees Erwin Roane's club members set out to take the place of the ones that were dying. Look, they've cut the old ones down and cleared the place off. What a lovely thing to do. I think it really amounts to a parable, my dear—a parable of human life. A generation grows old and decayed and stops blooming. The new generation comes on, fresh and flowering. That's the way it is, my dear. Erwin's a grand man, but something vital was locked in him from the beginning and it has stayed locked."

"Neely Barrow is a dear child."

"None dearer, and the time will come when she'll bloom like a cherry tree in the spring."

They drove by the Howard School and on by Peabody College, then turned west and presently were passing along Base Street. The place was active. The crackle of hammers sounded from two houses under construction.

Just then a workman carrying hammer and saw came around the corner of the house. There was a sort of shambling buoyancy in his walk and he was whistling a little air much more merry than tuneful.

"Why, I know that man!" exclaimed Mrs. Polk. "Once he repaired my back porch. Fortunately, he had his young son with him."

Somewhat surprisingly, it was the driver who interrupted. "It was him, ma'am, that come out with me that Sattidy."

"Him?"

"Yes'm, that boy. You ricollect, Miz Polk, I come to your house the day he was a-fixin' your po'ch, and that boy was inside a-talkin' with you."

"That was just after I overheard him rebuking his father for leaving rough places in his work. Of course, I remember."

"So that is his father. Well, the son was a very pleasant guest at Kingsley. It was Gordon Hicks's birthday and we asked Gordon and some other children out for the afternoon—and Neely Barrow told me after he left that he said he was going to build a fine home someday. She said very solemnly that she believed he would, too. He must have been very convincing."

"He convinced me, Ellen. I won't forget that child reproving his father for clumsy work, nor will I forget his admiration for my house. Those are things one doesn't expect of a boy that young."

"His ma looked like a right nice woman," said the driver.

"Probably so. What's the boy's name? I'm getting old."

"Hunt Justice, ma'am."

"Ellen, that boy will build his fine house. Something tells me he will. I'll stand with Neely Barrow on that."

They drove on through Base Street. The street was a short one but an active one. The crackle of hammers and the rasping whine of saws sounded its entire length. Buildings were springing up on both sides of the street. Some of them were ornate with much scroll work and gingerbread effect, but all were ugly; their bare little porches were ugly, supported by frail and ugly posts, topped by cornices whose ornaments were an offense. The roofs were mis-shapen with dormers and gables, from each of which a single stark window looked out as a malicious eye searching for deformities among men. One house was already painted, a saffron yellow with trim that was an evil make-believe of mahogany.

It was with a sense of relief that they drove out onto Spruce Street. They turned toward town. Before them rose the twin towers of the First Presbyterian Church. On the hill above it the classic outlines of the Capitol climbed toward the sky. To the east Fort Negley frowned impotently. The sun was already sprinkling gold upon the wooded crests and slopes of the Harpeth Hills. Mrs. Polk waved an eloquent hand. " 'The heavens declare the glory of God.' " Then she paraphrased a bit. "And how marvelous is the handiwork of man."

A gentleman passing on horseback saw them and lifted his hat, reining in his horse as he did so.

"Why, it's Eugene Lewis. Let's visit with him a moment."

The rider dismounted, and pulling his horse to one side of the street stood at the door of the carriage, hat in hand.

"The glow of spring is in your face, Mrs. Polk," he said.

"In the years I spent in Washington I don't remember a speech as delightful, or with so little effort. Don't you think Ellen Cole is entitled to a speech, too?"

"I was coming to that," he said gravely. "There are not many ladies, Mrs. Polk, who can sit so becomingly at your side. She borrows wisdom from you and pays with grace." He turned to the driver. "Your fame is known to me, sir."

"My word," said Mrs. Polk, staring at him, "the railroad must have had a good day."

"The railroad? Oh yes, the railroad. That's right: I do have some connection with the railroad. Yes, for a part of each day I give thought to bridges and tunnels and grades. I love it really. And, oh, yes, I had a charming visit to the Academy this morning."

"Anything special at the Academy?"

"Most special. A young boy became so interested in an account of the Grecian Parthenon that he substituted it for Latin grammar. It was a matter temporarily of great chagrin to Professor Clark; most gratifying, however, to me."

"I dislike to flaunt my ignorance, but what precisely was the Grecian Parthenon?"

"I find it embarrassing, too, Mrs. Polk, but I'm afraid I am a bit vague about it. I know it is one of the most famed of the classic buildings of Greece, but I didn't know some of the things that boy knew."

Mrs. Polk's eyes grew brighter. "Hunt Justice," she said almost in a whisper.

"That's the boy's name. How did you know it, Mrs. Polk?"

"Something tells me that I—I mean we—are going to know him better."

"Mrs. Cole already knows the boy. I saw him at her home not long ago. By the way, Mrs. Cole, just who is he? Professor Clark knew very little about him. He knew him for a satisfactory scholar—well, anyhow until he mixed the Parthenon and the genitive case—but he knows little beyond that about him."

"That gentleman—" Mrs. Cole pointed to the driver—"brought him out home the day you were there and we invited him to the party."

"Professor Clark gave me a very favorable account of him, said this was the first time he had ever faltered in a recitation. But then I suppose this is the first time the boy had ever had the Parthenon on his mind."

"I can tell you something else about him," said Mrs. Polk. "At the same moment the boy was dreaming of the Parthenon, his father was helping build one of those atrocities on Base Street."

"Base Street! I rode through it this morning. His father! Are you sure?"

"Quite sure. And that adds merit to the son. I propose to keep my eyes on young Hunt Justice. I think I'll be rewarded."

The man hesitated a moment, then he said, "There's a matter I'd like to speak with you two ladies about."

"We shall listen, sir."

Eugene Lewis smiled at the grandiloquence of Mrs. Polk's speech. "It, too, is about a building, a most memorable building. But it is, alas, even now losing its fineness." He paused and his eyes unconsciously sought the hills to the eastward and lingered there. Then they came back to Spruce Street and the two ladies who sat in the carriage. "I am speaking of the Hermitage, the home which General Andrew Jackson built. Well, I was out there not long ago. The beauty is there, of course, but decay has set in."

"Yes," said Mrs. Polk, and there was sadness in her tones, "it would. I never saw General Jackson many times, and when I did he was old and slowly dying; but the man's power shone out through his eyes and sounded in his voice. Once I got the fantastic notion that he was saying to death, 'Not yet, not yet; Andrew Jackson is still the master.' Is the place pretty much run down?"

"It is becoming so."

"I haven't been to the Hermitage since before the war. I loved the place. General Jackson was an amazing man. He was entirely without benefit of academy, and yet his speech had about it the flavor of elegance. I never heard him say, nor read from his pen, a sentence weak or cheaply phrased. He loved stateliness. Every view of the house is eloquent of his inner culture. I knew young Andrew, the adopted son. He was a charming man. He tried hard to carry on the General's tradition but something always frustrated him. He did well at the University but he never could quite match any phase of strength with the General. His widow still lives there, doesn't she?"

"Yes, she lives there with her son and her sister. She is an admirable woman. The place, as you know, was taken over by the state before the war. It permits the Jacksons to remain there, in fact desires it, but it furnishes them nothing."

"You said the house needs repair. Doesn't the state see to that?"

"I doubt if new paint has touched any part of it in thirty years. Even a slight breeze rattles the windows. Really, it looks a bit desolate."

"What could be done about it?"

"I don't quite know. It is, of course, by any right whatever, the home of Mrs. Jackson as long as she needs it, but it is a reproach to the state of Tennessee to permit the slightest unnecessary deterioration. A dozen selected prisoners from the penitentiary could in one day do wonders in cleaning up the debris that for almost twenty years has been accumulating on the grounds."

"I have heard some talk of converting it into a home for Confederate soldiers," observed Mrs. Polk.

"So have I, and it mustn't happen. We must provide a home for the soldiers—and a good one—but not the Hermitage. The soldiers would wear the Hermitage out too fast. It must be preserved for posterity."

"This is the fourth Hermitage, and in a way symbolizes the ascending scale of General Jackson's culture. There were strength and dignity in the log house which was the first, to which the fourth, this one, adds grace and spaciousness. And in this one are gathered the fine memories of all four. This is a fortunate meeting for me,

Mr. Lewis. It has given me something worthy to think about. The Hermitage must be saved—I like your phrase, sir—for posterity."

"I'm going to visit the Hermitage again before long. I'm going early. I want to stand in the garden and watch the sun come up."

"We have just been complaining about the houses on Base Street, and while we complain decay goes on in one of the greatest of our homes. Isn't that ironic?"

Ellen Cole spoke then. "When you go out to watch the sun come up at the Hermitage, take Hunt Justice with you."

Mrs. Polk stared at her. "My dear, you discourage me. I should have thought of that first."

"Why, I think that's a fine idea," said Eugene Lewis. "Of course, I'll ask him to go. Where does he live?"

The driver decided to participate in the conference. "I'll tell you whereat he lives."

As they drove away the driver slew an early horsefly and then engaged in song.

"Ol' Joe Hooker, won't you come out of the wilderness?
Come out of the wilderness . . ."

13

On Easter Sunday morning Major Eugene Lewis and Hunt Justice went out to the Hermitage. On Saturday the Major had visited the house on Oak Street. He introduced himself to Mrs. Justice, told her that he had met her son at Kingsley and that later at the Academy their acquaintance had been amplified, that they had established certain interests in common. He therefore would esteem it a privilege if Hunt would accompany him on a trip to the Hermitage early the next day. He explained to her what and where the Hermitage was.

"Tomorrow's Sunday. Hunt always goes to preaching on Sunday."

"He needn't miss tomorrow then. There's an early service at the little church near the Hermitage. I expect to attend. I'd like for him to go with me."

Hunt had come into the house then, from work in the garden in the rear. He recognized immediately the gentleman standing in the hall. He bowed and stood waiting a bit nervously.

"Good morning, Hunt. I have thought of the Parthenon a great deal since you called my attention to it."

"Thank you, sir. I have, too." A slow smile broke through the boy's timidity.

"I have just asked your mother's permission to take you with me tomorrow to see the Hermitage."

"Oh yes, sir. General Jackson's home. I'd love to go."

"I want to get there before sunrise."

"I'll fix him up a snack tonight," said Mrs. Justice.

"No, I'll take care of his food. He's my guest."

It was thick dark as they drove out the Lebanon Pike. They met no one, and the silence, except for the beat of the horse's hoofs and the grind of iron-rimmed wheels against the stones of the turnpike, was as one with the dead in Mount Olivet Cemetery to their right. Presently, they were passing through Donelson, but no gleam of light shone in any window. The village was sleeping soundly. Then they were at Clover Bottom, their road cutting in two the faint outlines of General Jackson's historic race track. They clattered across the Stone's River Bridge, and just beyond the first rooster crowed, at first tentatively, and then with great volume and ecstasy. The horizon was still of inky blackness, but even as they watched a tinge of pearl grew in the eastern horizon. By the time they had reached the Hermitage gate, the rose pink of the pearl flowed out into streamers of gold.

Eugene Lewis hitched his horse to one of the cedars that bordered the driveway and, walking rapidly, led the way to the garden at the right.

"They are not up," he said in a low voice. "I told them I would be coming early."

They walked through the path to the graves at the back. The day was breaking. The full light came almost suddenly. The line of hickory trees stood clearly revealed, their sturdiness a token of the strength of the man from whose earth they sprang. And there were magnolia trees, southern and luxuriant symbols of the warm chaste sentiment of the man who composed those noble lines above his wife's grave. The myrtle that bloomed among the graves, and the roses that bloomed in the garden were memorials to the gentle Rachel. The sun came up, rising on the crest of a sea of gold. The birds caught from somewhere the fall of an invisible baton and poured out upon the garden a joyous flood of song. The light deepened and the sun came through the trees and cast fantastic shadows upon the garden behind them. Far behind the house a cow lowed, and out beyond the road sounded the sharp, staccato barking of a dog.

Eugene Lewis turned to speak to the boy, but he was no longer at his side. He had moved a dozen steps away from the tomb and was standing in the garden path looking intently at the house. The sun was falling upon the eastern side of the house and upon the maple trees that stood near it. The boxwood and crepe myrtles which General Jackson had planted made rich the picture's foreground, and a rambler rose lay in masses of bloom upon the garden fence. The warming day was freeing the fragrance of a million honeysuckle blooms. The air grew heavy with the incense of spring.

Hunt Justice was not aware of Eugene Lewis's approach till the man stood at his side. The boy spoke quickly.

"Sir, I wish you would tell me about General Andrew Jackson."

"You know something already, don't you?"

"I read about him in a book but I want to know more."

Eugene Lewis told him more, told him of Andrew Jackson riding westward through the wilderness till he came to the new settlement on the banks of the Cumberland, told him of the young lawyer's early struggles, told him how he became a great man not only in his home but in his nation. And while he was talking there sounded the measured tolling of a bell.

"It's at the church. Every year they hold on this Sunday what they call their 'Sunrise Service.' We'll go to the church now."

"Look at that." Eugene Lewis waved his hand. Two trees lay in a tangled jumble. Another had fallen across one of the giant cedars. The grounds bordering the drive were foul with the accumulated debris of more than a decade. "And if you look closely at the house you can see how much it needs paint and good carpentry. Neglect doesn't damage the brick much, but it is ruinous for the wooden parts."

"Some of General Andrew Jackson's kinfolks live there, sir?"

"Yes, the widow of his adopted son, and the war stripped her of almost everything except the ground and the bare house."

"It looks to me like people ought to keep it fixed up."

"They should keep it fixed up. And they must."

They crossed the road and entered the church lot. Several horses, some harnessed to buggies, were hitched to the trees in the church lot. By carriage or buggy or horseback or on foot the countryside was arriving. There was a great deal of handshaking and neighborly comment. Both history and prophecy were fitted to the weather and to crops, and the health of the neighborhood was duly commented upon. A lady on foot arrived in some haste, evidently fearing that she was late. She saw Eugene Lewis standing with Hunt at one side and went across to him, holding out her hand.

"Good morning, Major Lewis," she said smiling, "I saw you in the garden but I was in no position to greet you then. I am afraid I overslept this morning."

"I knew we didn't trespass, Mrs. Jackson. To stand in the Hermitage garden and watch the sun rise on Easter morning—I shall not forget it."

"I watched the gate to see you as you came out, but I missed you. I was glad to see your horse still there and know you hadn't left."

"This, Mrs. Jackson, is Hunt Justice, a very dear friend."

She shook hands very cordially with Hunt but was plainly a bit puzzled. She couldn't place the boy. After a moment she spoke again.

"Now you both are going home with me for breakfast."

"We couldn't abuse your hospitality, Mrs. Jackson. I brought some food for us both."

"No," she said firmly, "you are going to have breakfast with me at the Hermitage. Dr. Lindsley will be there. I'll be expecting you right after preaching."

"To have seen the Easter sun rise from the Hermitage garden, to have eaten Easter breakfast in the home—well, we shall try to bear our favors modestly. It's all right with you, isn't it, Hunt?"

The boy turned to Mrs. Jackson. "I wouldn't want to put you to any extra trouble," he said.

She smiled. "Extra trouble is sometimes extra pleasure."

They were singing within the church.

> "I will sing you a song of a beautiful land
> The faraway home of the soul."

They went into the church, and sat near the fire whose gentle crackle was restful and friendly. Berrien Lindsley was in the pulpit. The teacher had become preacher—or perhaps he had always been one. Berrien had had lately many interests, prison reform, public education, public health, but his two great passions were still teaching and preaching. He had preached at the Hermitage Church before he was twenty years old, had preached with the eyes of the broken old warrior burning upon him from the pew beneath. New interests sprang from his fertile mind, but the old ones held. He was a frequent visitor to all the city's colleges, and usually on Sunday he preached somewhere. Three years before, Mrs. Andrew Jackson, Jr., had conceived the fitness of a Sunrise Easter Service at the church, and the idea caught on in the community. Mrs. Jackson had another suggestion, and it, too, was considered appropriate. Berrien Lindsley was invited. He pleased the congregation so much that the Sunrise Service was growing into a tradition in the Hermitage community.

When Berrien preached there was little of the cold, polished style of his father in what he said. His illustrations were gathered not from the realms of classical mythology or scholarship, but from the woods and fields lying about the Hermitage. Then the sermon was over, an Easter song was sung, and those in the church moved in unison toward the pulpit to shake Berrien's hand. For a little while after that they stood in the churchyard, scattered about in little groups touching now soberly, now jestingly, upon the community's major conversational themes. Mrs. Jackson, Eugene Lewis and Hunt Justice walked back to the Hermitage, and Berrien Lindsley led his horse and walked with them. The day had become warm and the sun, clear of the trees, was turning its full light upon the front of the home. It revealed the paint-hungry pillars and the colonnaded porch in clear reflection of its old-time glory. They went into the house, passing between the columns and through the door by which so many of the nation's great had entered. The great hall was bright with the wallpaper which the old General had selected, though a close view revealed the dinginess with which years of neglect had coated it. Toward the rear rose the circling stairway held in place as far as the eye could determine solely by its own artistry. Mrs. Jackson guided them into the parlor at the left.

"Make yourselves at home," she said brightly. "Breakfast will be ready right away."

She bustled out of the room.

"I don't believe, Dr. Lindsley, that I have presented my young friend. This is Hunt Justice. He is a scholar in the Academy. He came with me because he has a special interest in common with one of ours."

"Indeed," said Berrien cordially, though inquiry was in his voice.

"Yes, in beautiful buildings. That's right, isn't it, Hunt?"

"Yes, sir, I have thought about them as long as I can remember."

"Why, bless my soul! I never heard of such a thing in one so young. May I inquire what started your interest, how it began?"

"I do not know, sir. I just know that I love them—I mean beautiful houses."

Berrien stared at him. "Why, bless my soul! This is most interesting."

"By the way, Dr. Lindsley—" a quizzical light shone in Eugene Lewis's eyes—"what do you know about the Parthenon?"

"The Parthenon? The Parthenon? At the moment I don't believe . . ."

"Tell him, Hunt."

Hunt hesitated. It didn't seem quite fit that he should know something not clear to a great man. But Berrien sensed the cause of the boy's reluctance.

"Yes, yes, what about it? I should like to know."

"It is the most beautiful building in the world. It is in Athens, Greece, and was built in the days of Pericles in 438 B. C."

"Why, this is astounding! I do recall something of the Parthenon now. Young fellow, I crave your further acquaintance."

Eugene Lewis felt the indelicacy of exploiting further the lad's taste for fine homes, so he gently changed the subject.

"Doesn't the condition of this home distress you, Dr. Lindsley?"

"I haven't been here since last Easter. It was bad then; it is worse now. I didn't mention it but I was deeply saddened from the moment we turned in at the gate a few minutes ago."

"Was it the war that has done all these things to us? I have been at Cherry Hill lately. Decay has set in there, too."

"Yes, I know. Directly, it was the war, of course. But there wouldn't have been a war if terrible forces had not been at work within men."

"Terrible forces? And where would that place the blame?"

"Upon all of us, sir. We matched our faults against those of the North. It is magnificent when men match their virtues. It is tragic when they match their faults. The blind from both sections got together and both fell into a pit."

"No, it was we who fell into the pit. This house proves it."

"Then what do those sixteen thousand Union graves on the Gallatin Pike prove?" He waited a moment and when he spoke again, his voice was tinged with sadness. "No, there was no segregation of guilt. It was everywhere, and it varied with the spirits of individual men. As long as men's lives are not freed of uncleanliness there will be wars, and as long as there are wars there will be melancholy graveyards by the side of turnpikes, and great homes decaying, falling away from their fineness."

"Will war destroy us in the end?"

"I do not think so, though while its fury is upon us it will sometimes seem to. We were speaking of this house. I have visited here while General Jackson still lived. He was a good farmer, a good householder. Disorder was to him an abomination. There were no sprouts in those fields while he lived and if a tree fell on his lawn it was cleared that day. He wouldn't tolerate a foul fence corner. His fences were always neat and trim. As for the house— well, I have the fantastic wish that General Jackson was not buried so close to it. It's too shabby now, too shabby and desolate."

"I never saw the place at its prime."

"I did. It was at its prime when the old man died. A month before he died he sat out in the yard and gave orders. This for one field, that for another, check the fences, take care of the stock, put a new roof on this slave cabin, and as he gave every order the old warrior would plunge the tip of his cane inches into the ground."

"How beautiful to die with the things one has created at their prime!"

"Amen! Too many of us live on to see our handiwork dwindling. I was here the day the General died. I preached at the church that morning. The word was out that he was dying. There were not twenty at the church, and though they strove to listen they heard not one word that I said. I came here as soon as the service was over. I was in the room with him until toward sunset when the end came. He was conscious to the last and when he spoke, though with some difficulty, it was with power. On that summer day I watched a strong man change worlds."

Mrs. Jackson came in with the word that breakfast was ready. They followed her into the dining room and sat at a small table placed toward one end of the room. The great table at which presidents had sat was not there. A sort of gray emptiness was in the room. But there was greatness and beauty there, too. The cheap little table was cheerful with newly plucked flowers and fragrant with breakfast.

They sat at the table and Berrien offered thanks. The food was brought from the kitchen across the area way. There was quality in the damask cloth, a quality that belonged to the dining room in its prime. The cloth was fine but frayed, scarred by the grind of countless dishes, and by the strain and tear of a thousand launderings. But the china and the silver were from the stock which the General and Mrs. Jackson had bought in Philadelphia for the Hermitage.

Mrs. Jackson took the cover from a heavy silver dish.

"What!" exclaimed Berrien. "But no. I thought for a blessed moment that it was turkey hash and it still does resemble it, but, alas, one dreams now of turkey hash—dreams but nothing more."

She smiled. "You may wake up, Dr. Lindsley. It is turkey hash."

"Not turkey hash like . . ." He stopped.

"Yes, Dr. Lindsley, turkey hash made by General Jackson's private recipe. It was," she said sadly, "our last turkey. I wish my son could be at home today. He has the true Jackson fondness for turkey hash, but I'll save some for him." She touched a bell and a young Negro girl, smiling broadly, came into the room carrying a platter topped by a dome-shaped cover. Mrs. Jackson set it aside and lifted to a plate a golden-brown crisp waffle. On that she poured from a silver pitcher some melted butter. Then the waffle was covered with ample servings of the turkey hash, and passed to a guest. "This," she said, "is a kind of memorial breakfast. General Jackson was always served turkey hash on a waffle. That combination afforded his greatest pleasure in eating." She bowed her head to Berrien Lindsley. "You, sir, are the guest of honor. General Jackson was very fond of you. It was mainly his idea that brought your father to Nashville. He read almost everything that Dr. Philip Lindsley wrote, and he never missed an opportunity to hear him speak. 'I study Dr. Lindsley for his gift of expression,' I heard the General say once. 'He has the classic style I covet.' "

"So do I covet it. My father's English was the most polished I ever knew."

"But the General said also that he preferred to talk with you. He said that you knew more things to talk about. He was fond of you, sir. And then I remember that you were here when he died. You are the guest of honor. We saved the turkey for you."

"I am made very humble, Mrs. Jackson."

"To be the companion of the guest of honor at breakfast here this morning is a tribute I can never pay for with merit." Eugene Lewis might well have been fitting his phrases to the memory of the General.

Mrs. Jackson replied in kind, "We have no less pleasure in your visit because it was unexpected." She included Hunt Justice in her hospitable smile.

The aroma of the turkey hash prepared by Old Hickory's favorite recipe was in the room, dominant and pleasing. It was not a solo but a symphony of breakfast smells that flavored the dining room on that Easter morning. Commingling with the pungent fragrance of the turkey hash was the delicate perfume of the waffles, and the invigorating tang of newly made coffee.

"General Andrew Jackson himself was never served a more delightful breakfast."

"Thank you, indeed, Dr. Lindsley. May I serve you some more turkey hash?"

Berrien, who was in some degree a trencherman, accepted with pleasure another serving, but Eugene Lewis and Hunt did not.

"You're not stopping!" Mrs. Jackson was insistent. "Breakfast isn't over yet. Some more coffee, Major Lewis? It's hot. Let's warm your cup a bit. And won't you have another glass of milk? We have plenty." The grinning Negro girl came in with a plate of hot biscuits with top and sides distended from their lightness, and flecked with brown and gold.

"When General Jackson had finished his waffle and turkey hash," Mrs. Jackson was saying, "he was always served hot biscuits and blackberry jam. We have tried to make this a true Jackson breakfast."

Eugene Lewis hesitated for no more than a split second when the biscuits were passed. He took one.

"Take two and butter them while they are hot."

He took two. And before the breakfast was over, two more. The blackberry jam made the round of the table in an oversized thumbprint preserve dish.

"We used to have cherry preserves for breakfast every morning, too, but the cherry trees all died. There are plenty of blackberries but we can never get enough sugar." She reached for the tiny bell. "Won't you have another biscuit? There are plenty of hot ones in the kitchen."

"The flesh would like another one but even my mind knows better." But they took more coffee and the Negro girl brought Hunt another glass of milk.

The light which had brightened was not very friendly to the room. It revealed too clearly its decline from former splendor. One corner was cluttered with an accumulation of unused furniture, even a sack of something, perhaps grain, and an unsightly roll of carpet added to its disarray. Was this the room in which Martin Van Buren had dined in such elegance? Or, for that matter, a great assemblage of other guests bearing names no less potent?

The three left together. Berrien opened the dragging highway gate, and when he had closed it, stood talking for a moment with Eugene Lewis.

"I'm not going your way," he said. "I've been asked to attend an early afternoon funeral at Spring Hill. Except for one thing alone this has been for me a perfect morning."

"And that one thing . . ."

"The same that saddens you. That." He pointed with a sweeping gesture to the chaos of sprouts and weeds upon the lawn, to the fallen trees that untouched lay rotting, to the untrimmed and unkept cedar trees, to the fences whose corners sagged ground-ward. "There it is," he said. "One of our great landmarks is being destroyed."

Berrien cantered away, down the river road toward Spring Hill beyond the river. Eugene Lewis and Hunt Justice drove toward town along the Lebanon Pike. They drove slowly for the air was heavy with the perfume of spring, and the countryside rich with its beauty. To reach too quickly the drabness of town was to end all of this too soon. In the distance the hills stood dimly outlined against the haze which seemed but the fringes of the sky pulled farther down. Birds hopped about upon the freshly plowed ground and dined and sang, and roses bloomed in dooryards. It was spring in the Hermitage country.

There was much passing along the pike. Nashville was out to greet the coming of spring. Suddenly Eugene Lewis felt the boy at his side straighten. He saw that Mr. and Mrs. Orville Ewing were passing in the family carriage drawn by a pair of sprightly bays. He saw, too, that Erwin Roane and his granddaughter sat on the back seat. He lifted his hat and those in the carriage responded. He saw the smile on Neely Barrow's face, but he saw that the smile was for Hunt Justice.

"Why, yes, you do know her. She was at Kingsley. I remember now."

There was an edge in the boy's voice. "She likes houses, too. We talked about them."

PART TWO: THE SECOND BREAKFAST

PART TWO

THE SECOND BREAKFAST

1

THE election of a building commissioner went off quietly enough. The aristocrats saved their consciences by voting for Ed Titus, but there weren't enough aristocratic consciences in Nashville to tally very impressively when the votes were counted. Titsy Harris was swept into office if not by a landslide at least by a convincing drift of democracy's ground forces. The ugly homes overflowed Base Street, swept out into all the streets of the area, into the streets of Nashville's other areas. The city had been passing laws against unsafe buildings since 1836, but these were of no concern to Mr. Titsy Harris. He sat in his office, his feet on his desk, an oversize cigar between his teeth, a brown derby cutting across his forehead at a rakish angle, and from beneath its brim large watery eyes peered at the world. He puffed at his cigar and toyed with a mammoth watch chain. There was a knock on the office door.

"Come in," said the Building Commissioner without moving.

The man who came into the room didn't take his hat off either. He put his hands upon the desk and fixed his bright, beady eyes upon the commissioner. That gentleman met his gaze for a moment. Then he said:

"Have a cheer and set down. What's on your mind, Nat?"

"I ain't gettin' my sheer o' bizness, Titsy."

The cigar inscribed a speculative oval.

"Maybe your prices ain't right, Nat. You thought about that?"

"I ain't in bizness just for fun, and I didn't carry the Tenth Precinct for you for fun neither."

The cigar moved in a cuneiform track through the air.

"What you want me to do, Nat?"

"See that I get my sheer of trade. I earned it, didn't I?"

The cigar spelled out a word in thin air. The commissioner seesawed his chair back from the desk and took his feet from it. A pale light burned in the watery eyes that looked now unwaveringly at the man who demanded his rightful part of business.

75

"All right, Nat, say your say. Only don't take more time to do it than I got to lissen. Who is it that ain't tradin' with you?"

"Ed Crayton for one. He ain't bought even a pound o' nails from me in two months. And he's been usin' plenty o' nails, too; nails 'n' other things."

"You spoke to Ed about it?"

"I wouldn't 'a' come to you till I had. He says he spends his money where it brings most in."

"You act any different from that, Nat?"

"I put out a wad o' money on your election. I didn't aim to waste it."

"Any o' the other fellers besides Ed stopped tradin' with you?"

"Ain't gettin' much from any o' 'em."

"Even if you chipped in a little cash on me you got to take your time gettin' it back. Git your prices down, and don't come botherin' me till you've done it. Maybe I'll talk to Ed. I ain't promisin'."

Nat Baker, a bit disillusioned, went back to his establishment dedicated to building supplies. The Building Commissioner became active immediately. He closed and locked his office, got in his buggy, and drove out to the houses that Ed Crayton was putting up on Base Street. At one of them a workman was nailing in the braces between the sleepers. He promptly recognized the visitor.

"Why, howdy, Mr. Harris," he said, jumping up and holding out his hand. "I was at them speakings the Sattidy before election. That was mighty good speakin'. Never heard better. I most hollered my throat out. You want to see Ed?"

"Nothin' special. So you liked them speeches?"

"Yes sir, sometimes you lifted my hair right straight up. Remember what you said about Gin'ral Lee? That was mighty fine. Yes sir. Lifted my hair right off my head."

Titsy Harris regarded the man with growing interest. "What's your name?" he asked.

"Courtney Justice. I'm from Franklin County. Been workin' for Ed ever sence I come here."

"That's a fine section you come from. Ed treat you right?"

"Yes, sir, he's a tiptop man to work for. He don't stand for no shenanigan. You got to work but he pays you. He's raised me twicet sence I been working for him."

Mr. Harris chose to be humorous. "Wonder if he could use me. Well, I reckon I'd better speak to Ed while I'm here. He around?"

"He's on that job second house down. Expect him here drekly."

"I'll run down and shake his hand. Pleased to make your acquaintance. See you later."

He found Ed Crayton at the job second house down. It was clear that Mr. Crayton was in an advanced state of indignation. If the noises and words which issued from his mouth could be accepted as proof, he had about reached the maximum of his endurance.

"Something vexing you, Ed?" inquired a voice from behind. Ed turned and saw that he was in the presence of the Building Commissioner. But the right of outrage was one of the dearest boons of Ed Crayton's life. So, though surprised, he yielded not one whit.

"Howdy, Mr. Commissioner," his voice boomed out. "The next man I kill will be named Nat Baker. Glad to have you with us. What do you reckon that mangy polecat charged me for that saw? Three fifty, that's what. Health good, Commissioner? That weasel said there wasn't a better saw in town. I love a liar but he suits me too danged well. Which you chawin', Mr. Commissioner, thick Greenville or thin Greenville? I got both. Something told me he was a scalawag the minute I set eyes on him. Ain't traded any with him lately neither. Trouble is I didn't quit quite soon enough. Wait a minute, Mr. Commissioner, I'll fix you something to set on."

The commissioner's gesture indicated a disinclination to sit. "Maybe, Ed, you ain't fair to Nat."

"I ain't," said Mr. Crayton firmly. "I ain't got the words. If he ever starts to starve, I want to set right there and watch him."

"No, no," said Mr. Harris soothingly, "you buy a lot of stuff from Nat, don't you?"

"Didn't you hear me say I'd stopped buying from him? I still got some o' the sense I was borned with. I wish to God I'd stopped before I bought this saw. Nice spell o' weather, Commissioner."

"Nat's a friend o' mine, Ed."

"Then tell him to put some decent stuff in that store of his. And tell him this ain't the Californy gold fields like he thinks it is from the prices he charges. Last time I bought any nails from him he charged me two cents a pound higher than at Hillman Brothers. Three fifty for a hand saw that when the wind blows it breaks half in two. No sir, Commissioner, that friend o' yours ain't doing himself justice. He ought to rob banks. Like a little fruit, Commissioner? I got a right nice apple in my coat pocket."

The commissioner was becoming slightly annoyed. "Try Nat

again. I'll speak to him about his prices. Got to treat an old friend right."

Ed Crayton was becoming slightly annoyed, too. "The old friend I'm going to treat right most of the time from now on is named Ed Crayton."

"I believe I'd give Nat another try." The commissioner's voice had lost its unction.

"Might this visit be to give advice on where to buy stuff to put up houses with?" asked Ed Crayton bluntly.

Titsy Harris lighted his cigar, drew a deep draft upon it, then with lighted end first stabbed at some imaginary targets. "It might be good advice at that."

"Then I ain't in the notion to take good advice. Lissen, Commissioner, this—" he shook the stub of the broken saw—"ain't the first bad luck that happened to stuff Nat Baker sold me. Six hammers I bought from him at one time and they was made out of beeswax, the way nails dented 'em. All you can do is to scratch a plank with one o' his planes. You lissen, Commissioner. I hired a brass band for your speakings two whole days and a night. Paid 'em a good price, too. Every man I got working for me run all over town after you that last Sattiday and I paid 'em full wages. How come I ain't your friend, too, Commissioner?"

There was militancy in the question, and the irritation of the commissioner deepened. Besides he wasn't able to translate Ed's contribution in music and applause into a very impressive total of votes. He decided, however, not to bring the issue into the open yet.

"I'll speak to Nat about his prices. You try him again, Ed. We got to stick together."

Then he changed the subject. A matter had been running through the fringes of his mind. There was a bit of information which he needed.

"I saw a fellow on your other job—" he pointed up the street—"name of Justice. I saw him at my speakings. Purty nice feller, ain't he?"

"He's all right," said Ed, a bit glumly, his mind on the broken saw. "Works steady and got a cheerful disposition. He can put up a house tolable good."

"Purty lucky to get a fellow like that," was the commissioner's parting comment.

As the commissioner on his way to the buggy passed by the house at which he had stopped first, Courtney Justice, whistling cheerfully, was carrying an armload of debris to a trash pile in the corner of the lot. He waved cheerfully and Mr. Harris waved back. He was very thoughtful on the way back to town. Courtney Justice was on his mind.

2

Hunt Justice was deep in the study of his lessons. His mother darned a snagged place in a pair of her husband's overalls. Courtney was reading the weather forecasts in a patent medicine almanac.

The boy spoke out suddenly, triumphantly. "I've got it, I've got the answer."

"I thought you would, Hunt," said his mother calmly.

The father looked up from his almanac. "What is it you got?"

"My algebra problem. I've been working on it ever since I got home."

"Yes sir, I reckon nobody can doubt, Hunt, you goin' to get an education." Mr. Justice sighed broadly. "I wisht I had one."

"I got the right answer." The triumph was unmistakable in the boy's somewhat shrill voice. "And I understand it. I can explain it. I wish tomorrow would hurry up and come."

"I wisht I had one," reiterated Mr. Justice. Mrs. Justice continued calmly with her darning, but her eyes at intervals would stray fondly toward Hunt.

There sounded a knock upon the door. They looked at one another, a bit startled. Company was very infrequent at night.

"You see who it is, Courtney. Must be Mrs. Elrod. I'll straighten things up a little."

Mr. Justice bore a lighted candle into the hall and to the door. He wasn't able at first to identify his visitor, but there formed quickly upon his field of vision the form and features of the commissioner of buildings. Courtney Justice rallied from his initial confusion and grasped the great man's extended hand.

"Howdy, Mr. Harris. Come right in." He held the door open with one hand and lighted the entrance way with the candle held in the other.

"Thought I'd drop in for a friendly visit. The family's at home, I reckon."

"Yes, sir, all right here working away," said Mr. Justice with great cheer. He had become adjusted to the honor now being conferred upon his household. In fact, he was himself again. The commissioner was duly presented to his wife and son. He cleared his throat preliminary to speech. He elected an adventure in oratory.

"It warms my being to see a family dwelling together in peace and unity."

"Me, too," said Mr. Justice heartily. "I feel the same way about it." He said to his wife by way of explanation, "Mr. Harris is one of the big men at the city hall. He's the one I went to hear speak that Sattiday."

"I remember, Courtney. Maybe you better punch up the fire some."

"I will, Lizzie. This is my—our son, Hunt. He goes to the Academy."

"Fine!" said Titsy Harris, enveloping the word with the honey of his approval. "If more of our lads would improve their minds and hearts it would make our great nation stronger. You goin' to make a carpenter, son?"

"No, sir. I am going to plan houses—I mean nice houses, sir."

Lizzie Justice's fingers that held the needle stopped suspended in midair and she looked at her son as does one who seeks to discover the nature of a new and strange phenomenon. Courtney Justice looked at his son momentarily, speechless from surprise. Mr. Harris rubbed his hands in appreciation.

"A chip off the old block," he said beatifically.

"I expect he'll build 'em, too," affirmed Court Justice, his inevitable cheer returning. "When he was a little shaver he'd rather look at pictures of houses than eat a fine dinner, wouldn't he, Mama?"

Mrs. Justice's level glance moved across to her son. He was finding uncomfortable the focus of attention into which he had involuntarily thrust himself. "Yes, Courtney," she said. "You better put some more wood on the fire."

Courtney Justice had had experience with the signals. "I was jest about to forget the fire," he said cheerfully. "Lot o' houses going up, Commissioner?"

"Nashville is spreading like a green bay tree." The commissioner evidently intended to continue speaking, but a sudden stoppage in his throat prevented. When his paroxysm of coughing had subsided, Courtney Justice, a trifle nervous but entirely cheerful, said:

"Yes sir, Judge Garland Higgins from Fayetteville used to be my favor-ite speaker. He's good, too, specially when he gets started on Ol' Bed Forrest. But I never did hear speakin' like you done that Sattiday, Commissioner. Yes sir, that made music to my ears."

The commissioner's speech returned. "I didn't have hardly no time to prepare," he said modestly. "It was just what come to me at the minute." He arose. "I just thought I'd drop in. Have to go now; terrible lot o' work piled up on me." He sighed appropriately. "But we all got to work. It's work that takes a feller from a log cabin and puts him in the White House. Good even', ma'am, I don't see how your husband could have chose a nobler wife. Good even', my lad; do your best on your lessons. This is a land of freedom. Maybe you can rise even higher than your daddy. Accompany me to the gate, will you, Justice? A word with you, sir."

At the gate the visitor cleared his throat. "My time is valuable. I will come to the point. What I am going to say is man to man. You understand that, Justice."

"Oh, yes, yes. Won't even whisper it."

"I reckon you've done a lot of carpentering, Justice."

Justice's reply was slightly evasive. "I been carrying a saw and hammer sence I can remember."

"Very commendable, Justice. The way to go far is to start soon and keep goin'. Would you look with favor upon the opportunity to rise in your profession?"

"Why, yes, yes . . ."

"You might have a chance someday, even before long. Nothing can stop a good man." He opened the gate but midway through it he stopped to continue. "You are loyal to Crayton. You speak favorably of him. You doubtless render him labor commensurate to your wages. Justice, you impress me favorably."

"Thank you, much obliged." Justice was rendered slightly uncertain by the good impression he was making.

"If a more favorable opportunity than the one you now enjoy should present itself, you would not be adverse to giving it consideration?"

"Oh, no, not at all."

"Such could happen, Justice. Opportunity is golden. In the meantime, not a word to nobody. Good night, Justice."

The commissioner drove east on Oak Street. When the sound of his buggy had dwindled into stillness, Courtney Justice still stood at the gate, his fingers tapping nervously upon the latch. The night was as still as those who slept in the graves across Oak Street. He stood there for a few moments hidden in silence, save for his breathing and the nervous tapping of his fingers upon the gate. Then he turned and went into the house. Mrs. Justice's cool, level glance rested upon her husband very briefly, then she withdrew her eyes to her darning.

"Courtney, I don't trust that man."

"Don't be 'spicious, Lizzie. Maybe he's better than you think."

She did not reply. An uneasiness had crept into her eyes.

3

Courtney Justice took to the kitchen the small pail in which he carried his daily dinner. His wife turned about from the pan of dough she was kneading. He had not come into the house whistling as was his custom. She knew that something was wrong even before she saw his face. Her level voice was touched with anxiety.

"You sick, Courtney? You got the headache?"

"Not a thing the matter, Lizzie, not a thing."

She turned entirely away from the pan before her. "What is it, Courtney? You tell me. What is it?"

He swallowed, moved across the kitchen, and hung his pail on its peg. He turned to his wife. "I've changed jobs, Lizzie."

She took a quick step toward him. Her eyes were frightened. "He turned you off, Courtney?"

"No, no, Lizzie. I changed jobs, that's all. Got a better one."

"A better one? What do you mean, Courtney?"

"A better job, that's what I mean. Set down, Lizzie, and I'll tell you."

She sat down, wiping her hands on a dishcloth, never taking her frightened eyes from her husband's face. He told her about changing jobs. Ed Crayton was off somewhere figuring on another contract. In the middle of the morning the Commissioner of Buildings had made his appearance. Mr. Harris was accompanied by another man, introduced as Mr. Pres Vick. The commissioner desired speech with Mr. Justice. They sat each on a barrel of lime, and then Mr. Justice learned the reason for the great man's preoccupation.

Mr. Harris reached the gist of the matter with considerable indirection. Mr. Justice had been recognized as a man of character and professional adequacy. Mr. Vick, who was a dear friend of his, needed the services of such a one. Mr. Vick had recently purchased some lovely lots that languished for those symbols of American greatness, the home, to arise in encouragement of our national ideals. The commissioner then had inquired as to the wages paid by Mr. Crayton to Mr. Justice. On being advised that it was one dollar and a half, he told Mr. Justice that beginning tomorrow he would be paid two dollars. In short, he had been selected to direct the rise of those cottages on Mr. Vick's lovely lots. Two other carpenters had been employed. Mr. Justice would work himself and direct the other two men. Mr. Vick was a tried and true friend of the commissioner's and as soon as Mr. Harris had heard of Mr. Vick's need for professional services, he had hastened to recommend Mr. Justice. He presumed that the arrangement would be gratifying to Mr. Vick.

The commissioner mentioned further details. Mr. Vick had building projects in various sections of the city. He had to spread himself about among them all. Mr. Justice would act as carpenter, overseer and timekeeper. He would report the next morning to the building sites on Fern Street. That was the way the matter stood. Mr. Justice neglected to mention to his wife that his acceptance apparently had been wholly assumed. He had been relieved of all thought in the matter. Perhaps Mr. Justice did not himself notice the omission of that formality.

"Courtney, what's that man—the one who was here that night—got to do with it?"

"He's the one, Lizzie, that thought about me first. He recommended me."

"Courtney, I don't trust that man. Don't you do it."

"I've already done it, Lizzie. I go to work tomorrer."

"I don't like it, Courtney."

"Two dollars a day ain't bad, Lizzie. I worked down at Huntland for six bits."

"Mr. Crayton took you when you didn't have any job. He's treated you fair."

"I hated to leave him. I really did, Lizzie."

"Courtney, I don't want you to change."

"I've already changed, Lizzie. I told Ed before I left. It made him ter'ble mad, but a feller's got to look out for hisself."

She stood looking at him for a moment, then walked slowly back to her dough.

Courtney Justice reported the next morning to the lovely building lots on Fern Street. He was chastened from his wife's reproaches, stung a bit by the memory of Ed Crayton's withering indictment of both his sense and loyalty, but still cheerful. Two men were there awaiting him, and from his first sharp glance he suspected that their art in carpentry left much to be desired. Presently Mr. Pres Vick arrived. Mr. Vick had achieved some renown as a builder able to get the house up quickest with the least outlay of materials. It was true that Mr. Vick's patrons, on various occasions, had been greatly outraged by the accumulated weaknesses which the strain of use revealed in his houses. But in such emergencies he always had been able to employ his political resources to an advantage. He had been a bit worried the time the chimney collapsed. That had approached being serious since it set the house on fire. But his forces had rallied and made the lack of lime appear as an act of God. It was later that Mr. Justice learned of the regrettable instance of the chimney. He did not know then that Mr. Vick's business affairs once had come under such pressure as to require his retirement into inactivity for an extended period. Mr. Vick was known to be without capital at the time of his withdrawal. How then could he buy building lots? It cost money to put up even cheap houses. The fraternity speculated upon the matter for a while, then shrugged its collective shoulder. Let him build his houses; who would buy them from one so discredited?

Mr. Vick came bustling up, breathing heavily from fast walking. His little beady eyes made a malevolent trip over the three men. He carried a yard length of lath in his hand and when he was talking he whacked things with it for emphasis. He moved over near a sapling and whacked it.

"Hope you fellers got your fill o' restin'. We got two houses to put up here, and I want 'em up. I mean *up!* The sooner they're finished, the sooner I sell 'em, and the more houses you get to help build. These houses goin' to be nothin' fancy but good enough to live in. The chimbly's got to draw and the roof's got to keep rain out, and it won't hurt to make the house look nice. But we ain't going to put no doodads on it. There's enough stuff here to start on, and you'll get the rest when you need it. Justice runs the job when I ain't here, and I'm tellin' him here and now this ain't no settin' down job. You two fellers get to work settin' them corner posts. You 'n' me, Justice, better run over things."

He whacked the lath viciously against the timbers from which the two men were preparing to cut the corner posts. As they talked Courtney Justice's words were cheerful but there was uneasiness in his heart.

4

Neely Barrow Roane stood out on the portico at Cherry Hill with her eyes fixed anxiously on the front gate and the stretch of street beyond. Her grandfather should have been at home an hour before. The note which he had left for her to find upon returning from Dr. Price's College for Young Ladies said plainly that he would be at home by five o'clock. It was almost six. He had no taste for idling downtown, and he did not go often, but when he did his return to Cherry Hill followed immediately the conclusion of his errand. Beyond the front gate, the ground dipped rapidly until it fell to the level of Broad Street. Then it lifted steadily to the Capitol on its high hill. There rose the twin towers of the First Presbyterian Church, to its right the stately outlines of the Maxwell House, on out Summer Street the spire of the Baptist Church, and beyond it that of the Cathedral searched for the same God. From there Cedar Street ran westward up the hill whose dome was crowned with the Grecian temple that Tennessee had built for its Capitol. A low-lying, horizontal plume of smoke traced vaguely the course of the railroad.

Neely Barrow's eyes moved again to the First Baptist Church. The Roanes had been among Nashville's earliest Baptists. Then her eyes searched again for her grandfather and her anxiety grew sharper. He was not yet in sight. He should have been at Cherry Hill an hour ago. There sounded the faraway wail of a railroad train blowing for the bridge, and while Neely Barrow watched the train clanged into sight. A thunderhead of dazzling brightness had climbed high into the sky above Edgefield. Neely Barrow's gaze traveled again down toward College Street. It was then that she saw her grandfather coming up the hill. She knew that something was wrong. That uncertain labored walk told her something was wrong. He came closer and his haggard face frightened her. She ran down the walk and met him at the gate.

"Grandy, what's the matter? You're sick."

"No, child," he said, "I am not sick. I'm tired."

The tone in which the words were spoken concerned Neely Barrow more than an admission of illness.

"What is it, Grandy? Tell me."

"I'll be all right when I have had a little rest."

Inside the house he lay for a while upon a sofa, but when Neely Barrow came into the room with a cup of hot tea, he was standing at a window looking with unseeing eyes at the beauty that lay before him.

"Sit down, Grandy, sit down and drink your tea."

He obeyed the gentle tug of her hand and sank into a chair. He swallowed a little of the tea and then pushed the cup aside.

"I'm all right, child; just tired."

Neely Barrow came and stood directly in front of her grandfather.

"Grandy, you said once that we would not have any secrets from each other. Don't you remember? What's the matter?"

A wan little smile played nervously on Erwin Roane's face, and his features were less haggard.

"You are right, child. We will both sit down and I will tell you what is troubling me."

"Maybe I can help, Grandy. What is it?"

When he replied his features were haggard again. "I went to the bank and got the money on the bonds. Then I went to the city hall."

"You didn't lose the money, Grandy?"

"No, child, but it would have been just as well. I can't pay the taxes, Neely Barrow."

"Why, Grandy?"

"Because there won't be enough left to pay them after we have bought what we must have—must have, Neely Barrow!"

"Are taxes that much, Grandy? They didn't use to be."

"Something is wrong, I don't know what. They are more than double what they were last year."

"How can they be, Grandy?"

"I don't know, but we can't pay it. We simply haven't the money. It's outrageous!"

"Grandy, who raises taxes?"

"I don't know. I know where they are paid. I go there every year at this time. It wasn't the price alone. The man's manner, child, was insulting."

"What will they do, Grandy, if you don't pay them?"

"They'll take the house. He said they would sell it, sell it like a common cabin!"

"How long will they give you to pay them?"

"One month."

"Oh," said Neely Barrow relieved. She clapped her hands. "Why, it's just like those grammar lessons. You remember, don't you, Grandy? Miss Thomas said if I didn't get the lessons before a month was out I'd fail. Well, I didn't fail, Grandy. I don't think I ever did learn just what a participle is, but I made her think I did. We'll pay the old taxes. You just see if we don't. You sit there. There's some hot tea in the kitchen. I'm going to bring you a cup. I bet that man made a mistake when he added the taxes up. You can make mistakes adding things up, Grandy."

He was quieted, his pain was allayed. Her touch always bore healing for his troubled spirit. Neely Barrow looked at him in silence for a full minute. Then she said:

"Thank you, Grandy, for telling me about the taxes. I have a secret, too, but I won't bother you with it right now. I'll tell you tomorrow."

5

Dr. George Price sat in his office on the main floor of the Nashville College for Young Ladies. Dr. Price was troubled and he characteristically tugged at the lobe of his right ear as if to shake loose his thought processes, which were stuck at the moment. A problem was staring Dr. Price in the face and crying aloud for solution. Two of Dr. Price's young ladies, accompanied by two of his younger ladies, on the afternoon before had set aside most flagrantly the institution's standardized routine of performance. Instead of going directly to their homes from the college, they had routed their homeward course by the Capitol and had spent considerable time on the grounds and porticos. According to the report which had reached Dr. Price, for them it had been an enjoyable occasion. Happily, no other blot marred their records. But, even so, one ripple upon the smooth flow of their behavior might become the precursor of disturbances infinitely more serious. The ripple must be flattened out before it swelled into a wave. After a while Dr. Price relaxed, his eyes settled into the focus of preoccupation, and his ear-tugging hand fell gently to his desk. For minutes he remained so. Then he laughed loudly and with great satisfaction. The ripple was no longer in sight. Dr. Price's preoccupation had been concerned with a paper which he was due presently to prepare for delivery at a meeting of the D.K.E.'s. The subject which had been assigned him was "The Tennessee Capitol." What a coincidence! A great conspiracy of details had required all of Dr. Price's time lately. He hadn't been able to spend a minute upon his paper. He nodded his head. He had reached a decision. Each young lady would be asked to write a carefully prepared paper upon the Tennessee Capitol. That would serve many purposes. It would enact the purest letter of poetic justice. They had visited the Capitol in violation of law; let them write about it in obedience to law. What a delicate balancing would that achieve! It would be educative in that it would help the young ladies to gain and resolve knowledge of a subject itself most worthy. Lastly, the papers would without doubt ornament their true worth by the assistance they would yield him in the preparation of the D.K.E. assignment.

But the younger ladies? They could hardly be expected to prepare material of this sort. What about them? They had been at the Capitol, too. He tugged at his ear again and a decision fell into place in his mind. He would assign one of the younger ladies to each of the young ladies, as an assistant in the project of the Capitol. She could bring reference books from the library, copy down details and quotations and make herself generally helpful. The younger ladies would find themselves identified with a most stimulating adventure in learning. That was as it should be.

Dr. Price pushed his chair back and with military precision lifted himself to his full height. He would send for the offenders, discuss with them their offense, and assign punishment. He started to the door but was halted by a timid knock.

"Come in."

The knob turned and one of the young ladies entered his office.

"Why, good morning, Neely Barrow."

"Good morning, Dr. Price. May I speak with you, sir?"

"Certainly."

"Dr. Price, yesterday I went to the Capitol instead of going directly home."

"Really, Neely Barrow! You surprise me."

She smiled wanly. "I don't know what made me do it, Dr. Price. Some of us girls talked about the Capitol and I thought it would be nice to see it. It was nice, too. It was beautiful."

"You surprise me doubly, both by going and then by telling me about it."

"Why, certainly I'd tell you. I'm willing to be punished now."

"What punishment do you think would be suitable, Neely Barrow?"

"I don't know, sir. Maybe it was pretty bad for me to go, but it doesn't seem very bad to me, Dr. Price. Really it doesn't."

"It violated our rule, Neely Barrow."

"I know, and that was bad. But it was good to be up there. I am ready to be punished, Dr. Price."

The teacher looked at the child and his face wore a puzzled look. His plan was being thrown out of balance.

"What about the other girls?" he asked.

Her eyes brightened with quick surprise. "Why, then, you already knew about it, Dr. Price?"

"Yes," he said gravely, "I know about it. I think I would like for you to carry a message to them from me—no, that won't do. I'll send word to all of you to come to see me. We'll not mention this present visit, Neely Barrow."

Her hand tightened on the books she was carrying, but she did not leave. "May I ask a question, Dr. Price?"

The schoolmaster felt the imminence of further surprise. "Certainly," he said gravely. "What is it?"

"Why do we pay taxes?"

"What a curious question, Neely Barrow. Our taxes pay the expenses of running the government."

"Does it cost much more to run it some years than it does others?"

"Perhaps. I'd never thought of it that way. What are you driving at, Neely Barrow?"

"Our taxes are so much this year Grandy can't pay them. I guess I'll have to stop coming to school." There was the film of tears in her eyes, but her voice was steady.

"Are the taxes on Cherry Hill much higher this year?"

"Oh, yes, sir, more than twice. And Grandy can't pay them. You are so wise, Dr. Price, that I thought I'd ask you if there is any way to get taxes lowered when they are very high."

"Now that you mention it, my taxes this year seemed high, too."

"Do you think it would do any good if I went down to the city hall and talked to them about Grandy's taxes?"

His brow wrinkled in thought. "You let me see if something can't be done. Perhaps it can. You go on back to your lessons now. I don't think you'd find the city hall as interesting as—as the Capitol."

Later in the day Dr. Price summoned the four girls into his office. He was assured, he told them, that their illegal visit to the Capitol was in most respects an innocent one. But it was unauthorized, and if winked at it might spread and result in great mischief among the less dependable young ladies. He reminded them of the motto of the school, taken from Psalms and graven on the cornerstone of the college building: *That our daughters may be as cornerstones, polished after the similitude of a palace.* That ideal, he explained to them, required of his young ladies decorum and obedience at all times. For them to make unescorted and unauthorized trips would end in the complete dissolution of that ideal. He therefore would be required to impose a penalty. He outlined the conditions and demands of the penalty. Each girl looked at the other three. This was no punishment. In order that they might study the Capitol with more purpose, he would authorize for them a trip to the Capitol, perhaps two, accompanied by his daughter Elizabeth. He would expect two essays, eloquent essays, packed with facts and fine sentiment. Were the conditions clear? They were. Clear and most agreeable.

Dr. Price stood in the doorway of Mac Dickinson's office. He was tall and symmetrical, as straight as a grenadier, hair long and lustrous white, side whiskers that curved gracefully to a union at the point of the chin, the white of his hair at strange variance with the youthful pink of his cheeks.

"Come in, Dr. Price," said Mac Dickinson.

"You're busy, Mac; I'll be brief."

"I'm never busy when you come to see me, and I never wish you to be brief."

"It's a labor of love, Mac."

"I'd welcome the opportunity to do a little first-class reforming gratis, Dr. Price. You never come to see me if it's anything else. Sit there and tell me what's untoward in our body politic today."

"It's Erwin Roane's taxes, Mac. They've been raised so high he can't pay them."

"So? That's hardly what I would call news. A good many people's taxes have risen unceremoniously this year. How'd you find out about Erwin's taxes? He'd never tell you."

"It was Neely Barrow who told me. She asked if she shouldn't go to the city hall to see about getting their taxes reduced."

"That child?"

"Their taxes are more than twice as high as last year. She is afraid they will lose their home."

"Twice as high!" He laid some papers on his desk. "This is a case for pay. It can wait. Ordinarily I'm a peaceful and tranquil citizen, but it looks as though I'm about to be ruffled." He thought a moment. "I have a friend who is a right remarkable fellow. It's surprising, the extent of his acquaintance among all the walks of life. Well, we'll see. Tell Neely Barrow not to worry. They'll not lose Cherry Hill. Sorry you have to tear yourself away and hurry back to the college, but I must go to see my friend."

6

Mr. Adonijah—"Nige" to his familiars—Overall was indeed a remarkable fellow. He lived alone in a curious house on Lamar Street, a house which was itself a measure of his capacity for sentiment. It was built entirely by Mr. Overall, its walls from stones gathered from the vicinity of Montgomery's Hill on which Mr. Overall had been painfully wounded on the sanguinary afternoon of December 15, 1864. "Built out o' rock sprinkled with my blood," was his poetic conception of his home.

"Your blood wasn't more'n a drop in a bucket, Nige," a realistic friend had responded.

"No, I guess it wasn't, though I bled a right smart."

Mr. Overall's eyes faded into a reminiscent vagueness. "If I had it to do over I wouldn't 'a' got shot that day. They wasn't hardly any sense in it. They wasn't hardly any sense in nothin' that day. Ever'body tried his dead level best to git killed that day, and it look like most ever'body did. All I done was to git shot in the laig. It was right funny, too. I reckon I fought in ever' battle in the wah that was any 'count. I might 'a' missed a few. Shucks, I reckon I heard mo' bullits whiz 'n any livin' man. I started out hearin' 'em whiz at Shiloh an' I reckon from then on ever' three bullits that whizzed I heard two o' 'em. Purtiest whizzin' I ever heard was at Chickamaugy. It started out loud but it jest died away 'cause them Yanks was a-gittin' further off all the time. That Chickamaugy whizzin' was jest like music. Mostly the whizzin' got louder 'cause the Yanks was a-gittin' closer and we wasn't a-goin' nowhere."

Mr. Overall paused, his vision fixed upon battles long fought, hearing the ghastly shriek of bullets across a battle-swept terrain.

"It's right funny, the only bullit I didn't hear whiz was the one that hit me in the laig. I guess it's safer to hear 'em."

When Private Overall's leg had healed, the bullets whizzed no longer. Man's obligations were those of peace. It was Mr. Overall's obligation to provide himself with shelter, a reasonable ration of food, and clothing that adequately answered the demands of society and climate. All of these three necessities he had provided.

"Hardest work I ever done was a-buildin' my house. After the wah I jest lived aroun' anywhere I could stick my haid under a roof. An' it got right tejus. Well, my oncle in Texas died and he owned that piece o' groun' on Lamar Street. I was the nearest kinfolks he had, so I got it. Right then I made up my mind to build a house. Befo' the wah I'd worked some at the carpenter's trade and I'd helped put up a few chimblys. It was in the summer I got the piece o' ground. It wasn't much later I went to a old soldiers' reunion. We had us a big time, lots to eat, and more speakings than you cud listen to if you had four ears. I liked one of the speakers fine. He put on the rousements. He said ever' rock a Reb soldier had bled on ought to be used to help build a temple with. Right then I ricollected that Montgomery's Hill is plumb covered with rocks that Reb soldiers bled on. I never heard another word that man said. I was a-thinkin' about them rocks out on Montgomery Hill. Befo' he finished I made up my mind to build me a house out o' them rocks. And I done it. It took a lot o' contrivin'. A house jest don't build itself, specially a rock house. It took figgerin' with my mind and workin' with my hands. Anyhow, I'm a-livin' in it. I reckon it's the only real Reb temple they is. And Lamar Street is filled with people who come by to see it, some o' 'em people I don't know from Adam's off ox."

If Mr. Overall didn't know them, didn't even recognize them at sight, they were by that token obscure people. Mr. Overall knew everybody. He made it his business to know everybody, and he had available a carefully arranged assortment of information about each. The pigeonholes of his memory were remarkably complete. He was indeed a veritable walking encyclopedia of local biography. It was this expert knowledge that enabled Mr. Overall to meet the obligations of food and clothing. Mr. Overall made a living by the exercise of his native wits joined to his acquired knowledge of Nashville citizens. For three months every year he worked for the people who prepared and published the city directory. He performed yeoman service for candidates in need of more specialized knowledge of the city's sovereign voters. He had a few times been called in for consultation by the managers of stores who sold extensively on credit. Mr. Overall's expertness yielded him food and clothing with time left over for both investigation required for the continuance of his research, and for the philosophic reflection which gave him a sort of serene overview of humanity in general.

He was planting gourd seed by his paling fence when he became aware that a buggy was stopping at his yard gate and that he was about to be visited by Mac Dickinson. He was fond of the young lawyer and immediately became the very substance of hospitality.

"Howdy, Mr. Dickinson, come right in. Welcome to Bloodstone."

"Bloodstone?" Mac Dickinson was puzzled.

"Took me five years to name it when it ought to come to me in five minutes."

"I've been afraid," said Mac Dickinson, "that this would happen. Even a mind like yours, Nige, can stand just so much."

"It's my house," explained Mr. Overall, "I've named it."

"So that's the cause of your collapse?"

"Ain't all the fine houses around here got names jest like a fancy trottin' hoss? Ain't Belle Meade got a name? Ain't the Hermitage got a name? Ain't Tulip Grove got a name? Ain't your granddaddy's place named Traveller's Rest? Ain't my place got jest as much right to be named as any o' 'em?"

"The right of your place to be christened is clear, but why Bloodstone?"

"They isn't a single other name would do but that, and it took me five years to think of it." Mr. Overall was aggrieved by the sluggishness of his invention.

"Five years! How'd you *ever* think of it?"

"Why, Mr. Dickinson! Ain't I brought ever' rock in that house from Montgomery's Hill? Ain't ever' one o' 'em got Reb blood on it, shed between four and half past the evenin' o' December 15, 1864? Anyhow, if they wasn't no blood shed on it they could a-been. They was plenty shed. This is a reg'lar temple, Mr. Dickinson, and it's got a right to be named. I first thought I'd call it Bloodrock, but that didn't sound so good. Stone's a lot purtier than rock, Mr. Dickinson."

"I'm convinced. It's a noble name. By the way, how much taxes do you have to pay?"

"Taxes, Mr. Dickinson? What'd I want to pay taxes for?"

"I believe it's a bit customary for people whose houses have names to pay taxes on them."

"Don't talk about taxin' this house, Mr. Dickinson. It was enough trouble to build it. Brought ever' rock from Montgomery's Hill, more'n a mile. If I'd a-aimed to pay taxes I'd a-put up a shack. I got more sense 'n to put up a house people'll come five miles to see and pay taxes on it besides."

Mac Dickinson smiled. "I wish we had talked of this sooner. I could derive some very thrifty ideas from you. Has no effort ever been made to reduce you to the tax paying level?"

"You mean, did anybody ever try to get me to pay taxes?"

"Yes, that's what I mean."

"Twicet they've tried it, Mr. Dickinson. Twicet! I reckon they learned, though."

"Dear me," sighed Mac Dickinson, "I miss so much. If Will Shakespeare should play the gravedigger at the Masonic I'd hear of it a week later. How'd you frighten off the tax gatherers?"

"Used spizzerinktum on 'em. Yes sir. First time it was that Eph Hutchings that come snoopin' aroun'. He was deppity then. 'I come to get your assessment for taxes,' says he. 'They ain't none,' says I. 'Eight hundred dollars about right?' says he. 'You aim to buy it?' I asts. 'I aim to tax it,' he says. I seen right then vinegar's better for what ails men like Eph than molasses, so I used some. 'I ain't payin' no taxes,' I says. 'Then the law'll collect 'em,' he says. 'And I'm goin' to tell you why,' I says. 'First place, my house wasn't built so I could pay taxes. That's no house, that's a temple, a temple to Reb soldiers that shed their blood for the South. You don't pay taxes on temples. You shed any blood, Eph? Second place, even if I was turnin' this place in for taxes, I shore wouldn't to a feller whose uncle skipped the country with seventeen hunderd dollars tax money back in 1848—August, wasn't it? And if the word got out it wouldn't do you any good, Eph. Folks might get to sayin' you got skippin' blood in you.' The other time they tried to get taxes out o' me it wasn't no uncle I knowed about, it was the feller hisself. It was Ol' Man Lod Duncan. He never was much good at nothin' and he was jest about played out gin'rally, but somebody got him a job listin' land and houses for taxes. So one day he come traipsin' up. I met him at the gate. 'You actin' as tax deppity now?' He said he was. I told him I druther they'd send some feller out from the office who hadn't been arrested for stealin' a ham on Saturday before Easter Sunday back in '58, besides forgin' a check for ten dollars the very next June. They was some other things I was goin' to tell him, but he left. Any feller that tries to get taxes out o' me better be without sin, as the Good Book says. Law business purty good, Mr. Dickinson?"

"Fair, but if you don't mind let's stick to taxes a minute longer. The commissioner is sick, isn't he?"

"Yes, he's a right ailin' man. He's off somewheres a-drinkin' the health-givin' waters fresh from nature's fountains. Lucky for me he didn't come hisself. They ain't nothin' agin Truman Gilbert as fur as I know. But I'm not goin' to take no chances. He's not goin' to get my vote. Suits me to get people in office that I can handle personally."

"Who's doing the work while Gilbert is away?"

"Two fellers, both of 'em scalawags, and they ain't got nobody fooled but Truman Gilbert. He needs to drink some of them health-givin' waters for his haid same as the rest of his insides. One o' the fellers is Perk Bowles. He's a-livin' in style and finery at the St. Cloud, though what on ain't meetin' the naked eye, like the poetry book says. His wife left him last July, and that's the only time she showed sense. I like him less'n I do a Yankee with blue chin whiskers. The other feller's named Elmer Byron. He lives on Locust Street just this side o' the railroad. He ain't as big a scalawag as Perk, jest sort o' helpless like a one-armed fiddler. He had a baby borned the twelfth of las' month so maybe he'll spunk up some."

"Let us hope so. What I'm getting around to is this: They've raised the taxes of a dear friend of mine so high he can't pay them. I'm going down to the city hall to call on Perk and Elmer about getting my friend's taxes reduced. I thought maybe you could tell me a few things about these fellows that might help me. You know what I mean. For instance, do any of their kinfolks or close friends go untaxed? Things like that."

"Laws-a-me, Mr. Dickinson! Move over in the shade. They's plenty to tell."

There was plenty. Mr. Overall talked and Mac Dickinson made notes, and when he left Bloodstone the light of battle was kindled in his eyes.

Mac Dickinson went directly to the city hall. He asked to see Mr. Perk Bowles of the tax commissioner's staff.

"Come right in. Have a chair." Mr. Bowles was too oily in

manner, too gaudily dressed, his eyes too close together, his face too red. "Now, what can I do for you, sir?"

The answer was brusque. "You can reduce Erwin Roane's taxes to the proper level."

"Ah, Erwin Roane? Erwin Roane . . . ?"

"He lives at a place known as Cherry Hill."

"Oh, yes, I remember now. He came in here several days ago but didn't settle."

"Nor would I. Why was his valuation raised so outrageously?"

Mr. Bowles shifted in his chair. "It had been too low."

"I shall approach that point comparatively, and I hope convincingly. Just what value is placed on the property of your uncle, Cletus Morse, on Hazel Street?"

The red in Mr. Bowles' face deepened and he stirred in his chair. "What—what . . . ?"

"Were you about to ask what business is that of mine? All in good time, sir. But continuing—how much taxes did your cousin Elmer Bowles pay on his place at 242 Woods Street? Or, in further instance, your close friend in several devious affairs, Alex Rector on Dillard Street?"

Mr. Bowles got even redder, shifted about in his seat more violently, and made vocal noises that resembled gurgling.

"I see that my argument is being followed," said Mac Dickinson. "By the way, what is the status of the indictment brought against you in July 1873? Filed away, doubtless. Well, that procedure has been often used, I believe. I have had some experience in unfiling such documents. . . . No, don't speak, Mr. Bowles. I think perhaps the sound of your voice might annoy me. You listen." There was savage emphasis in his voice. "I wish you to reduce Erwin Roane's taxes to the old level. And further, I want you to see that assessments in the instances I have named be made and the taxes collected. You understand me, I believe. I shall within four or five days examine to see if my suggestions have been carried out. Good day."

At the threshold he paused and looked back at the apoplectic Mr. Bowles. "Also, see if some error has not been made in the taxes charged to the College for Young Ladies. I shall expect justice for Dr. Price. One more thing, I advise strongly against your shooting me in the back as I leave the office—or later. A friend of mine thinks you might be tempted to do it. He insists that your brother, Everett, shot a man in the back—1869, wasn't it? Well, quite likely that family trait has weakened." He closed the office door behind him.

7

Erwin Roane was relaxed, the strain in his face gone.

"I've good news, Neely Barrow, excellent news. The tax people made a mistake. I'm going to the city hall tomorrow and pay them."

"Oh, isn't that fine, Grandy? What was it that happened?"

"It was just a mistake they made, child. I have a courteous letter from a Mr. Bowles explaining it. That's curious, too, for it was he who was so ill-mannered when I was there, or perhaps I imagined it."

A quizzical smile overspread his granddaughter's face. She was silent for a while, then she spoke upon another topic.

"Grandy, I have to write something on the Capitol. Couldn't you help me some? Just talk about it, won't you, please?"

Her grandfather's face indicated then even further relief. Some old and grateful memory was revived.

"How delightful! No one, child, is more entitled to write the essay. My father was one who helped to direct the building of the Capitol. It was for him a labor of great love. And when it was finished, he served in it in an office highly honorable."

"I knew about those things, Grandy. I thought about him when I was up there last week. You remember, Grandy, I told you about it?"

"Yes, child, I remember."

"Well, that's the reason I am writing the essay. It's for punishment, Grandy, though I think it's mighty funny punishment, don't you?"

"I know, child, but you must obey the rules of the college. Try not to forget that. I remember so well something I heard my father say once: 'The cedars that grew on Capitol Hill were nature at her best, and the Capitol that was built there is man at his best.' "

Neely Barrow clapped her hands. "Why, I think that's beautiful. Wait till I write it down. Do you know anything else beautiful he said like that?"

"I have heard Father say many beautiful things about the Capitol. When William Strickland, the architect, died and was buried within the Capitol's wall, Father spoke at the services. I was there. I shall never forget one thing Father said. 'We offer as a sacrifice upon the altar of the temple of Tennessee the body of its builder.' "

"Oh-h," said Neely Barrow. "Say it again, Grandy, so I can write it down."

Erwin Roane repeated the words. "Another thing he said, child, that same afternoon was, 'From the top of that tower a thousand square miles of Tennessee are visible to the physical eye, but to the inner eye the whole state becomes revealed.' "

"A thousand square miles! Oh-h," said Neely Barrow, with a sibilant intake of breath. Her pencil flew across the paper.

"My grandfather and my father were great men, Neely Barrow. I never look at the Capitol without thinking of them. I have not been fair to them. I have not been fair to the home my father built. I have not been fair to you, child. I have . . ."

"Please, Grandy. If it hadn't been for you I wouldn't be here at all, and I'm so glad I'm here."

Jacob Shofner stood in the hall testing the merits of an assortment of walking canes. He was already wearing his special railroad board hat and he was about to fare forth to the quarterly meeting of the railroad directors. From upstairs came the rustle of a dress and the sound of running feet.

"Wait, Papa."

He waited while his young daughter ran down the steps to the hallway.

"You in a hurry, Papa?"

"Not that big a hurry. What is it, dear?"

"I need some help, Papa. I'm writing an essay on the Capitol. You know all about it, don't you, Papa?"

"By no means. It is, though, one of my special interests."

"Then was it Grandfather who knew all about it? Somebody did."

"I'll say he did. He didn't think of anything else for ten years. He didn't know anything else to talk about. Why, Mr. Sam Morgan, the chairman of the Capitol Committee, told me himself that he never came to an important decision without consulting Father."

"Tell me something I can put in my essay."

"Father's particular love of the Capitol was the tower, The Lantern, he always called it." Mr. Shofner had forgotten that he was due presently at a railroad board meeting. He was striding up and down the hall, his cane catching and accenting the rhythm of his steps.

"Papa, I need something for my essay."

"One time there was a man, a railroad man from Cleveland, visiting us. Father as usual was talking about The Lantern. 'Why do you call it that?' the man asked. 'The Lantern of Demosthenes was what they called a structure in Athens from which this was patterned.' Father was speaking very loudly as was likely to be the case when he was talking about The Lantern," said Mr. Shofner, speaking very loudly.

"Papa, my essay . . ."

"The man tried to joke with Father. 'Ah yes, The Lantern to find one honest man in Tennessee.' 'No, you wouldn't need a lantern to find an honest man in Tennessee. The state is filled with 'em. We use it to look for rascals that come down here from the North!' Father was shouting then," shouted Mr. Shofner.

"Wait, Papa, I can use that in my essay."

"And the man said, 'Rascals, ah yes, we do raise a few of them for the export trade.' 'Export trade, my hind foot,' snorted Father," snorted Mr. Shofner. " 'You keep the biggest ones at home.' The man saw he couldn't put anything over on Father, so he changed the subject. I think Father was clever though when he said The Lantern wasn't needed to search for honest men, just for scoundrels."

"Something more for my essay, Papa."

"I've heard Father say in a speech he made that the Capitol cost $900,500 to build and that every one of those dollars was sanctified by the ideals of the greatest people on earth. Father said . . ."

"Wait, Papa, till I write that down." She finished writing. "You have your cane. Weren't you going somewhere, Papa?"

"No, I'm not going. . . . Why, yes, I am too. To the board meeting, and they can't start till I get there. Don't you fail to prepare your lessons. I heard Father say once . . ."

But Argie Shofner was gently pushing her father out the door. She was ready to begin writing upon her essay.

8

Professor Yeatman sickened and died and so the boys lost the helpful influence of a good mind and a gentle spirit. Professor S. M. D. Clark succeeded to the principalship.

"That's bad," said James Parkes. "I guess I'll be covered with bruises from now on. Smack Me Down's got a spite at me. The last time he whipped me I didn't regain consciousness for nine days."

"You ain't yet," said Bart Halloran with Irish crispness. "Smack Me Down's all right and if a boy complains when Smack Me Down licks him, I'll lick him over."

"Who, me?" asked Jim indignantly. "I am not complaining. I'd appreciate it if Smack Me Down would lick me oftener. Make a lot better man out of me." James sighed for the man he probably would never be.

"I'm quitting the Academy," said Bart. "It's all right, but I don't think it's much help to a railroad man." Bart cocked his head, Irish fashion, and stuck his thumbs in the armholes of his vest.

"Railroad man?" inquired several voices in unison.

"That's me. Going to start in working for the railroad the first of the month."

The boys looked at Bart incredulously.

"Betcha I get to be a conductor or maybe an engineer. Yes sir, quitting you the first of the month."

"We'll miss you," said Hunt Justice.

Bart looked at Hunt for a full moment, his Irish eyes warm. "Oh, you will? Well, kid, if you ever get in trouble just send me word."

Gordon Hicks came around the corner of the building in a run.

"Guess what?" he asked, panting.

James Parkes struck a pose. "You look just like I did the last time I was the only one that got out of a burning building alive. . . ."

"Let him tell it," said Bart.

"We're going on a trip," said Gordon. "We are going to the Capitol."

"How extraordinary!" said Ivo Burns.

"Listen," said James Parkes. "Ivo has got a new word. Who's going to the Capitol, Gordon?"

"All of us. I was waiting in the office for something Smack Me Down's sending Papa, when Professor Garrett came in the office. I don't guess he saw me. He told Smack Me Down he wanted to take all of his class to the Capitol next Tuesday. He said there was going to be some speaking there that he wanted to hear, and he thought it would be education-al, I mean, fine for us. Smack Me Down thought awhile, then he said it might be all right. He asked if Professor Garrett would be responsible for us, and he said he would. Smack Me Down just sat there for a while. Then he said we could go. So we're going a week from tomorrow."

"How are we going?"

"Walk, and take our dinners. We're going to stay all day."

"Really," said Ivo. "How interesting!"

"I don't think Professor Garrett ever saw me. I was over in a corner. Smack Me Down went out into the hall with Professor Garrett, and when he came back and saw me he seemed to think I had come in while he was gone. I'm not supposed to know about our trip. So when Professor Garrett tells you, act surprised."

"I'll be surprised if he ever tells us," remarked James Parkes. "Once I dreamed I was at the Capitol and a lot of men wanted me to be governor, but I outran them. Lucky I did, too."

"Lucky? How was that lucky?"

"I'd be dead now. You ever read in a history book about a governor that's still alive?"

9

Professor Garrett took the boys on the trip to the Capitol. They left the Academy immediately following their second class period. He led the boys north on College Street, and they gathered as closely to him as possible, for he was telling rich stories of the history that had been made along the way they traversed. There on the right was the college building whose erection General Andrew Jackson had supervised. Then they were crossing Broad Street at the identical place where the dogs loosed by Charlotte Robertson had created such havoc among the Indians. He halted them at the market, for too many things had happened there to be related while in continued progress. There the Marquis Lafayette had been given the famous dinner. There General Jackson had engaged in the duel with the Benton brothers. It was there that General Jackson had halted the boys who had deserted the college in protest against the expulsion of Cave Johnson. There was the stone which in less happy days was the auction block for slaves. The stories which the professor told carried such a contagion of interest to the boys that they were a bit surprised when they reached the Cedar Street entrance to the Capitol grounds; they went first into the gallery of the Hall of Representatives where sat a great crowd of gray-clad men, soldiers of the Confederacy in their state convention. Professor Garrett found places for the boys to sit. Almost immediately they were standing again for a brass band on the main floor had swung with great triumph into "Dixie." One soldier yelled but the quiet rigidity of the others stopped him, held him chastened until the band stopped with a thunderous climax.

"I'll live and die in Dixie."

As if that were the signal for which they had waited, those men in gray opened their throats and translated into sound their memories of battle. They were following Breckinridge across that open field at Stone's River, they were climbing Little Round Top with Pickett, they were surging through the woods with Pat Cleburne at Chickamauga, they were galloping through the dark of a winter night with Ol' Bed Forrest, they were swinging around that Osage orange hedge at Franklin, they were lifting that free full-voiced yell with the little curling undertone of prairie melancholy that they had learned from Jawn Hood's Texicans. Then their shouting died away and the boys could see that some of the men were crying, sprinkling tears upon the altar of memory.

General William B. Bate, who had ridden ahead of his men in that march of death at Franklin, then spoke, and he put into clever and resounding phrase the same memories that had echoed in the shouts of the men but a moment before. He did not speak long, for in the early afternoon there was to be a great picnic for the men at the Hermitage. A long line of buggies and carriages was even then waiting in front of the Capitol. The Academy boys stood on the terrace and watched the soldiers climb in the waiting vehicles. The queue of buggies and carriages moved out of the Capitol grounds turning eastward on Cedar Street. Professor Garrett came back and rejoined them. His face was tinged with sadness.

"Professor Garrett, I wish you could have gone on the picnic," said Hunt Justice timidly.

"Thank you, Hunt. For a moment I confess that I felt deprived. But I was with them for a while. Now I think it is better to be with you."

"I loved to hear him speak, that general," said Gordon Hicks.

"So did I, but he does it almost too well. To keep alive the comradeship, that is well; but to make us wish we were back in the war, that is not well. We lost the war; we mustn't lose anything else."

"What could we lose, Professor Garrett?"

"We could lose the opportunity to help rebuild the South. We could lose time in rebuilding it."

"The South was right, wasn't it?"

"Don't ask me that. I thought so then. I fought in six major battles thinking so. I am sure I'd do the same thing over again, but that will not be required of me. I'm not so sure of right and wrong as I used to be. The past, young men, can be most alluring but it would be dangerous to let it obscure our view of the future. No. I have been with my old comrades for a while. Now, I am glad to be with you. Wouldn't you like to go up into the tower now?"

They climbed the steps which twisted constantly upward within The Lantern of Demosthenes. Presently, panting but happy, they reached the tower room and feasted their eyes upon the panorama that in all directions stretched out and out until lost in low-lying masses of purple hills. Professor Garrett pointed eastward to a long wisp of limestone dust lying low against the countryside.

"There go the soldiers," he said. "They will be at the Hermitage in less than an hour."

Hunt Justice spoke as one does remembering some precious experience. "I've been to the Hermitage. I ate . . ." He became aware of what he was saying and stopped suddenly. The boys were looking at him curiously.

"What was it you ate, kid?"

Hunt caught some quality of reassurance in Bart Halloran's question. "Breakfast," he said quietly.

"General Andrew Jackson set a good table when I used to eat with him," said James Parkes.

His levity was ignored.

"We envy you, Hunt," said Professor Garrett. "I have never eaten at the Hermitage." He left an obvious question unasked.

"Mr. Eugene Lewis took me."

"Oh, I see. I've heard, Hunt, that you interested Major Lewis in the Parthenon. Certainly, he could do no less than take you to the Hermitage."

They came down from the tower and ate their dinners at the spring behind the Capitol. They ate with great heartiness for the morning had been vigorously spent. Each one insisted on sharing his package with Professor Garrett, who refused, saying jestingly that such rich, fine food would render him incapable of guarding the boys from any and all harm, that being his main duty for the day.

If they would refrain from eating their dinners until they returned to the Academy, he would with considerable pleasure eat all of their dinners. During the meal the professor manifested a quality of humor of which the boys had not suspected him.

"You must be as big an eater, Professor, as Big Foot Spencer," said James Parkes.

Professor Garrett smiled. "I know something about Big Foot, but I don't believe I've heard of his capacity as an eater."

"Why, Professor Garrett." James' surprise was obvious. "Well, once he worked right hard all morning. So he was hungry and he shot and cooked a lot of game and sat down on a log right close to the Cumberland River, and there came a rise in the river and he had to quit, before he'd half finished. It made him terrible mad."

"I didn't know about that," said the Professor, speaking very casually. "Perhaps you have not heard of it, but Big Foot was a great jumper. He couldn't swim at all but usually he didn't have to. When he came to a stream he jumped it. One time he wanted to get across Stone's River. He backed up two or three miles and got a fine running start and jumped." The professor stopped and whistled a little random tune. The boys looked at one another in amazement. James Parkes could wait no longer.

"He made it, didn't he, Professor?"

"No, he didn't. There came a big rise in the river while he was in the air. He saw he couldn't make it. He couldn't swim a stroke either. . . ." Again the whistled tune marked an anticlimax.

"What happened, Professor?"

"He stayed up till the river fell."

They sat about the spring talking, but presently Professor Garrett arose. They climbed the hill to the Capitol. Both the building and the grounds seemed deserted. Many of those in the offices had gone out to the Hermitage with the Confederates. Out on the portico of the Capitol the teacher stood in the center of the boys and pointed out many spots of historical interest. James Parkes touched Gordon Hicks on the arm, and surreptitiously pointed out a spot of less historical interest.

"What are they doing up here?" he whispered. "Wonder if they've run away from Dr. Price's College."

"Then they've run away with his daughter," whispered Gordon. "That's Elizabeth Price in front."

"They've all got notebooks. That doesn't look as though they've run away."

"The Whig Convention of 1854 was held in the First Presbyterian Church," Professor Garrett was saying. "It was there they nominated . . . !" He broke off suddenly. "There are some friends of mine! Excuse me a moment. I must speak to them."

The girls had reappeared around the corner of the east portico. The teacher left the boys and walked across to the girls who stood clustered about the portico railing. He spoke first to Elizabeth Price.

"My dear, how delightful! Has education gone out-of-doors? How are your charming parents? My dear, what does this visit mean? What has come over Dr. Price's College?"

"Professor Garrett, what has come over the Academy?" Elizabeth pointed to the boys whom she knew.

They stood talking about the College and the Academy. Hunt Justice had moved away from the boys and was using the interlude to feast his eyes on the columns that gave the building strength and classic symmetry.

"Good afternoon, Hunt."

At the sound of the greeting, he turned quickly to find Neely Barrow standing at his side. He had been only vaguely conscious of the arrival of the group of girls, or of Professor Garrett's discussion of the Whig Convention. Even then the beauty of those columns had been claiming. But there stood Neely Barrow Roane, and the faint crimson flowed into his face.

"Good afternoon," he said. "You surprised me."

"Do you know the names of those columns?"

"No."

"Well, I do, Hunt. They are Ionic columns. Elizabeth Price told me a while ago. I thought you'd like to know."

"Ionic," he said, tasting the word as was his wont when it carried special appeal. "Ionic."

"What are you doing here, Hunt? I suppose you are with them."

"Yes. Professor Garrett brought us to see the Capitol."

"Isn't it strange that we came the same day? Now, isn't it? Elizabeth Price—she's Dr. Price's daughter—brought us. Well, I'm glad I could tell you that they are Ionic. I wish I could tell you how we happened to come but I don't guess I would have time."

"I'm glad I know they are Ionic."

"I doubt if you know the next time I see you. Boys forget a lot."

"I haven't forgotten I saw you out driving the day I went to the Hermitage."

"I saw you. You were with Major Lewis. I wondered where you had been. When are you going to build a house?"

"I'm going to. You just wait and see. Maybe I'll have some Ionic columns in it."

"I like Ionic columns."

"Come on, Hunt. We must go now."

Hunt Justice chilled a bit, for the voice was that of Professor Garrett. Hunt turned quickly. Professor Garrett had returned to the boys and they were all looking at him.

"All right, Neely Barrow," a tinkling voice called from the other direction, and Hunt saw that Elizabeth Price, standing with the group of girls, was summoning her charge. They were all looking at him, too, and the crimson in his face deepened.

"I'm coming." Neely Barrow's voice was warm and clear. Her black eyes were sparkling. She held out her hand to Hunt.

"Good-by, Hunt. When I get home I'm going to see if our columns are Ionic. I hope so."

It was time to be setting out on the return to the Academy. Professor Garrett walked on down the steps toward Cedar Street, and the boys followed.

"I remember it just as well as if it happened this morning. . . ."

"Remember what, James?"

"The time we went to the Capitol and one of the boys got to talking to a girl. . . ."

Bart Halloran looked for a brief second at Hunt, then he interrupted James Parkes' flow of reminiscence.

"You don't remember nothing."

At that, James's memory went completely blank.

10

The D.K.E.'s were holding a special meeting in the home of Dr. Price. The night was warm and no fire burned in the grate. They sat for a while in the living room. The fragrance of spring came in through the open windows, and the sleepy calls of night birds sounded from the trees without. The men talked casually of various things. The papers had said that the days of the horsecar were numbered and that men then alive would see the streetcars apparently unpropelled running along the street. Jacob Shofner expected to live long enough himself to take a ride on a horseless carriage. President Stearns, a cautious and canny son of Massachusetts, thought it was entirely within the realm of the possible to move cars by electrical force. But a horsecar was always under control. Its speed, it was true, was limited, but what besides mere whim would make a faster rate imperative? Yes, a horsecar started and stopped to fit the need. It was reasonably comfortable and entirely safe. Electrical force, on the other hand, was as unpredictable as powerful. No, he did not expect ever to ride on a car propelled by electricity. Men would experiment with it, but in the end they would choose transportation in which arrival would be more certain and progress safer.

"I imagine," replied Jacob Shofner, "that you came from Massachusetts to Nashville by the steam cars. Why didn't you ride a horse so as to travel more safely and to reach your destination more surely?"

The president, who pondered everything before he spoke, gave this gem of sarcasm due thought. Certain movements suggested that a reply was about to begin. But his rebuttal was blocked by testimony from another angle.

"Come, come, Doctor," chided Jacob Shofner. "We have a first-rate contraption now for talking at a distance—I don't mean yelling, I mean talking. I've talked over the telephone myself; so have all of you. Now be fair, Doctor. What did you say about it when it was first mentioned?"

A thin, dour smile softened momentarily the New England face. "That is the most convincing response you could have made. I confess that I was a doubting Thomas then, too."

"You doubted whether it would work, too, now didn't you, Chancellor?" inquired Jacob somewhat impatiently as if eager to array the colleges against progress.

"I waited to see," said Landon Garland. "I am not acquainted in that field. If it didn't work, I had nothing to lose; if it did, I had something to gain."

"I am not exactly a doubting Thomas," said Dr. Ward, "but I confess that I may have had a few doubts that day. I was on Mrs. Polk's gallery the day it was first tried. The town was filled with doubting Thomases. It seemed to me that they were half afraid it might work. There were fifty crowded in on the front gallery at Polk Place, and almost as many at the Adams' place across Union Street. They stood around waiting until the signal that all was ready came just about noon. Mrs. Polk held the receiver at her ear, and the crowd held its breath.

" 'What did you say?' asked Mrs. Polk into the mouthpiece. 'Oh, what do I want? Well, play a piece of music. Play *Dixie*.'

"She listened a moment. 'Why, that's it.' She listened a moment. Then she said, 'Here, you all listen.'

"I was standing up close and it was *Dixie* sure enough. 'Play *Lily Dale*,' said Mrs. Polk. They played it. Then they played *The Blue Danube*. Mrs. Polk motioned to Dr. Summers. 'Here, you ask them something.' He spoke into the phone very distinctly: 'Do you call it tel-e-phone, or tel-e-pho-ne, or tel-eph-o-ne?' We couldn't hear what was said but the Doctor laughed and said, 'That isn't respectful.' Mrs. Fall and Sadie Polk played some more music, and after a little while we left. Even then, there were some who had heard the whole thing who remained doubting Thomases."

"Some claimed the sound traveled through a hole that ran the length of the wire," said Dr. Ward. "I heard that said the same afternoon."

"Fiddle faddle!" snorted Mr. Shofner. "I went to Polk Place that night and talked over it myself. It takes a whole door for my voice to get through."

"You never scoff at progress, do you, Mr. Shofner?" asked the host.

"Me? No sir, I don't. If man can contrive a railroad, he can do anything. If anybody told me we'd be making regular trips to the moon in five years, I'd give him one of my best seegars."

"I have found it unwise to scoff at progress," said Dr. Ward. "I have usually remained to pray."

Dr. Price, who had left the room for a moment, came into the parlor and asked them to come out into the dining room for "some trifling refreshments," as he modestly put it. Of course, the trifling refreshments turned out to be a feast—to the surprise of no one. For almost two hours the feasting continued. There was choice of Maury County ham, or buffalo steak, the latter procured by Dr. Price through the special co-operation of the steward of the Maxwell House. There were oysters brought by very fast steamboat from the Gulf Coast. There were individual dishes of spring wild greens, laboriously gathered that day from fields lying about the city, and cooked with hog jowl as required by the very integrity of the greens. There was fresh asparagus from Dr. Price's own garden. There was spoon bread, without which Dr. Price always insisted perfection lacked in any supper. There were hot biscuits which brightened the eyes of every man there, votaries with one exception at the altar of Southern cookery. Then sillabub, and great towering cakes—coconut cake, caramel cake, jam cake, lady cake; take your choice, one or all. And all the time they feasted, Elizabeth Price sat at the piano in the parlor across the hall and played softly a repertory of songs dear to Southrons—*Fairy Belle, Little Old Log Cabin in the Lane, Listen to the Mocking Bird, Believe Me If All Those Endearing Young Charms, Darling Nellie Gray*. The D.K.E.'s and their guests feasted, the perfumes of spring drifted into the room, and the music across the hall was soft and alluring and far away.

They went back into the parlor, there were some formalities, and then Dr. Price read his paper on "The Tennessee Capitol." He read with fine vigor and a challenging voice. In finely phrased detail he revealed the Capitol's story. His auditors listened eagerly, for it was a topic of great appeal to all. His voice rang out with clarion force. "The cedars that grew on Capitol Hill were nature at her best, and the building that we have placed there is man at his best."

The antique chair on which Erwin Roane sat creaked from the violence of its occupant's sudden motion. He sat forward on his chair, his eyes unwaveringly upon the speaker.

"Please pardon me, Dr. Price, but this is indeed remarkable. I have heard my father say that, word for word."

"My poor mind is honored to follow one so worthy." The speaker bowed gracefully to Erwin; then he continued with his paper. "The strain of turning a magnificent dream into reality proved too great and the dreamer died for his dream. On April 7, 1854, William Strickland died and was buried within the Capitol foundation walls. We laid as a sacrifice upon the altar of the temple the body of its builder."

"This is uncanny!" exclaimed Erwin Roane, gripping the arms of his chair.

"The building was finally completed on March 19, 1859. It rose to a height of 392 feet above the Cumberland River. Its tower pierced the sky 206 feet above the brow of Capitol Hill. It cost $900,500 to build and every one of those dollars was sanctified by the ideals of the greatest people on earth. . . ."

"Father was a prophet," roared Mr. Shofner, half rising from his chair. "He said that twenty-five years ago."

"Again, I am honored to repeat the words of a gentleman so distinguished."

Dr. Price's eyes again sought his paper. "The building that I have described has known the true grandeur of a great people. It has also felt the stress and strain of war. The thunder of cannon has echoed within its chambers and the smoke of battle has drifted about it. . . ." He wound to his peroration. "It is a beacon light on a high hill. From its tower a thousand square miles of Tennessee soil is visible to the physical eye, but to the eye of the spirit the glory of the whole state lies revealed."

Mr. Roane's hoarse and strained voice was above the applause. "That was what Father said, his very words."

Dr. Price heard him, looked at him, then he looked at Mr. Shofner. A slow, bright smile began to kindle upon his face. He tugged at an ear, and then he laughed aloud. He was still laughing when the applause quieted. Those within the room regarded him with inquiry in their looks. Such uncontrolled laughter was not quite the appropriate response to their appreciation. It was within their experience that one whose pronouncements met with applause ordinarily sat with head half bowed as in humility. They found something jarring in Dr. Price's mirth. Ill at ease, they sat waiting for the laughter to cease. Presently, he was again able to use his voice for purposes of speech, though the laughter still glowed on his face and crinkled about his eyes.

"Forgive me, my friends, if my behavior has been somewhat unseemly. It so happens that the passages in my paper which you recognized, Jacob, and you, Erwin, are enclosed in quotation marks. Also, there is a note stating that these passages were taken from some essays written at the college. I had planned to give due credit to Argie and Neely Barrow at the close of the paper. I do give them credit. They were most helpful, but it seems that the credit goes farther back—to their grandfathers. I give them credit, too. On further thought, I wish to include both of you in my acknowledgments. You have used excellent judgment in your choice both of ancestors and descendants."

"May I mention myself in this distribution of credit?" inquired Chancellor Garland. "I have heard an excellent paper. My admiration for my adopted state has been increased. My credit as a citizen has been enlarged."

"I am not as artful in pretty speeches as you Southerners," said Dr. Stearns, "but I would like to say that I have found particular profit in this paper, even in its florid parts. Somehow, the Capitol here reminds me of the State House in Boston. They are unlike architecturally, but both are on a high hill. Each seems to look out over its constituents with a sort of mystical brooding. Each . . ."

"Pretty speeches, my word," said Chancellor Garland. "For one with such brief experience in pretty speeches, you manifest unusual promise."

Again the chill smile moved across the puritan face. "Give me time, Chancellor Garland. I will endeavor with all dispatch to accommodate myself to your ways."

"I have no doubt, Dr. Stearns, of your rapid progress."

"I have heard," said Dr. Ward, "that we are losing one of our best citizens."

"Who?" asked several voices in unison.

"Eugene Lewis. The Du Pont Company from somewhere in the east is building a big powder factory at Sycamore, and he will manage it."

"This is a loss," said Dr. Price. "He is one of our best citizens."

"He is indeed," said Chancellor Garland. "In his feeling for beauty, Eugene Lewis is an oasis in a dreary generation. And that isn't merely a pretty speech, Dr. Stearns."

"I've noticed," said Dr. Stearns dryly, "that plain statements of fact come well embellished in the South."

"I love beautiful things," said Dr. Price, "but I do not create any. I merely talk about it. The same is true of most of us. The best we can do is to love the beauty which others have made. Nor do we offer much effort to protect that which already exists."

"The Hermitage, for instance," said Dr. Ward.

"Precisely. A noble place but decaying fast. We all know that it's a great place. Now, when the house needs help, we stand in sheer apathy. I love the Capitol, but if it should start to decay all I would do would be to grieve, perhaps to write a protest to the *American*."

"But that isn't true of Eugene Lewis."

"Indeed, it is not. I heard this morning of his new connection and it saddened me. He can join to the conception of the artist the performance of one."

"He's an A-1 persuader," testified Jacob Shofner. "I say a bridge is a bridge, but Eugene Lewis can persuade the board of directors of the railroad that it is not only a bridge but a bouquet. Just give him ten minutes, and we'll give him five hundred dollars extra to beautify, so he says, a culvert or a bridge. Sometimes we hold our meetings in secret just to keep from beautifying everything the railroad's got. That man would tie a cravat on a steam engine."

"So Eugene is a good persuader," said Chancellor Garland jestingly.

"Listen, many's the time I've gone to the board meeting with my mind made up to vote against Eugene's extras; and I did if he didn't show up, or we got the meeting over before he did. But give him five minutes and I'd help vote him anything from flower seeds for the right of way to a statue of a handsome young fellow standing on one foot with the other hand stuck up in the air for the top of a depot. I certainly wouldn't take any personal cash to a board meeting when Eugene was going to do some persuading."

"We'll miss him greatly," said Dr. Ward. "I can understand how convincing he was before your directors' meeting, Jacob. But the railroad is young and eager. Its destiny lies in the future and it knows it. Nashville is old and a bit stale. Some think its great period lies in the past. It is just now rebuilding itself from the anemia of war. It isn't as easily persuaded as the railroad."

"Yes, but if anyone could persuade it, it would be Eugene."

"Yes, it would be Eugene," said Dr. Ward in his quiet, rich voice. "And I think it is being Eugene. For five years he has been patiently developing the sentiment of the people in favor of parks, and prettier homes, in favor of the heritage in artistry bequeathed us by nature and our choice ancestors."

"I doubt if he withdraws entirely from Nashville. Sycamore is only thirty miles away."

"I know that, but the Du Pont project is too big not to require all of his energy and time." He looked at his watch. "Vanderbilt University is very covetous of my time and energy. Its demands place limits even upon a lovely evening. I shall have to leave now. My body and my spirit have been refreshed, Dr. Price."

"To be entirely frank," said Jacob Shofner, "my interest in the Capitol up to now I borrowed from my father. You have made me suspect, Dr. Price, that the Capitol is deserving in its own right."

"Please report to Argie about my paper, Mr. Shofner. And will you, Erwin, tell Neely Barrow that I mentioned my indebtedness to her?"

11

Mrs. Polk climbed the steps of the railroad building to Eugene Lewis's office. Panting a bit, she knocked on the door.

"Come in. Why, Mrs. Polk, what an undeserved honor! Sit here, please. This office has never received a visit from one of such quality."

"But a very disillusioning one. Those stairs inform me that I am no longer a young girl."

"The years, Mrs. Polk, have simply added the graces of maturity to the young girl you used to be."

"Lately I have thought much of that young girl, but she seems so far away now. I wonder if you know, Major Lewis, that I left the White House more than thirty years ago."

"I am reasonably young, Mrs. Polk, but I have studied with some interest the influence of the years upon different people. Some they leave richer, finer, and from some they seem ruthlessly to strip away all good."

"I have watched that, too. The years either give or take away."

"According to one's character, I imagine. May I not bring you a glass of water? No? Then please tell me why you climbed my stairs. I await your command."

"Sit down, Major Lewis. I have no command, but there is something about which I wish to talk. Thank you. I left home merely to take a walk. I walk a little every day and the air this afternoon is delicious. Perhaps you have heard that I sometimes have vivid glimpses denied the physical eye. Well, I thought of him as I was crossing the street."

"Thought of whom, Mrs. Polk?"

"My congratulations, sir. I had heard that you are leaving us presently. We shall miss you greatly."

"I expected to come to see you before I leave."

"Of course. But as I was saying, I thought of him as I was crossing Spruce Street. Then I thought of you, and then I climbed your stairs, which I think were built for the young alone." She fanned herself vigorously for a moment, then continued. "It was Hunt Justice I thought of, sir."

"How extraordinary! My mind, too, has been upon him today."

"The last time I saw you you came to my house to give an

account of your trip with Hunt to the Hermitage. You seemed to have a glimpse then. I wonder if you remember a prophecy you made then."

"That Hunt would become an architect?"

"Exactly. Well, I thought of Hunt while I was crossing Spruce Street, then I thought of you, then of what you said. Then I decided what you and I ought to do. And here I am."

"That makes it easy, Mrs. Polk."

"Yes. Prophecy requires an investment. We'll go half and half."

He smiled. "I am poor at riddles, Mrs. Polk."

"There is no riddle at all. When Hunt finishes at the Academy he should go to college for at least two years. That, I imagine, will be arranged by the family. We have colleges available here, good ones. Then he should go where he can study architecture in earnest. That is your problem and mine. Mr. Jackson most considerately persuaded the Congress to vote me a pension. I do not require much money and I can easily spare half of the boy's expenses. Will you, Major Lewis, provide the other half?"

He stared at her. "Why, yes. I'll pay for the whole matter. I'll be glad to do that. I can afford it."

"But I can't afford to let you. I have had glimpses of that boy, I tell you. I want a part in his future. I saw him looking at my home with something akin to rapture in his eyes. I overheard him rebuke his father for incomplete work."

"Whatever you say, Mrs. Polk, I'll accept."

"It will be some time before the money will be needed, but when I've decided as firmly as now I like to get the thing settled. Otherwise it might go out of my mind. No, I don't think we should give him the money. I want him to promise to pay it back. I think that is good sense, besides being helpful to the character. I am assuming, of course, that he will want to use it."

"I have no doubt of that. By the way, his record at the Academy is superior, so Professor Clark tells me. They regard Hunt as very unusual."

"He discovered the Parthenon, didn't he? I mean locally?"

"It seems that the general opinion holds to that belief. By the way, Hunt has added to his fame, I hear."

"Indeed."

"Professor Clark told me. Recently Professor Garrett took a class and spent most of the day at the Capitol. Each of the boys chose one phase of the Capitol and made a report on it in class. Hunt's was so good that he was asked to read his essay in chapel. Professor Clark said there was more applause than he had ever heard at chapel."

"My glimpses were not in vain! What was his subject?"

"Ionic columns."

"Ionic columns! Are those at the Capitol Ionic?"

"Yes, they are Ionic. S. M. D. Clark said that he now considers himself an expert on Ionic columns. He said that since reading Hunt's paper he has the tendency to feel sorry for people who don't know practically everything there is to know about Ionic columns."

"Then I deserve a double portion of his sympathy. But tell me, what will become of the Hermitage?"

"I doubt if it is worthwhile, Mrs. Polk, to run very far ahead of public opinion, to save the Hermitage for those who are not particularly interested in its being saved. I know more people who are interested now than a year ago. I don't believe I'd leave Nashville at all if there was a chance to put on a great campaign of education, something that would pull people out of their indifference."

"You are resourceful, Major Lewis."

"Not that resourceful. I'll be back every time I can leave without harm to the powder plant, and I'll be active when I do come."

"I do not doubt it. Where, Major Lewis, could a boy study architecture to the best advantage?"

He pondered the matter. "Perhaps with Professor Letang in Boston Tech. That perhaps is the best place."

Mrs. Polk's eyes were shining very brightly. "Yes, Hunt will build his fine house. I may not wait to see it. but I'll get word of it."

12

The driver took the Coles into Nashville quite early. It was a bright Sabbath morning, and the air was alive with the sound of church bells. The streets were crowded with those moving churchward, and kaleidoscopic with Sunday finery.

The Coles alighted from the carriage at McKendree. Dr. McFerrin was preaching and they wanted to hear him, particularly Merrie, to whom the preacher was a compound between a prophet of old and a boon companion. The Coles were going to Mrs. Polk's for dinner. Dr. McFerrin would be there, and Greene and Susan

Cartwright. Weaver Cole told the driver that they would be ready to start home at five o'clock.

The driver stabled his horses at the car barn, he having a standing invitation to do that from no less person than Mr. Anson Nelson, the president of the company. He forked some hay down to them, and then went to pay a visit to his old friend and comrade in the wars, College Grove. He found no one at home. He knew that College Grove, by reason of his seniority, had been granted relief from Sunday driving. He was doubtless taking the air along some of the streets and presently would return. So the driver decided upon a brief walk himself. He walked along Cedar Street, stopping for a brief while to admire the courthouse. Lots of interesting things had happened at that courthouse. Yes sir, lots of them. That was where that scalawag, Maynard, had tried to auction off decent people's homes. Only it hadn't worked, thanks to Dr. McFerrin and Dr. Howell. Preachers were right useful people, yes sir.

"Where you goin' to preachin' today, brother?" asked a voice at his elbow. "I'm bound for a meetin' house that used to be stylish no end but now it's got religion. Can't you come along, brother?"

The inquirer was very tall, very thin, with shoulders so stooped that a long, small neck had to turn a bit upward toward its end so that the man's small, sharp eyes might view the world from a more horizontal position. His legs were long and thin, and bore the aspect of unco-ordination. One watching them might half expect the right leg to start off north and the other west. The voice was thin, clear and plaintive.

"I ain't been thinkin' I'd go to preachin' today, jest walk aroun' and look at things maybe."

"Brother, I'm a-askin' you to come with me to the Central Baptis' Church. Brother Williams is a reg'lar pillar of fire, as the good book says. I promised to bring a feller but he's flew the coop, seems like. So come along, brother, and take his place. I promised to bring somebody and it looks like you're him."

The driver made a quick decision. "I ain't much used to town preachin', but effn you say so I'll try it once. Whereat's this church with a pillar o' fire doin' the preachin'?"

"Cherry and Elm, brother. Jest enough to loosen up the legs."

Saying which he seized the driver by the arm, and his legs after a mismated series of motions started southward on College Street. The congregation was singing when they reached the church.

Brother Ed Hambrick—the man had so revealed his identity to the driver—still holding to the arm of the feller he had brought according to promise, marched proudly down the aisle. The church was generally crowded, but Brother Hambrick's quick eyes discovered the occupancy of the second bench from the front to be slightly under the maximum. He halted.

"Move over, Brother Gupton. I brought the feller I promised. 'Twon't hurt Baptists none to set in close communion."

Brother Gupton most obligingly and agreeably moved over. There followed some more singing, and scripture reading and prayer. Following this Pastor Williams preached—and when he did the pillar of fire burned brightly in the pulpit. No theologian was Pastor Williams, and the course of his sermon conformed not to any logical routine. His preaching was fervid and evangelical, a burning call for men to repent and forsake their old and wicked ways. His eyes glowed with fire, there was fire in his fierce impassioned gestures, his words were tinged with fire. There had been no futile rhetoric in Brother Hambrick's figure of speech. The sermon was long, but the driver didn't notice it. Then they were singing again, this time that old inquiry and promise of the revival meetings.

> "Oh brothers, will you meet me
> Oh brothers, will you meet me
> Oh brothers, will you meet me
> On Canaan's happy shore?"

The driver's mind slipped back, back. Before a half dozen measures had been sung he was in a log church from whose single door the ridges of the Kentucky mountains were plainly traced against a misty purple haze. He sat on a bench which was but a rough plank with legs, and his bare feet rested nervously on a bare clay floor. Curiously they were then singing the same song that swelled in such volume in the Central Baptist Church in Nashville. The driver's voice, shrill and boyish, had mingled with those of the worshipers in that church long ago. The years turned back and he sang again.

> "By the grace of God I'll meet you
> By the grace of God I'll meet you
> By the grace of God I'll meet you
> On Canaan's happy shore."

He didn't know he was singing. He hadn't sung the piece for more than a half century, but it came back to him as clear and fresh as it was in that olden church hard by the meeting of mountain and blue-grass. His mother was singing. She never missed preaching at that church, and when there she sang. It was said that her voice was the best of the community, and she knew all the songs, and all the words to all the songs which was itself no mean feat in memory. She was singing.

"By the grace of God I'll meet you"

But his father, where was he? Then he remembered that his father never went to preaching. But his mother did. It was her delight and refuge.

He didn't know that he was singing. He didn't know that he had caught some of the warmth from the pillar of fire, nor that the fountains of his youth had been reopened by the sound of men and women singing that old song. He didn't know that some in the rear of the church stopped singing and searched for the new quality that had entered the song of the Central Baptist Church. He saw some about him stop singing and look curiously at him. Brother Hambrick and Brother Gupton were staring at him as if a new planet had penetrated the range of their vision. Pastor Williams was looking at him intently. Then he remembered where he was. Then he heard his own voice. He started to stop from the sudden-ness of his discovery and from the impact of all the scrutiny directed at him. Then a wraithlike tendril of memory came to him from out of the past. One time, in the crude church at the foot of the mountains, something happened while a song was being sung, and all had stopped singing—all but his mother. Her voice never faltered. She was singing not only for the song but for her own dignity and for the decorum of the congregation. He did not stop, and presently those who had lowered their voices to listen to him came back into the song, and it wound to its triumphant finish.

When the benediction had been said, Brother Hambrick shook the driver's hand with great fervor.

"Brother, you have the gift. It's many a year since I heard such singing. How'd he sound to you, Brother Gupton?"

"The seraphim wouldn't 'a' sounded much better, Brother Hambrick."

Then Pastor Williams was shaking hands with him and inviting him to attend regularly. "We need a voice like yours to sing the good old songs of Moses and the Lamb."

"Thank you, Parson, but I gin'rally go to preachin' out in the country. Your sermon was mighty enlivenin', suh."

"Thank you, brother. I reckon it gain to lift my poor voice in the Lord's cause."

The pastor moved on to mingle among his brethren. Brother Gupton invited the driver to go home with him for dinner, but Brother Hambrick claimed that honor for himself by right of priority.

"Where you reckon I found him, Brother Gupton?"

"There isn't much tellin', Brother Hambrick," said Brother Gupton winking slyly. "I've heard say there aren't any fences you can't climb."

"I couldn't get over a two-rail fence if there's wickedness on the other side. Found him lookin' at the co'thouse. I figgered a feller who was a-standin' lookin' at the co'thouse ort to be rescued like a brand from the burnin', so I fetched him along. He's a-goin' to eat Sunday vittles at my house. That ort to give him a good start on the road to starvation of the body and meekness o' the spirit."

"Much obliged, but I got some vittles wrapped up over where I got my hosses hitched. And I got to give them critters water. I reckon I can't go with you for dinner, but I enjoyed the preachin' a right smart."

"I shore am sorry," said Brother Hambrick. "I was a-countin' on us raisin' our voices in song after we et. Yes sir, I found him standin' there in front of the co'thouse." He paused for a dramatic moment, then continued, "I'd just come from the jail."

Brother Gupton was disposed to jest. "I heard your sins'd been chasing you, but didn't know they'd got up enough speed to catch you yet."

"It's another man's sins done grabbed him hip and thigh. Couldn't see him though. Visitin' hours ain't till two o'clock."

"Who is it that's in jail, Brother Hambrick?"

"Feller that drives the streetcar. The one they call College Grove."

"College Grove!" exclaimed the driver in deep dismay. "College Grove! You mean he's in jail?"

"He ain't nowheres else. You know him?"

"We was in the war together. What's he done?"

"Some kind o' politickin', I'll bet," said Brother Gupton. "He gets a fever up ever' time there's an election."

"Yes sir, and when his fever's up he can't tell a scalawag from an honest man. Just as liable to keep company with one as the other."

"Streetcar company's threatened to fire him forty times for electioneering with the passengers," testified Brother Gupton.

"They'd 'a' done it, too, except for him bein' so good between elections."

The driver repeated his inquiry. "What's he done for them to put him in jail?"

"He's been politickin' again," said Brother Hambrick, "though I ain't believin' him guilty o' the charges. Yestidy we had a special election for councilman, and College Grove was appinted a officer in the Third Precinct. College Grove was powerful hot for Finis Gleaves, but it looked like Abe Otterson got most votes in the Third Precinct. It was College Grove's job to bring the election book in to headquarters, but something happened. He never got there with it. He says somebody stole it, but the law says how could anybody steal it when he had it in his own hands. They got out a warrant agin him for doin' away with a election book—and that's serious."

"College Grove didn't do that," said the driver. "They's times when he ain't got no more sense than a frizzled chicken with the yeller jaunders, but he ain't the kind that'd steal election books. I got to see about this. I'll meet you at the jail prompt at two o'clock."

He was there and Brother Hambrick arrived not more than a minute later. The turnkey was surly about it. They could stay twenty minutes but he'd be in plain sight all the time, and if they tried "any funny bizness . . ."

College Grove sat on a filthy bunk, the very essence of dejection. He took one look at the driver and then poured out his soul. "Pardner, I'll swear on a stack o' Bibles as high as the Maxwell House I didn't do a thing. That book was took from me. You got to get me out o' here. Effn I stay here much longer I'm liable to die. I ain't never been in a jail before."

"I have," said the driver. "You git used to it in no time a-tall. When they got ready to turn me out, they had to make me leave. Bet you it's the same way with you. Where'd you put that election book down so somebody could take it?"

"That's prezactly the point," affirmed Brother Hambrick. "Where did you?"

"I done told the po-lice that I come down Line Street. As I passed Clem Purvis' house, they was three men a-standin' at his front gate. One was Clem hisself, one was Ward Shirley and the other I didn't know. They got to talkin' about the election. They said that Abe Otterson was a shore winner over Finis, besides being twicet as good a man. I reckon I got excited-like and commenced jawin' with 'em, then I guess I put the election book down on the gatepost or somewheres. Anyhow, when I looked for it, there ain't hide nor hair of it in sight. I told that to the po-licemen and they jest laughed. I figger they're in cahoots with them fellers."

"Which one you reckon got it?"

"Fifty cents for one, four bits for the other; Clem Purvis and Ward Shirley neither one ain't got half the character of a common polecat. I never did hear the other feller's name. Pardner, you git me out o' here."

The driver and Brother Hambrick withdrew from the cell and held a consultation out in the jail yard.

"I miss knowin' a lot o' rascals, livin' out in the country like I do. I wish I knowed more about this Clem Purvis. It happened at his house."

"Brother, I was a-chinnin' my mind on the same pole an' my labors ain't brought no reward neither."

"Maybe a brick wall's one thing I can't see through," said the driver, "but it looks plumb funny to me, this feller Purvis talkin' it up for one candidate, and then maybe stealin' the election book to help the other. Looks like we're lookin' at somethin' we don't see."

"Got eyes and no eyesight, as the Good Book says."

"If College Grove done a thing like this, he's taken on new ways. We was together through thick and thin from Chickamaugy till Jawn Hood dee-serted us. Solomon's a lot smarter'n him but they ain't a stealin' bone in his whole skeleton. You know anybody who knows this feller Purvis that we could talk to?"

"Can't think of . . . wait a minute." An idea was forming rapidly. "Yes I can too. I know a feller that knows ever'body and ever'thing about him. Comes to preachin' at Central sometimes. Yes sir, we're goin' to see him right now. Looks to me like the harvest is gettin' ripe."

Mr. Adonijah Overall, having dined early, sat in the front yard at Bloodstone and tasted with apparent relish each minute as it passed. Mr. Overall always placed his chair so that with one small turn of his head his eyes could rest lovingly on the house he had built, or with one small opposite turn could rest inquiringly on the world without. Mr. Overall was in no minor degree a philosopher. It was, he considered, his profound conviction that unless a man loved his home his existence would never be warmed by loving anything. If he did not love his home, how could he love his community? A man who never loved his own community would never love Tennessee, and how could he love his nation unless he loved his state first, and from thence on out to the limits of the universe? Love began at the home and moved outward. Men were indifferent to their homes, so Mr. Overall reflected, because they were built of alien, unvital materials. That's odd, ran Mr. Overall's thoughts; love then doesn't start at the home but with the materials that compose the home. But why should one love brick, or stone? Mr. Overall loved the stone of his house because his blood was upon it. Love then began with the man himself, with his life and experiences. The home was merely the assembling into a romantic climax of the materials of his life which he held in great admiration or awe. It would be a better world, Mr. Overall thought, if all men could build their homes of stones upon which their precious blood had been spilled, but if such supreme experiences were not available, then of stones upon which as small boys they had sat and dreamed.

"Hello," said a voice at the gate, interrupting Mr. Overall's philosophic flow. He didn't rise, but there was friendliness in his invitation to enter the premises of Bloodstone. One of his visitors he knew rather well, the other not at all.

"Howdy, Brother Hambrick. How is your entitlements segasuating? Set down, gents, and air your cogitations."

Brother Hambrick mentioned the identity of the driver. Mr. Overall jumped to his feet and shook the driver's hand enthusiastically.

"Ain't a man in Nashville I'd druther you'd be. Never did hear so much about a feller not to ever set eyes on him."

"I guess mebbe I ain't who I think I am," said the driver modestly.

"I still say the funniest thing about the war was the Yankees helping you and old College Grove steal their wagons."

"They seen we needed 'em," said the driver reminiscently.

"I've laughed out aloud fifty times just thinking about that. I'm mighty glad to see you. Le's see, you've been in jail twicet, not to say anything 'bout the time them onery scounderls tied you up in the cabin. You drove that South Nashville streetcar for ten years, and you . . ."

"Wait a minute, Mister. Maybe you'd like to tell about the time I got choked on a catfish bone in Looeyville."

"Don't ricollect it. They's some things I miss. College Grove told me a lot o' things about you."

"It's him," said Brother Hambrick, "that we come to see you about."

"So it's him? You mean his predicaments ain't concatenatin' so good as formerly?"

"He's languishin' behind prison bars just like Paul and Silas."

"Who put him there?"

They told the story to Mr. Overall. He whistled a long-drawn note.

"Gee-ma-nen-til-ly!" he exclaimed. "The Amalekites has cast him into durance vile, and the Levites, that being us, has got to get him out." He stood. "Well, that isn't disimpossible. I guess we better go over to overcome the heathen, that being Clem Purvis." He waved his hat at his dwelling. "Stay here," he told it. "I'll be back just as soon as the evil doer gets busted where it's least soothing." He cast an inquiring eye at the sun. "I guess Clem's at home now. We'll see."

"Whereat's he live?"

"On Line Street. I forget the number. I know the house though."

They walked north on High Street to Cedar, then east to the car barn, where the driver excused himself and hurriedly ran in to see his horses. They were eating hay very comfortably. His quick eyes caught sight of his whip, and mechanically he lifted it out of the socket, and was carrying it in his hand when he rejoined his friends. Mr. Overall's quick eyes saw the whip.

"You expecting the Amalekites to resist? College Grove told me once the only time he ever saw you cry was the time you missed a horsefly. You won't need your whip today. I got facts on Clem Purvis that are as servigerous as an army."

They stopped in front of a disreputable-looking house on Line Street. Three men sat out on the porch. A whisky bottle half-full sat on the window ledge.

"Howdy, Purvis," said Mr. Overall. "We've come for the election book."

The one addressed pointed out Line Street. "Keep going. What business would I have with an election book? They ain't no election book here."

"Maybe yes, maybe no," said Mr. Overall whimsically. "No harm in asking."

"College Grove ought to stay out o' politics," observed Mr. Purvis. "Feller that can't keep his hands on an election book in broad open daylight ain't got no business with one. Tell him I said to stick to streetcar drivin'."

"He ought to of thought of that hisself," Mr. Overall said, "but he didn't."

"College Grove don't think well when they's an election on," observed Brother Hambrick. "He's from Williamson County where politics is second nature, as the feller says."

"Now about that election book," said Mr. Overall, sticking to the business in hand. "Don't you suppose College Grove might 'a' got excited by something he was saying and just put it down so he could wave with both hands, and then forgot it?"

"Lissen," said Purvis with conviction. "He had that book when he left here. You saw him, didn't you?"

The two men with him were entirely certain that they had seen College Grove depart bearing the election book.

"Sometimes you can't tell," observed the patient Mr. Overall. "You, Purvis, maybe forgot lots of things in your day and time."

"I said you git outa here," said Purvis. His two associates moved closer to him.

"A bit uppity for a feller that has three indictments agin him filed away. Better learn to be sociable or somebody might forget to disremember about them indictments."

The outraged Purvis jerked a wicked knife from some place of concealment and took one hurried step toward Mr. Overall—but no more. A whip hissed through the air and there was a quick, dull sound as it struck flesh. The stricken Purvis screamed once, dropped his knife, then clutched his wounded ear. The driver calmly drew in his whip, as he did so addressing Purvis's two companions.

"Ca'm yo'selves, gents. Or might you be a-hankerin' to lose your ears?" he inquired plaintively. "I ain't objectin' a-tall. I need me some practice."

"Looks like Gawd A'mighty's about to ketch up with Pharaoh's army," commented Brother Hambrick.

"Now, let's observe what's visible to the naked eye," said Mr. Overall. "There's the three indictments. I know a man that'd just delight to drag them out into daylight. I had a confabulation with him last month. And that isn't all either. Maybe you got some o' that stuff in your house that was stole from Grimes Store week before last. If a man would look inside your house this very minute, he might find some of that stuff."

"Stand still, gents," said the driver. "My right arm's a-twitch-in'."

"How much taxes you pay on this place?" asked Mr. Overall. "No need o' askin' though. I already know. Your brother-in-law on Base Street's got a better place 'n this. How much does he pay? I know that, too. Who was it got mad at Bud Chapple and poisoned his team o' mules? I know that, too. Don't you go daring me or I'll prove it. I haven't done any proving lately and I'm sort of restless to do some. Now you go in that house and fetch out that election book."

The three men stood rigid, staring at him.

"If you are not convinced yet—" a querulous note had entered Mr. Overall's speech—"I got more facts absotively relating to your iniquities. Like to hear some of 'em?"

Purvis hesitated a moment, then cursed obscenely and disappeared within the house.

"Keep a look on that window," said Mr. Overall. "Don't want anybody shootin' at me through it."

"I'll watch it," said the driver, "and effn anybody makes a move in it, I'll jest put an underbit on the right ear and the mark o' Cain on the forehead of these two fellers, jest to spite 'em. Stand still there, effn you wishes to stay in one piece."

Clem Purvis came out of the door. He handed a bulky sort of ledger to Mr. Overall.

"College Grove dropped it while he was standing here yestidy. I was goin' to take it to the sheriff tomorrer."

"Now that's just splendiferous of you," said Mr. Overall genially, "but we won't put you to all that trouble." His manner became a trifle austere. "Next time don't you find any election book no matter who loses it, and if that isn't wisdom pure and undefiled, I'm not the man who built Bloodstone."

They walked toward the jail. "I thought College Grove and Tom Linton was lying when they told me how you could use a whip, but I wish I could tell the truth like they can. Burnt up Purvis' ear and didn't scorch him anywheres else. Do me a favor, won't you? Show me how you do it. I didn't have time to see back there."

The driver stopped, moved to one side of the rough street. Suddenly his whip sang its venomous song. Four times it cut through the bright sunshine, and four small stones lying on the street fifteen feet away in turn leaped up an inch or two above the street as if suddenly rudely awakened from deep slumber and went careening away. Mr. Overall and Brother Hambrick watched the exhibition with popping eyes.

"Nobody's lied to me," said Mr. Overall. "Never saw anything in a sideshow like it. Don't you ever miss?"

"Once back in '57, or maybe '58, I disremember," answered the driver modestly.

"I couldn't do that even if I practiced a hundred years. I built Bloodstone pretty well, but I ought to. I guess I was inspired. I got a lot of facts about a lot of folks in mind, but I wasn't inspired then. That was business. But it's interesting. Sometimes I get a right smart fun out of it. I did back there with Purvis. It would have been awful funny if he had asked me how much taxes I pay. Funny, isn't it, I pay the same he does. But there isn't anything in Nashville like Bloodstone, and I don't feel I rightly owe any taxes."

"But suppose the city government wanted you to render taxes unto Caesar, Brother Overall?"

"Brother Hambrick, I'd look the feller that wanted me to pay taxes square in the eyes and if he didn't shut up I'd say, 'Remember the time your granddad was put in jail for stealing a hog. Stayed in a month, didn't he?' If that didn't shut him up, I'd come down to an uncle or maybe his own daddy. Anyhow, I'd stop him. There aren't a hundred men in Nashville I couldn't get mighty discouraging with if he wanted me to pay taxes."

They had reached the jail then. Most happily the sheriff was there, and it didn't take long to arrange for the release of College Grove. They told the sheriff where the election book had been found and that Clem Purvis had claimed it to be his intention to bring the book Monday morning. Oddly the sheriff seemed embarrassed and in a hurry to get the proceedings finished.

College Grove stood out in the jail yard and blinked at the sun and sniffed the air. He shook hands violently all around, the driver's longest of all.

"Pardner," he said fervently, "if I ever said a word agin your disposition, looks or character . . ."

"You never said it, no sir. The feller who said that didn't have hardly no sense a-tall."

"Less'n that. Me, I'd jest as soon speak agin Gawge Washington as agin you."

"I'll be lookin' for you at Central next Sunday morning," promised Brother Hambrick. "Your pardner attended this morning. You oughta heard him sing. Take us all the week to git the rafters fixed."

Brother Hambrick laughed heartily at his own wit.

"It was him that got you out." The driver pointed to Mr. Overall.

"It was that ornery reptyle, Clem Purvis, took it, wasn't it?"

"Clem sent you word to stick to streetcar driving," said Mr. Overall.

"Only decent remarks he ever made. He's joined to his idols." This from Brother Hambrick.

"I don't ask anything better than jest to drive hosses hitched to a streetcar. I'm cured. Any feller can git elected that wants to. I ain't helpin'."

At the time appointed the driver was waiting with the carriage at Polk Place. Presently the Coles were in the carriage that moved at a sedate trot out Lafayette Street, out the Murfreesboro Pike toward Kingsley. The sun cast shadows that almost while one looked grew fantastically long, and the air was filled with the very essence of things blooming and growing.

"Did you have an interesting day?" Ellen Cole asked the driver. A hungry horsefly died suddenly before he answered.

"Yes'm," he said, "I'd saved up a right smart advice for old College Grove."

13

The houses on Fern Street were finished in time that pleased even Mr. Pres Vick. Courtney Justice under the pressure of the challenges from his wife, under the sting of Ed Crayton's parting words, of Mrs. Elrod's summarily raising of the rent to ten dollars, and carried along by his native cheer had driven his two surly helpers at a rate that surprised not only Pres Vick but Mr. Justice himself. It is true that if an inquisitive person like Mrs. Polk had looked closely some very rough places would have stood revealed. But no one looked.

The two houses grew to completion, then Mr. Justice and the two men were moved farther down the street and another house begun. The house had not risen above the foundation when Mr. Justice was transferred to another job on Woods Street.

"These fellers can get this one done," Mr. Vick told him. "I'll be over here every day or two. The house on Woods is more particular. We aim for it to sell for real money."

So Courtney Justice went cheerfully to work on the Woods Street house. He quailed a bit inwardly when he saw how much more pretentious the house was to be. It was to be five rooms in size, and generally more refined than any assignment yet made him. It was, moreover, on a relatively good street, and that also added to Mr. Justice's obligations. Mr. Justice took a deep breath and plunged cheerfully into the task before him.

But matters on Fern Street didn't go so well. There was a lumber shortage in town and those builders unprotected by early purchases were having their troubles. The rafters for the house on Fern Street were late coming. The two men were laid off a day. Then the lumber came. They made ready to put it in place but discovered that it was cut a foot and a half short. They stood around dazed, looking at it helplessly. Then Mr. Vick arrived. He inquired why they were standing there doing nothing but drawing his good money. They pointed out the cause of their inactivity. He cursed the lumber company with force and continuity.

"Get 'em to change it," one of the men suggested.

"They can't change it. There isn't a two-by-four in Nashville. There isn't even enough stuff to piece with." He stopped, and a gleam brightened his bloodshot eyes. "Why can't you use this stuff?"

"You'd have to pull it down too much. Not enough pitch."

"Pitch? There'd be enough to shed water."

"It wouldn't have much strength."

"Have enough to sell it. That's what the house is for."

"Be purty dumpy lookin'. Wouldn't sell so well."

"People that'd buy this house not going to be particular 'bout its roof just so it sheds water."

So they lowered the roof and used the rafters. And in due time the house was completed. The two men were transferred to help Courtney Justice finish the house on Woods Street.

One day Mr. Vick called on Commissioner Titsy Harris. The cigar inscribed a command and Mr. Vick sat down.

"What's on your mind, Pres? Buildin' business purty good?"

"I sold flat top on Fern Street this morning."

"Flat top? Oh yes. Funny lookin' place. Rafters shrunk, didn't they?" The commissioner found his own humor appealing. "Git a good price, Pres?"

"Fair. Eight fifty."

"Fair! That's a hundred percent. Why, it's more'n that."

"We ain't in the business just to buy seegars."

"That'd been a good price even if it had a roof on it." The commissioner laughed heartily. "Still, as you say, money is what makes the mare go. The more money the faster she goes." He turned upon his partner. "Pres Vick, don't you let a word drop. You keep me out of this."

"I keep my mouth shet when I ain't usin' it."

"I can't take no chances, Pres. Got any more prospects?"

"Man's been twicet to see the house on Woods Street."

"Handle him right. Ought to make a wad on that house. Who was it you traded with for the other one?"

"Feller named Linton from out Hillsboro way. Paid cash."

"He goin' to move in?"

"His sister is. She's a widder woman. Got a boy six or seven years old."

"Flat top's the very place for 'em. Great place to raise a family." He started to laugh but changed his mind. "Handle your Woods Street prospect, Pres. Feed him the bait."

14

Tom Linton, a great hulking giant, hitched his horse out on Union Street and went in to Polk Place to see Mrs. Polk. Presently she came to the side door where he stood waiting, hat in hand.

"Mornin', ma'am, kin I ask you somethin'?"

"Surely, sir. How do you do? I know you. You're Tom Linton. Come inside, sir."

He went into the hall where he sat nervously fidgeting with his hands.

"I remember you well," said Mrs. Polk. "You know, the time poor Richard Winchester was killed. Greene Cartwright told me not long ago that if it hadn't been for you it would have been more than Richard."

Tom sat blushing and shifting his hat in his hands. "That was a terrible time," sighed Mrs. Polk. "What can I do for you, sir?"

"Me and my sister is movin' to town," the giant blurted out. "You know where my sister could git any work to do?"

"I might. What can she do?"

"She can sew and make things."

"Indeed," said Mrs. Polk, thinking rapidly. "She can do those things well?"

"Ever'body out in the country says so. They hate mighty bad to see her leave. She wants to put her boy in school."

"Could you bring her to see me? I might possibly be of some help to her."

"I could bring her tomorrow, ma'am. She wants to move to town, ma'am, because the school out in the country is mighty pore. She's a widder woman with a little boy seven years old, and she's awful anxious for him to git schoolin'. Could I bring her tomorrer, ma'am?"

"Would it suit you to come about ten o'clock?"

"We'll be here, ma'am."

"Bring the boy, too. I'd like to see him. What is your sister's name?"

"Mrs. Coleman, ma'am. Mrs. Susie Coleman, and her boy's named Stanley. I'll have 'em here, ma'am."

"You say you are going to move to town? Where?"

"I bought a house on Fern Street, ma'am. We goin' to live there. It's right handy to the Howard School, I think they calls it, ma'am. She aims to start the boy in there."

Mrs. Polk stood watching Tom Linton as he unhitched his horse and rode away. "Fern Street," she said sadly. "It's worse than Base Street. Somebody has cheated that poor fellow sinfully." Then she brightened. "I'd hate to be whoever did."

Tom Linton brought his sister and her son to see Mrs. Polk. They sat in the hall and talked casually. Within five minutes Mrs. Polk felt that a problem was about to be solved. Within five minutes more she had offered Mrs. Coleman a place in her household. Tom Linton, surprised, whistled sharply.

"I need somebody rather badly, but I can't have sloppy people around me. I've been a bit unfortunate with the sloppy ones lately. My dear, I believe you'd suit me. Keep the boy here with you if you wish."

"I'm going to start him to school."

"Of course. It wouldn't be fair to the school to keep a child like that out of it."

"His daddy went to school," said Mrs. Coleman proudly.

"I think I am going to like your sister, Tom."

"Ma'am, I never dreamed we'd be this lucky."

15

Winter didn't wait for Christmas that year as in Nashville it's supposed to do. Nashville is in the South, not the deep South like Macon, or Mobile, Baton Rouge or Beaumont, but still far enough across the border to blunt the edge of winter. But that year winter overrode most brutally the conventional blandishments of Southern climate. It was as if winter had said, "I've been too gentle and squeamish with those Southern people. I've pampered them until they have lost all proper respect for my true and rightful authority. I'll show them." And winter did show them.

On Wednesday it was not very cold, but in the afternoon a thin, gray carpet of cloud spread across the western sky. It hadn't body enough to hide the sun, merely to dim it so that a dull blur marked its slow descent. There was no wind. Not even a slow breeze touched the elements with animation. The whistle of the trains on the railroad, the chime of the steamboats blowing for the landing at Broad Street seemed muted. The cloud spread and thickened but it did not grow cold, not yet.

In the morning it was snowing. Still no wind stirred, and the snow came straight down. The flakes were not small and harsh like sleet, nor were they large and feathery. There was nothing to sting those snowflakes into hurry nor to confuse the order and dignity of their descent. And there were enough of them to fill with their soft whiteness the infinite interstices of space. One could stand on the terrace of the Capitol and look down below toward the town so close and yet see no town, see not even the thin streamers of smoke that flowed upward from the chimneys until lost in the very orderliness of that white universe. The houses could not be seen, only the hint of vague shadows behind the snow. There would be Polk Place, there the Adams house, there the Zollicoffer house, there Gale Thurston's house. But those vague shadows would have dissolved without the verification of knowledge. There seemed to be the slow, certain rhythm of the universe in the fall of the snow. There was no cloud above, only an unending, unbounded whiteness which held those snowflakes impounded until it was their time to fall in orderly sequence.

Mrs. Polk did not expect Mrs. Coleman that day, but a little after nine she heard the side door open, and there was Mrs. Coleman, shaking her coat free of the snow which clung to it.

"My dear, I didn't think you'd come. How did you ever get here?"

"The only trouble was it was slow walking," said Mrs. Coleman. "It isn't cold at all. There wasn't many children at the school."

"Anyhow, sit before the fire and get warm through. I never saw it snow like this in Nashville."

It was still snowing at three o'clock when Mrs. Coleman left. And it was getting colder. The stores were deserted except for the clerks, and it was announced that the mail carriers would make no deliveries the following day. The trains were still running—but hours late. All over Middle Tennessee farmers were in the fields, patiently driving sheep and cattle into the protection of sheds and barns, and the sheep that broke the way could lift only their heads above the surface of the snow.

"It will be cold tonight," Mrs. Polk said. "Have you plenty of blankets?"

"No, ma'am, we haven't. We wasn't expecting bad weather so soon."

"I wasn't expecting this kind of weather ever. Would you be able to carry a pair of blankets home with you?"

"Yes, ma'am. They'd help out a lot. I'll bring them back just as soon as Tom can go down home and get some more."

She left carrying two blankets. Mrs. Polk watched her retreating form until she was lost in the whiteness down Union Street.

It took more than an hour for Mrs. Coleman to struggle through the snow to the Howard School. Stanley was waiting and together they went on to their home on Fern Street. The boy was happy, and as he struggled panting through the snow he told his mother of the day at school. They kindled a fire in the fireplace and in the cook stove in the kitchen. Working together, they prepared supper. When it was eaten, they sat before the fire. The boy read in his schoolbooks, and the mother knitted at a pair of socks.

"It's cold in here," she said.

"Do you think I can go to school tomorrow, Mama?"

"I guess so, Stanley. It won't snow much longer."

"I like to go to school, Mama."

His eyes fell again upon the page of the book he was reading, and her fingers fairly flew around the sock she was knitting. She stopped for a moment and went to the window and looked out. Dark was settling down upon Nashville but she could see that there had been no abatement in the fall of snow. The wind was stirring restlessly, as a captured giant about to be unleashed. She opened the door a moment to see the snow more clearly, and an icy gust caught her in the face.

"It will be cold tomorrow," she said. She resumed her knitting, drawing her shawl more tightly about her shoulders. "It seems cold in here. I wonder if I left that door cracked a little." She examined but found the door securely fastened.

"Mama," said Stanley, "listen to me read my lesson."

She listened proudly while the child read his lesson.

"You remind me more and more of your daddy," she said, and the pride glowed in her eyes. She sat looking into the fire, her supple fingers making with skill and rhythm the round of the sock she was knitting.

"What's that?" she asked sharply, sitting up erect. There had been a sharp cracking sound, but it was not repeated. The boy stirred from his reading.

"Mama, I wonder what makes it so cold."

"I'm going up in the loft," she said. "Maybe Tom left the window open when he was up there the other day."

She climbed the crude stairs that led to the unfinished attic above. The little window was open. She looked out. The snow was still falling. She could see that it lay deep on the roof. She had to clear the snow away from the ledge before she could close the window. She had taken probably two steps back toward the head of the stairs when the sharp crack sounded again, this time close to her. She stopped, held the candle high, and looked about her. Then she saw something and a scream started that froze upon her lips. The roof was moving, moving in a horrible sidewise motion, and the cracking and grinding sounds were all about her. She started to run to the stairway but the timbers caught her. One struck her viciously, then she knew nothing more.

"Mama, Mama, what is it? What is it?" The boy was calling in tones of terror.

It stopped snowing about midnight. It had become too cold to snow. Ordinarily in Nashville the wind would have died, and the next morning the weather would have been clearing. But this was winter which by some strange whim of the elements had become disengaged from the main body of winter in the Dakotas, or Minnesota or somewhere, and drifted maliciously southward. When the snow had ceased falling, the wind had risen, and its moan had become a shriek. The sky was pure thick lead.

Weaver Cole came stamping up the steps of the back porch at Kingsley, flinging the snow loose from his hat and his greatcoat.

"Whew," he shouted. "I never saw any weather like this. You about frozen?" The question was asked the driver who was replenishing the supply of firewood on the back porch from a rick by the backyard gate.

"A feller could get cold effn he was a mind to."

"Suppose he wasn't a mind to, he'd about burn up, wouldn't he?"

The driver considered this rebuke to his native conservatism. "I wouldn't say that," he said, "but a lot o' times colder'n this I've worked all day with my coat off."

Weaver stared at him. "Oh, you have. Well, that makes it easy. I need some help but I didn't like to ask you for it. Now, all I have to do is say the word and you pull off your coat and go to work."

"Go ahead and ast me. Jest so it ain't indoors."

"It isn't," said Weaver soberly. "Do you think you could make it in to Nashville and back? I mean with a team?"

"You mean me?"

"Yes, you're the only one I'd trust a team with today. One of my hogs is sick, cholera maybe. I've got it off by itself, but I'm afraid for the others. They have some medicine at DeMovilles' that I want. Could you go get it?"

"He's a-askin' me effn I can get to Nashville." There was bitterness in the driver's voice. The very inquiry had put a slight upon his professional capacity. "I've drove a stage coach for days and never did get up to the level of the snow."

Weaver smiled. "Take the spring wagon and bring back a couple of sacks of salt. You can get it at Mr. Orr's. Tell Mr. De-Moville to send me some of that medicine he was telling me about."

Since the trip was to be made, Merrie insisted upon sending Mrs. Polk a sack of Weaver's sausages made fresh the day before.

Mrs. Polk answered the knock at her side door. "Mercy! Come in. Whom do you think you are, Daniel Boone?"

"No'm, not him. He always stayed in when the weather was like this."

"I have been told that he was a man of intelligence. What have you got in that sack?"

"That's some sausidge Weaver Cole made yestidy. They ain't so very good, ma'am, but I 'spect you could eat 'em effn you tried real hard on a cold day."

"I'll make the effort. How are they at Kingsley?"

"They all well, ma'am." He told her of the occasion of his trip to town. "Don't be oneasy, ma'am, about the sausidge. The fattenin' hogs were kept in another fiel' from the one that got sick."

"I wasn't uneasy. Anything that Weaver Cole prepares for food gets top rank at Polk Place." An idea came to her suddenly. "You have a team? But you came for salt; of course, you have. Could I send you on an errand, sir?"

"Why, yes, ma'am. . . ."

"It won't take you very long, and it would add another instance to your role of the Good Samaritan."

"You don't mean me, ma'am."

"I mean you. I've been troubled for the last hour. There's a woman who works for me. She's Tom Linton's sister."

"Tom Linton? You mean . . ."

"The same one. Samson and Hercules in one."

"What about his sister?"

"She comes every day and works for me. She's a lovely woman, and the best help I ever had. Yesterday, she told me that they hadn't enough blankets and quilts. They moved to town three weeks ago. She took two blankets home with her yesterday. She needs more. She lives on Fern Street in one of those horrible new houses. Couldn't you drive out there and take her more blankets? She needs them. It'd be a favor to me."

"If she's Tom Linton's sister, it's no favor to you. It's my favor this time. Whereat on Fern Street does she live?"

Two hours later, Mrs. Polk, sitting by the window, saw the driver guiding his team up Union Street. He didn't hitch his team out on the street. He turned in at the driveway. There was something in the way he drove! She looked more closely. Those were not sacks of salt in the bed of the spring wagon.

"Merciful heaven!" exclaimed Mrs. Polk. "Frozen to death!"

But Mrs. Coleman and Stanley were not frozen. Stanley was

conscious but terribly frightened. He thought his mother was dead. She had lain all night unconscious, from the blows dealt her by the timbers of the collapsed roof. But those timbers, short and deformed, as if repentant of their incredible malice, veered into a low arch under which the woman lay all night, on into the morning when the driver arrived. Her head was bruised, and her side was crushed, but she breathed. The boy heard the crash of the roof, and the scream that stopped in her throat unuttered. He cried out asking what it was, but there was no answer. He took their remaining candle and ran up the stairs. He saw the broken roof and screamed for his mother. He found her where she lay under the little crude arch. She would not answer him but he saw that she was breathing. She lay, banked away from the wind and the snow.

The boy brought up the two blankets and placed them over her. He thought quickly and went down the stairs and stripped the bed of all its covers and brought them up and placed them over her. It was cold, terribly cold. He made another trip and brought up all the clothing he could find. He kept calling for his mother to answer him, but that timber had struck her too grievously on her temple. He could see that she breathed.

He made other trips and brought up whatever cloths of any kind he could find in the kitchen, and then a rag rug which she had woven. He carefully placed all these upon his mother, put on his cap, his heavy wool gloves and his overcoat, and sat down by his mother. All night long he sat there. Sometimes he cried, but he knew he mustn't do that. He didn't know what he should do. Perhaps he should go out and try to find help, but then his mother might awaken while he was gone and need him. Besides he didn't know where to go. Nobody had moved into the other houses near by.

All night long he sat there by his mother under the broken roof. Sometimes she stirred and he called to her to speak to him. A section of the roof had caught so as to bank them from the wind that blew in such icy fury. But the cold, not so easily turned aside, sought them out. Their bodies were sturdy and resistant, and in their veins ran blood which through the night turned aside the thrust of the cold. The boy didn't know what to do except to wait. All night long he waited. He must keep awake. His mother might need him. He would grow drowsy but then he would move and shake himself till wakefulness was restored.

The night passed and a dull slate-colored daylight came over the land. The boy could resist no longer. He lay gently down by his mother and sank to sleep.

The driver knocked on the door and waited. Then he knocked again. There was still no answer. He turned the knob and the door opened. There was no one in the room, and no fire burned in the fireplace, though he could see that there had been one recently. He called out "hello," but there was no answer, no sound. It was cold in the room. Why, that was funny, somebody had torn up the bed. His spine tingled, for there was something wrong there. He called out again a vigorous "hello." After a moment he went to the kitchen. There was an odd sort of disarray there, too. After a moment he shook his head and started to leave. He closed the door behind him. His eyes fell upon the newly painted number upon the house. It was the number Mrs. Polk had told him. He was sure of that. In the yard he turned to look again at the house. What was the matter with that roof? He stared at it uncomprehendingly at first. Then he ran inside the house and climbed the crude stairway.

Unmindful of the cold, Mrs. Polk met the driver before he reached her side entrance. She saw that the boy, a grotesque bundle, was sitting up in the bed of the spring wagon. But there by him . . .

"Is she dead?"

"No, ma'am, but I'm afeard she's right bad hurt. The roof caved in."

Mrs. Polk tried to help, but it was the driver who carried the woman in the house, carried her in with the same consummate skill that had enabled him to get her down the stairs and out to the spring wagon on Fern Street. The boy very gravely followed him into Polk Place and watched while they placed his mother on the bed. The terror had gone from him. Help had arrived. His mother would live.

"What happened?" Mrs. Polk asked the driver. "No, don't tell me now. Go get Dr. Briggs."

Dr. Briggs came. When he had finished his examination, he told Mrs. Polk that he didn't believe there was any skull fracture but that obviously something had struck her a hard blow. Perhaps some ribs were broken. Her native strength, he thought, would overcome the effects of both the blow and the exposure. The boy should go to bed for a while.

"I'll see to that," Mrs. Polk promised, "but first I want him to tell me what happened."

The driver and Stanley told her their stories.

"That snow was heavy, ma'am, and the roof jest caved in. I don't think it was built right."

"Is our house ruined?" Terror was back in the boy's mind.

"You get to bed. No, your house isn't ruined. We'll see to that."

One who knew Mrs. Polk would have realized from the way she said it that the wrecked house was consigned to the category of business unfinished—but to be finished.

On the second day that spell of alien cold began to weaken. On the third day the snow degenerated rapidly into slush and clogged all the streets with its half-liquid ooze. On the fourth day the South rallied and took charge again of its own climate. It was then that Tom Linton, whom word of the trouble had finally reached in Giles County, came riding into Nashville.

"Is she alive?" he asked Mrs. Polk, who met him.

"Quite so. A Linton must be hard to kill. Yes, she's alive and very eager to see you."

16

As luck would have it, Eugene Lewis came to Nashville that day. Something had gone wrong with the delivery of a bit of machinery required for the powder mill and he had come to town to see what. That problem being solved, he rode up to Polk Place, holding several matters of major interest in common with Mrs. Polk. A towering young giant was in the library with her and an angry light burned in his eyes. Mrs. Polk introduced the two men and told Eugene Lewis the story.

"Tom's going out to Fern Street now and I want you to go with him. Unless I guess poorly, here's the opportunity you've waited for."

"Of course I'll go, and if there's any shenanigan about the way that house is built, I'll go with him to see the man that sold it to him and, my dear lady, perhaps I shall call upon the honorable Titsy Harris before I see you again."

Tom Linton looked at the wrecked roof and the wrath on his face thickened. The moment Eugene Lewis reached the head of the stairs his trained eye caught the story.

"Great heavens! Look at those rafters. The roof must have been practically flat—to save a few miserable feet of two-by-fours. Look at the way that was toed in. Not an inch holding. Warped stuff, almost all of it. Look at that mitering. Not a true joint in the whole mess. I'd run a workman off the place who built a pig shed that poorly. In high heaven's name, why did you buy this house?"

"We wanted to move to town, and this one was new."

"New! Good God! Who built it? From whom did you buy it?"

"A man named Pres Vick. I aim to break his neck."

"I'll testify that you had just cause. But that won't repair your house so you can live in it again. Pres Vick? Where have I heard the name? I've heard something and it wasn't good either. Well, let's go see him."

Tom Linton knew where Mr. Vick lived and the two men went to the house. They were told that he had gone to Commissioner Harris' office.

"Aha," said Eugene Lewis. "Well, I'll be glad to see the commissioner too. It all fits in."

They rode in College Street. Suddenly Eugene Lewis whistled sharply. "I remember about Pres Vick now. It was chilly outside and a foreman and a carpenter at the powder plant were eating their dinner in my office. They were talking about Pres Vick. 'He's building houses,' the foreman said. 'Wonder who's putting up the money? Pres hasn't got any.' 'I wouldn't live in a house if Pres Vick put on the hinges for the back door,' the other said. 'Everybody in the building business knows Pres Vick and they all think the same thing.' They were describing a man who would build a house like yours!"

They hitched their horses, then went into the city hall and down the long, deserted corridor. They knocked on the door.

"Come in," a hoarse voice bawled.

"That's him," said Tom. They opened the door and entered the office. Mr. Pres Vick was there, but the commissioner was not.

"Commissioner's out. I'm a-waitin' for him." Then he recognized Tom Linton. "Oh!" he said hoarsely.

"You remember Tom then," said Eugene Lewis pleasantly.

"Don't know when the commissioner'll be back. Can't wait." Mr. Vick started for the door, but Tom Linton blocked his way.

"You sold him a house recently." The voice was still pleasant.

"Yes, he got a bargain, too."

"But the snow caused the roof to break."

The man's eyes were shifting constantly between Tom Linton and Eugene Lewis. "What's that?"

"It crushed the roof like an eggshell. Very faulty construction."

"Act of God," the man mumbled hoarsely.

"This ain't," said Tom Linton, and knocked him down.

Pres Vick lay groaning upon the floor, nursing a wounded jaw. He raised himself on an elbow, saw Tom Linton waiting for him to get up and sank back to the floor.

"Excellent, Tom. Maybe you won't have to do it again." Major Lewis addressed the man on the floor. "My business in part is building. I might very reasonably be regarded as an expert. That's all right, Tom, let him up. Here, sit in that chair. If necessary, Tom, hit him on the other jaw. As I was saying, I know buildings. The one Tom bought violates all the building laws and standards. That makes you guilty. He wants his money back."

"Money back! It was a fair trade."

Eugene Lewis ignored that. "Now what we want to know is who's backing you. Everybody knows that somebody is putting up the money. Who is it?"

The frightened man said nothing, his eyes flicking from Tom Linton to Eugene Lewis and back again.

"All right, Tom. I've given him a chance. Now I'm turning him over to you."

Tom Linton's right hand fell to the man's collar, grasped it, and with a bone-shaking jerk, lifted him to his feet. And then the knob of the door turned and Commissioner Titsy Harris came into his office. His eyes darted about the room.

"No violence, gents, no violence," he said nervously.

"By no means," answered Eugene Lewis pleasantly. "Mr. Vick was just telling us who is putting up money on his building projects."

And then the identity of Mr. Vick's backer was revealed to Lewis, even before Titsy Harris spoke.

"He's a dirty liar. I never let him have a cent."

That denial, added to the pain which Mr. Vick was suffering from injuries to teeth and jaw, was enough to unbalance his estimate of the situation.

"He's a liar himself," he yelled. "He let me have every cent of it."

The commissioner saw the error into which he had fallen. "If you gentlemen will excuse us, me and Pres'll settle this all right. I'm sorry . . ."

"We're going to get this settled now. Tom, knock the face off anybody who tries to stop us. Commissioner, this man bought a house on Fern Street two weeks ago. He paid cash for it, eight fifty. The other night the roof caved in and seriously injured his sister. He wants his money back—now."

"Money back! Tell it to Pres."

"No, we're telling you. One of you is going to give Tom his money back."

"I give the money to him," growled Tom Linton, jerking his head toward Vick.

"I give it to him the next day." Vick's evil look was fixed on the commissioner, his hand clutching a bruised jaw.

"You see where that puts it," said Eugene Lewis pleasantly. "You see, Mr. Harris, you are Commissioner of Buildings for the city of Nashville. Unfortunately, there were enough bad and indifferent citizens combined in the city to elect you."

The commissioner was no longer bland and oily. "Get out!" he yelled.

"It is generally known, I believe, that you are an ornery, filthy crook, that you have used your office only on this or that pretext to extort money from builders and dealers in construction supplies. I happen to have some instances available, Mr. Commissioner. . . ."

"Get out o' here!"

"The next time you open your mouth," said Tom Linton, "I'll shet it."

"Tom wants his money back. His house is ruined and his sister is badly hurt. Eight fifty, wasn't it, Tom? Pay him a thousand dollars. His sister was quite badly hurt. One hundred and fifty dollars is very little for that."

"Even if she got hurt, what's that to me?"

Tom Linton struck him then with sudden and unrestrained fury. The commissioner crashed lengthwise to the floor. Pres Vick leaped toward the door, but Eugene Lewis was there before him.

"Sorry," he said, "but we're all staying for the closing exercises. Lift him up, Tom. Put him in the chair. Listen, Commissioner, unless you pay this man back the money the house cost him and a reasonable amount for injuries caused his sister, I'll spread word of this all over town. We'll go directly from here to Mac Dickinson's office—I see you know him—and there file suit against you.

Then I'll take everybody I can get to go with me on a trip of inspection. I know of some preachers, some lawyers, some teachers, and at least one editor who'd go gladly. We could publicize your buildings pretty well. I think the newspapers would be glad to tell how that house collapsed and almost killed a lady—that makes it almost murder, doesn't it? Pay Tom that money. He'll give the deed back to you. It hasn't been recorded. You said you paid him cash, Tom?"

"Yes, I did. Money I got for the farm."

"Did you pay the same money to the commissioner, Vick? If you think he lies, hit him, Tom."

"Yes, the next day. He put it in that safe yonder. I saw him."

"Sounds like the truth. All right, Commissioner, one thousand dollars; and if you don't pay it promptly, Tom Linton will beat you into a pulp for his sister's sake and I'll go to jail with him for the town's sake. Take a good look at Tom Linton. Ever hear of him killing the four scoundrels in the cabin off the Nolensville Pike? But I see you know about it already."

"They was better men'n him," said Tom.

"Keep your hands offen me. I'll give you the money."

The commissioner paid Tom the money, and Tom handed him the deed. Then Eugene Lewis and Tom left.

"He could put us in jail for that," said Tom.

"He could, yes, but he won't. To put us in jail would start a lot of talk, and that's the last thing he wants. I've had such a good time, Tom, that I had forgotten that I am due back at Sycamore tonight."

Back in the commissioner's office, Titsy Harris was pointing an outraged finger at Pres Vick. "Git out o' here, you mangy traitor," he said in a hoarse, cracked voice, "git out o' here and don't let me ever set eyes on you again."

17

Courtney Justice came home about four o'clock. "There isn't a thing there to work with," he explained to his wife. "Hasn't been a stick o' lumber all day. I piddled around and got things straightened up a little. I don't know what's got into Vick. He promised to have the stuff there this mornin', but it ain't come yet."

Pres Vick did not appear the second day, nor the third. Courtney Justice made a trip to the boss's house but no one was there. He felt greatly depressed. He made a trip to the house being built on Fern Street. No one was there. He had heard that the two men had finished one of the houses and that it was occupied, but it looked deserted to him. No smoke was coming out of the chimney. His eyes fell up the roof. What was wrong there? It looked like something crumpled, broken. Uneasiness gripped Courtney Justice's inwards. He went back to the house on Woods Street, gathered up his tools and started home. On Ewing Avenue he met one of the workmen who had been engaged on the Fern Street houses. The man stared at Mr. Justice in surprise.

"Who you workin' for now?"

"Why, Pres Vick I reckon. Ain't you?"

"No, nor you neither. He's flew the coop. Left owing me fourteen dollars, too."

"What you mean?"

"Ain't nobody workin' for him. Ain't you heard?"

Courtney Justice shook his head.

"Well, they ain't. He's gone—to hell, I hope. Nat Baker saw him at the railroad deepo' gettin' on the cars and asked him where he was goin'. He told Nat he was leavin' and never comin' back. Nat asked him about the sixty dollars he owed him for nails and lumber. He was still cussin' Nat when the train pulled out. I'd love to drill auger holes clear through him. I need that money."

"What you goin' to do?"

"Nothin', looks like. I been trampin' all day lookin for work."

Courtney Justice sat at the table but he wasn't eating his supper. Out of the depth of his wretchedness, he heard his wife's cool, even voice.

"You've been like this three days, Courtney. Now you tell us what it is."

He told them.

"I'm not surprised much. How much did he owe you?"

"Eighteen dollars."

She waited a moment, thinking. "Courtney, you go see that man—named Harris, wasn't he? The one that got you to quit Mr. Crayton. You go see him. Maybe he'll do something about it. He owes it to you."

Courtney Justice knew something was wrong the minute he entered the commissioner's office. Titsy Harris sat at his desk, but his feet weren't on it in their old nonchalant way. An odd discoloration spread over one side of his face and a sullen anger burned in his eyes. He smoked vindictively at a long cigar. He did not get up or speak to the man who stood fumbling with his hat.

"Mornin', Commissioner. Can you tell me where Pres Vick is?"

The commissioner's cigar stabbed angrily at his visitor.

"You work on that job on Fern Street?"

"Yes, sir," thinking of the earlier assignment.

"Git out o' here, git out and don't you never come back. If I ever see you again, I'll kill you."

The sounds of profanity accompanied Courtney through the hall. He imagined he could still hear it when he reached the street. His wife was in the front room knitting. He sat wretchedly in a chair by the window.

"What'd he say, Courtney?"

"He cussed me something terrible, Lizzie. Said he'd kill me if he ever saw me again. What've I done, Lizzie? I can't think o' anything."

"I expect you just got in bad company, Courtney, like the prodigal son in the Bible."

"Looks like we'll be movin' back to the country, Lizzie."

His wife laid her knitting in her lap and faced him.

"We're not going back to the country. I wouldn't 'a' come here to begin with if it hadn't been for Hunt. He's doing fine now. He's going to graduate before long and we're going to stay here anyhow till he does."

His wife's firmness always re-established Courtney Justice. "All right, Lizzie, but work's pretty scarce now. If we had the money that scalawag owes me, it'd sure help out."

"No use saying *if*. When you keep the wrong company, you're apt to lose your money. Who is that knocking?"

It was Mrs. Callie Elrod, standing in the doorway, hands on hip.

"It's time for the rent," she said. "Pay the rent on time and save nine, I always say."

"Come in, Mrs. Elrod. Lizzie'll pay you."

Mrs. Justice went to a press in the corner. From it she took ten dollars which she handed to Mrs. Elrod. "Sit down and visit awhile."

"Much obliged, but I have a whole passel o' work to do." She fronted Courtney Justice. "What's wrong?" she asked crisply. "You lost your job? I saw you comin' in yestidy and agin while ago like a whipped houn' dawg. Pres Vick treated you wrong?"

"Yes, he did," said Courtney Justice.

"Don't be surprised if I ain't. Pres was born a scamp. But you didn't think you was workin' for Pres, did you? Pres was standin' in front o' a bigger scamp so you couldn't see him. I think I know who he is but I ain't sayin' right now. What'd Pres do?"

"He run away. He ain't been here this week."

"Skedaddled, huh? Owe you any money?"

"Eighteen dollars."

"That'd be cheap if it learned you who to let alone. You got another job?"

"No, work's mighty skeerce."

"You asked Ed Crayton for your job back?"

"He wouldn't give it to me. We might have to move back to the country."

"I told you we're not going back to the country, Courtney."

"What was that essay you said Hunt was writing, Mrs. Justice?"

"On the Hermitage, the house General Andrew Jackson lived in. He's making the essay so it reads mighty pretty, I think."

"I want for you to read it to me sometime. Funny, ain't it, that boy takin' to houses like he does."

"When he was a little boy he used to go with me to Mr. Power's store at Huntland, and every time he'd stop and look at Mr. Moore's house like he was seeing a vision. I'd hurry him to come on. 'Mama, let me look at it just a minute longer,' he'd say."

"He's different. I can't hardly figger him out. Dreams a lot, don't he?" She turned to Courtney Justice. "I'd try Ed Crayton. Might not do no good, but you can't tell till you try, as I always say."

"I'll go see him today," said Mr. Justice, his purpose kindling.

"No, not today. He ain't here. He'll be back tomorrer. I want to know one thing though. If Ed hires you—and I don't guess he will—you goin' to stick this time?"

"Till I die." Mr. Justice's sincerity was emphatic.

"You go see him early tomorrer. He might be needin' a hand, but I don't guess he is."

Mrs. Elrod went to see Ed Crayton early that afternoon. He disengaged his attention from some drawings he was studying.

"Even', Callie. If I had a son who was a plumb eejit I'd start him to work drawin' these things. Once I asked a feller who'd drawed one to explain it to me and he couldn't. You feelin' all right, Callie?"

"I ain't got time to feel anyways else. I ever give you any bad advice, Ed?"

"Oh, lots o' times, Callie."

"Name oncet."

"Ain't it funny that out of them thousands o' times I disremember 'em all. Sorry, Callie, but I ain't takin' him back."

"What you talkin' about . . . ?"

"Bein' in the buildin' business still leaves me a little sense. I know what happened to that striped polecat, Pres Vick! Sorry to disappoint you, Callie, but I'm not taking him back."

"I didn't say anything 'bout you taking Pres Vick back."

"Well, I'm not takin' Justice neither."

"Who asked you to? For all you know I come to borry a handsaw."

"Take your pick of handsaws, Callie."

"How's that boy o' yours doin' in school, Ed?"

"Better'n ever. He can read the Third Reader through without a bobble."

"How about his 'rithmetic?"

"Knows the multiplication table to the sevens."

"You set a right smart by that boy, don't you, Ed?"

"What you drivin' at, Callie?"

"Nothin', Ed. Just hopin' nothin' would happen to you. Be mighty bad for that boy to have to quit school now. It just wouldn't be right, I always say. Last time your boy was at my house we had a big talk. That boy's mighty set on school. He's expectin' to go to college, too, when he gets grown. I sure hope nothin' ever happens to you, Ed. That little feller o' yours just natchelly belongs in school."

Ed Crayton stared at her. Then he burst into laughter.

"All right, Callie, I'll take him back. I'll learn him the carpenterin' trade all over. I'll lose money on him every time he cuts a scantlin' the wrong length. Then, by the time he's makin' me a decent hand some dead beat'll come along and take him away from me. I'll take him back, but I'll probably kill him before the year is over. I got to get to work on this here Chinese puzzle that the feller that made it thought was plans for a house. If that's a stairway, my name's Titsy Harris. And it ain't!"

"Much obliged, Ed."

"Don't mention it. I wouldn't a-took him back if I didn't need him. Gawd A'mighty, look where he put that fireplace!"

18

There was spring in Courtney Justice's walk, good cheer on his face, and his eyes were bright with resurrected hope. He was whistling a merry little tune as he came up the walk in his own front yard. His wife stood in the door waiting for him.

"It's all right, Lizzie. Ed took me back. Begin in the mornin'. He's startin' in on a mighty purty job on Base Street."

"I couldn't stand to see Hunt leaving the Academy now. He's going to finish his essay on the Hermitage tonight. I wish I could be there when he reads it."

"I ain't felt so spry since the day I finished Mr. Moore's barn." He saw and partly understood the transfixed look on his wife's calm face. "Hunt won't have to build barns or houses on Base Street, Lizzie. He'll build courthouses and things like that. You'll see."

They saw Mrs. Callie Elrod cut across her yard into theirs. "Have any luck?" were her first words.

"Plenty. Start tomorrow. I'm goin' to make Ed a good man. The way I feel, Mrs. Elrod, Ed's goin' to be purty lucky to have me."

"I want you to read Hunt's essay on the Hermitage," said Mrs. Justice. "Could you come over tomorrow or the next day?"

"Either time," said Mrs. Elrod. "Funny about him writin' a whole essay on one house."

She gathered herself to depart. "After this rent'll be eight dollars," she said.

19

President Stearns of Peabody College was receiving Principal S. M. D. Clark in his office. The day was pleasant and genial and a wood thrush, just outside the window, sang its liquid trill over and over again. The president, prim and erect, sat behind his desk. In his eyes was a faraway look. His inner vision was seeing Massachusetts and always his old guide and philosopher, Horace Mann, stood in the foreground. The Principal of the Academy was addressing him.

"Dr. Stearns, it is, I believe, the policy of your college to accept only those students who plan for a career of teaching."

"It is, definitely."

"But there are, sir, conditions under which you would be willing to make an exception."

"There are times when we would like to do so, but the program of our college is too firmly established to permit the least evasion in administering it."

"Even so, I must make my appeal, Dr. Stearns. We have a lad in the Academy who in some ways is the most remarkable scholar I have ever taught."

"May I inquire what profession the young man intends to follow?"

"Architecture, sir. I have rarely if ever seen anyone with such singleness of purpose."

"In that event, may I suggest, Dr. Clark, that Vanderbilt University offers courses of study much preferable to ours for young men entering the field of architecture."

Mr. Mann was seen to smile in gentle approval. Curiously Dr. Clark did not seem greatly concerned by the refusal. In fact, he had foreseen it almost word for word; it was time to use the guile he had planned.

"Of course, Vanderbilt is known to manifest the virtues you name; there are two reasons which make your college the more desirable for him. First, it is two miles nearer to his home. Second, the fees are lower. Both items are of importance; the second is serious."

"I can understand that. But you can see, Dr. Clark, that to admit one not committed to a life as teacher would start the process of dilution which ultimately would greatly weaken us."

"I would not have you diluted in the least. This lad would not dilute the strength of your courses. He wishes to study freehand and mechanical drawing. Your Miss Bloomstein is said to be excellent. I remember hearing you say recently that you considered her the best in the city. You selected her, I believe."

The president did not answer.

"Then I should like for him to study the sciences under Professor Penfield. I understand he was considered very good even in Massachusetts."

Some pink showed in the marble of the president's face. "I am sorry, Dr. Clark . . ." he began weakly.

"The study of mathematics is the firm foundation of the practice of architecture. Where could anyone find more thorough instruction in mathematics than under Miss Julia Sears?"

Where indeed? Miss Julia Sears, herself of the essence of Massachusetts, bearer of a name venerable with honor in all the areas of the state, graduate of Bridgewater which Mr. Mann had founded and dedicated, Miss Julia Sears whom Dr. Stearns had personally chosen to come south with him. Dr. Clark mounted to his climax of appeal.

"When the lad has had his college preparation it is very likely that he will enter the School of Architecture of Boston Tech, and there study under Professor Letang. Somehow or other it seems appropriate for the lad to study under the instructors in your college if he later is to carry on his educational work in Boston. Very regrettably Vanderbilt University has no instructors from your state, sir."

"What is the lad's name?"

"Hunt Justice, sir. He is, I assure you, of superior quality."

"It had not occurred to me but I can see now that to build better homes, to raise the people's taste, has much in common with teaching. I feel that we can admit this young man, but we surely must guard against his admission being used as a precedent."

S. M. D. Clark arose from his chair. "Thank you, Dr. Stearns. I think you may count on Hunt's presence when the college opens in September. He will represent your college very creditably in Boston."

"It is possible that we may be able to find a small scholarship for his use."

The principal of the Academy left. Dr. Stearns could see very clearly that Horace Mann was pleased. He was pleased, too.

20

That afternoon Eugene Lewis rode in from Sycamore to attend the monthly meeting of the Old Table Club. S. M. D. Clark drew him to one side of the parlor just before they went in to supper.

"I've done my part of the bargain. President Stearns has agreed to admit Hunt."

"Indeed! Just what logic, Smack Me Down, did you use on his rock-ribbed mind?"

"I wasn't logical at all," said S. M. D. Clark modestly, "merely psychological." He told the story.

"I'd never suspect you of such artfulness. Well, they do good teaching out there, and that's the main point. I'm remaining in town tomorrow on business. In the afternoon I'll go to see Hunt and his parents." He burst into an explosive little laugh. "Beware of the Greeks bearing subtle compliments to one's birthplace—particularly Massachusetts."

S. M. D. Clark took a folded manuscript from his pocket and handed it to Eugene Lewis.

"Here, read that. It's an essay on the Hermitage written by Hunt. Mail it back to me when you've finished with it. It's rather remarkable."

Hunt Justice and his mother were setting out some chrysanthemum plants, when Eugene Lewis arrived. The memory of the visit to the Hermitage was still vivid in the boy's mind and he had told his mother so often of it that it was almost as if she had gone with them. They invited him into the house, but he preferred the little front porch.

"It's not the season for indoors. Let's sit here if you don't mind."

Hunt brought out two more chairs and they sat on the porch.

Eugene Lewis turned to the boy. "You've just about finished at the Academy, haven't you?"

"Yes, sir."

"Is it still your wish to become a planner of houses, an architect?"

"Yes, sir."

"I have come to talk with you about it. Have you planned for anything after you graduate at the Academy?"

"I'd like to go to work for someone who builds houses, not ugly ones."

"That's what Courtney thinks," said Mrs. Justice, "but I say he isn't rightfully finished with school yet. He ought to go to school longer. Don't you think so, sir?"

"I surely do. I suggest that you spend the next two years in Peabody College. That also is Dr. Clark's opinion, as he has authorized me to tell you. It is Mrs. Polk's opinion, too. In fact, arrangement has already been made for your admission. After that you should go east somewhere for training in architecture. We think Boston Tech is excellent."

"Is that a college, sir?"

"Yes, perhaps the leading college of architecture in the nation."

"But I couldn't ever go to it."

It was his mother's cool, clear voice flavored with the overtones of the country that answered. "Maybe you could go to college. Your grandpa did."

"I know, Mama, but they had some money."

"Anyways, don't say you can't ever go, son."

"Let me think out aloud a little," said Eugene Lewis. "Just suppose—there's no harm in supposing—that Hunt could go to Peabody College and study drawing, and science and mathematics, and then suppose he could go on to the College of Architecture. Just suppose he could. It might mean the difference between an ordinary architect, and a good one. Do you see what I mean?"

"Yes, sir. Yes, sir, I do." The boy was breathing heavily.

"If you went now into an apprenticeship you would, I think, grow into the ability to plan houses quite above the average; that would be good but it wouldn't be your best."

"Yes, sir, but how could I . . . ?"

Eugene Lewis bowed his head slightly to Mrs. Justice. "Would it be possible, madam, for you and Mr. Justice to keep Hunt in the college here for two years?"

"Yes," she said without hesitation. "Of course we can." Hunt's eyes were upon his mother.

"Then," said Eugene Lewis, "I am here to tell you that the money for him to attend Massachusetts Institute of Technology or some similar institution will be available when he is ready for it. Mrs. Polk and I will each put in half of the required amount. It is no gift. We expect Hunt to sign notes for repayment at six percent—at such a time as he finds it convenient to settle the notes. Please—" he raised a hand gently—"let me finish. Mrs. Polk has been thinking of you, Hunt, since you helped your father repair her back porch; I, since you became overwhelmed by the picture of the Parthenon in your Latin book that day at the Academy. We are not at all unselfish in what we have done. Nashville needs an architect who is not only good but unusual. It is Mrs. Polk's belief, and entirely shared by me, that you, Hunt, can become one. It so happens that we have the money. We are willing, indeed eager to invest it, through you, in the city we both love."

Presently Eugene Lewis rode away. Mother and son sat on the porch together. For a while they sat in silence. It was the boy who spoke first.

"Mama," he said, "Mama." But he said no more.

"Yes, Hunt." She arose and went into the house. From the table she took a well-worn Bible and sat in the rocking chair by the window.

21

Time marked the days from the record. Pres Vick was never seen in Nashville again, though sundry word reached the city that as a corrective agent Tom Linton's fist seemed to lack in permanent efficacy. Titsy Harris saw fit to resign his commissionership not very long after Mr. Vick's departure. The gossip was bandied about in political circles that the honorable Titsy resigned under pressure brought against him no less by his friends than by his enemies. The gossip alleged that in affairs of his office he had cheated his friends as effectively and with as good will as the enemies who were his natural prey. While all of this was doubt-less very straining to Mr. Harris' broad back, the straw that broke it was the circulated report of the thrashing which Tom Linton had administered him. Mr. Harris was not without fame in the more violent episodes of his life. Titsy was a big man and strong before success and dissolution had wrought their mischief upon him. It had been his policy if oratory, blandishment or guile failed, to resort to his fists. But this time according to the report, embellished by much telling, Tom Linton, using only his right hand, had greased one side of his victim's office with the bruised and pulpy body of the commissioner, while greasing the left side with the body of Mr. Vick. Mr. Harris knew that his day was over in Nashville, and he sat no more in the councils of the mighty. The commis-sioner who was appointed in his stead was not only willing but able. Under him builders conformed to law, and generally there was im-provement in the taste and style of the houses. Frequently they were too close to the street, their fronts too severe, their roofs too covered with excrescent growths, their front porches too varied from the general style of the house itself. But they were good houses. The time might again come when the grace of Melrose and Mansfield and Burlington might prevail. But not yet! There was no leader yet available. The general movement was toward better homes. Ed Crayton sensed it.

"People gettin' finicky. You better learn how to make a clean joint, Justice. Yes sir, things have changed. They hung a feller over in Edgefield yestidy who put down a floor that squeaked. Yes

sir, you better learn the carpenterin' trade or you'll be back workin'
for Pres Vick."

"I'll have it learned by dinnertime tomorrer," promised Mr.
Justice cheerfully.

22

Mrs. Polk gave a picnic on the lawn at Polk Place for the graduating class of the Academy. The boys arrived at four o'clock. Mrs.
Polk stood out on the veranda to greet them. They passed back
through the hall and into the dining room where lemonade was
served them. They stood about drinking the lemonade gratefully,
for it was a warm day. Mrs. Polk came back and reviewed with
them pleasantly their days at the Academy. Wouldn't they have
some more lemonade? They would. Mrs. Polk wryly suggested
that from their thirst the teaching at the Academy must have been
very dry. She would speak to Dr. Clark and Professor Garrett, who
were coming presently, about it. They heard then wheels grinding against the stones of the driveway. It was the driver bringing
Merrie Cole. Weaver had felt that it was best for him to plow
corn. The driver let Merrie out and drove the team on back to the
carriage house. As he unhitched them he sang the old Southern
soldiers' song of vainglory.

"I marched to Old Manassas and my heart was full o' fun
And I killed me forty Yankees with a single barrel gun."

He heard another carriage approaching, and he saw Dr. Green
driving into the lot.

"Well, here we are again," said the preacher heartily, "and it
wouldn't surprise me a bit if refreshments are included in the
order of business. Last time I saw you was at a conference meeting—and you weren't listening to preaching either."

"As I ricollects it, Brother Green, you didn't have your mind
hitched to the Word neither."

"You wouldn't have any indirect reference to a piece of chicken,
would you, brother?"

"Not jest a piece o' chicken, Brother Green. The rest o' the
chicken was a-keepin' the piece company."

"Maybe so, maybe so, that wouldn't be unlike me. Bethesda is
a noble community, but very seductive to the spirit."

"I took the Coles to that meetin', they bein' powerful Methodist people, but all they talked about comin' home was Miz Grigsby's custard pies and Miz Eggleston's barbecued mutton and Miz Windrow's deviled eggs, and Miz Cullom's fried chicken, and Miz Vaden's chowchow, and Miz Page's baked ham, and Miz Moss's potato salad. Weaver Cole said it seemed like all he heard that day was Miz Seay askin' Miz Carter how did she make that chicken salad, and Miz Beasley askin' Miz Battle where did she learn how to make beaten biscuits like them she brought. Weaver said it looked to him like there was more recipes than religion at that meetin'."

"I fear that food is the Achilles heel of the Methodists," said Brother Green, becoming faintly classical. Then he relaxed. "I wouldn't be surprised if we are called upon to refresh our bodies here this afternoon. Mind you, I have no direct proof, but a Methodist preacher's inferences as to food are more dependable than cold logic. Mrs. Polk asked me to lend her my daughter Lena May for the day. So I brought the child over about nine this morning. Now, what would Mrs. Polk want with Lena May? I'll make a guess. My daughter, she's only fifteen, but she can make just as good a cake as any Methodist sister of the Bethesda community. She's positively gifted. You mark me, there'll be cakes visible to the physical eye here this afternoon, and where cakes are gathered there are the pies also, et cetera, et cetera. Oh, there's Dr. Clark. I must go speak with him."

Mrs. Polk was saying to the graduating class, "If your thirst is quenched, go out into the yard. Some of your friends are there."

"Come here, Hunt," called Gordon Hicks. "You going to Peabody next year?"

Hunt inclined his head affirmatively.

"Ever think that tomorrow is our last day together? I'm going to Vanderbilt."

"So am I," said James Parkes, "and I'll bet you I make real smart men out o' them Vanderbilt professors. Why, you look what Smack Me Down was before I started out with him. Look what I've made out of Professor Garrett. Any fellow that tries to teach me learns fast. I miss old Bart Halloran."

"He's helping to drill holes in a cut between here and Clarksville, where they are going to put the new railroad."

"Bart'll make a mighty good railroad man. I bet you he gets to be an engineer," prophesied Jim Parkes. "I used to think I'd make a railroad man but—" Jim sighed—"there isn't enough money in it."

"An engineer gets good money," said Gordon.

"You might call it good, but I wouldn't. When I get about thirty years old I want to sit out in my yard with a plug hat on all day long. I'll call a servant and hand him a greenback. 'There's ten dollars. Run down to the Nicholson House and buy me an *American*. Don't wait for the change. I'm in a hurry. I want to read about what I did yesterday.' It's going to take money for me to live right!"

"Where you going to get all that money?"

"I guess I'll buy me a mint and make it," answered James Parkes, sighing.

Mrs. Polk came then and seated them at small tables placed conveniently about that part of the lawn. "Wait a minute," she said, "that isn't the way I want it. Move that table over here, will you, please?"

It was Ivo Burns who reached the table first and supervised moving it. Ivo cast an inquiring eye over the terrain.

"Wouldn't that be preferable, Mrs. Polk?" he asked, pointing.

"Yes, really I believe it would," she said, surprise in her tones.

"Lord help the Vanderbilt professors," whispered Jim Parkes to Gordon. "Ivo's going there, too."

Then two visions of loveliness came bearing trays of food.

"What's Lena May doing here?" asked Jim Parkes of Ivo Burns. He whispered out of the corner of his mouth, "You suppose she knew we would be here?"

"Rother," said Ivo.

Hunt Justice, sitting at the table with Gordon Hicks, Berrien Lindsley, and President Stearns, saw Neely Barrow bearing a tray of food across the lawn. His heart missed a beat and his face grew crimson. Neely Barrow's keen eyes flashed over the lawn and came to rest upon the table where Hunt sat. Without hesitation, she turned to it. "May I serve you?" she asked President Stearns. Then she served Berrien Lindsley, and then the two boys. "Hello, Hunt. I want to talk with you before you leave—about the columns." She passed on.

Ellen Cole was carrying a pitcher of lemonade from table to table. Merrie Cole was carrying a platter of sliced ham, and Mrs. Coleman, fully recovered from her harrowing night on Fern Street, was making regular trips from the kitchen to the main supply table.

"They've enough ham to last for a few minutes, Merrie. Suppose you offer them the fried chicken."

"I've known elephants that ate less, Mrs. Polk," said Merrie, a bit inelegantly but smiling.

"But what good were the elephants?"

"I was merely complimenting the boys, Mrs. Polk. I married an appetite."

Neely Barrow was making a round with a large platter laden with an ample assortment of pickles. Lena May was carrying fried chicken.

"Could it be, Dr. Stearns," asked Berrien Lindsley jestingly, "that you left Massachusetts because the people there have never learned to prepare chicken properly?"

"No," said President Stearns, "it was because the people in the South have never learned to prepare teachers properly."

"We've never eaten them," said Berrien.

The president answered Berrien in kind. "You've hardly used them in any way," he said, smiling dourly.

Neely Barrow held the platter at Hunt's side. "Ours are Ionic," she said.

"I thought they would be " said Hunt and watched her move on to the next table.

Lena May placidly lifted the best pieces of fried chicken onto Jim Parkes's plate. A sudden idea took hold of Jim's mind.

"I bet you've been making cakes."

"There really are people who like my cakes," she said, her placidness unmarred by a ripple.

"I like your cakes, Lena May. Goodness knows, I ought to. I taught you how to make them, didn't I?"

"You did stand around in the way once."

Jim changed the subject. "Just look at the way Hunt watches Neely Barrow. It's positively disgusting. It must be that he watches her hoping she'll come back with more cake."

"If you'll watch me I might bring you a piece of cake."

"My eyes will never leave you if you'll make it a big piece."

"I don't think Hunt is cake-minded. I think he is looking at her for her own personal worth. She is pretty."

"Fair," said Jim, weighing his words carefully. "Yes, just about fair. But fair's pretty good when you think of the millions of girls that aren't even that good-looking. Why, in Europe alone there are . . ."

Ivo Burns was finding the half-whispered exchange between Jim and Lena May somewhat irksome. "Of course," he said, manifesting a slight hint of petulance, "I could ask Mrs. Polk to serve the chicken but that should be unnecessary."

"Oh, I'm sorry, Ivo," said Lena May, hurriedly bearing the platter to Ivo's side. Ivo scanned the offering.

"I see that I come late," he said; "the best pieces have been retired from use, as it were."

"Try these," counseled Lena May, serving him; "maybe you'll be able to make out—as it were."

The air was sweet with the fragrance of spring, and the pleasant coolness of evening was tempering the warmth of the day. It was the season when the shadows of night thickened slowly. There was no hurry.

Then came Neely Barrow and Lena May bringing dessert—rich, ample strawberry shortcake heaped with corrugated folds of whipped cream. There was no hurry. Life lay ahead.

Mrs. Polk asked Ellen Cole, "Where is that driver?"

"He's where he likes to be, with the horses."

"Bring him here where I like for him to be—with the people."

Mrs. Cole went to the gate to the stable lot. The driver was sitting on the carriage seat flicking idly with his whip. Even as she was preparing to speak, she heard him break into a snatch of song.

> "I'm a good Ol' Rebel
> That's just what I am."

He didn't seem to relish the song for he shifted from Rebel defiance to Rebel gayety.

> "Just before the battle the general hears a row,
> He says the Yanks are coming, I hear them shootin' now;
> He turns aroun' in wonder and then and there he sees
> The Georgia militia eatin' goober peas."

She knew that song was conjuring up old visions: the campfires of John Hood's army, the long, creaking westward movement of Hood's tired wagons—westward, westward, following the autumn sun. He stopped singing, then sat bright-eyed gazing at scenes long dead except in memory.

"Mrs. Polk wants you to join us for some refreshments."

"That's mighty nice o' her, ma'am." He folded his whip with

care, and laid it on the carriage seat. Mrs. Polk waited for them at the nearest table.

The sun had fallen behind the hill. The windows of Polk Place and the Adams' home across the street, being higher, caught the last rays and transfused them into splashes of gold. The vesper chorus of the birds was in full throat. The traffic on Church Street had quieted almost to silence.

Hunt Justice felt rather than heard Neely Barrow standing at his side.

"They don't need you, Hunt. Let's go sit at this table and talk —about columns."

They sat at the table.

"What are you going to do, Hunt, when you graduate at the Academy?"

"I'm going to Peabody and then to Massachusetts Institute of Technology."

"Massachusetts ... what's the rest of it, Hunt?"

He told her.

"What will you study there?"

"Architecture," he said.

"What is architecture, Hunt? It's about columns, isn't it—and things like that?"

"Yes, columns, and everything else about buildings. I want to learn how to build houses—like yours."

"It's not as fine as it used to be. We're dreadfully poor."

He looked at her in surprise. Then he said hurriedly, "So are we. I couldn't go away to school but some people have promised me the money. I am going to pay it back."

"That won't be much trouble when you learn how to build fine houses. I'm going to Peabody, too, Hunt. No, not now. I must finish at Dr. Price's first."

"You going to Peabody College? Why, I didn't know it."

"I haven't had a chance to tell you, Hunt," she said gently. "I'm going to be a teacher. I have to do something. We're dreadfully poor." She said placidly, "Besides, that's what I want to do, I guess. Grandy'll have a fit at first." She paused a moment, then, "Isn't it funny, me telling you all of this?"

"I want you to tell me," he said, a touch of hoarseness in his speech.

"I want you to know. I want you to tell me, too. You must write me a letter, one every month while you are in Massachusetts Institute of Technology."

"Yes," he said huskily, "yes."

"The columns at Cherry Hill are Ionic," she repeated. "I look at them every time I walk up to the house."

"In the Parthenon there is a room which is called The Maiden's Chamber. In that room are six Ionic columns that for perfection have never been equaled. . . ." He stopped suddenly, flushing from the half-consciousness of his pedantry.

"It sounds beautiful. I wish I could see them."

"I wish I could, too."

"I'd like to be with you when I see it. Don't you think we ought to see it together?"

"Yes," he said hoarsely, "yes, I do."

"Wasn't Mrs. Polk a dear to let me come? I don't think I ever have enjoyed a talk as much as this one."

The shadows thickened slowly. Mr. Bowen, the lamplighter, was making his evening rounds. He stopped his light buggy in front of Polk Place. He worked his gadgets and a glow softened the twilight in front of the home.

"I'm sorry . . ." said Berrien Lindsley to Mrs. Polk, rising tentatively.

"Sit down, Berrien, I want to talk with you awhile. It isn't dark yet. Am I to conclude that the Board of Health is a hard master?"

"Not the Board of Health, Mrs. Polk, but the diseases which plague man. They are starting early this year."

"That should keep the doctors busy."

"It takes more than drugs, more than doctors. They are last resorts. The Board of Health begins far earlier. I firmly believe that most of our diseases are the products of our own ignorance and triflingness. Here's a sobering thought, Mrs. Polk. If we had known as much about Asiatic cholera—no, if we had been willing to use what we knew even then, President Polk might be alive today."

"I've thought of that," she said, then was silent.

Her eyes drifted about the lawn, coming to rest on Neely Barrow Roane and Hunt Justice seated at the table near the lower side.

"Very, very interesting. I wonder . . . do you recognize that boy, and girl, Berrien?"

"Oh, certainly. That's Neely Barrow Roane. The boy, I know

him, too, though his name has escaped me. He was at the Hermitage one Easter when I was there. He was with Eugene Lewis."

"I will tell you a secret, Berrien. Eugene and I are lending that boy money, when he is ready for it, to attend Massachusetts Institute of Technology."

"When you and Eugene Lewis have faith, who am I to doubt? Is there need for further funds?"

"Oh, no, that's our own private and sacred investment."

"It comes back to me now. Interested in architecture, isn't he?"

"Very greatly. That's the reason for the Massachusetts Institute of Technology. I am very fond of my glimpses, Berrien. This lad is one of the best glimpses I ever had."

"If only I could have been one of your glimpses, Mrs. Polk!"

"You have always been a most special glimpse, Berrien. Ever since in Murfreesboro I saw you as a boy, not so old as Hunt Justice. Your father preached at the Presbyterian Church and brought you along. You sat on the front bench and at intervals nodded your head in approval of the sermon. Don't smile. Your father's sermon was worth a nod even from his son. You are a born crusader, Berrien. I want to solicit your support for a new crusade, but I'd rather talk more at length than I can tonight. It's about General Jackson's home. Mary Dorris and I talked about it the other day. She is exceedingly concerned about it. I went out there recently with Ida and Gale Thurston, and unless we make the Hermitage into a shrine, we will by neglect make it into a wreck. But we'll talk later. The driver seems to be holding a levee. Let's go listen. If he's telling the story of the supply wagons that he and his friend stole from the Yankees, it's worth hearing."

But it wasn't that story. It was one that Mrs. Polk had never heard. There had been one or two tales already, one a choice though brief account of the lady passenger who would neither stay in the coach and ride nor get out and walk while traversing a flooded stretch just south of Bowling Green. Gale Thurston cast an expert eye about and saw that the entire party had gathered about. The time was ripe for the climax.

"Tell about Colonel Vaughan's leg."

The driver waited a moment, summoning old memories. "I think it was the Fourth o' July, 1864. We hadn't got to Atlanta yet but was havin' a right smart skirmish with the Yanks. I had the wagons hid back safe in the woods and was up where the excitement was. Colonel Vaughan of the Thirteenth Tennessee, who was a case effn I ever see one, was eatin' a snack. Then he got out his pipe, an' effn the Yanks had ever smelled it they'd a-been licked right then. Matches was awful hard to get and we didn't have any fire kindled on account of it bein' so dry. Colonel Vaughan had a sunglass, so he held it up to light his pipe. That give the Yanks somepin to shoot at and a big shell come a-whizzin' and then Colonel Vaughan didn't have but one leg. The other one was shot off right above the foot. What you think was the first thing the Colonel said—'Get my pipe and sunglass.' Some doctors come tearin' up and dosed him with morphine and whisky. The Colonel was a drinkin' man then, but after the war he quit teetotal. 'If that's the best licker you got I'm a goner,' he yelled. We got him in an ambulance and they appinted me to drive it. We started to the field hospital. Purty soon we was a-passin' Gin'ral Frank Cheatham's headquarters. He come out an' started sympathizin' with the Colonel. 'What you need, Colonel,' he said, 'is some first-rate whisky.' He brought out a bottle and the Colonel took it all. 'That's fair licker, Frank,' he said. We kept goin' and then we come to Gin'ral Hardee's headquarters. He come out to see the Colonel and said he was powerful sorry and maybe some good whisky would help. The Colonel took all he had left in the bottle and said it was better licker than Frank Cheatham kept on hand. We drove on about a half a mile and we passed Gin'ral Joseph E. Johnston's headquarters. He come out and shook hands with the Colonel, and said it would be purty hard on the army but he expected they'd have to do without the Colonel for a few days. 'Got any licker, Gin'ral?' said the Colonel. The Gin'ral went back in his tent and brought out a bottle about a third full that he said was twenty-year-old apple brandy. The Colonel swallered it all down, and said that effn the Gin'ral ever had any mo' like it to send him word and he'd get shot in the other leg. The Colonel dropped off to sleep then and when he waked up the next day the doctors had him all fixed up. It really wasn't so very long till he was back with the Thirteenth Tennessee. But," the driver concluded, "on account of some o' that bein' pore licker his leg never growed back."

"I suppose," said Gale Thurston, prompting him, "that a great many lost limbs have been restored by the prompt use of fine liquor."

"I wouldn't say as how very many have, but it's been done. Yes sir. Well, me, for instance. Had both legs shot off at Chickamaugy, but I was drivin' a supply wagon and I knew where Gin'ral Pat

Cleburne kept his special leg-growin' licker, so I reached back and got his bottle an' took a swig...."

"What happened?"

"Never missed a day drivin'. The only trouble my two legs is forty years younger'n the rest o' me."

"Why couldn't they provide the whole army with that liquor?"

"The still house burned down and they lost the directions how to make it."

A baffled look spread upon President Stearns' face. These Southerners! No man in New England would believe a monstrous tale like that. Yet it was clearly accepted in Nashville.

23

"The trouble with Dr. Stearns," affirmed Miss Julia Sears, "is that every time he opens his eyes he thinks he is seeing New England. The man is the soul of honor—New England honor—and he understands education—New England education. Now don't jump to conclusions. I was born in Massachusetts and I plan to die there, but right now I'm in Tennessee, and that's the place I see when I look at it. When in Tennessee, do as the Scotch-Irish do, say I. Temporarily I've traded John Carver's *Mayflower* for John Donelson's *Adventure,* and the trade sticks as long as I'm here."

"It was the trade of wisdom, Miss Sears," commented Professor Garrett.

"I've courted wisdom," said Miss Sears placidly. "Sometimes she has evaded me, and sometimes I have won her favor, though never more pronounced than in my exchange of boats—temporarily, however, as I have explained. Emma Cutter who came with me to Tennessee retained the *Mayflower.* So, she went back to Massachusetts, which, I think, for her was itself a matter of wisdom."

"How are the scholars in your classes, Miss Sears? Do they unfold mathematically according to your wishes?"

"Oh, no. I always manage for my wishes to run ahead of a scholar's performance. It would be boresome if they came up to expectations."

"Your expectations are subject to eloquent report, Miss Sears."

"I cultivate my expectations very earnestly, Dr. Garrett. In fact, I have to. It's almost a race lately between my expectations and the achievement of two of my scholars. Up to now I have kept ahead," she added grimly.

"May I guess the name of one of them?"

"No need to guess. They are perfectly well known, both of them. Dr. Clark told me in confidence, just as I fancy he has told fifty others, how he maneuvered Dr. Stearns into admitting Hunt Justice. He bamboozled—a perfectly good Southern word, Dr. Garrett—Dr. Stearns into the notion that Hunt was practically just as bright as a Massachusetts boy. Of course the president wanted to have a part in a miracle like that, so he let him in. Do you know what I told Dr. Stearns yesterday? I told him to get word to the Massachusetts Institute of Technology to start improving. But from the way he looked, I fear that I was too subtle."

"Is the other scholar Charles Little?"

"Of course. Neck and neck—the South is rebuilding my speech, Dr. Garrett—is the way those two young men keep. Charles is the more fluent, the more precise, the more at ease. Hunt has a remarkable capacity to put mathematics into its proper perspective. Somebody in Boston is going to be sharply surprised one of these days. Hunt not only understands his mathematics but he also understands why it exists. Lizzie Bloomstein who teaches drawing insists that she is studying drawing under Hunt. She thinks that if she can have another term with him she can learn to handle the work very well. Don't think those two are the only students I have worth reporting. The others are good. Willard Brister is good, so is Joseph Blankinship, so is William Romine, so is Charles White; but Hunt and Charles are experiences that do not come to a teacher very often. We live in the uplands with good students, but we climb the peaks with Hunt and Charles."

Time moved ahead. Hunt graduated with the fond blessing of the College and made ready for his journey to New England.

24

President and Mrs. Cleveland visited Nashville, and were house guests at Belle Meade. On Sunday afternoon they drove into the city to call on Mrs. Polk. The presidential carriage returning to Belle Meade was barely out of sight when Berrien Lindsley dropped in to pay to Mrs. Polk the respects of an old friend. Then Neely Barrow and Hunt came. Mrs. Polk had invited them before she had known of the visit of the President. Mrs. Polk seemed strangely tired as they sat in the parlor, but her eyes were bright with excitement. She sat for moments saying nothing, looking straight ahead but seeing the past. Presently she spoke in the monotone of one who communes with the long ago.

"They live in the White House now. I have never been back to it. It must be finer than when we left. Oh, much better furnished. Once at a reception we ran out of silver, but no one noticed. Those servants could handle an emergency like veterans. It frightens me to remember how long ago that was. I think the President is an honest and reasonably wise man, but that he could become dreadfully stubborn. Did you notice his jaws? They're not the sort that yield. It's odd that a man so fat should keep his coat buttoned so tightly. That accents not only his stoutness but his lack of ease. Mr. Polk was of slight build but he, too, was stiff and formal. I never in my life heard him call anyone but me by a Christian name. Isn't Mrs. Cleveland appealing? A very lovely woman, but I think she's a bit frightened. The strain upon Mr. Polk was almost incredible. And it wasn't much less on me. It's a little curious about the wife of the President of the United States. No one realizes—certainly not the President himself—how much she is concerned in her husband's success. I suppose he thinks that she knows that he will be all right. But she doesn't, I fear. There are times when she lives in agony until some specially important issue is settled. And he thinks that she is as serene as a summer day! Of course, the President never gives a thought to the White House —except that it is where he eats his food, receives his guests, works and sleeps. All of that he takes for granted. It's his wife's obligation to arrange so that he can take it for granted. And yet by being maladroit she could wreck the neighborliness of nations." She paused a moment, then continued in an even, detached voice. "I have never flinched from my age. Till now it has always seemed so irrelevant. It isn't so this afternoon. The President's visit has made my age so real. I am eighty-five years old, and there are many days in eighty-five years. So many! Some of those days have been great, and some have been terrible. . . ." She stopped and looked at Neely Barrow and Hunt as if surprised to find them there.

"Good gracious, I've been talking like one about to depart. Well, I'm not. I've a lot of life left yet. I'll live to go to weddings not yet arranged—" she smiled, turning to Hunt—"to see houses built that do not yet exist in a man's imagination. When do you leave, Hunt?"

"Next week, Mrs. Polk."

"God go with you. I am greatly interested in you for several reasons. I think you will work diligently keeping your work tempered by a balanced mind. I think you will be held to a straight course by a great and enduring purpose. I think that the time will come when you can give my beloved city a service greatly needed." Again, she stopped. "There I am preaching again."

"Mrs. Polk, I intended to see you before I leave to thank you for your faith in me, for the money you have let me have. Let me do it here."

"Oh," she said, her eyes flashing to Neely Barrow.

"I know about it, Mrs. Polk. Hunt told me."

"My mother asked me to thank you for her."

Mrs. Polk's eyes rested speculatively upon Hunt. "I am sure that you have a good mother, Hunt."

"Yes, I do. She is good."

"Of course, she is. You have nothing mean nor coarse in you. I am inclined to favor your father also."

She did not miss the boy's narrowest margin of hesitation. "Yes, Mrs. Polk, my father is a good man. He worked for you once. You remember."

"Certainly, I do." She had only that morning looked at the hidden places in her back porch, smoothed out because the son had required it of the father. She was silent for a while. Then she spoke very quietly.

"I have since the others left this afternoon been greatly in need of the strength of the young. You do not know how you have helped me by staying awhile. Neely Barrow, you will tell me all the news from Hunt. He will be writing to you."

"I will write to you both."

"Isn't that lovely? Anyhow, Neely Barrow, come to see me and we'll talk about what he writes to each of us, at least within limits."

"If I should come often, Mrs. Polk, would it annoy you?"

"Oh, my child, that's not the way to annoy me. Quite the contrary." She stood, holding out her hand to Hunt. "Good-by, lad. Come back bearing your shield."

Berrien Lindsley invited Neely Barrow and Hunt to ride home in his carriage. And presently they drove away.

No rain had fallen in three weeks and there had been much travel on the streets of the city. The air was faintly gray with limestone dust.

"Tomorrow will be a big day," said Berrien. "A reception for the President at the Capitol, and one for Mrs. Cleveland at the Maxwell House. I don't think they will be glad to leave Nashville, but their bodies will. Oh well, he courts fatigue who wears a crown. Here we are at Cherry Hill."

Neely Barrow laid her hand upon Hunt's. "You will write to me, won't you?"

"Yes," he said huskily. "Yes, if you want me to, Neely Barrow."

"Well, I do. And if you don't want me to answer when you do you'd better say so now."

"Looks as if this is going to be a hard winter on letter carriers," said Berrien humorously.

25

The Justices sat at supper. On the table was their best cloth, and to eat there was everything for which Hunt had a special preference, for that was the last supper he would eat at home before leaving for Boston. There was already a box tightly packed with food for his use on the cars. Most of it his mother had prepared, but the cake had been baked by Mrs. Callie Elrod.

"I'm ashamed to tell you how much o' that kind o' cake Mr. Elrod could eat. He wasn't no finicky eater 'bout nothin', but he could down a jam cake before you could say skat. One minute there'd be Mr. Elrod and the cake and the next jest Mr. Elrod a-wipin' off the crumbs."

Hunt thanked her.

"It's good cake," she said. "I expect travelin's right appetizin'. I never thought I'd know anybody that'd be going that far. I sometimes think I'd like to travel and see places. When you comin' back, Hunt, next summer?"

"I don't know, Mrs. Elrod. Mama thinks if I can find the right sort of work to do somewhere next summer I ought to take it."

"I never knowed her to be wrong yet."

He nodded, smiling appreciatively. "I'll feel better about Mama when I remember you live close."

"She'll be all right. And your daddy'll be all right, too. Ed Crayton thinks he'll stick this time. Ed says he's a-makin' a right good carpenter. Nothin' fancy, but when he nails two planks together they stay nailed. Ed'll give him steady work as long as he stays deef to fox houn's and don't get no fancy notions from dead beats like Titsy Harris. You goin' to the deepo tomorrer, Miz Justice?"

It was Hunt who answered. "Yes, Mama is going and Papa, too. Mr. Weaver Cole's driver is going to take us in their carriage. He's a mighty nice man, that driver."

"The Weaver Coles! Sendin' their kerriage! You've gone up fast. But you stay on the good side o' that driver. From what I hear it's courtin' the graveyard to pester him. Well, I'll try to see you long enough in the mornin' to say good-by. Remember the day you rented the house? You stood out in my yard and told your daddy he was a contractor. I didn't ever forget that. I knowed right then that they was something different about you. My goodness, I'd clean forgot about that settin' hen. She's my hope for Christmas fried chicken."

When Mrs. Elrod left, Mrs. Justice wrapped each piece of jam cake separately and placed them very precisely in the box into which she had already put the delicacies she had prepared. Then she fixed supper, timing its completion nicely to her husband's arrival from work. They sat at the table.

"Hunt, you say the blessing," his mother said.

Hunt said the words he had learned as a little boy and when he had finished, to his and his mother's surprise, his father added a high-pitched "Amen."

"Yes sir," said Courtney Justice, spearing a chicken dumpling. "Ed acted right nice when I asked him for tomorrer off. Said if he had a boy leavin' he'd want off, too. I guess I been plain lucky."

"Take another piece of chicken, Hunt," said Mrs. Justice. "Courtney, give him a good piece. Maybe chicken is scarce where he is going."

"I'm going up to that Capitol sometime and look at it," said Mrs. Justice, as he accommodated with the chicken. "You've talked about it so much, Hunt, you've sort o' got me interested. Maybe if this one wears out they'll want you to put up the next one."

"Those peach preserves, Hunt; take some o' them. You've always liked them. I wish you could take that jar with you."

"Wisht I could 'a' gone to college and learned about house

building. It might 'a' been a right smart help. Still I been mighty lucky. We got some money in the bank, Lizzie."

"It's going to stay there," said his wife evenly.

"I started out lucky," said Mr. Justice. "I was lucky when I picked you, Lizzie. I reckon the only sorrer I ever had was when I done somepin that didn't please you."

"That hasn't been often, Courtney. Hunt, there's two kinds of pie, gooseberry and egg custard."

"May I have a piece of both, Mama?"

The spell of fine weather still held and they sat out on the porch and talked. Two nights before, the moon had been full, so it rose a little late. Its mellowed light flooded the side of the porch nearest Cherry Street. It gleamed a silver white on the tombstones across the street. Hunt stood and said:

"Mama, Papa, will you excuse me? I want to walk around awhile."

When he had gone, walking east on Oak Street, Courtney Justice watched him until he faded from sight. "That's funny. Where do you reckon he's goin', Lizzie?"

"Maybe out to the college, Courtney."

But Hunt did not turn in at the college. He walked resolutely on to Cherry Hill. There was no thought that he would see Neely Barrow. He had always held treasured the memory that she had asked him to her home. But there was always before him the disparity between Cherry Hill and the little house on Oak Street. He had gone to Kingsley when invited and to Polk Place. But that was different. Cherry Hill was a challenge. He would not go there until he had found himself worthy. He stood by the side of the gate. There was no light in the great house, so silent in the moonlight. To the right was the cherry orchard, and on the other side the ground dropped sharply to the Cumberland River, a half mile away. Behind him was the glow of the gaslights on Broadway and above that, those on Church Street. And then church bells added their solemn sweetness to the October evening. It was, Hunt recalled, Wednesday evening and those bells were calling the faithful to prayer meeting. Then the bells of the new First Baptist Church began tolling. The Roanes were Baptists. They were probably at church. With what quiet and gracious dignity the house sat there in the moonlight. How dark and rich were the magnolia trees! Near the street was a little pagodalike summerhouse, thickly draped with morning-glory vines, the thick spread of blooms now opening in the recreating cool of the evening. The sweet and lonesome whistle of a steamboat sounded from down the river. Hunt Justice stood there gripped by the thrill of Cherry Hill. Then a voice that he would never forget spoke from the shadows of the summerhouse.

"Isn't that you, Hunt?"

"Yes," he said, surprised at the hoarseness of his voice.

"I thought it was. Come in, can't you, Hunt?"

He lifted the latch of the gate.

"I didn't think anyone was at home," he said by way of excuse for standing at the gate. "It is so beautiful here."

"Isn't it?" She held out her hand. "I want you to know Grandy. Grandy, this is Hunt Justice. He is the one who is going to Boston to study architecture. I told you. Remember?"

"Oh yes," said a voice from the darkness. "Sit down, Hunt."

The boy saw the outlines of the chair and sat down. Neely Barrow sat in the chair next to him, and her nearness was precious.

"I walked by the college," said Hunt, his mind still upon the necessity of an explanation. "Then I stopped to look at Cherry Hill in the moonlight. I am leaving tomorrow."

"When will you be back, Hunt?" asked Neely Barrow.

"It may be two years."

"Two years!" The words as if in protest escaped Neely Barrow's lips.

Hunt could feel his heart pounding but he answered steadily. "Yes, if I can find work to do, Mr. Lewis thinks I should take it. So does my mother."

"So do I," said Neely Barrow, "and then when you do come back you'll stay."

Hunt's tones were ragged with hoarseness. "It might be best to work during the summers."

"Yes," said Neely Barrow, "it might be best." She was giving him her consent to work during the summers.

"The buildings in New England are sturdier than ours," said Erwin Roane, "but they are harsher; they lack our grace. Only in churches do they surpass us. Their churches are the most beautiful in America."

"Our homes, I think, sir, are the more graceful because of our use of columns."

"Precisely. The Greeks were great benefactors in many ways,

but it is my notion that Phidias gave more to the world than Plato."

"I see what you mean, sir."

"So do I," said Neely Barrow. "I told you, didn't I, Hunt, that I am going to college. I may be a schoolteacher when you come back."

"I do not wish it," said her grandfather stiffly.

"If I should make a very good teacher, Grandy, you'd be proud of me."

"It isn't a question of pride. No Roane has ever taught school."

"Then it's time they started," said Neely Barrow calmly. "Did any Roane ever make an architect, Grandy?"

"No."

"It seems to me, Grandy, that there are a lot of nice things we have never done." Her hand, raised in a gesture of regret for the fields hitherto unoccupied by the Roanes, fell upon Hunt's hand lying on the arm of his chair. Surprised, she looked quickly but did not withdraw her hand. Above the drumming of his own pulse, Hunt could hear Erwin Roane saying:

"I imagine architecture is very fascinating. I have sometimes thought that the highest expression of a man's culture is the home he builds. No, Neely Barrow, I do not mean to discredit any needed labor. It has always seemed to me though that a family limiting itself to a narrow range of activities has the better chance to retain its strength. . . ." He sat for a while in silence, then he stood.

"I am tired," he said in a strained voice. He held out his hand to Hunt. "I wish you well in your studies. Good-by, sir. I think we had better go in now, Neely Barrow."

"I will go with Hunt to the gate, Grandy."

He seemed very old as he walked toward the house in the moonlight. Neely Barrow and Hunt stood at the gate and looked into each other's eyes. He held out his hand and she placed hers in it.

"You will not change while I am gone." It was a statement no less than a question.

"No," she said almost fiercely, "I will not change, not even if you do."

"You know I will not."

"Yes, I know it. Write to me, Hunt. I'll be waiting for you to come back." Her fingers tightened their clasp. And then she was gone. He watched her until she passed the columns of the porch into the shadows beyond. He heard her speak to her grandfather. Then he turned and walked rapidly toward Oak Street.

Erwin Roane waited for his granddaughter on the porch.

"Who is he, Neely Barrow?"

"I told you of him, Grandy."

"Yes, I know, about his fondness for buildings, and all that. But who is he?"

She sensed the impatience, or was it anxiety in his tone. She waited through a moment of silence for her own decision. But it was he who spoke first.

"Does he mean anything to you, Neely Barrow?"

"Everything, Grandy," she answered clearly but gently.

"Neely Barrow," he said sharply, "you are too young. You do not know."

"I have known for a long time, Grandy."

"Who is he? Who are his people?"

"I have not seen them, Grandy, but I have seen him."

"I do not like it, child. What has he to match your name?" He stopped, and again Neely Barrow knew of what he was thinking. And that knowledge drained Neely Barrow of her resentment and defiance.

"You are tired. I think you should go to bed now, Grandy. I'm proud of my name. I'm proud of you. Nobody in this world ever had a lovelier Grandy. I don't know about the Justices. I think they are poor. Hunt told me that Mrs. Polk and Mr. Eugene Lewis are lending him money to go to college. You like aristocrats, Grandy. If Hunt isn't one now, he'll become one."

"People of themselves do not become aristocrats."

"I am concerned, Grandy, with what people themselves may become."

"I, child, am concerned by what they already have become. This will pass. You are young. . . ."

"Listen, Grandy, Mrs. Weaver Cole told me that she met Weaver at a supper at the Maxwell House. She saw him just a second, and from right then never doubted that he was *the* one, and from that time on he thought the same about her. They were mere children but they never changed. She wasn't an aristocrat. She said so herself, but if she isn't now, I don't want to be one. Wasn't it strange that I saw Hunt first out at her home and from that very second I've been perfectly certain? I didn't then know what I was certain of, but I do now. You can trust me, Grandy."

Without replying, he turned and went in the house.

"He doesn't understand now," said Neely Barrow to herself, "but he will."

26

Mrs. Elrod had come over for a moment after supper, and they were talking of Hunt's departure that morning.

"Hunt looked fine sitting there by the car window," said Mrs. Justice. "He was waving at us as far as I could see."

"Seemed like the cars left there mighty fast," observed Courtney Justice. "I walked by the winder a piece, but it got away from me."

"Courtney went on the cars with Hunt," said Mrs. Justice.

"Somebody had to carry one of his valises for him. If there's anything left in this house beside the furniture, I can't remember it."

Mrs. Elrod indulged in a bit of unwonted sentiment. "Wisht I had a boy like Hunt. You'll miss him a lot, Miz Justice."

"Yes," she said, "I'll miss him, but I never have been as happy as I have been today. It's something I've dreamed about all of my life."

"He got a mighty good seat," said Mr. Justice, "right by a winder so he can see everything. Guess he'll see a sight of things before he gets to Boston."

"I knew there wasn't anything common about Hunt almost since he was born," said Mrs. Justice.

"Gracious, Lizzie, there oughtn't be. Your own daddy was a big bug till he got wiped out by the war, and the same about my granddaddy. That war sure upset things. Hadn't been for it we might be big bugs, too."

"I don't put much store by granddaddys and such," said Mrs. Elrod. "Don't know as I ever had one. Where you reckon Hunt's at now?"

"Up somewheres the other side o' Louisville. He gets to Cincinnati at ten o'clock. Train runs jest as fast after dark as it does in daylight."

"It was mighty nice o' Mrs. Cole to send her kerriage to take you all to the deepo," said Mrs. Elrod. "I've heard quite a bit o' talk about that feller that was drivin'. They say he used to swaller folks alive when he didn't like 'em. He set out there in the kerriage while you was gettin' ready and the way he killed hossflies with his whip was a sight to look at. He kept a-singin' all the time, too. I couldn't hear the words but the music was soft and sweetlike."

"He's a nice man," said Mrs. Justice. "He's been nice to Hunt ever since we moved here. One day a long time ago some boys were mistreating Hunt, and that man made them stop. He did it without hurting the boys' feelings, too."

"They was right smart people on the car," said Mr. Justice. "Looked like nice folks, too."

"Don't you go to leavin' this woman by herself o' nights. I know how it breaks out. One hour Mr. Elrod'd be workin' like a Christian, the next he'd be fox huntin' like a sinner."

"I ain't a-aimin' to," promised Courtney Justice. "I'm cured— well, jest about."

"Jest about?"

"I ain't denying that fox houn's still make purty music. But I won't go huntin' while Hunt's off in Boston. I'm promisin' that but I ain't promisin' I won't about a week after he gets back, jest to celebrate."

"You put it off till then and Miz Justice and me'll give your fox hunt a blessin' like they do in furrin countries. I'll even fix you up a snack to take along."

"Maybe I'll take you up on that, but right now I'm goin' to stick to carpenterin'. Ed Crayton's done right by me and I aim to do right by him."

"I guess I better be goin'. I jest run over. You need rest, Miz Justice. You look a little peaked."

"This is the happiest day I ever had. Come again when you can, Mrs. Elrod."

Mrs. Elrod left. Mrs. Justice looked with unseeing eyes out through the window at the shadows outside.

"My boy, my boy," she said in low tones. And then she reached for her Bible.

27

At Sycamore Eugene Lewis received a letter from Mrs. Duncan Dorris requesting an interview when he came to Nashville. If it was not his plan to be in the city presently then he should rearrange matters and come. She needed to talk with him. He knew Mrs. Dorris. So he half invented an errand of business and went into

Nashville the next day. He found Mrs. Dorris at her home on Spruce Street.

"All right," he said when they were seated in the library. "Here I am. What is it?"

"Of what did we talk when I saw you last?"

"The Hermitage, of course."

"Exactly, and it's the Hermitage I want to talk about now. Mrs. Andrew Jackson came to see me Sunday."

"Yes?"

"I think her idea's a grand one. She believes the Hermitage might be made into a shrine just as important as Mount Vernon."

"It might, but somebody would have to go to a lot of trouble."

"Of course. I'm willing."

"I used to be not only willing but eager. I thought the railroad was demanding, but at Sycamore . . . ! Today's the first time I've been away from the plant in three months. One time in an emergency I went sixty hours without sleep. Perhaps my zeal for some very worthy causes has weakened somewhat."

"Then renew it. The proposition to make of the Hermitage a home for Confederate soldiers will be pressed vigorously at the next session of the legislature. A great deal of sentiment will support it. If it is done, it will destroy the place even more surely than neglect is doing now. We must, of course, provide for our needy soldiers. We can't do less, but there are other places just as satisfactory for living purposes and without the sacred memories."

"An argument will be to award the sacred memories to the soldiers."

"Surely, and bolstered by the economic plea that the state already owns the Hermitage."

"The state has owned it for thirty years."

"And let decay accumulate for exactly that period. General Andrew Jackson had faults that are least hidden from his greatest admirers, but he was a great and virile and colorful man. He built here a home, a great home, a home of strength and dignity and excellent taste. He and his beloved wife filled it with furniture from the best markets of Philadelphia and New Orleans, some of it of superb quality. That belongs to the Jacksons. If the Hermitage becomes a Confederate home the priceless furniture, beds, chairs, tables, everything will be scattered and the lovely memories that clustered about them lost. Mrs. Jackson thinks the Hermitage can become the Mount Vernon of the South."

"Perhaps it can," he said. "Your eloquence is very contagious. What do you want me to do?"

"I don't know. I just wanted to talk with you. We need ideas."

"At the moment I have none. If one comes to me, I'll ride all the way from Sycamore to tell you of it."

"I knew I could depend on you. By the way, when are you moving back to Nashville?"

"What gave you the idea I'd be coming back?"

"Oh, nothing, except that life for you in a factory in a wilderness would in the end become wearing. It would take an entire city to absorb your good impulses, Eugene."

"The salary at Sycamore is fabulous, really. And I've been worth it. But I'd move back tomorrow if I were really convinced I could add some beauty to the town."

"There has been some improvement."

"Yes. Some respectable homes are going up now. I passed some as I came in, heavy and overornamented but quite fit to live in. I imagine I'll be coming back. But let's get back to the Hermitage."

"I have thought about it for a long time, as you know, but always vaguely. Since Mrs. Jackson came to see me, however, I've tried to think to a point. I'm not willing for the state to maintain it as a shrine. Go look about our lovely Capitol and you know why. One of our great shrines—that's really what it is—filthy with tobacco juice. I've quit going inside. I'd rather the Hermitage would go on to normal decay than be treated like that."

"Yes, I think perhaps I would, also. The continuity of politics is too uncertain."

"I wouldn't be willing for the Hermitage to be maintained by the state. It wouldn't work. Would it work for the ownership to continue with the state even if the home is privately administered?"

"No, it would be best for a Hermitage Association both to own it, and to direct it."

"The Hermitage Association! Why, that's the phrase I've been looking for."

"Is it your definite decision to follow Mrs. Jackson's cue?"

"Yes, but I don't quite know what her cue was. You've helped me. The Hermitage Association—that's decision number one."

He amended the phrase, "The Ladies Hermitage Association."

"Ladies? Why that?"

"I have an idea that you ladies would be amazed if your real power were ever discovered. I think every lady in Nashville of any strength would join the Ladies Hermitage Association. In the first place, she'd believe in it. In the second place, she'd like to try herself out in some public enterprise. Mark my words, we are standing on the threshold of the era of women."

"But we need men."

"Oh, you'll get them. Every worth-while man hereabouts will be standing in line to help the Ladies Hermitage Association any way he can."

"All right, Eugene, tell me how to get the Association going. I feel terribly helpless."

"I'm helpless, too, but I never let that limit my counsel; first, I'd see Mac Dickinson. Mac has perhaps the best legal mind in the city. He has, too, an ardent fondness for the old landmarks and traditions. Unless I don't know Mac at all—which I do—he will be heart and soul for the Association. He will tell you how to proceed in order. Then, your husband can be enormously helpful. As editor of the *American* and correspondent of some Eastern papers, he can use leaven to transform the lump. You will need publicity. He can give it where and in the form that will do most good."

"I can depend on Duncan, bless him. But, Eugene, who should lead in this? I can't. No, I'm not asking you to contradict me. I'm brave only in private. In public I'm terrified."

"Then, dear lady, brace yourself for the reign of terror. It's upon you. The finger is pointed at you."

"Stop jesting, please."

"You'll need a committee—steering, executive, whatever you choose to call it. May I offer suggestions as to membership?"

"Oh, yes, and please appoint the officers."

"Please do not use sarcasm on me. It dulls my best effort. It slows me down. I'd say, first off, Mary Baxter, Sallie Lindsley and Bettie Donelson. . . ."

"That's a perfect beginning. It covers everything, even family connection with the Hermitage. There'll be others, of course? What about Mrs. Morrow and Mrs. Albert Marks and . . . ?"

"Certainly. Nashville has more than its share of feminine leadership, possible and actual. And that, dear lady, is where you belong—to see that every woman who has ability is made responsible for its use. For instance, I'd assign the legislature to Sallie Lindsley. She is a sight reader of men's minds. She has the proper touch, and knows the proper word. Trust your publicity to Duncan. He has an uncanny sense of the public's response to a headline or a column of print. I doubt if you have ever thought of the curious influence of matter printed at a distance. A citizen of Nashville who reads something in the *American* says, 'It may be so'; but if he reads the same item in the *New York Herald* he says, 'It must be so.' Duncan can be invaluable. Be sure to attach Berrien Lindsley to your cause. He's a sort of crusader and prophet combined—Elijah, Saint Thomas Aquinas and John Knox combined into one man. That's a bit emphatic but you understand what I mean."

"I imagine you will move back to Nashville soon. The railroad would like to have you back, wouldn't it?"

"Its officers say so. Perhaps they do need me since another railroad is being insistently rumored."

"Why? Wouldn't another railroad help the city?"

"No," he said emphatically, "it would hurt it. The two railroads here now serve Nashville far better than three or ten could. Furthermore, I regard the promoter of the new road as an entirely unprincipled man. It's an American tendency to dilute quality by excessive competition. Yes, I think I'll come back. I am greatly interested in the Hermitage. My wife claims my greatest concern is houses. I think that it is beauty in any form. I can not understand why a railroad is willing to provide a bare dirty room for its travelers to wait in. Even as economy I think it's stupid. I am interested in homes, beautiful and enduring homes. I think the tide of our ugliness is ebbing somewhat and it seems to me that the rescue of the Hermitage would cause its more rapid retreat. Destroy the Hermitage, Belle Meade, Belmont, Myrtlewood, Polk Place, Mansfield, and Tulip Grove and I wouldn't put foot in Nashville again."

"Polk Place," said Mrs. Dorris softly. "I saw Mrs. Polk the other day. She's getting old, Eugene. I never thought age could lay a finger on her."

"Time, dear lady, will perhaps not wait so long for you."

"I do not expect it. All in my power to do will have been done long before, and I do not care to remain after that. What is the word from that young man in whom you and Mrs. Polk have such interest?"

"Very favorable. I get a letter from him every two or three months. I think Mrs. Polk hears oftener."

"Are you still as ambitious for him?"

"I only reflect the enthusiasm of his instructors in Boston when I say I am more so than ever. They understand my interest, and send me an occasional report. Professor Chandler considers him a very remarkable pupil. The boy is moving toward a specialty in Southern Colonial. Chandler regards him in some degree as an authority in the field now."

Her mind was back upon the Hermitage. "I'm going to put all the strength and sense I have into this. I'm going to talk to those we have mentioned before the sun sets, Mac Dickinson first of all. I think you'll be needed presently, and when I send for you come immediately. I shall not until this is concluded apologize for asking anything of anybody."

28

On the seventh of January, the driver came in early from Kingsley. He stopped the carriage for a few minutes at Polk Place, then he drove back to Spruce and turned north. Two blocks ahead he brought the carriage to a sudden stop and addressed a man who was hurrying along the street.

"What's your hurry? Been bit by a snake?"

"No, but effn I see a snake I aim to bite it. You better not get too clos't to me."

"You still got a job for steady vittles, or has the streetcar comp'ny done come to its senses?"

"I been permoted."

"Which way, down or out?"

"Up, an' they goin' to pay me same as President Grover Cleveland an' give me a body servant six feet high besides."

"How come you're two hours late gittin' to work?"

"The smile o' the Lord's fell on me. It used to be hosses but now it's lightning that's goin' to be hitched to my chariot."

"I knowed a feller oncet who was took sudden jest like you. It didn't run in his fam'ly neither. Yes sir, took vi'lent jest like you. Folks felt powerful relieved when he hung hisself."

"I ain't goin' to relieve 'em that-a-way. I'm a-goin' to relieve 'em by gettin' 'em where they goin' while they still young. Last week a young and beautiful lady got on the car out at St. Cecilia and when she got off at DeMoville's corner she had to use crutches on account o' old age. Now a streetcar that's got e-lec-tric-i-ty in it jest natchelly burns the wind."

"I read in the paper about these newfangled contraptions. They say the undertakers done passed resolutions in favor o' 'em. When they goin' to start manglin' people with 'em on the streets?"

"Somewheres about April. They done ordered the e-lec-tric-i-ty."

"They ain't a-goin' to let you slaughter women and little children with 'em, I hope."

"That's what I been tryin' to tell you for an hour and a half. I'm a-goin' to run the first one. I'm a-goin' to start practicin' jest as soon as they get the e-lec-tric-i-ty."

"Why ain't you drivin' today?"

"Water pipe busted on Stonewall Street and the track's out. They aim to have it fixed by tomorrer."

"Say, you hop in and let me take you for a ride. That'll cool your mind off so you can use it for somethin' besides skull fillin'."

"Whereat you goin'?"

"Somewheres down in the wilderness. Place called Sycamore."

"When you comin' back?"

"This evenin'. Gotta bring a man back. Big doin's goin' on, I reckon."

"Effn you'll go by the car barn for my overcoat I'll go along. That'd give me a chancet to rescue you from your evil ways."

So they drove back to the car barn. College Grove got his overcoat and was swinging himself up in the carriage seat when the door of the office opened and a gentleman came hurrying out.

"Wait a minute," he said. "I want to talk to both of you. We planned quite an affair last night and you two gentlemen belong in it. I'm Frank Morrow, the president of the company."

"I know you, Mr. Morrow," affirmed College Grove.

"I thought perhaps you did, but I wasn't sure that you did, sir. We wish to use your fame. Sometime in the spring we are going to change over from horsepower to electricity. We want to make quite a ceremony of it. We should like for you—" with a nod to the driver—"to drive the last trip we make with horses, and you—" with a nod to College Grove—"to take the first trip with electricity. Of course, no passenger will be carried either time, but a picked delegation of citizens. We are going to advertise the two events and we expect to make it quite an occasion. Will you, sir, do us the honor to accept?"

"I took hosses the first trip; effn you say so I'll take 'em the last."

"Then, that's settled. This gentleman's services belong to us so we'll assign him the first trip with electricity. The arrangement pleases me. Thank you very much."

They drove away.

"Looks like this means you're ending, pardner," said College Grove, "and I'm jest beginning."

"Looks to me like they're not so certain 'bout this newfangled contraption and if anybody's got to be sacerficed it better be you."

They drove out the White's Creek Pike. The driver broke into song.

> "I'm jest a pore wayfarin' stranger,
> And this world is not my home."

"Hist it a little, pardner, and I'll sing bass."

The pitch was histed and College Grove's bass rumbled its complement. The day was crisp, and there was little warmth in the sun that shone only at intervals. Singing and talking, the two men drove through the wilderness toward Sycamore.

They reached their destination about one o'clock. Before two they were on their way back to Nashville.

The note which Mrs. Doris had written him was an imperative summons, so Eugene Lewis disengaged himself from the immediate affairs of the powder company, and after making brief preparations for the journey joined the men waiting at the carriage. He was to spend the night, the driver informed him, at Polk Place. The next morning, very early, he would be driven to the Hermitage. Breakfast would be served there and some important people would attend and discuss an important matter. The arrangements had been planned at Kingsley the evening before. Mrs. Dorris had said that Eugene Lewis's presence was necessary. It was too late to get a letter to him. Someone would have to go for him. Weaver Cole then offered the services of his horses, his carriage and the driver. That was how the trip had come about. The driver had stopped at Polk Place to tell Mrs. Polk of the breakfast at the Hermitage, and to express the wish that she could attend, offering transportation in that event. Mrs. Polk lacked strength to make the trip to the Hermitage. But she did desire that Eugene Lewis spend the night at Polk Place. She wanted very much to talk with him. She would see that he left Nashville early enough to arrive at the Hermitage on time. The driver concluded his message. "Weaver Cole has jest natchelly turned me over to you. You say where and there we go."

At nine o'clock on the morning of January eighth the guests sat down at the great table in the Hermitage dining room. They were there by invitation of Mrs. Andrew Jackson III, though really the hostess was Mrs. Bettie Donelson, daughter-in-law of General Jackson's secretary in the White House. But it was Mrs. Dorris upon whom the responsibility of the gathering rested most heavily. They were served waffles heaped with opulent portions of turkey hash, made according to the recipe held dear by General Jackson. There was coffee, rich-bodied and fragrant; there were hot biscuits and finally blackberry jam from the Tulip Grove pantry. No work of business was mentioned until breakfast was eaten. It was the code of the Hermitage. General Jackson himself had set the pattern. He would not tolerate the introduction of politics or business into mealtime conversation. When the food had been eaten and the dishes removed, but not before, he would say, "Now, Mr. Grundy, let us consider the claims of your candidate."

And so, when the proper moment arrived on that morning of January eighth, they were welcomed by Mrs. Andrew Jackson III. She then introduced Dr. T. A. Atchison who would serve as chairman in the discussions to follow.

Dr. Atchison whose bedside manner was the envy of the physicians of the city was at his best. He complimented Mrs. Jackson as one though not born in the Hermitage at least born to it. He referred to Mrs. Donelson as one truly kin to the Hermitage by mind, spirit and marriage. He made graceful and general references to all present. A new idea in medical technique had occurred to him. He saw among those present his dear patient, Felicia Love. He paid her a professional visit only three days before. He had used all of his professional skill and cunning in her behalf, but he doubted whether she would leave her house before spring. But there she was, the incarnation of roseate health. If instead of medicine he could only administer motives such as a breakfast meeting at the Hermitage seemed to inspire, then his fame as a practitioner would travel to the far quarters. Mrs. Love was heard to remark very crisply that the morning carried an advantage outside of motive since in one biscuit she could get the equivalent of a hundred of his pills, which were derived from the same major ingredient. Dr. Atchison replied that hereafter on his visits to his dear friend he would carry not a bottle of pills but a pan of biscuits. He thought that it was fitting that a few men were present, a division of humanity rapidly disappearing, and doomed to ultimate extinction. In the meantime, there would doubtless be some chores which the remaining members might perform. Even the ladies themselves might be surprised by the amount of service which men were still capable of performing.

But enough! His place was in the sickroom, not in the forum. One of the most inspired and dominant women of his acquaintance was his dear friend Mary Dorris, wife of his dear friend Duncan Dorris. It was his very great privilege to present Mrs. Dorris. He sat down.

Mrs. Dorris had not shared entirely in the general appreciation of Dr. Atchison's good humor. Her mind was upon but one thing and she wasted neither time nor words in presenting it. Before she had spoken a full paragraph all smiles had disappeared and intentness had come into all faces. "Today," she said, "is the anniversary of the battle of New Orleans. It was on this day in 1815 that General Andrew Jackson and his gallant army set such a memorable pattern in gallantry. Today the legislature of the State of Tennessee convenes. We are going to ask that this legislature perpetuate that hero, give him to the ages. The General loved his home. He made it into one of America's great homes. The next few weeks will decide whether it is to be assigned to a worthy though temporary purpose and let presently to perish, or be preserved and its beauty and memories offered to the generations to come. There are two options available and only two!

"Mr. and Mrs. Jackson do not plan to remain longer at the Hermitage. When they leave they will take with them the furnishings of the home, that is, unless arrangements can be made for their purchase. I will be frank. The finances of Mr. and Mrs. Jackson are at such low ebb that they feel it necessary to dispose of some of the pieces. This places an additional obligation upon us. Besides persuading the legislature to assign the ownership of the Hermitage to the Association we will have to raise funds to retain for the home the furniture which has mellowed within its rooms. The sum required will not be small. It will indeed challenge our ingenuity. But whatever the challenge we will meet it. We will meet it in the legislature, too. I will not compliment you except to say that you were invited because you have something to give and can give it."

Eugene Lewis arose promptly. "I realize, sir," he said nodding to Dr. Atchison, "that all we need now is an organization ready for action. The Ladies Hermitage Association may proceed appropriately to its complete organization when it has a Hermitage to administer. Until then all we need are a general and some good soldiers. We'll try to be the latter. I move, sir, our unanimous choice of Mary Dorris as general."

Dr. Atchison remarked that he had entertained some fear that residence in the remote sections might have dulled his dear friend's perspicacity, but the remarks to which they had just listened proved happily this was not the case. Unless someone present found a flaw in Eugene Lewis's reasoning—which he was not able to detect—his dear friend Mary Dorris would by acclamation be accepted as their commander. He nodded gracefully to Mrs. Dorris and said, "You have but to speak, brave general, and we will translate your word into deeds."

Mrs. Dorris spoke, grimly and pointedly. She had developed a clean-cut and incisive program for their campaign. It was outlined in explicit detail and each woman assigned to the service she could render best. Mrs. Dorris wound to her finish. "The legislature as you know meets at noon today. One of the first measures introduced will be to convert the Hermitage into a home for Southern soldiers. That proposition will have a strong initial appeal. It will raise a false but most alluring sentiment. What are our answers to the advocates of the soldiers' home? Not to deny a home, of course. Every one of us will support a measure providing such a home, but not the Hermitage. Within thirty years all the soldiers will be dead. What then? If the Hermitage lasted that long it would then be an irrecoverable wreck, one of our precious landmarks gone forever. Another point, and perhaps the most convincing. Andrew Jackson was President of the United States. General Jackson was Southern, by birth and by sympathy, but we must not forget that it was he who once said, 'The Union must be preserved.' This must be as true at the Hermitage now as in the mind of its builder then.

"Now I have not gone into this casually, nor am I the convert of a single hour. I have been thinking, though somewhat vaguely to be sure, of this for a long time. Two people have given my thoughts form and content, Eugene Lewis and Mrs. Jackson. I am expecting all of you to help give them reality. Mistakes will be forgiven as a common quality of us all but not inactivity or neglect.

If I have spoken somewhat boldly I ask you to remember that I would not have spoken at all except in love and faith."

She nodded to Dr. Atchison who stood beaming. It was, he said, a meeting long to be remembered. Never had he witnessed such a courageous and intelligent display of leadership. He could not resist the temptation to refer again to the impressive nature of the meeting composed of the finest of Nashville's womanhood, and a large and respectable representation of its men. He stroked his beard and with a merry twinkle in his eyes added a humorous postscript to the effect that he was large, and Dr. Elliott was respectable. It was his intention to adjourn the meeting but Mrs. Dorris had not the slightest intention of permitting them to disband on a jesting note. She stood. She had her idea for the meeting's proper benediction.

"Mrs. Jackson, Mrs. Donelson, bring the candle, please." The two ladies left the dining room but returned a few seconds later. Mrs. Jackson held in her hand a small dark candle, perhaps two inches long. She handed it to Mrs. Dorris who held it out for all to see. "This candle was found in the tent of General Cornwallis at Yorktown. After the battle of New Orleans it was presented to General Jackson and he was asked to light it every year on the battle's anniversary, which request he never neglected to observe. The candle has not been lighted for more than two score years, but on this eighth of January we honor Old Hickory most significantly. It is, I think, fit for the flame of that candle to burn again this morning in solemn commitment to the memory of him and in devotion to the home he loved so well. Mrs. Jackson, will you hold the candle? Mrs. Donelson, will you light it? Let it burn by the clock one minute. We will stand in silence gathering light for our work ahead."

In the historic room the candle burned steadily and there was no sound save of restrained breathing, and the stately ticking of the mantel clock. The snow was gently falling outside, and an overlay of white was obscuring the waxen green of the great cedars. Inside the candle burned and its light shone clearly on the faces of those gathered about the table.

PART THREE: THE THIRD BREAKFAST

PART THREE

THE THIRD BREAKFAST

1

THE proposal to turn the Hermitage into a home for Confederate soldiers was appealing to a great many people. It joined two of Tennessee's great traditions: Old Hickory, and the soldiers who had galloped untiringly across the war on the scarecrows that carried Bed Forrest's army. Mary Dorris was not unaware of the power of that sentiment.

"We made a mistake," she said to Dr. Atchison. "We pitched our campaign too narrowly. We must have thought that as goes Nashville so goes the state. I've been counting noses, the noses of those who vote. Right now we'd lose. Tell your doctors and lawyers that if they know a representative or senator outside of Nashville—the farther outside the better—to go to work."

"All right, General, it will probably ruin my practice, but I'm a foot soldier in your war. I'll do what I can, General."

"The senate isn't causing us much anxiety. We have a majority there."

"The house, then?"

"Yes, there's our trouble, and we might be able to handle it but for one man, Captain John H. Savage, from one of the mountain counties!"

"Savages are frequently a bit difficult."

Mrs. Dorris, frowning, answered a trifle hurriedly. "He was a Captain in the Southern army, and I doubt very much if he ever surrendered. He's a very determined man, somewhat crude but studiously polite, and a natural leader. I wish I could think of some strategic approach to him."

"Isn't he Sallie Lindsley's assignment?"

"Yes, and she has an appointment with him this morning, but I'm not hopeful. I've talked with him. Still, Sallie's likely to think of something. She's a resourceful woman."

"If he's susceptible to Southern sympathy or ancestry, Sallie will interest him."

Just then Sallie herself came into the room. "I thought I should

187

report," she said. "Well, I saw him. It was an agreeable visit, but I don't think it did any good."

"You mean . . . ?" Mary Dorris hesitated to ask the question.

"Yes, I mean he's still against us, and—" she added grimly—"it looks as if he intends to remain so. I find the man interesting. But I'm stumped. I talked with him for more than an hour. I told him the story of General Jackson, that he was President of *all* the people. I explained how beautiful it would be if all the people could visit his home. He asked whether the General would prefer for *all* the people to visit his home or just *his* people. He said he reckoned there were people I wouldn't want in my home. I told him that all of my men fought under the Stars and Bars. He said, 'Excuse me, ma'am, but if they did you ain't being rightly respectful to 'em. Looks like I am standing up for my Rebs better'n you are for yours.' He had the answer ready for anything I could say. I'm afraid I've failed, Mary."

"If you have no one could have done more."

"I met Martha Dickinson as I came away from the Capitol. She said Governor Taylor has become so enthusiastic that he thinks he thought up the matter first."

"My feeling exactly," said Dr. Atchison. "I remember perfectly when the idea first came to me."

The lines on Mrs. Dorris's face sharpened, but Mrs. Lindsley permitted a faint smile to rest briefly upon her face. "I liked very much the fondness of Captain Savage for his grandson."

"His grandson?"

"Yes, a boy eleven or twelve, a likable lad. He's a page in the house chamber. I think both the child's parents are dead."

Apparently Mrs. Dorris was not listening. "We have a majority in the senate if we can hold it. You've done fine work there, Sallie. If the opposition, though, shows too strong in the house I'm afraid we can't hold the senate." She shook her head angrily. "What's the matter with me? Of course, we can hold it." She paused a moment, then continued, anger edging her tones. "Why can't Captain Savage see that what we should give our soldiers is a comfortable home, and good food, and love and kindness—but not a chance to wear out the Hermitage's floors, to tear down its doors, to let fall into complete decay the garden, perhaps even the grave? Why can't he see that? There must be some way. Anyhow the speaker has promised to keep the Confederate bill from coming to a vote for another week. In that time . . ."

"In that time, Mary, I'll have another talk with Captain Savage. I don't know what I'll say but I'll think of something. I'm not quitting yet."

"Dr. Billy Rhett's cousin from Giles County is one of the leading anti's in the House. Billy promised to have a talk with him," said Dr. Atchison stroking his beard. "I'll run over to his office and remind him of his promise."

2

On Monday morning of the following week, Sallie Lindsley arrived at the Capitol for her final appeal to Captain Savage. The appointment was for half after ten and she waited out in the hall. It was cold in the building and she walked briskly about, always keeping her eyes upon the carved oaken doors of the House Chamber. Captain Savage did not appear at the appointed hour, but she knew that a member's plans were subject to unexpected interruptions.

She rehearsed again the argument she wished to make. She would begin with a statement which her brother, Randall Mc-Govock, had made the year before the war began. There had been a meeting at the Hermitage and Randall had made an address. Most happily she had by sheer accident found his manuscript only two days before. Randall must have been a prophet for his address had outlined for the Hermitage almost exactly the career proposed by the Ladies Hermitage Association. "I can foresee," Randall had said, his eyes doubtless burning with the fires of Scotch-Irish prophecy, "I can foresee the time when men from the far north, from the far west, yea, from all of our sections, will come here to rekindle from this altar the radiance of their spirits."

She would read those words to Captain Savage from Randall's faded manuscript. Randall, who had died on a Southern battle-field, Randall who was one of *her* Rebs. She tried to anticipate Captain Savage's answer to that. He would say that Randall made the speech before there were Rebs. If he had made it later he would have said something very different. And she would reply . . . Then she saw the carved doors swing abruptly open and Captain Savage come out. He was walking rapidly, and his face was set as if in strain. He saw her and halted grudgingly but without rudeness.

"I'm sorry, ma'am, but I can't talk with you."

"Oh . . ." The word was sharp with disappointment.

"Charley's sick, ma'am. I'm terrible afraid he's bad sick. I got to go back. The woman where we stay is watching him till I get back. I had some business and I had to come up here. I'm sorry, ma'am."

"Wait a minute," she said, her mind moving rapidly. "Where do you live?"

"On McLemore Street." He was moving toward the stairway. She fell in beside him.

"I'm going with you. I might be able to help."

"I'm obliged, ma'am, but I wouldn't want to put you to any trouble. But you could tell me a good doctor to get. I'm uneasy, ma'am."

"Let me go see Charley. I've seen a lot of sick boys. I ought to know something about them. Yes, I can tell you a good doctor to get."

They left the Capitol, walking rapidly. Sallie Lindsley, who was a bit fat, was panting a little by the time they had reached Cedar Street.

"If Charley isn't any better," she said, "I'll get a doctor for him."

"I'm mighty uneasy, ma'am. Charley wasn't ever sick before."

He turned in at a house on McLemore. Captain Savage mounted the worn stairs and entered a room on the right, Sallie Lindsley following close behind him. A gaunt woman sitting by the bed arose when they entered.

"How is he?" Captain Savage asked almost as he passed the threshold.

"They ain't no change that I can tell," she answered. "He's been out o' his head a little, but nothing vi'lent."

Sallie Lindsley slipped gently into the chair in which the woman had been sitting. She knew what it was. She had seen it before. She knew that incessant rasping cough. Lung fever, pneumonia! The boy was restless and turned his head constantly.

Sallie Lindsley arose. "I'll go get a doctor. It won't take long."

"Get the best one you can, ma'am," said Captain Savage.

Luckily Dr. Atchison was in his office on Spruce Street. He looked up from the medical book when his visitor entered the room.

"Did you tame the Savage?" he asked. Then he saw her face more clearly. "I beg your pardon, Mrs. Lindsley. What is it?"

"It's that boy, Captain Savage's grandson. Pneumonia. Get your bag, Dr. Atchison. You're going back with me."

"How women have taken to ordering me about—Mary Dorris and now you!"

"Get your bag. That boy needs help."

A knock sounded at the door. "See who that is, please," said the doctor. "I'll be ready in two minutes."

It was Mary Dorris. "Sadie Fall said she saw you coming in here. I couldn't wait for the news."

"There isn't any news, Mary, except that Captain Savage's grandson has pneumonia—bad, I'm afraid. I've just come from there."

Mary Dorris said "Oh" three times, understanding growing on her face. "I'm sorry he has the pneumonia, but, Sallie—" she broke off—"where's Dr. Atchison?"

"Here I am," said the physician coming into the front office, his overcoat on, his bag in his hand.

Mrs. Dorris stood, her eyes darting from one to the other. Suddenly brightness overspread her face. "Sallie Lindsley," she said, "you dear woman. Dr. Atchison, you cure that boy."

"It is my custom to try," he answered with dignity.

"Don't you see? Don't you see, Dr. Atchison? Cure that boy."

"I shall treat him, not the Hermitage," he answered, his professional propriety nettled for a moment.

"But if in curing him, it helps us, would your precious medical ethics be violated?"

He was smiling again. "I get your point, lady. First things first, second things second, and if they tie together, great is Allah. I find no impingement upon my medical conscience. Are you ready, Mrs. Lindsley?"

"Yes, except I want to send some word home. Could you take it, Mary?"

"You couldn't ask anything, Sallie, that I wouldn't do."

"Then tell Louise to send me anything I need for the night. I think I'll be staying. The number is 870 McLemore. That boy appeals to me. Tell Annie to watch out for the house. I'm ready."

All that afternoon and on until midnight the grandfather, the lady and the physician sat at the bedside of the fever-stricken boy. At midnight Dr. Atchison looked across at Mrs. Lindsley.

"You go sleep awhile. I'll call you if you're needed."

Captain Savage said, "The woman said you could sleep in the room across there." He pointed. "The man that's in it won't be back for a week."

"How is he?" she asked the doctor.

He shook his head gently. "He's a sick child. I'll call you the moment you are needed."

She went into the room across the hall.

"I want Charley to get well, Doctor." Captain Savage spoke with the forthrightness of the hill country.

"Lung fever, Captain Savage, is a willful disease. Of all the diseases I treat it gives me the most helpless feeling. But, sir, I promise to use all the skill I have."

"Thank you, suh. Charley's all the kinfolks I got and . . ."

A spasm of coughing interrupted him. Later Captain Savage completed his statement. "If Charley'd die there wouldn't be any of the family left. I'm seventy-four years old. I don't count. Charley's got to get well."

The boy spoke from the bed. "Grandpa, my side hurts. Please make it stop."

The hurt eyes of the old man relayed the boy's plea to Dr. Atchison. "My side," gasped the boy. "Stop it, please, Grandpa."

The doctor took from his waistcoat pocket a small pasteboard box. He opened it and took from it a very small white tablet. He carefully cut it in half. "Swallow this, son." The boy's eyes, unnaturally bright, softened from the reassurance of the doctor's presence.

"Yes, sir," he said, and swallowed the medicine. Ten minutes later he was sleeping but breathing heavily.

"I don't know whether I should have given him that morphine or not," the doctor said speaking half to himself. "It relieves the suffering, but I always fear that it charges for the relief it gives. Frankly, I have given morphine over a long practice, but never once without apprehension. I'm always afraid that nature would rebel against buying so much for so little."

"I want Charley to get well, Doctor." There was a dogged sort of pain in the monotone of the words.

"I have always done my best to cure a patient."

"Our family was one o' the first in the mountains. My granddaddy knowed Dan'l Boone right well. One time we had the say-so in our parts. But somehow we seemed to run out fast. When the war come on I was the only Savage left to fight. Charley's daddy died when the lad was four years old. Charley's got to live. I'm depending on him."

The night passed and Charley still slept, though his breathing was edged with metallic shrillness. Mrs. Lindsley came into the room. "How is he?"

Dr. Atchison's eyes rested on the flushed face outlined on the pillow.

"About the same," he said gravely. "He has been sleeping for several hours."

"You men go in there and sleep awhile." She looked keenly at the old soldier. "When did you sleep last, Captain Savage?"

"A little while Saturday night, ma'am."

"My gracious! This is Tuesday morning. Go on to bed. I'll take care of Charley."

She sat there looking out the window with eyes that did not see the gnarled limbs of the old sycamore tree, nor the drab roof tops across McLemore Street.

The boy on the bed, almost panting from the strain of speech, said, "Where's Grandpa?"

"He's tired, Charley, and has dropped off to sleep for a little rest. Do you want me to call him?"

"No, ma'am, I just wanted to know." He was sleeping again.

The gaunt woman came in with some breakfast. "How is Charley?"

"About the same," said Mrs. Lindsley, thanking her for the food.

"It'd be a shame for anything to happen to him," said the woman and withdrew from the room.

The breakfast was palatable and Mrs. Lindsley ate all of it. Charley was restless and moved constantly and his face showed plainly the fever that burned within him. Sometimes he was delirious, and then he would open eyes clear with understanding and ask where his grandfather was.

The gaunt woman came saying that some folks waited in the hall below to see Mrs. Lindsley.

"I'll stay with him while you go see what they want," she said.

It was Mrs. Dorris and Berrien who waited. "How is he?" asked Mrs. Dorris even before she had reached the bottom of the stairs.

"I think we'll know by this time tomorrow."

"It's critical then?"

"Yes, decidedly."

"You go home and rest," said Mrs. Dorris. "We'll stay with him."

"No," Sallie Lindsley smiled faintly, "he's my case, mine and Dr. Atchison's."

"I'll stay today," said Berrien, "you go home and go to sleep. I'm not entirely unaccustomed to such matters. I'm a graduate physician, you know," he added whimsically.

"No, the boy is my case. Thank you for coming. You all go on back and take care of things."

The faint smile lingered on her face as Sallie Lindsley climbed the stairs.

"Is that you, Grandpa?" called the boy as she entered.

"No, Charley, but he is coming right away."

"He says his side hurts," said the gaunt woman as she left the room. She paused in the door long enough to add, "Do the best you can."

"My side, Grandpa. It hurts," panted the boy. "My throat hurts, too."

Some change had come into him. She didn't know what it was but there was something. She went quickly across the hall and, rapping upon the door, called, "Dr. Atchison."

In less than a minute the physician came out into the hall fully dressed and with no hint of sleep upon his face. Behind him came Captain Savage.

"What is it, Mrs. Lindsley?"

"I don't know, Dr. Atchison. I think you should see him."

The physician moved his stethoscope gently about over the boy's chest, then held it over the heart so long that those who watched him sensed the sinister meaning of that delay. He looked up.

"You did right to call me. I'm going to give him a bit of strychnine."

"What is it?" asked Captain Savage hoarsely. "How is Charley?"

Dr. Atchison's eyes never left the child that tossed upon the bed. "I think he'll be better presently." But there was strain in his tones.

"Get him well, Doctor." The old man's hoarseness blurred the words out of all true form. "I'm depending on Charley."

The morning passed and the afternoon came. Gusts of late winter wind beat fitfully upon the house and shook the window frames with dry brittle sounds.

Dr. Atchison stood. "Send for Billy Rhett," he said. "If there's any new treatment for lung fever he'll know about it."

At three o'clock Dr. Billy Rhett arrived. The gaunt woman brought him into the room. He was of medium height and build.

His hair was jet black and his features were of olive tinge and classic form. His eyes were dark and deep and fine. He was the choice product of the Webb School at Bellbuckle, and lately of the Vanderbilt College of Medicine. His voice was inclined to softness, but the words came with surprising abruptness. There was something subtle about his manner of speaking which led an understanding hearer halfway to expect him to break into classic phrase—which he usually did. His Latin apothegms together with the habit of speaking in droll asides offered welcome relief to an intense preoccupation. He listened while Dr. Atchison explained the case, listened with his ears but all the while his eyes searched the fevered face outlined against the pillow, the faces of the others in the room, and the room itself for their testimony.

"Open a window!" he said. There was the briefest hesitation. "I know it's cold, but you can put on more clothes. This air is intolerable. Of course, you've been keeping that child warm, but *aegrescit medendo.*"

Dr. Atchison raised a window and propped it up. Sallie Lindsley calmly put on her coat and tucked the quilts about Charley.

"The lad's name is Charley Savage, and this is Captain Savage, his grandfather," she said by way of introduction.

Captain Savage repeated his ritual. "I want Charley to get well, Doctor."

"*Si diis placet.* This air is better. Let's have a look at him."

Shielding Charley from the open window he made the routine examination with his stethoscope, pausing in deep concentration at the heart. "Strychnine, Doctor?"

"Yes," said Dr. Atchison, "one twentieth of a grain. An hour ago."

"Then the only thing to do is to let him have all the air he can get into his lungs. Give a hand with the bed. Let's get his face as close to that window as we can."

All three, almost startled, looked at the young physician. That was something new in lung fever. But they helped move the bed, and the air which Charley with such labored struggling effort drew into his lungs was cold and pure. The gaunt woman came into the room, and saw the open window and the bed by it.

"Is he . . . ?" She could not complete her question.

"No," said Dr. Rhett, "he'll likely outlive us all. We'll know for certain before many hours."

"I'll fix supper for you all," she said and went down the stairs.

It cleared toward sunset and the wind quieted.

"Captain," said Dr. Rhett, "do you think you could find an orange at any of the stores? I want one for Charley just as soon as he is conscious again. Get several if they are nice ones."

They heard the door clang behind Captain Savage. Dr. Rhett took his gaze away from the restless figure on the bed for just a moment.

"Now tell me what this is about. Of course, the orange juice will be good for him, but did you notice how rigid that old man was? He needed to get away for a few minutes. He needed to get some air into his lungs, too. I'm a curious person. I need to know what all of this means. What's it all about?"

"It's about a young lad with pneumonia," said Mrs. Lindsley.

"And a very sick young lad. Excuse me a moment." He put two sticks of wood into the stove. "That serves another purpose besides warmth. The draft pulls more air through that window. That boy needs air."

A spasm of coughing interrupted. He pressed his stethoscope against the boy's chest and listened.

"He has a little breathing space left, but not much. There isn't a thing to do but wait. Do I hear the story?"

"I think Dr. Rhett is entitled to be told what we know of the situation, Mrs. Lindsley."

"So do I," said Sallie Lindsley and proceeded to relate the story. Dr. Rhett listened carefully.

"Well, well. I knew there was a scrap on about the Hermitage, but I never expected to get into it. But here I am, *nolens volens*. I suppose that is Captain Savage returning with the oranges."

It was Captain Savage and he had two oranges.

"All I could find. How's Charley?"

Dr. Rhett examined the boy again, pouring all of his concentration into the sounds carried by the stethoscope.

"Jubilate Deo! He is better."

Then the woman, the two physicians and the boy's grandfather all were standing.

Dr. Rhett handed his stethoscope to Dr. Atchison.

"You listen. You've heard more of this than I have."

Back and forth and across Charley's chest Dr. Atchison moved the base of the stethoscope, pausing time and again in the area of the heart.

"I have never known so quick a change. Yes, he's better."

A little later the gaunt woman came in again. She stood listening. "He ain't wheezin' so bad," she said.

Dr. Atchison answered. "He's better."

She said nothing more for a full half minute. Then she said, "Ain't it too cold in here?"

"No," said Dr. Atchison, "Charley needs the air."

She pondered that phenomenon. "Oh!" she said. "Oh! Well, I baked a pie. I want you to have it."

It was a good pie, and they sat eating it. The woman stood watching them, her puzzled eyes moving from them to the bed to the window.

"Lady," said Billy Rhett, "you're not by any chance from Giles County?"

"Grundy County," said the gaunt woman.

"Another illusion gone. I had always thought that the champion pie makers were from Giles County."

At nine o'clock Charley's breathing was decidedly more even, less labored.

"I suppose," said Dr. Atchison, "that I should have some credit. It was I who thought of sending for you, Billy."

"I suspect you would not have lost any credit by not sending for me at all. The young have an amazing capacity to turn away even from the doors of death itself, especially if they are healthy-bodied like that boy. Still," he said, a whimsical note in his voice, "it was I who suggested opening the window. Keep that in mind, please."

"I read Sir William Osler's statement, but I didn't know it was being followed."

"It isn't very much, Dr. Atchison. To me it makes excellent sense. When I came in here there was almost no oxygen in the room and that was what that boy needed."

A weak voice called from the bed. "Grandpa, where are you?"

"Here I am, Charley. Do you want something?"

"No . . ."

"Yes, he does." Dr. Rhett moved quickly to the bedside. "Wouldn't you want a glass of milk, Charley, if I wanted you to want it? You are getting better fast."

"Yes, yes . . ."

Dr. Rhett went down the stairs two steps at a time. "Oh, lady," he called.

Immediately the gaunt woman appeared.

"Have you an egg and some milk?"

"Yes."

"Beat an egg into a glass of milk."

She went quickly, even gratefully into the kitchen.

"Here's another gem from the pages of Osler." He slipped his hand under Charley's head and skillfully lifted it a few inches from the pillow. "Take this, son. It's guaranteed. Here, now, drink it."

The boy took a swallow, and his hand quickly clutched at his throat. "It hurts."

"I knew it would, but it's the way to get well soonest."

Charley drank the milk and a few minutes later was sleeping soundly.

Dr. Rhett looked at his watch. "Heigh ho," he said. *"Omnia bona bonis.* It's a lovely world. It's ten o'clock. I'm going home."

3

Mrs. Dorris sat in the parlor of her home on Spruce Street. Some members of the Ladies Hermitage Association would arrive presently to consider their further course. Mrs. Dickinson came first, then Mrs. Baxter came in her carriage, and Sallie Lindsley came on foot for she lived only a few doors away. Last, Mr. and Mrs. Alex Donelson arrived from the Hermitage community.

They were seated in the parlor. Mrs. Dorris was speaking. "I am sorry to report I don't know anything that I didn't when we met last. The meeting of the legislature has only another week to run. I have no knowledge of any member who has changed his opinion. Mrs. Dickinson has just told me that the Speaker of the House told her he expects the Confederate bill to be brought out of the Committee for a vote tomorrow or the next day."

"I heard," said Alex Donelson, "that Mrs. Lindsley practically saved Captain Savage's grandson's life. Oughtn't that to give us some advantage?"

Sallie Lindsley didn't answer sitting. She stood. "I will not talk with Captain Savage further about the Hermitage. That would seem to me a sort of base trading. I'll work day or night using whatever sense and wit I may have with any other member, but not with Captain Savage. While I am on my feet let me say that I was at the Capitol yesterday. The house was in session, but not a member with whom I wished to confer was there. I have no further report to present. I'm going up there from here. Perhaps I'll know something by night."

"I am perhaps a little discouraged," said Mrs. Dorris. "We haven't lost yet, but we are farther from winning than I thought we'd be. The only mistake that has been made was by me when I organized the campaign. I saw Nashville too well and Tennessee not well enough. All of you have been superb, and you, Sallie Lindsley, you have been an angel. Win or lose, I've won. I've lived much more closely with you dear people. But I still believe we'll win. . . ."

The maid came in and said that someone at the door wished to see Mrs. Lindsley.

It was Captain Savage. He held his broad gray hat rigidly in his hand. A sharp pain pierced Mrs. Lindsley's heart for it was in her mind that Charley was worse. That must be the reason Captain Savage had not been at the Capitol the day before.

"Charley's getting well fast, ma'am. They told me at your house that you'd be here and I wanted you to know about him. I'm mighty thankful, ma'am, for your help."

"I am so glad to hear from him. You can be proud of Charley. He is a lovely boy, Captain Savage."

"He won't ever forget you, ma'am. The woman where we stay, she's been mighty good to Charley, too. Reckon you could tell me where I can find them two doctors? Seemed like they knew just exactly what to do for Charley. I'd like to pay them and get that off of my mind."

She told him where to find the physicians. "I don't think they're in any hurry for their pay, but they'd like to see you."

He took a tentative step toward the door. "One other thing, ma'am. I guess I better tell you that the Confederate Home bill will pass the house today maybe without any votes at all against it."

"Yes," she said numbly.

"We just had to give 'em a home, ma'am."

"Yes," she said.

"But we made some changes, ma'am. Some of us went out there yesterday and we fixed things up a little different. We are leaving the Hermitage and part of the land for you-all, ma'am. That'll pass too, maybe late this evening. Might I bring Charley to see you, ma'am, before we go back home?"

4

Neely Barrow came into the library with a copy of the *American* in her hand. "They got it, Grandy."

"Got what, Neely Barrow?"

"The Hermitage. It looked as if they wouldn't for a while. But it says here they did."

"You mean that it has been sold? Who bought it?"

"Nobody bought it, Grandy. The legislature gave it to the Ladies Hermitage Association. You remember, don't you? It's what Dr. Atchison talked about with you."

"Oh yes, I do remember now."

"I'm so glad they got it. They say Mrs. Dorris has barely slept or eaten in three months. Grandy, I'm going to graduate this summer. I saw Mr. Mac Dickinson on the street and he said he believed he could have me elected to teach in Howard School. I would like to, Grandy."

"We've discussed that already, Neely Barrow."

"What am I to do after I graduate this summer? Tell me that, Grandy."

"Why should you do anything?"

"Yes, why?" The two words were sharp with irony. Her eyes were upon the frayed carpet, and in her mind was the back gate which lay where it had fallen when its hinges parted from the rotting wood. There was great beauty at Cherry Hill, but there was also accumulating decay.

Her grandfather came and stood before her, his forearm resting upon the marble mantel.

"Neely Barrow, I have never compromised. I have never sullied our name by any action of mine."

It was in her mind to ask whether a family might not be sullied by inaction, but she held the inquiry back. "What makes you think, Grandy, that I wouldn't make a good teacher?"

"You twist my meaning. I did not say that at all."

"Then why do you object?"

"I know our ancestry for two centuries back. It is my greatest pride. I do not believe that teaching quite fits into the pattern of our family."

"Then ours is a family to which nothing new can ever be added?"

He did not answer and she continued. "I do not have many

dresses. I do not need many. But I will need a new one when I graduate. The other day I went to Thompson and Kelly's to buy the goods for one. The lady was so gentle and patient and understanding that she made me want to work there. Of course, I don't guess I ever will, but what would be wrong if I did?"

"You don't understand, Neely Barrow?"

"Yes, I think I do. I understand that for two hundred years we haven't had a saleslady in our family. We haven't had a dressmaker either. And yet I wish I could be as skillful in something, and as pleasant personally, as is the lady who is making that dress. Tell me, Grandy, why I can't make my own dresses. Why have I never learned to make a dress? Is it because no woman of our family in two centuries has made one?"

"You are the first one of our family that I have failed to understand, Neely Barrow."

"You find it easier, Grandy, to understand the dead than the living?"

"No, easier to understand those who accept the family code than those who refuse it."

"Since I refuse the code I think I'll tell Mr. Mac Dickinson that I want the place at Howard."

"No," he said harshly, "it is not something a woman should do."

"Miss Julia Sears does. . . ."

"A Northerner. . . ."

"And therefore not of our family and therefore not to be trusted!"

"Our conversation seems a bit unpleasant. Since it is, there's a question which for a long time I've wished to ask. I have assumed that the relationship with the young man in Boston has been broken off long ago. Am I right?"

She didn't answer for a long moment, but stood tapping with her finger upon the window sill. When she spoke her voice was curiously gentle.

"It is interesting, Grandy, that a minute ago you were exalting our family because it has not changed. Now, you ask me hopefully if I haven't changed. No, Grandy, the relationship has not been broken off."

"You have not seen him?"

"Not since that night he was here. That was a long time ago. I do want to see him very much."

"You have never mentioned him to me."

"How could I, knowing that it would pain you, would anger you against me? There have been many times when it would have made me very happy to talk with you about Hunt."

"You told me then that you did not know his family. Do you now?"

"No, but that is my fault. . . ."

"For two hundred years our family has been zealous not to dilute itself."

"It would be Hunt who'd be diluted."

"That, Neely Barrow, is perfectly silly," he said, and started to the stairs that led to his room. But he stopped, stood for a moment stock-still, then came back across the hall. Erwin Roane looked at his granddaughter and there was pain in his eyes. "Neely Barrow, may I tell you a story?"

"Yes, Grandy."

He waited a moment before he began, summoning strength. "My grandfather Roane was not far behind James Robertson and John Donelson. He was already established when Andrew Jackson arrived in Nashville. He lived here forty years and died. I have been told, and I do believe it, that all the city mourned his loss. He was greatly rich in his neighbors' esteem and reasonably rich in money. He had built Cherry Hill, even in its disrepair today the loveliest place I ever saw. My father succeeded him, and did so worthily, I think, though I doubt if he had grandfather's strength in equal measure. He loved Cherry Hill with his father's ardor. He knew how to keep it grand and gallant. It was a home. And so our neighbors loved to come to it. We had many guests. On New Year's Day, Neely Barrow, my mother and father stood continuously almost in state to receive those who came to bring their New Year's greeting. I remember one time vividly. General Jackson and Mrs. Jackson brought Sam Houston, and while they were here Mr. Felix Grundy and Mrs. Grundy came, and then Dr. Boyd McNairy and Mrs. McNairy. I remember that the air seemed to thicken when Dr. McNairy came into the room for he was General Jackson's enemy. General Jackson stiffened and hardened and stood even more erect. Dr. McNairy was entirely at ease, however. He shook hands with my mother and father. Then he held out his hand to Mrs. Jackson. For a short moment she hesitated, then flicked an inquiring glance to her husband. He stood looking straight ahead. Mrs. Jackson extended her hand to

Dr. McNairy pleasantly enough but she did not smile. 'Good afternoon, General Jackson,' said Dr. McNairy, and held out his hand. I remember how clear and distinct his voice was. It seemed to me almost that the clock, time, everything stood still. I'm sure my heart did. For a few seconds General Jackson stood unbending and grim. Then he held out his hand. 'You are my enemy, Dr. McNairy,' he said, 'but out of respect for our hostess and host, and remembering that once you saved my life I will shake hands.'

" 'Enemies only politically,' said Dr. McNairy. 'I have great admiration for you personally, General Jackson. It was a pleasure to save your life—if I did—for the companionship of so gracious a lady.' He bowed very gently to Rachel. At that General Jackson's face lost its grimness. 'It may be a weakness of mine, Dr. McNairy, not to be able to separate enemies, political and personal. You are the first, sir, to tempt me to try to do so.'

" 'You call your party *Democrat*, General Jackson. I have been told that the word itself freely permits me to be a *Whig*.'

" 'I have never taken my political faith so lightly.' General Jackson's face was grim again, but only for a moment. Then he really smiled. 'I think you saved my life, Dr. McNairy. I know you saved my arm. Whig or not, I thank you again, sir.'

" 'I wish that my poor skill could often serve so worthy a use.'

" 'We have another bond.' General Jackson smiled ruefully. 'The only time I have ever run from anyone was from a kinswoman of yours.'

" 'I remember,' said Dr. McNairy dryly. 'It's no wonder you— er—retreated, sir. Amanda was a very determined woman.'

"Then a servant came with cakes and cordial, and the talk became more general. That day is imprinted indelibly upon my memory. There were many such days at Cherry Hill." He paused. Then he said with exquisite sadness in his tones, "Days that can never come again." He looked about him with a look of surprise on his face. "Of what am I talking? Oh, I know, of the past. It is always with me. It stands at my side always. Something snapped within me when Rebecca died. We had been married but two years, and when she died the light went out at Cherry Hill. It was dark for thirty years—until you came. I never knew my son very well. There was always something between us—some sort of a barrier, invisible, untouchable but real. We loved each other, I think, but it was a love owed by each to the other. Then he married and went away to live. You know what happened. Fourteen years ago he and his wife died of the plague the same week, and you, then five, came to Cherry Hill."

"Yes, Grandy, I know."

"I haven't talked—I've been silent because—I've—I've had nothing to say."

"Pride can destroy one, Grandy."

"It's been destroying me. Pride from two directions, nay, from four, only I've nothing in myself to anchor pride in. Since I am talking, let me talk a bit more. My father was a wise man. I think he understood me. He left me Cherry Hill, and some money. I think he foresaw the war, for mainly the money that was to be mine he put in trust for me. Even then he had little faith in my ability. The other money was used long ago and that put in trust has dwindled."

Before he resumed his story there was in the room only the sound of the languid crackle of the fire. "You came here fourteen years ago. Before you came I had seemed dead—even to myself. When you came I came back to life. You are all I have, child, all the name Roane has. It is in your keeping. It will die unless you keep it alive."

5

Breakfast at Cherry Hill was a bit formal the next morning. Neely Barrow went on to her lessons at Peabody. Charles Little was teaching at the College then, and her last class for the day was in Latin taught by him. She waited until the other students had left the room.

"Mr. Little, may I ask you a question?"

"Sit down, won't you? I am asked too few questions by my best pupils."

"Thank you, Mr. Little. I wish I could think of nice things like that to say to people. Mr. Little, do you think I'd made a good teacher?"

"Yes," he said, "a very good teacher, indeed."

"Miss Julia Sears thinks I would, too."

"Yes, I've heard her say so several times."

"But my grandfather thinks I wouldn't."

"I'd shrink from opposing your grandfather in most things, but not in this."

"Do you know any reason, Mr. Little, why a woman shouldn't be a teacher?"

"Only one, and it doesn't apply to you."

She smiled. "Mr. Mac Dickinson said he could get me a place in the Howard School. We really need the money."

"My connection with such matters has not been academic," he assured her. "It is a condition more or less common among teachers."

"I have plenty to eat and wear," she said, "but we need so many things. So much of the house needs either painting or repairing. We need a lot of new things. Curtains don't last always and ours are forty years old."

"They were doubtless of excellent quality to begin with," he said.

"I think they are still beautiful. Excuse me, Mr. Little, for talking about personal things. I wanted to know what you thought of me becoming a teacher."

"Very highly of it," he said, "but if your grandfather doesn't wish you to teach I don't quite see how I can advise it."

"You've been very kind. Good afternoon, Mr. Little."

The teacher watched her until she reached the door. "It's my turn, Miss Roane. May I ask you a question?"

She stood waiting and he continued. "If there is any imper-tinence in my question please consider that it has not been asked. One of my classmates was a remarkable fellow named Hunt Justice. He left for an eastern college almost immediately after he finished the course here. I have heard that there was an attachment exist-ing between you and him."

"Not *was*," she said, "*is*."

"I would compliment him if I had the chance. I do compli-ment you. Hunt had excellence of mind and beauty of spirit. . . ."

"*Has*, Mr. Little."

"That makes you almost a specialist in the present tense," he said laughing.

"As far as Hunt is concerned, past, present and future."

"*Was, is* and *will be*," he said. "How lovely!"

"Tell me, Mr. Little, did you ever see Hunt's mother?"

"Yes, twice. Once when we graduated and again two weeks ago."

"Tell me about her."

"I spent Saturday afternoon in the City Cemetery. As I left I came along Oak Street. A woman was working in a flower bed close to the street. I had met her when we graduated and I knew her at once. I introduced myself. We had a very pleasant conversation—most of it, of course, about Hunt. I think she is terribly lonesome for him. He wanted to come home last summer, but she told him not to come. He was helping Professor Letang with the plans for the World's Fair buildings at Chicago. She was wise and patient enough to wait another year."

"I, too, told Hunt not to come."

"A very interesting expansion of Mrs. Justice's wisdom and patience. I found her plain, but poised and at ease. Her voice is deep and even, a rich contralto whose beauty a sort of country flatness cannot hide. I have never seen Hunt's father. He is a builder of some kind but his mother offers at least a partial explanation for the boy's strength."

"I don't guess you can imagine, Mr. Little, how much this talk has helped me. I just had to talk with someone about teaching— and other things."

He bowed. "I have found it pleasant to talk about teaching— and other things."

Neely Barrow did not turn toward home when she left the college grounds. Her course indeed lay in the opposite direction. She crossed Market Street and walked along Ash Street until she came to Cherry. There she turned south. The sweetness of spring was in the air and the grass in the yards was green and growing.

Mrs. Justice worked in her flower beds. It was a quiet day and the breezes were gentle and caressing. She was thinking of her son who studied in a faraway college. She was seeing him sitting by the car window, as she saw him when he left for Boston on that autumn morning.

Someone was speaking to her. She straightened and saw a young lady standing at her side. Suddenly, by some subtle and inner revelation, she knew who her visitor was.

"Good afternoon, Mrs. Justice."

For an instant there was silence. Then Mrs. Justice held out her hand. "You are Nee . . . you are Miss Roane," she said.

"How did you know me?" asked Neely Barrow.

"Hunt told me about you. Maybe that was it. Won't you come in?"

"Let's stay out here. Your flowers are so pretty. I love to look at them. It's pleasant here and the view is lovely."

"We had lots of jonquils but they're gone now. I think the flags are pretty, don't you?"

"Indeed I do. What are you planting?"

"Zinnias and marigolds. Hunt is right fond of them. There is a rambler rose on the garden fence. It bloomed a little the summer before he left, but it's filled with buds now. He could stand and look at it by the hour."

"Let me see it, please," said Neely Barrow.

Mrs. Justice set her hoe firmly against a tree and led the way back to the garden which behind the house slanted slightly upward toward the brow of the low hill lying behind Oak Street. The garden was a brief panorama of greenness, the dark green of onions, the lighter green of potatoes, the light green of peas, the gray-green of cabbages, the neatly spaced rows bearing their crowns of green in modest triumph. A rose vine wreathed its way along the length of the paling fence.

"Oh, it's beautiful back here. Did you make this garden, Mrs. Justice?"

"I helped, though Courtney did most of the work. He's Hunt's father. He's getting to be mighty handy with a garden."

"When did you hear from Hunt, Mrs. Justice?"

"Last Saturday. It seems like it's been an age since I saw him."

"I know it has. Did Hunt work in the garden when he was here?"

"The last two or three years he did most of the work that was done. He's a good worker."

"How did he become so interested in houses?"

"We've wondered about that. We bought him a book when he was little. It had a lot of pictures of fine houses in it, and for a year he had it in his hands all the time he was in the house. Maybe that got him started, I don't know."

"He said in the last letter he wrote me that he thought he would come home this summer."

"I look for him to come. He's going to be at work this summer helping them get ready for a big fair they're going to have up in Chicago. He's going to come by home as he goes back to Boston."

"I wish I had come to see you sooner."

"I thought maybe you would. Sometimes I almost expected you."

"Did you?" asked Neely Barrow happily. "I wish I had come when you expected me. Wouldn't that have been nice?"

"Hunt sent me a book with some pictures of places in Boston. Can't you come in awhile and look at it?"

"Oh, I'd like to." Neely Barrow did not mention that Hunt had sent her a book of Boston scenes—likely the same one—and that she might reasonably be regarded as an expert in the pictures since she had studied them for hours and with great intentness.

She sat in the front room and looked through the book though every picture was already vividly etched in her memory. Perhaps Hunt had stood on this corner. Perhaps he had gone into that building. She rose to leave. "Hunt will seem much closer in Chicago. He wrote to me about what he is going to do there."

"It's more than a thousand miles to Boston and it's not more than five hundred to Chicago. I measured it on a map."

"Were you surprised when you heard about it?"

"You could have knocked me over with a feather when I heard about it. It wasn't that I didn't have faith in Hunt, but a world's fair! I went to a Franklin County fair once, and I heard Mr. Moore at Huntland tell about the time he went to the state fair. But a world's fair!" The wonder of it was again in Mrs. Justice's eyes. "Now, Courtney, it didn't excite him a bit. He said he thought it would happen all the time. Courtney's that way, though. To tell you the truth, I don't think he'd ever heard of a world's fair any more than I had."

"When Hunt comes home you keep him most of the time but divide him with me a little."

"I guess Hunt will do the dividing," said Mrs. Justice smiling.

Presently Neely Barrow left, and as she walked along Cherry Street she was curiously happy. Mrs. Justice prepared supper for her husband who was due home from work. She was singing a little song from the Tennessee hills and in her heart too was happiness, new and lifting.

6

The word was out that, on April 29, the mules and horses which had pulled the streetcars of Nashville would be retired, written into those records in which men preserve the story of their lost institutions. The town's citizenship knew two extremes, the doubters, disbelievers in progress, electrical or otherwise; and the accepters who could with no effort whatever expand a good deed into a millennium, or a light shower into a good crop year. In between were the saner folk who had faith in the promises of the experts but resolved to study the new device in transportation with a speculative eye and mind.

"It won't work," said the doubters. "Besides if it did a lot of people would take to gadding about who've got work to do at home."

"We are standing on the threshold of a new era," said the accepters, falling into the threadbare phrase of the swallowers of the swords of progress. "Today in Nashville, tomorrow, who knows? Maybe Paris, or London or China, you can't tell."

There was much bantering on the streets.

"You can't tell me they won't run," affirmed one whose optimism was strengthened by experience in faraway places. "I saw them run in Cincinnati—made ten miles an hour right down the main streets."

"Wouldn't believe a word a feller said who'd been in Cincinnati," countered a doubter.

"Well," said the traveler cheerfully, "I guess I'd feel the same way if I'd never been further off than Flat Rock."

"It ain't the fellers who go the fartherest whose children has got most to eat."

A third bystander recalled the main issue of the day. "I expect it'll run all right. Company knew its business when it spent all this money making the change. Besides I've seen other fellers who'd seen 'em run just like you say—" nodding to the man who'd been to Cincinnati—"but—" nodding to the man who'd been to Flat Rock—"I ain't going to paternize till they get the accidents out o' their system. They say they do a lot o' damage till they get the hang o' 'em."

The speaker didn't know, of course, that College Grove had spent weeks getting the hang of them. An instructional track had been built within the carbarn on Cherry Street, and, while it was a bit microscopic, it provided for all foreseeable emergencies and College Grove had met them all with reassuring *savoir faire*. If he rounded a sharp curve and found a log most surprisingly on the track his reactions were equal to the situation. In short, College Grove was ready. Furthermore, he had understudies who closely approached—though did not reach—him in readiness.

It was a perfect day. The delicate grace of April was blending into the warmth and certainty of May. The charming young girl was becoming the lovely young woman. The hackberry trees wore their new gowns of lacy wistful green.

It was a busy morning in the stores for the town was crowded. Everything was to close at noon so that all might witness the grand metamorphosis. The change was to be made with ceremony and with proper sensitivity to the dramatic values involved.

When the stores closed the countryside moved out of the stores and lined the sidewalks of Cherry Street, and the townsfolk found their vantage places in windows or on balconies and waited comfortably for the pageantry to begin.

At the carbarn on Cherry Street the driver sat placidly waiting for the courthouse clock to sound the hour of one. It was then that horses were to step out of harness, so to speak, in favor of a power new and mysterious—to yield to progress, but with a fitting and impressive climax. The last horse-drawn car in Nashville was to retrace the route of the first one almost a quarter of a century before. It was to move out Cherry Street to the Old N & D Depot, then across to College Street and back into town. A full car of specially invited guests were to make the trip. The guests were Weaver and Merrie Cole, Constantine and Amanda Watson, Greene and Susan Cartwright, Colonel Thomas Craighead, Governor Bob Taylor, Professor A. D. Wharton, Reverend M. B. Dewitt, Mr. Joel Cheek, Mr. Walter Stokes, Mr. Eugene Lewis, Mrs. James K. Polk and Neely Barrow Roane.

"Certainly, I'll go," said Mrs. Polk when they asked her. She eyed them keenly. "You don't happen to be surprised, do you? Sooner or later, I suppose I'll get to be an old woman, but I'm not one yet. I'll be there in plenty of time. By the way, who's going?"

They told her.

"An excellent list. Someone with sense made it up. But there's something a little heartbreaking about it. It suggests so many who would belong in it if they were still here. Wait a minute," she said a bit excitedly. "Who's driving the car?"

"The gentleman who drove on the first trip."

"Perfect. How well I remember that day. The war was over. It was sunrise after a long night. The day was fresh and lovely, a little earlier in the year than this, sometime in March, I think. I remember that a yard in Priestly Street was gold with jonquil blooms. Yes, I'll go. I'll feel honored to go. I helped welcome the horses, I'll help say good-by to them." She wrinkled her brow in thought. "May I suggest one more passenger?"

"You have that right eminently."

"Then ask Neely Barrow Roane. I have reasons."

"I have not once known you, dear lady, without your reason," said Anson Nelson. "We will add Neely Barrow's name very gladly."

Eugene Lewis brought Neely Barrow and Mrs. Polk in his trap. He helped the ladies to the ground, then handed his horse to a stable boy to be hitched. Anson Nelson came over to greet them.

"We are here," said Mrs. Polk gaily. "Can you think of any reason for not starting?"

"Only one, Mrs. Polk, and perhaps it's a good one. Six of our guests have not arrived."

"Not a good reason at all. Much easier on the horses without them." She saw the driver standing at the front step, his whip in his hand. "You, sir," she said, "have you no greeting for your fellow traveler on life's streetcar?" She turned to Constantine and Amanda Watson. "Good afternoon, dear friends. I'd love to see your whole family. But, of course, not right now. From what I hear there wouldn't be any room for anybody else."

"Seven," said Amanda, smiling. "Boys, all sizes, and all just like Constantine. They fight all the time. Most quarrelsome man I ever married. I hate to think what would have happened to the Yankees if the boys hadn't come along a little late."

"Constantine by himself was almost too much for them," said Mrs. Polk. "Well, we'll be prepared next time." She turned to greet Greene and Susan Cartwright. "Delighted, my dears. Does Old Hurricane bloom like the rose?"

"Sometimes the crops don't do so well, but we have a garden of memories in full bloom," said Greene.

"A farmer turned poet! That, I assume, assigns the care of the crops to you, Susan."

"All abo'd," yelled the driver. "Effn you want to take a trip without loss of life, limbs and laigs now's yo' chancet. Streetcar leaves in five minutes. Jest a few mo' seats left. Step right abo'd. Travel in style. Last chancet you'll ever have to go somewhere and git back too."

College Grove standing over by one side laughed with a great display of sarcasm. "Effn you like your happy homes take a last look at 'em. You won't never be seein' 'em no more."

"Pay him no 'tention at all," advised the driver. "He was kicked by a steer when he was little."

"I've set by the hour listenin' to him brag about the passengers he'd left daid and dyin' right in the street. Yes sir, drove right off and left 'em."

Anson Nelson and Frank Morrow frowned. Levity did not become a meeting so in step with the very dignity of progress.

"Before the trip is started," said Frank Morrow, lifting his voice to carry to the limits of the barn, "it is appropriate for us to hear a few words spoken by a citizen who for fifty years has been in the forefront of every worthy movement in Nashville. I present Colonel J. P. McGuire."

The brief address that followed made graceful reference to the inevitable yielding of old orders. It was the way of human development—serve and depart. Serve well; depart in honor.

He brought his remarks to a close and Frank Morrow nodded to the driver.

"Giddup," said he, and his whip cracked like a rifle.

"Wait a minute," called Anson Nelson. "There are Mr. Giers and Mr. Thuss to take a picture."

The two photographers who always arrived at the last possible moment came rushing in unfolding their paraphernalia as they came. They fussed about viewing the streetcar from all angles. They spread a flowing black drapery over the camera and Mr. Thuss crawled under it. The cloth moved in violent undulations. Then Mr. Thuss reappeared shaking his head ominously and motioning for Mr. Giers to crawl under and take a look for himself. Mr. Giers crawled under and again the surface of the drapery became agitated. Mr. Giers came back into view. It was plain that he added full corroboration to Mr. Thuss's fears. Another place would have to be found. Presently, Mr. Thuss and Mr. Giers were satisfied. Posterity was protected. Mr. Thuss in rich German accents addressed the driver.

"Ach, das ist goot, Buffalo Beel. Do now your capers."

The whip cracked with a sharp abruptness suggesting that even for posterity there'd be no more delay. The car moved out of the barn and south on Cherry Street. Applause in great volume arose from the crowds assembled on the sidewalks.

But the driver's heart was heavy. He had been at the beginning. Now he was at the end. He was watching a beloved institution die. He was indeed helping it to die. Then his native optimism asserted itself. An institution had to die in order that a better one might be born. The streetcar company had sense. It wouldn't have spent all that money if it hadn't known what it was doing. Things would be better. They always were. He cracked his whip and lifted his voice in song, pleasantly satirical of a neighboring community.

> "If I were a young man
> And my life was still ahead
> I'd move myself to Gallatin
> And act like I was dead."

But his song quieted, for ahead of him arose the stirring strains of "Dixie." It was Professor J. E. Bailey directing his chorus from the veranda of the Maxwell House. The driver turned his head and spoke to Mrs. Polk.

"Sounds like Jawn Hood's army's come to life," he observed.

"Professor Bailey seems to be in the spirit," said Mrs. Polk.

Professor Bailey was in the spirit. Tall and thin and as angular as one of his notes of music, he was directing with such a sweep of beats that he had to hurry back from each beat in order to be in time to start the next one. Suddenly his right hand would be extended horizontally, his long index finger pointing in a fierce demand for more volume from the tenors.

The streetcar passed the Maxwell House and dropped down the Cherry Street hill toward Broad Street.

"It seems like yesterday," said Mrs. Polk.

"It is yesterday," said Susan Cartwright. "It is yesterday, and I am standing on the porch at brother's and you have just asked me to ride. No, it is today and I'm twenty-five years older."

The driver was singing again.

> "Oh if I was a young man
> Somewheres in my teens
> I think I'd move to Lebanon
> And live on turnip greens."

Again he was interrupted, indeed silenced. The choir of the Central Baptist Church was assembled on the corner of Elm and

Cherry, and when the car came into view it entered with great resonance into:

> "How firm a foundation
> Ye Saints of the Lord."

The driver could see Brother Hambrick and Brother Gupton standing in the choir and they, too, were plainly in the spirit.

"I'm glad the foundation has improved," said Mrs. Polk. "It wasn't any too good on the first trip. Remember, Susan?"

"No," said Susan. "If anything was unfirm that day I didn't notice it. It was more like a flowery bed of ease to me."

"Ah, yes, there are times when youth lacks discernment."

"But I hadn't met Greene then, Mrs. Polk."

Again the irreverent lilt of the driver's voice fell upon the soft spring air.

> "If I were a young man
> And didn't have a dollar
> I'd move up to Bowling Green
> And wear a paper collar."

Neely Barrow's eyes had been searching for something. She found it as they passed Oak Street. She pointed.

"There's where Hunt lives, Mrs. Polk. I went to see his mother the other day. Mrs. Polk, I liked her a lot."

"Of course, dear. She's his mother, you know."

"I know the lady," said Eugene Lewis who sat near. "She doesn't have to depend upon her son to merit respect." He bowed gently to Neely Barrow. "Though, of course, if she lacked quality he'd have enough to go around. Have you told Neely Barrow about the money?" he asked.

"No, I haven't. Suppose you do."

"Very naturally, you know, Neely Barrow, that Mrs. Polk and I have had the honor of investing some money in Hunt's future...."

"Purely selfish," interrupted Mrs. Polk. "We saw the boy had unusual promise, so we wished some of the glory."

"Exactly," agreed Eugene Lewis. "Hunt being what he was, we didn't stand a chance to lose the money. Besides that, we were sure that Hunt sooner or later would plan a great building and we could

pose as its godparents and get some credit for it. Surely you understand that, Neely Barrow."

"Exactly," mimicked Neely Barrow. "You understand my part,
too, I hope. I wanted some of the glory myself."

"I still think we will get the glory, but the cash is already coming
in. Hunt has already sent us two hundred dollars."

"Two hundred dollars! Where did he get it?"

"Very honestly, it seems. He drew plans for the front of a
building merely as a class exercise. Professor Homer was so pleased
with it that he showed it to one of the leading architects of Providence, Rhode Island. It happened the fellow was drawing plans
for a public building in the city. He asked immediately to see
Hunt. And the meeting ended with him buying the plans for $200.
Of course, they will have to be recast to fit into the building as a
whole. It was an unusual honor. Anyhow, Hunt sent the money
immediately as a payment on his notes. I have never heard of anything like that either."

Constantine Watson pointed. "I rode by there the first day of the
battle of Nashville."

"Why, Constantine, you might have been killed!" exclaimed
Amanda.

He looked at her tenderly. "Would you have married a man,
dear, whom the Yankees *could* kill?"

"Anyhow, I wouldn't marry one who'd ever surrender." She
addressed the guests. "Did you all know that Constantine never
did surrender? The Yankees were too scared of him to get close
enough for him to surrender. Besides, he wouldn't have anyhow.
One couldn't have married a stubborner man than Constantine."
She paused a moment, then added reflectively, "Though I never
tried."

"Here's one Yankee who got close enough to a Rebel for him to
surrender," said Merrie Cole.

Weaver Cole's face lighted up with his slow smile. "You have
it inverted, Merrie. Don't you remember how you surrendered
when I had you surrounded that day at Mrs. Polk's?"

Again the driver lifted his voice.

> "If I were a young man
> And didn't know a thing
> I think I'd move to Shelbyville
> And live just like a king."

Then they were bound back to town. There to the right was Peabody. Mrs. Polk saw it and it raised a question.

"You going to teach school next year, Neely Barrow?"

Neely Barrow sighed. "I wish I knew. I want to and I ought to, but Grandy won't consent. Can you imagine any harm it would do me to teach next year in the Howard School? Mr. Mac Dickinson said he could get the place for me."

"It'd help you, dear. I think it would be a lovely experience. But your grandfather is a unique breed, child. I can't advise you to disobey his wishes."

"I suppose I'd better not disobey him this time, but I'll have to later."

"Later?"

"Yes. About Hunt. I don't think he'll ever agree to that. I'll have to disobey him then," she added.

Neely Barrow was silent for a while. Then she said, "I think I'd like very much to be a teacher. I think Miss Julia Sears is a fine teacher. I told Grandy so. Perhaps that was a mistake. Grandy said she was a Northerner. I oughtn't to have led him on to say that. If he halfway believed before that no Southern lady would be a teacher, just as soon as he said that, he was so certain of it that nothing could ever change him. I asked Miss Sears once if she ever regretted becoming a teacher, and she said she'd quit the schoolroom only to go to heaven."

"I know your grandfather, child. I can't advise you to become a teacher, but somehow I wish you would."

"Unless you two are talking secrets," said Eugene Lewis, "I'd like to tell you that I am moving back to Nashville this summer."

"How delightful!"

"I've never been quite happy at Sycamore. There are others who can do the work there. Maybe I am impardonably vain, but I have the feeling there is work to do here than I alone can do."

"You will return to the railroad?"

"That's the plan. But there is another matter that interests me greatly. It is about decided that Tennessee will celebrate her centennial with an exposition rivaling the various world fairs. I want to have a part in that."

They were climbing the College Street hill, nearing Church. The trip was about over. Greene Cartwright looked at Mrs. Polk and knew what she was thinking—but not all she was thinking. She hurriedly wiped the tear away, and her eyes rested warmly and reminiscently upon Amanda Watson, then upon Susan Cartwright, then upon Merrie Cole. Mrs. Polk's eyes moved on to Neely Barrow.

"You are a bit young, my child, but you fit this trip perfectly. You give me a sense of completeness, dear. I'm glad I asked for you."

"I'm glad, too, but how do I fit?"

Mrs. Polk's eyes moved back to Amanda, and Susan and Merrie. "They were my girls but they've outgrown me. They do not need me any more. Maybe you do need me. I wanted you along because I need you."

The driver's quick eyes spotted Brother Hambrick on the side-walk. Evidently the Central Baptist Choir after finishing "How Firm a Foundation" had scattered to find vantage places for the streetcar's return trip. Brother Hambrick directed his voice at the driver and yelled, "What's the matter, pardner? Cat's got your tongue? Sing us a piece."

And there slipped back into the driver's memory a piece that he had sung in Brother Hambrick's presence. He cracked his whip viciously at an imaginary horsefly and began singing rather low at first but in tones that grew in fervor and volume.

> "Oh brothers, will you meet me
> Oh brothers, will you meet me
> Oh brothers, will you meet me
> On Canaan's happy shore?"

College Grove was a restless man while the first trip was under way. He walked up and down and over and across within the car-barn. He would climb aboard the new electric car and reassure himself as to the feel of the various gadgets. Every now and then he would pause to announce publicly that in his opinion they were wasting their time waiting for the return of the first car. He claimed that while Methuselah might have been a good driver in his young manhood the very laws of nature would render him a menace if entrusted with the reins in his advancing years. He hated to think of what in all likelihood had already happened to the passengers, without doubt men and women of value to the community. It was his contention from the very beginning that only those be allowed to take the trip who wouldn't be missed anyhow. In fact, he could think up a good carload whose loss would leave

the city improved. At a climax in his pessimism the sounds of shouting reached them, swelling in volume. But he was not one to yield
without protest even to overwhelming odds. "Count their arms,
count their legs," he shouted. "I lay you five to one they ain't all
there."

There have been exceptions but Nashville has usually regarded
its landmarks with affection and has witnessed their departure with
sadness. There were a few who regarded the ceremonial of the
departing horsecar as an empty and senseless gesture. *When they
are through with the old one, stop, and when ready with the new
one, start,* they said in effect. But the realists were few and the
sentimentalists many. Their parents, their friends had ridden on
the horsecar. For a quarter of a century no street scene had been
complete without one. How fitting and how sad then to bury it in
full honor! The driver handed the reins to one of the carbarn
stable boys, and stood looking at the horses in deep and tender abstraction. Mrs. Polk said in a low tone to Eugene Lewis, "This
might well be the last time I'll ever be on a streetcar."

"Oh, Mrs. Polk..."

"Yes. I am old. I wouldn't have missed this trip but I borrowed
time for it."

In Nashville all ventures new or old are accorded the honor of
dedicatory speeches. Mr. George Armistead made an address which
omitted none of the phrases of the proper hallowing of the new
electric car. Then they were ready to start. But Mr. Thuss and
Mr. Giers arrived in an advanced state of perspiration and heavy
breathing. They had had a heavy run of business at their studio and
had been compelled to run every step of the way to the barn carrying full equipment.

"Hold it," Colonel McGuire ordered College Grove who stood
braced and with a stern grasp upon the gadgets of control. "Hold
it. I want a picture of this for my grandson's office—if I ever have
a grandson, if he ever has an office."

Mr. Thuss and Mr. Giers performed their rituals and presently
the city's first electric car was ready to depart.

The passengers were the directors of the company, the board of
public works, Chief of Police Clack, wearing an even higher collar,
representatives of the press, Mr. Godfrey Fogg, Reverend Jere
Witherspoon, and two ladies, Mrs. G. W. Stahlman and Mrs. H.
B. Stubblefield.

The driver's eyes rested at length upon the new car. Then he addressed College Grove. "Even a hossfly wouldn't get messed up with that contraption."

When the laughter had subsided, College Grove received the official nod. He braced himself even more rigidly and moved to the right the gadget he held clenched in his left hand. Certain under parts of the car literally writhed in the birth pains of electrical impulse. The wheels began to turn with a great grinding sound. Sparks flowed from the points of contact between wheel and rail as from a forge. But the pessimists were confounded. The car moved. With a noisy clumsy dignity it moved southward on Cherry. At the Maxwell House corner, College Grove pulled the gadget in his left hand back to its starting point, and with a great clicking of ratchets began to apply his right-hand gadget. The car slowed to a stop. The switch was turned, for the new route ran out Church Street. College Grove released the brakes and applied the power. The underneath part of the car was stricken with convulsions, the car shook with great tremors and the wheels began grudgingly to revolve. The car eased around the corner. Then they were passing the First Presbyterian Church, many of whose members stood on the steps and in the little areas between the building and the street. They applauded with great vigor not only the new car but their pastor who was aboard. Fresh volumes of applause arose from the yard of the McKendree Church and from the Bailey House across the street.

At Vine Street a citizen had most thoughtfully provided himself with a reserved seat. He had driven his horse hitched to a light trap close into the sidewalk facing south. There he sat comfortably awaiting the event. He didn't seem particularly disturbed by the caustic remarks of those who wished to stand in the space so pre-empted. He sat and waited and took his ease. The applause out by the McKendree Church and the Bailey House announced that the feature event was about to be presented. The occupant of the reserved seat anchored his whip securely in its socket and threw his reins around it. He stood and faced Church Street, towering above the crowd and doubtless rejoicing in his uninterrupted view. So intent was the gentleman that he neglected to observe that his horse, having caught some odd glimpses from the corner of its eye, had turned its head about and stood quivering from what it beheld. And as the horse considered these matters a stream of sparks flew with a crackling sound from the wheels. The horse crouched, sprang and went away from there entirely unaccompanied by the gentleman in the trap. For with the initial onward surge of the horse and vehicle he had transferred to a horizontal position on the street, and, as if in revenge, cushioning his fall with several who but a few minutes before had complained so bitterly against his beforehandedness.

College Grove turned his eyes just long enough to witness the more active parts of the drama. They impinged heavily upon College Grove's sense of humor.

"Some hosses and some folks jest like that," he observed through the open window to Godfrey Fogg who sat nearest him. "It jest natchelly scares the fillin' out o' them to see somethin' new."

In the excitement of this episode College Grove forgot an important item. He had reached even then the Nicholson House. Just ahead the route of the streetcar turned southward into Spruce Street. He had been carefully rehearsed in the procedure to use in rounding a curve. The current was to be switched off, or, at most, only enough used to creep safely around. That went completely out of College Grove's mind. The car clanged down upon the curve. It hit it with bone-shaking momentum. For a dreadful instant it stood poised, undecided whether to leave the track for an unsponsored career all its own. Fire spouted from its wheels in a stream. But the flanges held, and the car righted itself and proceeded out Spruce Street. The passengers disentangled themselves from the floor and from one another. It would be something to tell about for a long time to come. College Grove, a philosopher of no mean quality, said in a loud voice plainly audible to all, "You couldn't do that with hosses."

He was ready for the next curve and the car eased into Broad Street gently and becomingly.

There was a wave of feminine applause from Dr. Price's College for Young Ladies, and the Episcopalians cheered in their dignified way from the front of Christ Church across the street.

The directors had told College Grove that the trip was to be made slowly and in proper decorum. But the track ran straight ahead into the west. The invitation of that uninterrupted vista broke down his restraint. His memory of his orders faded away. He pressed the gadget in his left hand farther around. And so delighted were the directors with the feel of fresh speed that their memories weakened, too. The car ran straight ahead into a future rich in promise.

7

Neely Barrow yielded to her grandfather's determination for her not to become a teacher in the Howard School. But, in doing so, she urged a point which left him impressed and depressed.

"Do you wish to know, Grandy, why I wanted to do this?"

"If you care to tell me."

"For one thing I would like to find out something about me. Am I good for anything? Do you know of anything that I am good for, Grandy? Then, we need the money dreadfully, I'm afraid. I'm twenty years old, Grandy, and I've never seen a drop of paint put on this house. If something breaks we never have anybody to fix it. I can bear our carpets wearing thin because that cannot be helped, but I cannot bear for a gate to rot from its hinges and stay where it falls. When it rains we set a bucket in a closet upstairs to catch the drip, but we do not have the roof repaired. Now do you know why I want to make some money, Grandy?"

"No," he said harshly. "Because I have lowered the family name it should not follow that you must too."

"Lower the name! Lower the name! Would it lower our precious name to get our house painted?"

Erwin Roane's face was an ashen white. There was a period of silence. Then he said in tones old and very tired, "You're quite right, Neely Barrow. It is I who have lowered our name. I shall try to raise it. Perhaps I can find some paint for Cherry Hill. Will you excuse me, please?"

He went up the stairs slowly, with great effort. Neely Barrow stood looking at him, her face touched by contrition. She caught up with him at the head of the stairs. "Grandy, forgive me. Please, Grandy."

"Isn't that beside the point? Forgive you for what? It is I who have lowered our name, who have cheapened Cherry Hill."

"Grandy, please . . ."

"Perhaps I can find some paint for Cherry Hill. Anyhow, I'll try. Good night, Neely Barrow."

He went into his room and gently closed the door.

Not many days after that Neely Barrow came home from the college to find her grandfather excited. He saw her coming and met her as she came up the walk to the house. His face was brighter, more animated, than she had seen it in a long time.

"We are going to paint Cherry Hill . . . right away."

"Why, Grandy . . ."

"Yes, and repair it, too."

Something chilling blew across her heart.

"I have sold the lots across the street," he said.

"Sold them? Why did you, Grandy?"

"You did right, Neely Barrow, to complain the other evening. I had felt the neglect to Cherry Hill but . . ."

"Not that, Grandy?" She pointed to the lots.

"Yes, to a Mr. Dilly. He had been to see me about it before, but when he came to see me today . . ."

"Grandy, who is he?"

"He is not the sort one would care to know. But he paid cash."

"But why, Grandy? What does he want it for?"

"As a speculation, he said. He has some friends in the city administration and he thinks he can sell it, for a small profit, of course, to the city to make into a park."

"A park? Right across from Cherry Hill?"

"But it would improve it. They will plant shrubbery and care for everything."

"But it divides the place. How could you, Grandy?"

"Divides it to preserve the better part. It was you, Neely Barrow, who gave me the idea."

"But not to sell the land, Grandy!"

"I know. Don't think, child, that it was easy for me to do." He paused and passed his hand wearily across his brow. "Easy! Good God!"

Neely Barrow knew then the agony through which her grandfather had passed—was still passing. But quickly and characteristically her mind jumped to his defense. He had been treasonable to a little part to save Cherry Hill itself.

"He gave me three thousand dollars for it and I intend to use every cent to make the place like it used to be. You have never seen it at its best, Neely Barrow. It was glorious then. I can die happy if I can see it that way once more, if I can show it to you as my father showed it to me."

She had never seen her grandfather so excited, she knew that. It was for Erwin Roane more than a simple barter in real estate.

It was as if he had sold one of the courts of the temple to rebuild an outworn altar.

8

Jim Parkes was en route to the Green home. His horse cantered along the pike and a strange light burned in his eyes and glowed on his face. "Now, what would you do if you were in my place?" he asked, though it wasn't clear whether he made the inquiry of the horse he was riding, or of the world at large. The answer seemed to come promptly.

"You sure you would? Well, I guess you're right. That's what I think. I say again that *there's a tide in the affairs of men which the crest if taken—taken*—taken where I'd like to know. How does it go anyhow? Funny, I'd forget that. It seemed just the thing to start off with. Leave Professor Baskerville practically wrecked if he knew I'd forgotten it. Let's see now. *There are affairs in the tide of men.* That won't do. Well, what will do? You still think it is a good thing to say, Professor? So do I if I can get the hang of it. *There is a tide in the affairs of men which, taken*—that's right so far. Now how does the rest of it go? Anyhow it means if you are going to do it at all now's the time. Why, that's funny. How'd you know where we were going?"

His horse, having a special wisdom in such matters, had turned in at the Greens' driveway.

Mrs. Green answered the fall of the knocker. She didn't seem in the least surprised to see him. In fact, Jim Parkes was such a surprising young man that she made it a point never to be surprised by anything he did. So entirely unruffled she accepted the fact that with no hint of an appointment he was calling in the middle of the morning.

"Come in, Jim." She led the way into the parlor.

"You pretty good in Shakespeare, Mrs. Green?"

"No, I'm afraid I'm not, though I have read several of the plays. What made you think of that, Jim?"

"Well," he said, "Professor Baskerville won't talk about anything but Shakespeare. It looks like the professor thinks that while he wrote it himself, he'd sort of like for Shakespeare to have the credit. You ought to hear him say that one about *A tide has taken the affairs of men.* Got me to thinking, too. How does it go, Mrs. Green, after I stopped?"

She smiled her gentle smile. "You had that a little wrong, didn't you, Jim? The way I remember it is: *There is a tide in the affairs of men which, taken at the flood, leads on to fortune . . .*"

"That's it. That's it exactly. Where's Lena May?"

The serenity of her face was not interrupted. "She's baking a cake. She'll be through before long. There's a book on the table."

"*There's a tide . . .* You mind if I go in there where she is, Mrs. Green? I might be some help to her, you know."

"Go on in, Jim. Maybe you could be some help."

"Thank you, Mrs. Green. Looks like any girl would be glad for somebody to quote Shakespeare to her while she bakes a cake. . . *leads on to fortune.* I think Professor Baskerville's got something there, don't you, Mrs. Green?"

She stood, gently smiling, watching him disappear into the kitchen.

Lena May's immunity to surprise by Jim Parkes equaled her mother's. "Good morning, Jim. Have a seat on that stool. Can't shake hands with you." She held out flour-covered hands in explanation.

"Certainly is a fine cake," he said.

"How'd you know? You haven't seen it. It's in the oven."

"That's funny about me. I can see a cake in the oven, just as plain as daylight. There isn't much you can hide from me. You pretty good in Shakespeare, Lena May?"

"I wouldn't think you'd have to ask. What do you want to know that for?"

"It's on account of something I've got on my mind. I wonder if you know that if a tide is taken in the affairs of man and seized . . . I think I've got it wrong."

Lena May was on the verge of being surprised but held herself in control. "We've got a book of Shakespeare. Would you like to see it?"

"No. I never saw a book yet that got its quotations right."

"I have some batter left over. I'll bake a little cake for you if you want it. Mother see you as you came in?"

"Perhaps she did. So many people see me I just can't keep them all in mind. When did you see Neely Barrow?"

"Last Sunday night at McKendree Church."

"She's a Baptist. What was she doing there? Who let her in?"

"I did," said Lena May, peering at the cake within the oven.

"She say anything about Hunt Justice?"

"He was mentioned."

"What a memory that girl has! Why, he's been away from here years and years. You don't suppose she's interested in him, do you? Well, if he is all I can say is that he'd better seize the flood at its tide. What's the matter with me? I don't think I got it right that time."

"I'll go get the book," said Lena May.

"And leave me alone with that cake! Do you know what happened the last time I was left alone with a cake? It fell. I heard it hit."

"Hunt is coming home this summer."

"Let's not tell Neely Barrow. The less girls know the more cakes they bake. What's happened at Cherry Hill? The Roanes got rich or something?"

"Why?"

"Well, I rode by there this morning and they had men working everywhere—some painting the house, some painting the fences, some at work on the roof. I don't know for certain but I think they've dug up forty-one thousand gold doubloons that were buried here when the Irish captured the city."

"Let's have a picnic while Hunt is here."

"I knew if I would just give you time you'd say something with sense in it. Now let's see. Who'd go on it?"

"Why, Neely Barrow and Hunt, and Gordon and Gertrude, and Ivo Burns and Sadie Polk, and Bart Halloran, and . . . maybe some others."

"Haven't seen Bart in a year. First thing Mr. Eugene Lewis did when he moved back to Nashville was to try to hire Bart for the big railroad. That means he's mighty good. But Bart stuck with the new railroad. That means he hasn't got good sense. Never stick to anything little when you can get something big. That's my motto."

"Are you going to have a big printing company, Jim?" she asked demurely.

"Well, anyhow, we're going to have some big type. I'm thinking about that Shakespeare again. You know that's what I came out here for."

Lena May steadfastly refused to indicate surprise. She peeped at the cake. "It's about done. You want me to get that book for you?"

"No. I've got to get it right. Professor Baskerville just can't get Shakespeare off his mind. Yesterday in class he came to that one about tides and affairs. Right there he almost went wild. Got me to thinking, too. It all amounted to, if you don't do a thing you ought to do when you ought to do it you don't get to. So here I am. But I got to get it right. One syllable wrong leaves Professor Baskerville practically wrecked."

"Is it that one in *Julius Caesar* that you are trying to think of, Jim?"

"Caesar? Caesar? Why, that's funny. There was a fellow named Caesar got killed not a half hour before. Why, how'd you know that, Lena May?"

"I think this is the way it goes," said Lena May very serenely: *"There is a tide in the affairs of men which, taken at the flood, leads on to fortune. . . .* Is that it, Jim?"

He looked at her, wide-eyed. If he couldn't surprise the Green family it could certainly surprise him. Suddenly he jumped off the stool and straightened himself to his thin six feet.

"Why, that's it exactly. That's a sign, Lena May. I don't suppose you could have any objection after that, could you?"

"After what, Jim?"

"After helping me out with that Shakespeare. It's a sign, I tell you."

"A sign of what, Jim?"

"That we're going to get married. It's what I been trying to tell you for a year or two."

She took the cake from the oven and set it on the table. "You didn't need a sign from Shakespeare, did you, Jim?"

"You mean you're willing?"

"Of course I am. I thought you understood that all the time."

"I'm not a good understander. There are times when I have to get Shakespeare to help me out. You know what, Lena May?"

"What, Jim?"

"Is there anything in Shakespeare about cake? That would be another sign. Because after we get married, you know what I'm going to eat? Not a thing but cake."

9

Eugene Lewis and Courtney Justice stood on the platform waiting for the two o'clock train to come in. Mrs. Justice had not gone with them to the station.

"I'd rather see him coming in the gate and up the walk like he was coming home from school," she had said.

They had driven away in the Lewis carriage. She moved her rocking chair to the front window and sat as she had so often waiting for the click of the gate. She sat there gently rocking, her eyes filled with memories.

Eugene Lewis and Courtney Justice stood looking down the track and waiting for the blast of the engine sounding for the Cumberland River Bridge.

"I thought Mrs. Justice would want to come to the depot."

"Women is funny," commented Justice. "I've heard her say a dozen times lately that she wants to see him first coming in the gate jest like he was a little feller gettin' back from school."

"Frankly, Mr. Justice, I suspect that Hunt is the main motive for my return to Nashville."

Mr. Justice for a moment looked troubled. The random thought intruded itself that Mr. Lewis might be a bit anxious for the repayment of the money owed him.

"I've been a bit uneasy about the possibility of Hunt's not returning permanently to Nashville. I have had some correspondence with his instructors. I never doubted that his record there would be excellent but it has surprised me. He has developed, they say, into a technician of unusual ability. But even more than that, he has ideas."

Mr. Justice was not able to follow this tribute to his son in its entirety, but he agreed with a series of emphatic nods.

"I have really been disturbed by the possibility that Hunt may prove so good that a larger place may try to get him. I want him in Nashville. There will be some important building here within the next ten years. How long is Hunt going to stay?"

"Two weeks," said Mr. Justice, glad that the conversation had been restored to a state of poise.

"I want to borrow him from you and Mrs. Justice for a whole day. I need him at least that long."

"There it is." Mr. Justice's quick ears had caught the whistle of the train, calling for the bridge.

Within less than a minute the train rattled over the Front Street crossing. Then it swept past them, the brakes screaming against the wheels. The conductor, with Irish nonchalance, swung off the train while it was still in noisy progress. He walked leisurely along with the train timing himself to his proper location when the cars drew to a stop.

"All out for Nashville," he roared, obviously fearing that unless discouraged some of his passengers might attempt to remain on the train. He roared his order in even louder tones. By that time the passengers were coming down the steps, but there was no sight of Hunt.

"You reckon he didn't come?" inquired the anxious father. "It'll tear Lizzie all to pieces. There he is!" His restless eyes had caught through the window the sight of Hunt coming along the aisle, the last in line, because of the heavy valise he bore. The boy came down the steps holding the valise before him braced against his knees.

"Howdy, son. You're a sight for sore eyes," said the father, grabbing the valise with one hand, and shaking his son's vigorously with the other.

"You look fine, Papa. How's Mama?"

"Never better. She's got enough cooked for a basket meetin'. Been starvin' us a month waitin' for you."

But Hunt was being greeted by Eugene Lewis. "Welcome home, Hunt. We're all proud of you."

"Thank you, Mr. Lewis. No one ever had nicer people to come home to." He stood on the platform, an inch taller and correspondingly larger than when he went away. His clothes were plain, but they were neat and fitted him. The boyish look was still on his face but something about him suggested a certain sort of new freedom. The overtones of Lincoln County were in his speech, but there were other overtones that Eugene Lewis knew well.

They walked along the street to the hitching rack by Link's Hotel. There they got into the carriage, drove across to Cherry Street and then westward, dodging the midafternoon traffic, slowing to a walk while an electric streetcar clanged by.

"Ever see one of them contraptions before, son?"

"Yes," said Hunt smiling, "I've even ridden on them."

"Next time I get a little time off I'm goin' to take me a ride on one. People say electricity will ruin a watch in the pocket of a passenger or feller standin' up close. Lots o' fellers leavin' their watches at home now. Anything to that, son? You think it would ruin a watch?"

"I don't think so. If it ruined the watch it would almost ruin the man, too."

"That's about what Ed Crayton said. Well, I'm glad to hear it. I couldn't get along without my watch."

They came to Oak Street. The gravestones gleamed white against a background of summer green. Then they were at the front gate.

"I'll not stop," said Eugene Lewis, "but could I have you next Monday, Hunt? All day?"

Hunt instinctively looked at his father, who was nodding his head very cheerfully.

"Yes, sir, Mr. Lewis, we can spare him by then."

"I'll be around rather early. Happy homecoming." And Eugene Lewis drove away.

Lizzie Justice heard the gate click, and looked up hurriedly from the Bible she was reading. There coming in at the gate was Hunt, her son, a man now. The tears welled into her eyes but she quickly wiped them away. It was against Lizzie Justice's code to shed tears in public. She went out the door and down the front steps. Hunt took four or five giant strides and reached her at the foot of the steps. He took her into his arms. For a while no word was spoken.

"I saw you coming in at the gate first," she said.

"I saw you coming out of the door first, Mama."

She moved back a step. "Let me look at you. Oh, how fine you look!"

Coutney Justice, who had carried the valise on into the house, came back to the porch. "Come on in. You can talk and rest, too, in here."

"I'm not tired. I don't feel like I'd ever be tired again," said Lizzie Justice. They turned to go up on the porch.

"Wait a minute," a voice called. It was Mrs. Elrod, coming across the yard and carrying in her arms a large watermelon. "Bought two off a wagon this morning. This one's for you, Hunt." She put the watermelon on the ground and, hands on hips, stood looking at him.

"You've been a right smart Yankeeized. You think it's really him, Mrs. Justice?"

"I'd know him if I was blind, Mrs. Elrod."

"You have to be careful. Lots o' times nice Southern boys been sent up north and when the Yankees sent 'em back it wasn't the right ones at all. Hunt have any birthmarks or maybe one toe off, Mrs. Justice? Better look."

"Couldn't anybody else come in the gate like he does."

"Well, I guess we'll find out for certain in a day or two. If it really is Hunt I'm goin' to bake him a cake for Sunday. And they's a lot o' questions I want to ask him, too."

"Even if I am a counterfeit I like watermelon. Thank you, Mrs. Elrod."

Mrs. Elrod turned to Courtney Justice. "Better put the watermelon in your cellar. Keeps cooler there." She went on back across the yard.

Mother and father and son sat on the shaded porch and talked. The summer sun slanted toward the west. At intervals trains passed, spreading clamor and smoke among the neighborhoods lying against the tracks. Touched by the sunlight was a faint hint of golden unreality, advance samplings of Indian summer. The fragrance of the harvest was in the air. They sat and talked, and Lizzie Justice's eyes never left her son's face. After a while she stood. "I know you are starved," she said. "I'll get supper ready. It won't take long."

"We'll go with you, Mama. We'll try not to get in the way."

That pleased her since she wished not to miss a syllable spoken by her son. Presently supper was on the table. Lizzie Justice had treasured in her memory all of her son's preferences for food.

"I haven't eaten fried chicken like this since I left home."

"We've got forty chickens now just the right size."

"Pass the gravy," said Hunt. "We got to talking and I almost missed it."

"Courtney, go in and get another plate of biscuits. Do they have good biscuits in Boston?"

"They don't have any. But they have some things that I like very much. They have something they call Indian pudding. . . ."

"How do they make it?"

"To tell you the truth, Mama, I don't know. They start with milk and cornmeal and molasses, but I don't know exactly what they do with them. These beans, Mama, I haven't had any like them. They have green beans up there, but they never taste right. Their fish is better than ours, though."

"You can have snapbeans every time you want them. We have a garden full."

"Been a mighty good season for gardens and crops. We've had more of everything than two families could eat."

"With me here that makes about two families. How have you been, Papa?"

"Haven't missed a day from sickness. Haven't missed a day from anything. I been raised twice since you left, Hunt."

"Mama told me in a letter. I'm proud of you, Papa."

"Oh, you are!" Courtney Justice beamed with pleasure. "We been savin' a little money. Don't owe a red cent to nobody."

They ate vegetables and more fried chicken and hot biscuits and cherry preserves. Lizzie Justice's eyes rarely left her son's face, and a happy light shone in her eyes. She went into the kitchen and came back bearing a deep pan in which was something golden and alluring.

"Peach cobbler!" exclaimed Hunt. "I never saw any in Boston."

They went back into the front room, and Hunt told them of some of his experiences in the College of Architecture. His mother noticed that his eyes would now and then stray to the clock on the mantel.

"Maybe, Hunt, you want to walk around some before bedtime. I guess there are lots of places you'd like to see."

There was gratitude in his answering smile. "Yes, Mama, if you and Papa will excuse me."

His mother went to the gate with him. "She came to see me."

"Yes, Mother, she thinks you are a fine woman. I know you are."

10

He turned in on Cherry Street, and then east on Rutledge. Ahead of him the street lifted its climax in Cherry Hill. The cherry trees were richly green and stood in sturdy consciousness of their own artistry. Then as he drew nearer he saw that the fences stood in fine symmetry and were freshly painted. He lifted his eyes to the house and the wooden parts of it, too, gleamed with virgin whiteness. Everything was clean and neat and trim, and that surprised him, for it was not so when he left.

He saw Neely Barrow standing out by the gate. And at the same moment she saw him. She opened the gate and ran to meet him.

"Hunt," she said, "Hunt, you've come back."

The setting sun poured its glory upon them and there was in the world a sort of holy stillness. Neely Barrow clung to Hunt as if to satisfy all the hunger of those absent months.

"Two years! Hunt, do you know how long two years are? Do you?" There was a touch of fierceness in the question.

"Yes," he said, "I know. Sometimes I've counted the minutes."

"Hunt, don't leave me so long again. Do you know how long it has been?"

Presently they walked up the street toward the house.

"How is your mother?"

"She told me about your coming out to see her. You couldn't have done a grander thing than go to see her."

"Did she like me?"

"So much that she was willing for me to leave her my first night at home. How is your grandfather?"

"Grandy has been very excited for weeks now. We're painting and overhauling and repairing Cherry Hill and while he's excited I think he's happier than I ever saw him."

"I saw it when I first came in sight of the place." He looked about him. "It was beautiful before, but it is much more so now. Whoever placed that house, whoever built it, had an almost perfect sense of fitness, of proportion, of unity. I've thought about Cherry Hill often. It has helped me to think about it."

"How has it helped you, Hunt?"

"It has been for me a sort of standard, a measure. And then because you were here . . . In my mind I'd see it and you would come between those columns and out on the walk."

"Ionic columns," she whispered.

"Yes, somehow you and Ionic columns go together. All true columns are beautiful but Ionic most of all. The Doric is severe, a bit sad, and the Corinthian a bit boastful. But the Ionic is graceful and modest. The Ionic seems to say: *There are generations of culture and breeding behind me.*" He stood looking at the house, his eyes bright. His voice when he spoke was vibrant but in the monotone of one who recites the routine of his craft. "*Twin chimneys at either end tied together with a brick parapet above the roof-ridge line. An entrance impressive and graceful. A two-storied projecting portico with four lovely Ionic columns supporting a pediment of the same order. The façades and the gable treatments extraordinarily interesting.* In my visions, dear, Cherry Hill has always stood in the background with you coming out between the Ionic columns and down the walk."

"Hunt, you are home again! Back with me!"

He smiled. "Don't you think, Neely Barrow, that I should see your grandfather?"

"You must see him, but he's not here. This is the night for his beloved Old Table Club, and this time he was really glad to go. Now that Cherry Hill is more like it used to be he is once more eager to be with his old friends. Let's sit down, Hunt."

There were chairs on the lawn, and they sat facing the city. To their right the Cumberland River skirted the bluffs. To their left the early evening traffic was moving out Market Street to Lafayette, out Lafayette to the Murfreesboro Pike. It was a favored drive for those who owned carriages, and their intermittent rattle sounded clear and near. There was still enough light to see in vague outline the Capitol, the Lantern of Demosthenes lifting high into the summer air. Then the tolling of a church bell was heard, its tones quiet, and sweet and a little sad.

"Hunt, you have two solid years to tell me about. You'd better start now. Two years, Hunt!"

"Before I begin there are a few arrangements I'd like to have settled. Next Tuesday morning I'd like for you to go up to the Capitol with me. I want to look at it inside and out and I want you to be along."

"Listen," said Neely Barrow, "I'm learning to cook. I'll fix some things to eat. It would be fun to have our dinner up there. Of course, I'll go."

"And in the afternoon I want you to go with me to see Mrs. Polk. She is one of the best friends I ever had."

"Mrs. Polk is one of the best friends I ever had, and I'm going to see her that afternoon, and if you'd like to go along I guess I could arrange it."

"Then I'm going to see Miss Julia Sears and Professor Smack Me Down Clark both Wednesday afternoon."

"I'll show you the way! That's when I am going."

"And my mother said to ask you to come to our house to dinner the Sunday before I go back."

"She's sweet. Of course I'll come. You haven't heard anything of a picnic, have you?"

"No. What about a picnic?"

"I think there's to be one. Gordon Hicks or Jim Parkes will tell you about it. You hadn't heard about Jim and Lena May, had you?"

"I haven't heard of anything."

"Well, they're going to be married."

"I'll look surprised if you think I should, but it will be somewhat of a strain."

"That's not very nice, Hunt. When they tell you, you act surprised. Say, 'Why, that's the last thing on earth I was expecting,' or something like that. You must learn to be polite, Hunt! And, oh yes, Lena May said she wasn't surprised at all when Jim popped the question, but the way he popped it, she said, was the biggest surprise she ever had. She said she'd tell me sometime."

How quiet it was at Cherry Hill, how gentle the air of that summer evening! In the town below the street lights were coming on one by one. The night itself was as a benediction said for lovers. Hunt rose and came over to her chair.

"Neely Barrow," he said softly, "will you marry me?"

"I have known I would since that day at the Capitol."

He took her in his arms and kissed her gently. When presently Neely Barrow spoke her voice was very tender, but she said lightly, "Now tell me about Boston. Start at the beginning."

He was still talking when somewhere downtown a clock struck nine. He stood. "I'll tell you the rest of it the next time. I must go home now."

"I want to see you every day you are here, Hunt. Even if it's for only ten minutes."

"Neely Barrow, I must say something. I have just got to say it. I want to marry you more than I want anything in the world, but . . ."

"Yes, I know," she interrupted him. "Not until you've proved yourself worthy. That's it, isn't it, Hunt?"

"Yes," he said, "that's it. It's been in my mind a long time. I'm not good enough for you, Neely Barrow. I know I'm not, but I intend to be."

She interrupted him again. "I think you're the stupidest person I ever saw, but I love you for it. If you weren't so stupid you wouldn't be Hunt Justice and I wouldn't care for you at all. What is it you're going to do to prove worthy of me?"

"I don't know what. Something that I do myself that's important, that's worth doing. If, for instance, I can plan and build a house that is as good and beautiful as Cherry Hill, I'll know that's a sign of—well, of my worthiness."

"You become more foolish every minute, and I love you more. I don't think we'll have so long to wait, Hunt."

"I must go now," he said hoarsely. "I'll come tomorrow evening."

"I'll be waiting."

Again he took her in his arms. A lazy summer breeze stirred among the trees of Cherry Hill. Somewhere in the distance a whippoorwill distilled the soft melancholy of the night into its song.

11

On Monday morning Hunt sat in Eugene Lewis's office, and turned the pages of an exciting book. It bore the title *The Great Buildings of Ancient Greece.* Eugene Lewis had excused himself from Hunt and gone on into the Director's room. Some men were already there. Presently they arranged themselves about the table.

"Gentlemen," Eugene Lewis said, "before we begin the consideration of our business, I should like your permission to include a young friend of mine, Hunt Justice, in our conference. Hunt has been for two years in Massachusetts Institute of Technology as a student in Architecture. He has been helping Professor Letang on the buildings for the Chicago Exposition during the present vacation. I should like very much—of course, with your permission— for him to meet with us."

"Bring him in," said John Thomas in his brusque and hearty way. "If he can build a world's fair we need him."

So Hunt was brought in and introduced to all the men about the table. Then they were seated, and Eugene Lewis was speaking. "In a few short years Tennessee will be a century old. And such a hundred years! What an incredible variety of Tennesseans have marched across that century! Pardon me, I have no intention of making a speech. The question before us is simply this, shall we permit our hundredth birthday to come and go and make no more than a perfunctory gesture, no more than a mere address by you, Dr. Dudley, as good as your addresses are?"

"I sometimes get around to the point," observed the professor dryly. "What is yours, Eugene?"

"A centennial exposition. Our first century brought into epitome!"

"I'm for it," said Gideon Baskette. "It would be manna to any newspaper."

"I'm for it, of course," said H. W. Buttorff, "but as a business-man I'd like to know where the money is coming from."

"We can get the money, gentlemen. It will not be easy but we can get it. The question to answer first is, do we want to do it? It will mean for us three years of hard work—I think that long at least."

"I'll take your word for it," said Van Kirkman. "I can give three years of time."

"Count me in," said L. D. Fite. "I'm not a young man but I fancy I have three good years left."

"And me," said John Sperry. The assents went the round of the table.

"Well, let's get started," said Ed Barthell. "I move that we hold the Tennessee Centennial, and that each man present entrusts the direction of his life for three or more years into the hands of Mr. Simon Legree Lewis."

John Thomas stood. "I'll take the vote. The *aye's* have it. We will have the Tennessee Centennial. Eugene, accept the Centennial and us, and let's get to work."

"All right. I want us first to decide at least tentatively a location for the Centennial."

"A moment, please, Mr. Director General," said Dr. Dudley very suavely. "As a matter of fact, haven't you already decided upon a location?"

"As a matter of fact, I have. I merely wished you to commend me for it. The site is West End Driving Park. I have canvassed every available tract of land in the community, and from every standpoint this is much the best. . . ."

"I move the acceptance of the site and that we empower the Director General to make due arrangement for its use," said Samuel Keith.

"Passed," said John Thomas.

"Thanks," said the Director General dryly. "Someday I hope to propose something that will cause enough discord for me to finish my address. I shall presently appoint a committee to see that your commands as to the site are duly executed.

"Now in order to fix our thinking somewhat, let's talk about the proper complement of buildings for the Centennial. . . ."

"*Complement!*" exclaimed Dr. Dudley. "A college professor might use that word fittingly, but not a railroad man."

"I am not a railroad man. I'm a Director General and I was speaking of the buildings. Let me mention a few merely to raise them for consideration. We will need an auditorium for addresses, for the presentation of opera or of plays, for band concerts on rainy evenings and for more purposes than I can guess just now. We will need a Commerce Building in which to present in vivid miniature the state's enterprise in buying and selling. Our state is mainly agricultural. We shall need an Agriculture Building, to give representation and dignity to the way by which most of our people live. Transportation is becoming increasingly important. We shall need a building to indicate our achievement and to forecast our future in modes of travel. . . ."

"How about the Streets of Cairo?" asked Clay Evans, winking broadly at his colleagues.

Eugene Lewis ignored his flippancy. "From 1854 until now we have not had built in Nashville a single distinguished home. Some lately have been hopeful, but no more than that. That is not true of Nashville alone, but all of Tennessee—perhaps all of the nation. Can't we make our main buildings—whatever their use—fine enough to start people thinking in such terms? We'll have the Streets of Cairo, and the Streets of Bagdad and the Streets of Paris, but we'll have them hidden, banked off from the main buildings so as not to violate the impression which we hope to establish. And then in the center, and as the chief glory of all, a building which will make the Centennial one of our people's great associations with beauty. If I sound a bit grandiose that's precisely how I feel. I've been groping for such a building for weeks. I haven't yet found it."

"A reproduction of the Hermitage," said Alfred Howell.

"I've thought of that. The real Hermitage is less than a dozen miles away. A great many of our visitors to the city will wish to see the original. Some interesting improvements are going on out there now. A reproduction here would but dim the glory of the original. There are special reasons now for that not to be done. Besides, the building I have in mind should be better established in the culture of men than is the Hermitage, as fine as it is."

"A replica of the *Mayflower*," said John McCann.

"A curious suggestion from a Scotch-Irishman, who doesn't know the name of the vessel in which his ancestors arrived in Philadelphia. The *Mayflower* was a very worthy boat indeed, but it doesn't fit the notion I have."

John Sperry suggested a great tower with a clock and chimes that played at sunset, but the questing look was still in Eugene Lewis's eyes. He turned to Hunt Justice.

"You perhaps, Hunt, have had more connection with great buildings than any of us. Do you have any ideas? You wouldn't suggest the Massachusetts State House, would you?" he asked with a touch of lightness.

"No, sir," said Hunt very clearly, "but—" He hesitated.

"But what?"

"The Parthenon, sir."

Eugene Lewis's hands dropped to his sides as if he were stricken. "My God! That's what I have been looking for for weeks, and too blind to see it right before my nose."

"The Parthenon?" asked Tully Brown. "What's the Parthenon?"

"There's a touch of Fate in this. I think I would have asked the same question if Hunt hadn't once told me. Tell these gentlemen about the Parthenon, Hunt."

Hunt sensed the parliamentary amenity of the moment and looked instinctively at J. W. Thomas. Thomas caught the look and said, "Go ahead. If the Par—Par—whatever it is—interests Eugene Lewis that much I'd like to know what it is myself."

Hunt told them about the Parthenon—about its history, about its Doric beauty without, and its Ionic beauty within. "It was one time," he said, "when men did their best, gave all they had. And there's another matter. Nashville is called *the Athens of the South*. I've read it in Northern papers and it made me feel very proud. But this building would give much more meaning to that phrase. It would really connect Nashville with Athens in its greatest period. . . ."

"But I'm a businessman," said H. W. Buttorff. "Wouldn't the cost be prohibitive?"

"I'll answer that," said Eugene Lewis, speaking with some sharpness. "We are not haggling over pennies. The Parthenon I do believe is the greatest notion one ever had in connection with an exposition. The idea grows upon me. It's epic, I tell you. We'll get the money. I can see it now."

"You mean the money?"

"No!" roared Eugene Lewis. "I mean the Parthenon. Of course, we'll build it. We'll group everything about it—that is, everything except the Streets of Cairo, and we'll move them still farther away. I tell you, it's what I've been looking for ever since the project has been in my mind. Let your frugal soul relax, friend Buttorff. I'll guarantee the money. Excuse me, Hunt. I interrupted you."

"The cost would be considerable for a permanent building," said Hunt. "The building is really enormous. But it could be composed of temporary materials and still give an authentic appearance."

"Wait a minute," interrupted J. W. Thomas. "Suppose we build this Par—what you call it. How do we know another one won't bob up in Seattle or Providence or some such place?"

"The Parthenon has never been reproduced." There was an impressive finality in Hunt Justice's words.

"You sure of that?" persisted Thomas.

"Perhaps models have been made. The building has not been reproduced."

"What use could be made of the interior?" asked James Demoville.

"I do not know, sir. That would have to be considered very carefully. The Parthenon was a temple and nothing should be done, of course, which would violate that fact."

"I am a far happier man than I've been in months," said Eugene Lewis. "Something better seems to be evolving slowly. The Hermitage is evolving; the Capitol is being dressed up. I was by Cherry Hill yesterday and it seems to have grasped again its old greatness. Now this . . ." He paused a moment, then continued. "There are a great many preliminary demands to be arranged in our program. I shall set to work tomorrow. I want you lawyers to help with the legal details. We will have to get somehow a great deal of money. I suppose that means the issuance of bonds, and that means some more free help from you lawyers and some expert counsel from you businessmen who go through life asking where the money is coming from. Then other states and communities will wish to have part in the Centennial. I happen to know that Ohio has made tentative inquiries. All right, gentlemen, I leave my railroad oxen standing in the furrow. The railroad has granted me relief for such time as may be required for duties as important as this. I am assured that my salary will remain unchanged. Therefore, anything I may do for the Centennial will cost it exactly nothing. I'm depending on all of you. As you drive along the street today stop and look at the Capitol. Look at it long enough to get a true glimpse of its beauty. If you can, drive out to the Hermitage. The ladies have in a few short months taken away the lost look that was about the home. It is on its way back to its greatness. Drive by Cherry Hill. Its improvement is amazing. Drive by Belmont. It was becoming disheveled and shabby. But a college has taken it over and it will be rescued."

"I should like to ask a question, Mr. Commissioner General," said Dr. Dudley. "Would it not be necessary, at least as a matter of good manners, for us to secure permission from the city of Athens to reproduce the Parthenon?"

"It would," said Eugene Lewis. "I'll take the responsibility for the permission."

"I'd like to see a picture of the Parthenon," said Lewis Baxter. "Is one available?"

"I know where there's one," said Hunt Justice rising. "May I get it, sir?"

"You mean your old Latin book?" inquired Eugene Lewis.

"No, it's in your office. I saw it a while ago."

"Certainly. Go get it, please."

Hunt came back with *The Great Buildings of Ancient Greece*. The book, opened at the Parthenon, went the rounds.

"Very beautiful, indeed," said Dr. Dudley. He nodded to Hunt. "Would you mind telling us again about this building, particularly in what esteem it is held by the great critics of architecture?"

"They would, I think without exception, call it the world's most beautiful building in respect to symmetry and simple dignity."

"Son," said H. W. Buttorff, lifting his eyes from the book, "you've sold me a house, and," he added, "I'm a hard man to sell a house."

"Wouldn't you like to know where the money is coming from?" asked Ed Barthel.

"I like the looks of this house, Ed."

12

Hunt Justice leaned back against the plush upholstery of the car seat and closed his eyes. The train was toiling up the ridge toward Twin Tunnels and the engine was laboring like a tired horse. The car window offered a varied panorama of harvest color, and the fringes of the fields and right of way gleamed with goldenrod. The blue haze that during the summer had clung to the distant hills had drawn closer. But of none of those things was Hunt Justice conscious, for he was recreating in his mind's eye and ear that precious period which had ended but little more than an hour before. He was still thrilled by the Monday he had spent with Mr. Lewis. They had eaten royally at the Maxwell House as the guests of Mr. Buttorff. The dinner had been fine, and Hunt smiled dimly as he recalled how some of the guests jested with their host as to where the money would come from to pay for their food, and some complained that their host being the sort of man he was they'd not order further but go through the rest of the day all but famished. But they had talked frequently about the Parthenon. It warmed Hunt to remember that most of them seemed a bit excited by the prospect.

After the dinner was finished each man had shaken hands most cordially with him with some kindly personal reference to his contribution to their preparation for the Centennial. Eugene Lewis had held him for a moment after the others had left.

"Your day isn't over, Hunt. You remember that I asked for you all day."

"It's been very pleasant so far."

"I want you to go with me out to West End Park. I need some help out there."

So they had driven to the park and there had spent the afternoon. Eugene Lewis had a plot of the area upon which throughout the afternoon he wrote cryptic symbols.

"There," Hunt had said, pointing, "is the place for the Streets of Cairo."

"My thought precisely. Why do you think so?"

"It is the most removed part of the entire area. Those who want to go can do so without much trouble. Those who do not care for the Streets will not have even to *pass them* to get to the other attractions."

They agreed upon the main entrance near the convergence of Church and West End.

"The Parthenon," Hunt had said, "should be somewhere about there. There it would dominate the whole scene best."

"The original Parthenon stood on a high hill, didn't it?"

"I've been thinking of that. What about that hill yonder?"

"No," Eugene Lewis had said emphatically. "That's a separate tract of land. Besides if it were built up there our people would take a distant look at it and say 'How magnificent!' but they wouldn't climb the hill for a visit to it. I want it where people will see it at close range, walk between its columns, meet their friends on the porch, absorb its beauty and so ultimately translate its beauty into other beauty."

Hunt was vaguely conscious that the train was stopping. He glanced idly out the window, and noted that the station was Portland. He sank back against the seat and closed his eyes. Then he was at the Capitol with Neely Barrow. They had gone with systematic care to all parts of the building while he wrote copious and rapid notes in a book he carried. He had been surprised by the keen observations Neely Barrow made and sometimes she had called his attention to something worthy of space in his notebook.

They had climbed the Lantern of Demosthenes, and had used an hour looking from the parapet walls out at the countryside stretching for miles in every direction.

"Oh," said Neely Barrow. "There's Cherry Hill." It fitted among the trees as if nature in a special burst of benevolence had placed it there. They had tried to find Hunt's home, but Oak Street lay behind a hill. But they had found the Academy, and Peabody College, and Vanderbilt and Polk Place, and several churches. Presently they went back down into the main building and there retrieved the package of food which Neely Barrow had prepared. Then they went out on the grounds and sat on a bench and ate the food.

After a while they went down the hill and in a few minutes were sounding the knocker at Polk Place. They were shown into the library and a few minutes later Mrs. Polk came in. She held out a hand to each.

"My dear children, God is good. Two of my best and youngest friends. And together! Do you mind if we sit down? No, don't you sit yet, Hunt. I want to look at you. How fine you are! I must compliment the Yankees. They've done well by you."

"Don't you suppose, Mrs. Polk, that Hunt has been a fine influence for the Yankees?"

"Oh, without doubt, Neely Barrow, I have no doubt that some of them have been greatly altered. But look at him. They deserve some credit. Sit down, Hunt. Now, let me hear you."

Hunt had told all over again—as he had told his parents, as he had told Neely Barrow, as he had told Eugene Lewis—the story of his experiences in the Massachusetts Institute of Technology, and with Professor Letang at Chicago. They had sat there in the library until the afternoon was almost used up. Neely Barrow did not want Mrs. Polk to miss anything, and time after time she prompted him as to some episode or byplay so that Mrs. Polk could hear the whole story. The clock had struck five. Then Neely Barrow stood and Hunt followed.

"I have always known the length of my years," Mrs. Polk had said. "Even so, I never knew that I was getting old till a very few years ago. I suppose I thought I could evade the wear and tear of time, but I have been failing, slipping back, growing more infirm. I think now I know why."

"Yes, Mrs. Polk?"

"I have not lately been enough with the young. Once they were my daily companions. Their hopes entered into me, and my mind was active with their problems. And so by some subtle and blessed alchemy their youth and vigor were transfused into me. Lately, the word has got out that I am old, and the old come to see me and we pool our oldness. That gives each one an added increment of age. Right now, I feel younger than I have for months. Neely Barrow, you have neglected me lately."

"I will not any more. I need you, Mrs. Polk. I feel wiser than I have for months."

"You need wisdom and I need youth. We'll get together often and make the exchange. Most delightful! Hunt, I haven't told you but Eugene Lewis came to see me last night."

"Did he tell you about yesterday?"

"As graphic an account as I have ever heard made of a day. Perfectly thrilling! Let no one tell me I had no prophetic glimpse that day when a small boy stood in my front yard and looked at Polk Place as one does who sees a vision. I'll warrant that within a month the Parthenon will be more than a word from the mists of antiquity to the people of Nashville. You'll forgive me, Hunt, if now and then with a considerable show of pride I say to someone— *a discovery of mine.* You see, I antedate even Neely Barrow."

Hunt felt the train losing speed and presently it stopped. He turned his eyes idly, half-seeingly upon the station without. It was Franklin. He saw the conductor shaking hands with a gentleman standing on the platform. The conductor was using his right hand in the rites of friendship, while in his left he held a watch. One eye he kept on his friend, and the other alternated between the watch and some packages which were being unloaded from the express car. Suddenly his hearty Irish voice enveloped every nook and cranny of the dingy station. "All abo-o-o-rd!" And the train was moving again. Again the sequence of recent events flowed across the screen of Hunt's inner vision. There was the trip to Kingsley. Merrie and Weaver Cole had sent the driver with the carriage for Neely Barrow and him. The driver sang every song about Yankees he could remember, chuckling between verses and watching Hunt with a sly eye. A horsefly swooped down, settled and bored for blood. The driver's whip cracked sharply, and the horsefly feasted no longer.

He winked broadly at Neely Barrow. "I hear it ain't so bad in Boston, ma'am. They say they's fellers there got right good sense."

The memory of the hours at Kingsley left Hunt warmed.

Neely Barrow had invited him to Cherry Hill for supper which in most part she had prepared herself. The food was good but the meal, in fact the whole evening, had been for Hunt a definite strain. It plainly had been a strain for Erwin Roane, too. He had watched Hunt closely. Plainly he was puzzled. Sometimes his eyes were kindly, for he could find no flaw in Hunt's behavior or poise. Sometimes his eyes were cool and remote, for he could not escape long from the consciousness that Hunt was a commoner. Hunt had known what he was thinking. There were statements which Hunt had expected to make to Neely Barrow's grandfather, but he couldn't make them. Neely Barrow's mind had played actively between the two men. With skill she directed the conversation, holding back here, pushing on there, raising little issues skillfully devised to evoke both men to their best. But Neely Barrow was under strain, too, and her eyes for all their brightness were a bit wounded. Toward the end of the evening a turn for the better had developed somewhat surprisingly.

"Why did you go North to school?" Erwin Roane had asked. "Are there no colleges of architecture in the South?"

"No, sir. Mr. Eugene Lewis suggested the Boston college, sir."

"Are you given a fair chance? The Yankees have never been very tolerant of us."

"In a class with Professor Winslow we were required to do a sketch of a home from memory. I made one of Cherry Hill. He chose it as the best of the class, and it has been on one of the display boards in his room for over a year."

"Indeed!"

"He has asked me a great many questions about Cherry Hill. He claims that the Southern Colonial—he means, of course, the Southern Greek revival—is America's most beautiful home."

"Oh, indeed." The eyes were kindly again. But the gap was still there and Hunt could not cross it.

It was much pleasanter to recreate the day he went to Cherry Hill for Neely Barrow and took her out to the house on Oak Street. His memories of that were pleasing. His father's appearance was the result of a great deal of care and effort. His wife had remarked favorably upon it.

"Well, I ought to look good after four hours' primpin'."

That was before Hunt had come with Neely Barrow. It was the first time that she and his father had seen each other. Very obviously he was for her a brand-new specimen and her eyes would leave him only reluctantly. He was vocal with statements of good cheer. The world, always in his high favor, had added recent and notable areas to its substance and charm. Then he would move an alleviating finger around his neck and offer the humorous suggestion to his wife that if she really wished to cut his throat she should use a butcher knife and not a collar starched like that one.

He fascinated Neely Barrow and she rarely took her eyes away from him. Cherry Hill had never been a cheerful place, and good cheer was a quality for which she instinctively yearned. Courtney Justice was for her a new experience, but she understood Hunt's mother. There was so much kinship between Hunt and his mother that understanding came easy. It was also easy to expand the affection she had for Hunt to include his mother.

"How did you get along making that cake?" his mother was asking.

Then, the picture changed, moved back a few hours, and Hunt and his parents were seated in the Central Baptist Church. A great many people had looked at Hunt with interest that morning as he came with his parents down the church aisle, for the word was out, not unconnected with certain proud statements made casually by Courtney Justice, that his son was exercising influence upon just about every building of importance under construction in the country. Pastor Lofton referred in his sermon to his great pleasure at having "one in our midst ordained to build temples."

Sometimes it seemed to Lizzie Justice that her husband went to church mainly to shake hands. On that morning Courtney was a trifle surprised to find the initiative in handshaking wrested from him. The brethren and sisters bore down upon him en masse. They shook hands with Courtney and Mrs. Justice, but their eyes were upon Hunt, and there was an appreciable lengthening of their handclasp when they reached him. There was a flush upon Hunt's face as he recreated the morning at the Central Baptist Church.

The train was stopping again. Hunt glanced out and noted the sign "Bowling Green" swung across the front of a long narrow station. Several boarded the train. A tall youth, of slight build and patrician face, came down the aisle, swinging before him a large valise. He saw the vacant seat by Hunt and courteously asked if he might sit there. Hunt nodded absently, for a part of him was still at the Central Baptist Church. The newcomer adjusted his valise and relaxed against the cushions. The conductor came down the aisle and held out his hand for the thin young man's ticket. "Virginia-bound, son? You keep an eye on them Virginians."

"Why?" asked the young traveler, somewhat stiffly.

"They're funny people. Yes sir, got to watch 'em. They got 'Piscopalians for engineers, and Presbyterians for conductors." His laugh was homeric.

"My ancestors came from Virginia."

"Don't take it too hard, son. You stick to Kentucky and maybe you can live it down." He passed on down the aisle, his sides quivering with mirth. The Virginia-bound young man opened a book and began to read.

Hunt was remembering the night before. How incredibly lovely was Cherry Hill! It lifted gently back from the street, and a four-day-old moon laid its silver fingers with tender grace upon the Ionic columns. How incredibly lovely was Neely Barrow, standing at the gate, her hand lifted in a good-by salute, the moonlight kindling dim glints in her hair.

The pictures were deeply satisfying, but now there was cast upon the screen one picture from which he flinched. He had gone unexpectedly the day before into a room in which his mother stood. Upon her face was the haggard and drawn look of one in pain.

"Mother, what is it?"

She started; her hand grasped the back of the chair as if for support. Then the look was gone.

"Mama, what is it? Are you sick, Mama?"

"No, no. I am not sick."

But he kept asking her, for that ashen haggard look had troubled him.

"Listen, Hunt, I'm not sick. Maybe I got to thinking about you leaving tomorrow. But even if I was sick I'd be the happiest woman in the world. I wanted my son to be somebody. And he is! When we moved to Nashville, Hunt, I didn't much want to come. Now I know the Lord sent us. Looks like everything has turned out right. I never thought Courtney would work as steady as he does, and he's been mighty good to me. Everything's all right, Hunt. You write to me as often as you can."

The conductor paused on his rounds. "You going to Virginia on a visit, son?"

"No."

The conductor regarded him critically. "You might be a preacher, but . . ." He paused on a dubious note.

"I'm going to the University of Virginia to study law."

"Goin' to be a lawyer, huh! Well, the railroad needs a good one right now to prove that scrub cow Number 8 killed at Bristow yesterday wasn't a pure-blood champeen Jersey and worth her weight in solid gold. We killin' a lot o' them pure-blood scrubs lately and when you get back maybe we can use you." He pointed to Hunt. "Funny, ain't it? He's goin' to Boston. As fur as I know he's the first feller to go to Boston sence before the Civil War, though why anybody ever went there. . . . You not going to be a lawyer, too?"

"I hadn't thought to," said Hunt smiling. "I could change, you know."

"There's money in it. My second cousin salts down a wad o' cash every year. Besides if you work for the railroad company you get a free pass anywhere you want to go." He broke off with a shout which for audibility vied with the whistle of the train then sounding. "Horse Cave, Horse Cave! All off for Horse Cave."

The Virginia-bound young man smiled gravely and extended his hand to his seat mate. "I'm John Rodes from Bowling Green."

"I'm Hunt Justice from Nashville."

"May I ask if you are going to Boston to attend school—Harvard perhaps?"

"No, I'm going to the Massachusetts Institute of Technology."

"Sounds impressive. I don't believe I know of it. What do you study there?"

"Architecture."

"Indeed. I was under the impression that one learned architecture by working on the job."

"Most architects have."

"Excuse me, but why do you spend a great amount of money learning something you . . ."

"Excuse me, but the University of Virginia doesn't offer training for the scrub-cow cases, does it?"

The conductor passed again and stopped for a brief display of repartee. "If I was as pore and hungry as some o' them cows I'd get out in front o' Number 8, too. You study up on scrub cows, son. Maybe the railroad can use you."

"He's studying building," John Rodes said, gesturing toward Hunt. "Do you suppose the railroad could use him, too?"

"Buildin', huh? You mean layin' tracks and things like that? You mean he's goin' clear to Boston for a p'fessor to show him how to spread rock? I got a nephew who ain't wiped his back on no college wall but you ought to see Bart Halloran put track down."

"Bart Halloran?"

"You from Nashville, maybe you heard o' him. He's my nephew. When he lays track it stays laid where he lays it. But he don't know no more about a college than a hummin' bird."

"I know Bart. I went on a picnic with him Saturday."

"You out picnickin' with Bart? How'd you know him?"

"We went to the Academy together. He gave me a thrashing once."

"He did! Well, ain't that just like him! You didn't say nothin' agin the railroad company, I hope."

"Positively, not a word." Hunt went into some details.

"Oh! when you was both little." A tinge of disappointment showed in Conductor Halloran's voice. But he rallied. "It's agin the rules but anytime you two want to stand on the back platform I'll unlock the door. Soon as we get by E-town and through the tunnel I'll let you out on the back platform. Goin' down Muldraugh's Ridge is the purtiest sight you ever set your eyes on. It's agin the rules to let passengers out there. But if you been out picnickin' with Bart you got rights on this railroad."

13

On a raw cold day in February Mrs. Elrod went across the yard to the Justice home. She rattled the doorknob and then opened the door and went inside. She called out loudly the moment she was inside. Something about the answer made her uneasy, and her uneasiness grew into terror when her eyes fell on Mrs. Justice, standing by the window, gripping hard the scrolled timbers of the bed, her face twisted and drawn in pain.

"What is it? You sick?"

"Yes, Mrs. Elrod, I'm sick. I don't feel well at all."

"Don't stand there, set down. You ought to be in bed. What's the trouble, Mrs. Justice?"

"I don't know. I've had a terrible pain off and on for a long time. I had it a little when Hunt was at home, but I didn't say anything about it. I didn't want to trouble him."

Mrs. Elrod expertly maneuvered Mrs. Justice into bed. "Your husband know you are sick?"

"He knows I don't feel well. He wanted two or three times to send for a doctor, but I thought I'd be getting better."

"Well, you're goin' to have a doctor this time," said Mrs. Elrod grimly.

Fright showed in Mrs. Justice's eyes. "You think I'm much sick?"

"You're not much well. You got any choice as to doctors? I'm goin' to get one."

"Wait till Courtney gets home."

"He's goin' to get home right away. I'm goin' after him."

Mrs. Justice objected, but that ashen drawn look on her face had brought Mrs. Elrod to a firm decision. She went for Courtney Justice, and he, frightened, came home immediately.

"She hasn't been well since last fall but I didn't think it was anything serious."

"Maybe it isn't, but we goin' to see. If I had the sense of a goose I'd 'a' noticed it before now."

So Doctor Billy Rhett came, and his face was grave from the first glimpse of the face that lay so gray against the pillow. It grew graver as he sat by the bedside.

"Am I . . . ?" Lizzie Justice couldn't finish the question.

"A pretty sick lady," he said cheerfully, "and—" his eyes moved about the room—"if I'm to be trusted as a judge, a first-rate house-keeper. We'll do what we can, and so must you."

"What—what do you want me to do?" The inquiry was made in a whisper.

"I think, madam, that about all required of you is to rest all you can and to let your mind dwell upon pleasant things. Do you have children?"

"A son."

"Think of him. Such thoughts are the medicine God prescribed." He stopped regarding her curiously. His gaze wandered to Courtney Justice, then back to her. "Is your son by any chance named Hunt Justice?"

"Yes, sir."

"That's his name," added her husband.

"Good heavens! If he's half as fine as I've heard you have more blessings than you can consider. Mrs. Justice, I want you to take one of these tablets every three or four hours as long as they last. Eat everything you can, especially eggs and meat. Drink all the milk you can. And think of your son all you can. He's worth thinking about."

Her eyes were brighter. "I don't want much to eat but I'll try. I don't have to stay in bed all the time, do I?"

"No, sit up some when you feel like it but not too long. My compliments, Mrs. Justice. Only a strong woman could bear the son Mrs. Polk described to me. Well, *palmam qui meruit ferat.*"

His eyes signaled for Mrs. Elrod and Courtney Justice to follow him. On the porch he talked with them.

"How long has she been like this?" he asked Courtney Justice.

"She never was a woman to take on much. She's been lookin' bad sence before Christmas, and I knowed sometimes they was something hurtin' her but she never complained. She got breakfast this morning. Is she bad sick, doctor?"

"Yes," said the physician. "I'm very much afraid she is. I don't know anything to do except to make her as comfortable as you can and wait."

"I'll take care of her," said Mrs. Elrod.

Neely Barrow went into the library where her grandfather sat reading the *American.* She had in her hand a small valise. "Grandy, Hunt's mother is dreadfully ill. Jim Parkes came by to tell me. I'm going out there and if they need me I won't be back tonight."

He looked at her without understanding. "What did you say, Neely Barrow?"

She told him again. "You understand, don't you, Grandy?"

"Is he there?"

"No, but Jim said Dr. Rhett told them to send for him."

He stood looking at her. "There has been no change, Neely Barrow? Do you—does the connection between you still exist?"

"Yes, Grandy."

He was silent again, his eyes turned toward her, but remote, fixed upon far horizons. "Neely Barrow, will you sit down a moment? Thank you, dear. I do not wish to trouble you. I have no greater wish than for your happiness. But I couldn't stand it for you to make a mistake. I've been depending on you to regain what I have lost. If you should fail me I'd be wretched even in my grave."

"No, no, Grandy . . ."

"I've never done anything evil in my life, but I have never done anything good, either. Somehow I've been blocked. Something happened inside me. It needn't have happened but I let it get started and I didn't stop it and then it hardened. I have been like a man in sight of the promised land, but powerless, paralyzed. You are my hope, child. If ever I should have a great-grandson I want him to take up the strength I laid down, to be what I yearned to be but never have . . ."

"Please, Grandy . . ."

"I do not dislike Hunt. I thought he was rather likable the times I've seen him. You are my hope, Neely Barrow, you and your children. I find in you the qualities lost in me, lost in your father . . ."

"Please, Grandy . . ."

"The one you choose must be your equal. I couldn't stand it if he isn't."

"Listen, Grandy, Hunt is my equal. You know he is. You tried to find that he isn't. I saw you; but you failed, and it puzzled you. You have been puzzled ever since. You have never heard of his family. His father is a common carpenter. They live in a plain little house across from the graveyard. How could he be our equal? You couldn't make it out. Well, he is my equal. Ask Mrs. Polk if he's not—ask Major Eugene Lewis, ask Mr. Weaver Cole, ask Professor Clark—no, don't ask them. You know he is. You watched him and you couldn't find a thing wrong with him. And you couldn't understand it. . . ."

"Please, Neely Barrow, let me say something. You are no longer a girl. You're a young lady. You have grown beyond my control. Make sure. You can't afford a mistake. I can't afford for you to make one."

The tears showed in her eyes. "I'll not make a mistake. I must go now, Grandy." Then her face brightened with a smile that shone through her tears. "It's going to be all right for all of us. I know it is. I'll be home just as soon as I can."

The driver hitched his horses to the rack at the side of the Link Hotel. It was cold and dark, and he rubbed his hands together and stamped his feet upon the flagstones as he walked to the railroad station. Merrie Cole had taken some things to the Justice home the day before and while there had promised Neely Barrow to send the carriage to meet Hunt the next morning. That was a relief to Neely Barrow who flinched from the prospect of Hunt coming into Nashville and riding a hack out to the home on Oak Street where his mother lay dying, dead for all he would know. For Mrs. Justice was dying. Dr. Rhett had told them so.

"Life is the very stuff of mystery. I deal daily in it—its incoming, its remaining and its outgoing," he told them, "but there is a sober and solemn beauty in its uncertainty and elusiveness. Sometimes it slips away with so little apparent reason as to leave us overwhelmed, and then again it lingers on and on, long after the signs seem certain for its passing. A physician can't say what is in the mind of God. Three days—four perhaps. I don't know."

It was then that they had sent the telegram for Hunt to come.

The driver stood on the cold platform and waited and there was sadness in his heart. He had stopped at the Justice house on the way in. Neely Barrow was asleep but Courtney Justice told him that she was "jest about the same," that she had been asking at frequent intervals when Hunt would come.

The driver stood out on the platform. The stars glittered crisply, and one's breath seemed chalk-white in the gaslight that flickered dimly at the platform's end. A hackman lounged against the lamppost. A baggage helper sat on a truck with his head between his knees and took a cat nap. The man on the truck awoke and slapped his hands vigorously for warmth. The driver's keen old ears heard the far, faint whistle of the train, sounding, he thought, for the crossing at the Federal Cemetery. The whistle blew again, nearer this time. The man on the truck awoke the second time, crawled down from the truck, and pulling it forward and then backing it a bit, placed it in proper position. It was still very dark. The driver saw the pale blob of glow that grew and brightened. The train was sounding for the bridge, and then it rattled into the station.

Hunt was the first passenger off the train. He saw the driver and his tired face softened into a dim smile.

"How is . . . ? Is she . . . ?" He couldn't finish the questions.

The driver nodded. "She wants to see you. Ready to go?"

On the way out he asked many questions. Since that day months before when he had seen the haggard look on her face, at intervals a dull fear had tugged at his heart.

"You well?" the driver asked.

"Yes, yes, I'm well. Mama knows I'm coming?"

"Yes, she knows you're coming, son."

"There isn't any chance for her to get well, is there?"

"I'm afraid not, son."

"I wish I'd never left," said Hunt fiercely.

"I wouldn't say that, son. They say that's what she is proudest of." He paused awhile, then continued, "I was younger'n you when mine died. She was a mighty fine woman. It's purty sad for her to have to go, son, but they ain't a thing about her that won't make good rememberin'. Ain't nothin' bad about her dyin', son, except how folks'll miss her. That scripture that tells about a good woman had her in mind."

Neely Barrow was waiting for them. Hunt took both of her hands. "I knew you'd be here. How is she?"

"You look so tired, Hunt. She's not in any pain now. She said for you to come in the moment you came."

They went into the room. He sat by the bed and talked with his mother. They talked quietly and sometimes her voice would fall to a whisper. "I'm so thankful you got here. It wouldn't be peaceful to die without seeing you."

"But, Mama, you're not going to . . ."

"Yes, Hunt, I am. The doctor told me so Wednesday. That doctor's a good man. I know he is from the way he told me."

"Don't, Mama."

"Don't worry, Hunt. I'm not afraid at all. Sometimes the things I've done haven't been very good, but I've never done a mean thing in my life. I'm thankful I've lived long enough to see my boy somebody. That was what I wanted most. I'm ready to go now. Hunt, I don't want you to stay here too long. Go on back and finish what you have to do."

"Mama . . ."

"Don't worry about your father. He wants you to go back, too. We've talked about it. Courtney's been mighty good to me. He'll get along. Don't worry about him. Go on back as soon as you can and get your work done. We both want you to. She wants you to. Hunt, she came as soon as she heard I was sick. If she was my own daughter she couldn't have been better to me. It used to be it made me afraid to think about dying. But I'm not afraid. Really, son, I'm happy. Everything has worked out all right."

Courtney Justice, who had been asleep when Hunt arrived, came into the room.

14

They buried Mrs. Justice just across the street from the house on Oak Street. One could stand on the porch or in the gate and see the freshly heaped mound of brown-red earth. It was decided that Courtney Justice would continue to live in the home. The Negro woman who worked at Mrs. Elrod's would go across every day and straighten the house, and he would get his meals at Mrs. Tanner's boarding house, only a brief walk around the corner at Cherry Street. He would go on working for Ed Crayton. His tones were still cheerful but there was a dazed and hurt look in his eyes. He and Hunt had a long talk the night before the departure for Boston.

That afternoon Hunt and Neely Barrow had called on Mrs. Polk. She was frail but of wonted quickness and vigor of mind. She went with them to the door when they left, and she charged Hunt in part precisely as his mother had a week before.

"Go on back, Hunt. Learn everything they can teach you. Gain discipline so that your visions may have in them no lack of orderliness, no excess of personal emotion, only an even movement forward toward Beauty. That is great architecture; that is great art anywhere. Come back to Nashville, Hunt, and put up your buildings. Let them rise to the service of man and glory of God."

Ed Crayton finished his supervisory visit to a house being built on Lamar Street. As he left, he spoke with Courtney Justice. "Stop at my house on your way home. I want to talk with you. I'll be there."

"Reckon I hadn't better go on home and change clothes first?"

"No, come just as you are. I want to be sure to know you. If you had on your go-to-meeting clothes I might think it was somebody else."

So Courtney Justice stopped. They sat by the fire in the living room, and Ed Crayton made the proposal he had in mind. The Nashville and Chattanooga Railroad was about to begin upon certain enlargement and revision of various parts of its equipment. Several small stations were to be built in the neighborhood of Decherd and Tullahoma, also freight warehouses at Wartrace, Decherd and Huntsville. He had been given the contract for all of these. He had pondered duly upon the matter because his hands were completely full of building in Nashville. But it was too favorable an item of business to miss. Finally, would Mr. Justice accept the commission as head carpenter for the railroad buildings? It would mean a small raise in salary and a considerable increase in responsibility. His headquarters would be at Decherd which he understood to be in the neighborhood of Huntland, Mr. Justice's old home. No need for an immediate answer. The railroad work would begin sometime late in the summer. He was much obliged for Mr. Justice coming by.

Mr. Justice did not reply for a full minute but sat apparently in deep study. Presently he lifted his head from its slump into abstraction.

"Ain't nobody got a finer boss man to work for than you, Ed, but right now I ain't a mind to take the offer. Used to be didn't make me no difference which rock I set on. I ain't that way now. I been mighty lonesome lately."

"That's one reason I offered it to you."

"And I take it mighty kindly, but I jest don't want to leave here—anyhow for a while yet."

"I guess I understand. If you change your mind let me know. You been working mighty good lately, Court."

15

Winter greened into spring, and then summer came marching along a hot dusty road. The sun poured its substance upon wood and field. Heat waves danced and quivered above the streets.

Mrs. Felicia Love was calling upon Neely Barrow Roane. At the gate the Love coachman sat dozing in the shaded interior of the carriage.

"How's your young genius, my dear? I hear he's cut quite a swath in Boston."

"Hunt is no genius, Mrs. Love."

"My dear, my dear! Whenever a young lady says that her affianced is no genius that means she fears he is an idiot."

Neely Barrow stopped in time the wave of anger which threatened to inundate her. Her guest was Mrs. Felicia Love, who by the town's social canons was permitted statements denied all others.

"In either case he is quite well, thank you."

Mrs. Love laughed heartily. "I suppose I'm the only woman in Nashville who hasn't seen this marvel. I won't claim I have been indifferent about him myself. I've made efforts to see him but I just didn't seem to have any luck. I always got there a little late."

Neely Barrow smiled a bit ruefully. "The next time Hunt is here I'll make it a special point for you to meet him."

"Fine," said Mrs. Love. "I'm no mean judge of humanity, my dear, and I'll be glad to tell you once and for all if he's a genius."

"I'd like to serve you a piece of cake and some lemonade, both of which I made myself."

"I do feel a trifle undernourished."

Neely Barrow came back with the cake and lemonade. Mrs. Love looked at the cake and her eyes widened.

"You didn't make that cake, Neely Barrow?"

"No one helped me."

Mrs. Love ate the cake, audibly appreciative. "I've not been well lately, but I'm no mean judge of cake. Would it annoy you, my dear, if I should request another piece?"

"You *must* be a judge of cake. Hunt likes this, too."

Mrs. Love was provided with more cake. "Dear me," she sighed. "I was born divided, my dear. One half of me leans toward the graveyard, and the other half toward the kitchen. I often wonder which half will win out."

An impish gleam danced in Neely Barrow's eyes. "May I get you another piece of cake, Mrs. Love?"

"Child, that slight note of expectancy in your voice that I'll say 'No' does you discredit. I should be delighted." Neely Barrow, the gleam still dancing, came back with the half of cake that still remained. She placed it on a table near Mrs. Love, and started slicing.

"What a lovely cake! Put it away, Neely Barrow, put it out of my sight. You shouldn't encourage my graveyard side like that."

Neely Barrow served her and took the rest of the cake to the kitchen.

"How is your dear grandfather?"

"He's playing chess with Colonel McGuire. He is well, thank you."

"Cherry Hill is so beautiful since you repaired and painted it. By the way, what is going on across the street?"

For no reason whatever a chill wind blew across Neely Barrow. "What do you mean, Mrs. Love?"

"Why, all those men, measuring with tape lines and driving down pegs. I suppose you knew about it."

"I didn't. Grandy sold the lot to a man who said they would make it into a city park. I suppose that's what they are starting."

"Didn't look like a park to me. Looked like a lot of cheap houses. Just the kind that wouldn't do Cherry Hill any good. Well, if I stayed any longer I'd finish that cake. So the question, my dear, is which is the wiser to do—with the cake, or without Dr. Atchison. This once I will choose the latter course."

Neely Barrow smiled, remembering how Mrs. Love had not wholly withdrawn from the former course. She was eager to see what was going on across the street, so she went out on the portico with Mrs. Love. And then the chill wind that had blown upon her spirit grew colder. There were four men busily plotting off the area, driving stakes and talking all the while. It was her first impulse to go across to the lot. But what then? No, the best thing was to see Grandy at once.

"Do you go by Colonel McGuire's, Mrs. Love?"

"I can without a bit of trouble." Mrs. Love's hand flew suddenly to her throat.

"Great heavens!" she gasped. "My brooch!"

"Oh, don't you have it?"

"No, I didn't put it on. I remember now. I must be losing my mind. My great-grandmother bought it in Paris. I have not failed to wear it in years. Without it I feel entirely unclothed. If you want to ride, my dear, let's go. I must get my brooch on."

She asked the coachman to drive briskly, and a few minutes later they stopped at Colonel McGuire's.

"I should be happy, my dear, to send Alex back to take you home."

"Oh, no, but I'm very grateful for this ride."

She lifted and let fall the McGuire knocker. A servant answered.

"My grandfather is playing chess with Colonel McGuire. Please tell him that I wish to see him."

Her grandfather came immediately, troubled, for this was not like Neely Barrow. "What is it?"

"Grandy, what are those men doing on the lot across the street?"

"I don't know. What does it look like they are doing?"

"I don't know. Mrs. Felicia Love said it looked as if they were getting ready to build some cheap houses."

"I guess it's the park, dear. Mr. Dilly told me it would be used for that."

"I think you ought to see, Grandy. I don't think that they're starting a park."

His face was haggard. "I'll ask Colonel McGuire to excuse me and go find out what it is."

"Go where, Grandy?"

"Why, to Mr. Dilly, of course."

"Shall I go with you?"

"No, you go on back to Cherry Hill. I imagine it is all right."

But it wasn't all right. Mr. Dilly was in his office. He was not at all interested in his visitor's concern. The matter belonged in the category of finished business. He did explain that something went wrong with the park deal. He couldn't afford to hold the property always, so finally he had sold it to a man named Ed Crayton, a respectable contractor. What he planned to do with it he could not say. It was regrettable but nothing could be done about it.

"They are starting to build something there," said Erwin Roane hoarsely.

"Houses, I expect. Good day."

Erwin Roane returned to Cherry Hill, haggard and panting from hurry. The men were still working on the lot. He sat down on the portico step and covered his face with his hands. Neely Barrow came out of the door and saw him.

"What is it, Grandy? What is it?"

He lifted his face then, pain stamped upon every feature. "They are going to build houses, Neely Barrow."

"How can they, Grandy? The man promised you . . ."

"Most stupidly I asked for no assurance but his promise. They will build slums across from the house my grandfather built."

She went across the portico and sat down by him. She felt that he was trembling. He stood and said, "I will not have my grandfather's memory nor the home he built violated."

He turned down the walk toward the gate, walking very erectly, but the look on his face terrified Neely Barrow.

"Grandy, where are you going?"

He did not answer her and she followed him. He went out the

gate. "What are you doing here?" he asked the man apparently in charge.

"Gettin' ready to build exactly six houses."

"For whom?"

"For Ed Crayton. Anything else you'd like to know, pardner?"

"You—these men are going to build the houses?"

"There'll be some more on the job."

"There is no job. You listen to me. My grandfather built that house." He pointed to Cherry Hill. "My father lived there; I was born there. My son was born there; my granddaughter was born there. That house and that granddaughter are all I have left in the world. I will permit nothing to cheapen or harm them . . ."

"Tell it to Ed Crayton."

"I am telling it to him through you. I will kill the first man who starts building a house on this lot. Tell him that, please. Tell him that I sold the lot under a specific promise that no house would be built upon it. If you come back tomorrow or the next day or any day, I will be here and I will kill the first one that starts working, and as many others as possible. I can do no less than that in honor. Good afternoon, sir."

Neely Barrow walked back to the house with her grandfather, her hand upon his arm. It was not the time to speak with him, to remonstrate with him. Later she would talk with him, but not until he had quieted a bit. She was trembling, too, and her mind was racing. The man had said that Ed Crayton was building the houses. Hunt's father worked for Ed Crayton. Perhaps Hunt's father would come as one of the carpenters on the six homes. She must see Courtney Justice at once.

"If you will excuse me, Neely Barrow, I will lie down awhile. I am very tired."

"Sleep if you can, Grandy. Everything will be all right."

She went with him into the library. He was trembling as though with a chill. "I'll lie on the sofa awhile," he said. "I'll feel better presently."

She went out of the house, and walked rapidly toward Oak Street. She knocked on the door of the Justice home, but no one answered. Mrs. Elrod came out on her porch and stood, hands on hips, regarding Neely Barrow with an inquiring eye.

"He's not home from work yet. Be here drekly." Then her eyes brightened with recognition. "Why, child, it's you. Come over and set on my front porch till he gets here."

Neely Barrow went and sat on Mrs. Elrod's front porch, and they talked of several things, though principally of Hunt. It was clear that Mrs. Elrod was burning with curiosity, but Neely Barrow merely told her that she wished to talk with Mr. Justice. Why didn't he come? She was restless and followed the conversation with difficulty.

"There he is now," said Mrs. Elrod. "I made some dressed eggs today. When you start home come by and I'll give you some."

"Why, if it isn't Miss Neely Barrow," said Courtney Justice. "Come right in."

"Mr. Justice, I want to talk with you."

"Must be something important. Have a cheer."

"Mr. Justice, you work for a man named Crayton, don't you?"

"Yes, Ed Crayton. Been working for him since the week I got here—that is, most of the time."

"Mr. Crayton is starting to build some houses across from my home."

"Oh, is that where they are? I haven't been over there yet, but I reckon I'll be sent later on."

"Mr. Justice, is there any way to stop Mr. Crayton from building those houses?"

"Why, ain't it all right to build 'em?"

"Let me tell you the story. Our house was built by my great-great-grandfather. You build houses. You know how people can love them. We have always loved our home as if it were, well—one of the family. We are very poor now. Recently my grandfather sold the lots across the street to a Mr. Dilly for some money with which to repair and paint the house. Mr. Dilly promised him it would not be used for building, but said he intended to sell it to the city for a park. Grandfather doesn't know how to handle business affairs, so all he got was the promise, nothing in writing. It will break his heart if those houses are built. You don't understand. Something dreadful might happen. For my sake will you ask Mr. Crayton not to build those houses—not yet anyhow?"

Courtney Justice sat looking at her, not saying a word.

"You don't understand, Mr. Justice," she repeated, "but I haven't anybody in the world except Grandfather . . . and Hunt."

"I'll try. I don't know what good I can do but I'll try. I'll go see Ed tonight." He looked at her, something kindling in his eyes. "I know something that might work."

Courtney Justice went to see Mr. Crayton. He walked briskly with the suggestion of one who has made an important decision. When he left his home on Oak Street he was a bit dazed by the decision he had made. Before he had gone two blocks his native cheer had reasserted itself, and he was considering his choice with apparent pleasure.

"It's just what Lizzie would 'a' wanted me to do," he remarked to himself.

Mr. Crayton was at home and greeted his visitor on his front porch. "Take that rocker," said the host heartily. "What you doin' all dressed up like a Chattanoogy drummer?"

"I come to make a trade, Ed."

"A trade? I didn't know you was a tradin' man, Justice. What you want to trade?"

"You've been after me, Ed, to take that railroad job. You started offerin' it to me back in the winter. You come to see me yesterday about it. All right, I'll make you a trade."

"What kind o' trade, Justice? What's the railroad job got to do with a trade?"

"I'll take the railroad work if you'll give up building them houses on South Market."

Ed Crayton stared at him, laughed, and said, "What's the matter with you, Justice? You gone batty?"

"I'm in my right mind, Ed. Let me tell you how it is—confidentially, you understand."

Ed Crayton nodded, the laughter still in his eyes, the half-puzzled look still on his face.

"You know my boy, Hunt? I never did know how I could have a boy like Hunt. He's got more sense in his little finger than I got in all o' me. You goin' to hear from Hunt. It was Lizzie he got it from. I don't know how it happened but Hunt got struck on one of the real high-up girls of the town."

"I heard about that, yes, but what has that got to do with the trade you been talkin' about?"

"I'm comin' to that. This girl liked Hunt jest as well as he did her. Well, when Lizzie got sick last winter she came and stayed. She knew what to do for Lizzie, too. . . ."

"Yes, but what . . ."

"I'm comin' to it. She lives in a fine house right close to the houses you are puttin' up. Her granddaddy is takin' it purty hard.

He thinks they'd kind o' take some o' the shine off his house. She—that girl—come to see me while ago and she asked me with tears in her eyes to ask you not to build them houses. If you won't, Ed, I'll do you a good job. I sort o' think I'd like it back in my old neighborhood. I'll go, Ed, if you'll make the trade."

Ed Crayton looked at his helper curiously. Then he suddenly broke into loud laughter. "You've made you a trade, Court. I really need you on them railroad contracts. I'll call them Market Street jobs off tomorrer."

"It's a promise, Ed?"

"It's a promise."

"I'm mighty glad to help that girl out, Ed. I think I'll like it fine down in the country. They're my folks down there."

After Courtney Justice had gone, Ed Crayton stood looking down the street after him. "Funniest thing ever happened," he affirmed between bursts of laughter. "I sure did need Justice on that railroad contract, and I'm goin' to pay him more'n I told him I would. Yes sir, funniest thing I ever heard of. City men wasn't any more'n out of sight with an option on that lot for a city park when here comes Justice hotfootin' it for a trade. I was goin' to call them jobs off first thing in the morning anyhow. Still, Justice'll like it fine down there."

Neely Barrow walked rapidly back to Cherry Hill. Courtney Justice's promises somehow left her reassured. It was some hope to offer Grandy. She ran into the house, through the hall into the library. "Grandy," she called. "I have something to tell you."

There was no answer. "I'll let him sleep," she thought, "and tell him when he wakes."

She turned to leave the room. Perhaps it was the stillness from the sofa that stopped her in the doorway. "Grandy," she said a bit sharply.

But only that deathlike stillness answered her. She ran back to the sofa. "Grandy," she called, "Grandy." She dropped on her knees beside the sofa. And then she saw that for the first time perhaps since his boyhood he was at peace.

16

Eugene Lewis was pursuing his favorite topic with Barksdale Reeves. "Lift us out of the doldrums, Barksdale. A really distinguished house hasn't been built in this town for almost a half century."

"I know some pretty good ones, Eugene. For instance the Drouillard home on Demonbreun Street."

"Too showy, too dated. General Grant at his architectural best—which wasn't good enough."

"Why should I build a new home? I have a good one now."

"A beautiful home, but being hemmed in by ugliness. The rag, tag and bobtail are moving in not three blocks away."

"Only in one direction. I still have three decent exits."

"Ten years from now you'll be lucky to have one. Your home is doomed, Barksdale. I wish you would build its successor. I wish you would set a pattern. You have the money."

"Yes, I have the money, and to tell you the truth, I've thought something of it. But, Eugene, no one but a Reeves has ever lived in my home. My grandfather would come back and haunt me if I moved out."

"Sooner or later you'll have to surrender."

"Don't be such a prophet of gloom, Eugene."

"I wouldn't even mention the matter if I didn't know something of your financial competence. I'm a director of the bank, you know."

"Yes, I know. I am not ashamed of my money. In fact, I'm proud that I who twenty-five years ago was penniless am now in a position to build a nice home—if I should so desire—besides stocking the place with a cow and some chickens—if I so desired," he added whimsically.

"The time will come, Barksdale, when you will build that house. When it does, put up a good one; no, not a good one, a great one."

"I'll think about it," said Barksdale Reeves, with an absent note in his voice. Then he spoke with sudden directness. "Eugene, have you got a few hours you could spare?"

"Why, yes; what's on your mind?"

"I want you to take a drive with me. I doubt if you knew—even though you are a director of the bank—that I have bought a place on the Cumberland River. It's a nice place and it seems to me an unusual site for a home. I'd like for you to drive with me out there. I have my buggy."

"I should be delighted."

So they drove across the river, bore to the right until they passed Shelby's Pond, then climbed the hill.

"There it is," said Reeves pointing.

"How lovely! I've been by here twenty times. Why hadn't I ever noticed it before?"

They hitched the horse and walked about. Eugene Lewis was excited. "The house should be there. What a view it would have from the portico! The river for at least two miles! I have not seen finer trees than those. One does not often find nature so completely helpful."

Barksdale Reeves wanted to walk about in the fields, but his friend had eyes only for the noble eminence fitted and garnished by nature for a home.

"If I should ever move here I want some cows grazing in that field, some fine Jersey cows. I have for a long time watched goods pass through my store. I want to see cows graze on my meadows."

"But consider how ennobled your cows would be if from the east portico of your home you watched them graze, a picture framed by lovely Ionic columns."

"I think I'd rather go down into the fields and watch them graze."

"Not if you had the sort of portico I've envisioned for you. And then, tired temporarily of the cows, you could go to the front portico and watch your friends arrive for a pleasant visit."

"Framed by other Ionic columns, I suppose."

"Certainly. Look, Barksdale . . ." He moved his hand in a broad sweep. "What a view! What loveliness would spread out from the bedroom windows. Your dining room would be there. There a window opening out, a broad bay. How lovely to watch the Cumberland flow turbulently by in the winter, crawl lazily in the summer!"

"Listen, Eugene, we're going back to town. One more passage of your eloquence and I'll start building tomorrow, and I'm not ready for that by a long time."

They crossed by the Haysboro Ferry and came back to town by the Lebanon Pike. It had been a long drive and they were hungry, so they stopped at Warwick's tavern for some food. They ate and talked and then rose to leave. A gentleman was entering as they left. He walked with quick nervous strides. His finely molded face was swarthy as from much exposure to sun. His hair was tousled as if the wind had run its fingers through it. He was not tall but he seemed to tower above Eugene Lewis.

"Good afternoon, Reeves. How do you do, Major Lewis?"

His voice was loud, touched with bluster, and yet in its background sounded the ring of iron. He extended his hand to Reeves. "I fancy from your looks, Jere, that you are in excellent health."

"My body, praise be, has never been a target for those pestilential slings and arrows that so harass other men. I am always in excellent health." He bowed slightly to Lewis, a faint ironical smile curling about his lips. "My health, sir, is perhaps the reason I love to build railroads. A great deal of strength is required, you know."

Eugene Lewis matched the smile. "Yes," he said evenly, "strength of one kind or another, Mr. Baxter. Each must do the best he can with what he has."

"Meaning of course that I have brawn and you brains."

"Precisely, and no discredit offered to either. It takes both to build a railroad."

"Then I must have both. The Central Railroad is being built into Nashville."

"Yes, I hear so. The city is very sturdy. It has survived a great many misfortunes."

"Oh, but sir, the Central Railroad is no misfortune. It, despite the frantic efforts of a great competitor to prevent its existence, will be a blessing to the community."

"Efforts, to be sure, but not frantic efforts. The railroad is too busy serving the people to waste itself by becoming frantic. Is this the extent of what you wished to say, President Baxter?"

"Almost. I do not wish even my—shall we say enemies?—to misunderstand me. I very greatly covet your understanding of me, sir. You are an intelligent man, but likely to jump to conclusions too early. For instance, you think that my main interest is power, glory, self-aggrandizement. It is not so at all. I have very little money, and no taste for political influence except to promote my projects. I never undertake anything, sir, unless after careful consideration I decide it is for the common good. When I decide that something is greatly needed I set about to provide it. I have not failed yet."

"Wasn't there the governorship?" asked Eugene Lewis quietly.

"Sure enough there was. It had gone completely out of my mind." He smiled with quiet ruefulness. "Well, I won't count it among my enterprises. I don't think now it was in behalf of the common good. Merely a postadolescent flourish. But the Coal and Iron Company. I achieved that, didn't I? The Central Railroad will come into Nashville. It will come into the city, and if I should become convinced that it would tend to the common good for it to circle the Capitol we'd build it around it, sir." He stopped for a moment, then continued angrily, his words coming fast like bullets. "I expected all of your devices to prevent my building the Central Railroad or to delay it beyond the contract period. I found them sometimes amusing, sometimes tiresome, but I didn't resent them, only once. That was when you attempted to slow us down by hiring Halloran from us. I doubt if that was allowed by the rules. It angered me, sir."

"The ethics would be the same, I think," said Eugene Lewis, "but it never occurred to me to hire Halloran to slow you down. I had already accepted your road then. We wanted Halloran simply because we needed him on that Lewisburg job."

"Then the pay you offered him suggests that you were in bad straits with your Lewisburg line."

"We were. By the way, did you raise him to match our offer?"

"Not one cent of advance, sir. I am not interested in loyalty that sells to the highest bidder. No, I didn't even hear of the matter from Halloran. As a matter of fact, he will have as much pride in laying the track into the city as I will to see it done. And if it is decided to circle the Capitol or to tunnel Capitol Hill, Bartley Halloran will lay the track, sir."

"A very interesting conversation," said Barksdale Reeves thoughtfully as they drove away.

"A very useless one," said Eugene Lewis. "It wasted time. It was annoying, nothing was said. . . ."

"I wonder. I got the idea that he was saying something between the lines. Jere Baxter would take considerable pleasure in reminding you later that he had called his shots beforehand. I wonder what he meant by that reference to building his road around the Capitol."

"That would be fantastic. It was merely an idle boast."

"Jere Baxter is an unusual man. I am aware, Eugene, of the hostility between you two. It might lead you to underestimate him . . . not in business canniness. You are aware of that, I imagine."

"Yes, I am aware of that. He is building his road into Nashville. That required canniness."

"I fancy he is right about not having much money. I think he was perfectly sincere about his desire to be of public service. I suspect that his greatest pleasure would be to feel that he had singlehanded overcome determined opposition."

"I could forgive him even now," said Eugene Lewis, "if he would put up a handsome building for his railroad station here."

17

Hunt Justice finished his course in Architecture with high honor and the unreserved favor of his instructors. The work with which he had been assisting Professor Letang at the Chicago Exposition was finished. He had an invitation to assist Professor Homer upon some public buildings in Providence, Rhode Island, which would not begin before the beginning of the next year. He wrote to Eugene Lewis asking for counsel as to acceptance. The reply came immediately. Take it. Very few buildings, even including the poorer sort, were in process of construction then, and fewer were contemplated. Nashville was overbuilt. The town was filled with new houses, some substantial, most ugly. It was his hope that a revival of taste would follow the Centennial. Indeed it was more than a hope. It was a faith. Hunt should be ready for that. The experience in Providence, a community of artistic qualities, would be most helpful. But come on to Nashville. They were about to begin on the plans for the Centennial buildings. An excellent architectural staff had been provided—Mrs. Sarah Ward Conley, Mr. Zwicker, Mr. Thompson, Mr. Gibel, Mr. Gaebler, and for the Parthenon, Colonel William C. Smith. He was happy about the whole arrangement, but would be happier if they could secure Hunt's counseling services for the next several months. The idea was for Hunt to advise the Board expertly as to plans submitted. He believed that everything could be checked completely in time for him to join Professor Homer in Providence. Nashville was discouraged by the financial depression sweeping the country. It was making the Centennial much more difficult. It would, however, be pretty bad if matters didn't loosen a bit by the time the gates opened.

Mrs. Polk was losing ground, he feared. And, oh yes, Neely Barrow was now teaching in the Howard School, though he suspected that item did not properly belong in the category of news. If looks had any meaning they were proof that it was very agreeable employment. She and the faithful Roane retainer were keeping

Cherry Hill in very presentable condition. Doubtless he had heard that the city, inspired by a hurried and peremptory visit from Mac Dickinson, had purchased the lot across the street for a park, but that was as far as the matter had yet gone.

One final item: Mrs. Elrod had said in the event of Hunt's coming to Nashville for a period, she would consider it an honor to assign her front room for his service. She had mentioned with some show of subtlety that her place was located in nice proximity to the Howard School—in the event, of course, that he should choose to enter that school and really try to learn something.

So Hunt came to Nashville and spent four intense months, time filled with delight and strain. The town was under strain, too, for there was widespread unemployment, and money was very scarce. Only the indomitable spirit of Eugene Lewis kept the Centennial from going into collapse. Whenever a member of the Board became doubtful, Lewis visited him immediately and warmed him again to the work in hand. The depression was manifest throughout the section. Projects begun in the fine fervor of hope dwindled into inaction. There were times when Lewis flinched inwardly from the prospect, but then he would stand suddenly erect, throw his shoulders back, and go to talk with businessman Buttorff.

"It is fortunate," Buttorff would say, "that the panic is this early. It will run its course and then we will have the Centennial."

"I don't understand you. To begin with you were the most skeptical one of us."

"Isn't that the time to be skeptical? It's too late now. Besides, it isn't good sense. I've got money in the Centennial, so I must believe in it. A depression couldn't be permanent where there are plenty of necessary resources and men have character. A depression means that something has got out of balance and must be got back in. Eight months, at the most a year, and the correction will set in. We will have the Centennial. People's minds will be right for it by then."

After a day of checking and rechecking tentatively drawn sketches, or of measuring for elevations and distance at the Centennial grounds, Hunt would walk to Cherry Hill and Neely Barrow would come down the street to meet him. She would tell him of her day at school and he would tell of his with the transit and tapelines. Sometimes they would go for a brief visit with Miss

Julia Sears, or Professor Clark, or with Charles Little, or to the home of Mac Dickinson, or to Weaver Cole's. One Sunday Hunt got on the train and went to Decherd to spend the day with his father. He found Courtney Justice well and very cheerful.

"I'm doin' the best work o' my life, Hunt. Not a hour off for sickness sence I been here, and I never felt sprier. Ed Crayton comes down ever once in a while and he acks like he's pleased."

From somewhere he borrowed a horse and cart and they drove to Huntland and out to see the house in which Hunt had been born. The people who lived there were friendly and they remembered Courtney Justice.

"Spent many a happy day here," Courtney told them. "Mighty nice place to live, but the schoolin' round here didn't used to be so good, so Lizzie 'n' me took Hunt to Nashville for schoolin'. It worked out fine. That little shaver there looks like he could take some schoolin'."

When they left the home of his birth and boyhood Hunt found himself eager to see Mr. Moore's home. They got in sight of it a few minutes later and Hunt found that he was trembling. There it stood as great and graceful as it had when he, as a mere lad, had watched it day after day from across the road, had watched it with shining eyes and dreams that stirred and swelled within his heart. There it stood and no marks of the years were upon it, stately and timeless, dreaming of the strong spirits it had nurtured, of great days gone, and yet to be.

It was pleasant for Hunt to be with his father. Some old vague restraint between them seemed broken down, and they had seemed closer than he could remember. When the train upon which he was to return to Nashville rattled into Decherd, Courtney Justice said to his son, "I'm proud of you, son. I won't ever forget today. I want to come up to town one day before you leave and get you to help me pick out a tombstone for Lizzie. Sometimes I get mighty lonesome for her."

18

Neely Barrow and Hunt had gone several times to see Mrs. Polk. They knew she was fading away, but her eyes were bright and her words were crisp and coherent. One day in August the word came that she wanted to see them. They went in the afternoon. She lay propped high on pillows. Her eyes were still bright, but her hands plucked continuously at the quilts, and an unearthly pallor was upon her face.

"Sit down, my children. This is my company day. I've had some important visitors today."

Hunt said nothing, knowing nothing to say. Neely Barrow said, "We mustn't tire you, Mrs. Polk."

"The first ones to come were Constantine and Amanda—the Watsons, you know. She was most the scatterbrained girl I ever saw, and she has made just about the best mother for a house full of boys. When he was young, Constantine sat and brooded about his honor; now it's about his crops."

"You mustn't become tired, Mrs. Polk."

"I'll have time to rest later. While they were here Gale Thurston came. He didn't stay long. He has seemed terribly lonely since Ida . . . went on before. . . ."

"Isn't there something I could get you, Mrs. Polk?"

"Just let me talk. It's a privilege I wouldn't want to relinquish now, my dear. After Gale had gone Merrie and Weaver came. It was so fine to have them, so lovely to carry the memory of what they said with me. Who do you think came with them? Their driver. Of course, I'm familiar with the demands of the sickroom. I know the manners that belong in one and I've not seen better than his. He's a patrician under the skin. . . . Bear with me a minute; I become tired so easily. . . . What do you think I had him do? I had him sing. One time I was out at Kingsley, and I sat with the Coles on the side portico. Their driver was singing out in the horse lot. Fifty years before that Mr. Polk and I had gone to a camp meeting in Rutherford County, and they sang that same song. It was a bit primitive, but sweet and appealing.

" 'Oh brothers, will you meet me
On Canaan's happy shore.'

"Well, this afternoon I felt very close to Mr. Polk—oh, very close. I thought he would like to hear it sung again. The driver didn't flinch when I asked him to sing it. He understood. He sang it, low and soft and very beautiful. I think Mr. Polk heard him."

She closed her eyes and lay in silence. She opened her eyes and motioned for Hunt to come closer. "Eugene Lewis had told me that there is no building here now. But there will be. Be ready when the time comes. Stand up a bit closer, Neely Barrow. Let me see you two together. How sweetly that driver sang. May I shake hands with each of you? I am very tired, very tired. But I will rest after you leave. How precious you look! I will rest soon. *He giveth His beloved sleep."*

19

The Commissioner General was exceedingly angry. All of the land needed for the Centennial had been secured except a small and very strategic plot jutting out from Lake Sevier. The owner had been offered a thousand dollars for it. He didn't choose to sell at the moment. They waited but apparently he had no notion of selling. Finally R. W. Turner was sent to him, commissioned to raise the offer to $1200 if an emergency should be found to exist. It existed. The owner had sold the lot to a Mr. Dilly. Turner journeyed downtown to see Mr. Dilly—and for his pains was informed that ten thousand was the lowest possible figure he would consider. Mr. Dilly said frankly that he was in business for other purposes than health. When Eugene Lewis's explosion showed some signs of dwindling into silence Ed Barthell said that he supposed the next step was to invoke the Law of Domain upon Mr. Dilly.

"And let it drag in the courts six months, perhaps a year!" stormed the Commissioner General. "We need that plot now."

"Who is this Dilly?" asked Mac Dickinson.

"You know as much about him as I do," replied Turner. "He's been here three or four years. He's mixed up in a lot of real-estate deals, most of them small, and some of them shady."

"Can't we build around his property?"

"No, we've got to have it if it takes murder to get it, and a thousand dollars is a fair price for it."

It was then that Mac Dickinson laughed out aloud. "I just thought of something," he explained. "Leave the lot alone a day or so. I think I'll go call upon a friend of mine."

The friend proved to be Mr. Nige Overall, who sat in his front yard at Bloodstone, and gave thought to his blessings. Ordinarily Mac would have given Mr. Overall free rein, but he was in a bit of hurry that morning.

"Do you know a Mr. Dilly who is in the real-estate business here?"

"Dilly? No, never set eyes on him. I know he bought that lot from Ol' Man Roane and tried to hornswaggle the town to buy it at a fancy price for a park, but he couldn't work it. Then he sold it to Ed Crayton. Ed started to build some houses but changed his mind and sold it to the city. I never did rightly know what happened but somethin' did. No, I don't reckon I know Dilly, but I guess I could find out somethin'. You much interested, Mr. Dickinson?"

"Yes, I am, and I'm in a hurry." He sketched briefly the situation.

"I got a right smart interest in this Cen—how do you say it? Any chance me gettin' a pass for some day while it's goin' on?"

"Listen, if you can turn this man Dilly into a notion to sell this lot reasonably I'll see that you get a season pass."

"What's a season pass?"

"It's one that admits you free every day as long as the Centennial lasts."

"Every day! You just watch me. Dilly's a-goin' to give you that lot."

"No, but we do want to buy at a reasonable price."

Mr. Overall thought matters over and decided to call upon Mr. Dilly. Perhaps that would open up something. He decided to play the role of a prospective house buyer. He found Mr. Dilly sitting at his very cheap desk in his very cheap office.

"Name's Overall. Might buy a house if it tickled my funny bone just right."

Mr. Dilly became all solicitude. "We tickled funny bones harder to tickle than yours. What size house you aimin' to call home?"

"About five rooms."

Mr. Dilly jumped to his feet. "We got the very identical place. Let's go see 'em. They sell for cash." He eyed Mr. Overall speculatively.

"I got the spondoolix, but it's got to buy me what I want. It's got to buy me a place with a shade tree in the front yard and a rocking chair by the front winder." His eyes were searching Mr. Dilly with great intentness.

"Let's go see them houses," said Mr. Dilly very earnestly.

"Ain't got the time now. Just wanted to find if you had anything. Might go tomorrow. Got any special offer to a feller with cash?"

"Anybody that waves the long green in my face is goin' to get a bargain."

"Be back tomorrer."

Nige Overall left the office almost but not quite convinced that Mr. Dilly belonged outside his practice. There was something—almost—but when he tried to put his mind upon it it vanished. Still something haunted him gently but persistently. And then suddenly he knew. He pulled out something from the long ago and hurriedly reviewed it. Then he nodded his head in a very satisfied manner. Everything fitted, even the name.

Mr. Nige Overall early the next morning was blithely on his way to see Mr. Dilly. But in the midst of his satisfaction somewhere within him a discreet nerve sounded a warning. He should take someone with him to his interview. Of course, Mr. Mac Dickinson would love to go. But Mr. Overall was committed to the drama. How much more satisfying it would be to walk into the Dickinson office and place very nonchalantly on the desk before him Mr. Dilly's agreement to sell.

And then he saw his old friend College Grove walking briskly along the sidewalk on the opposite side of the street. "Wait a minute," he called. "What you doin' the next half hour?"

"Who? Me? I thought everybody knowed what I'd be a doin'. Jest a-pourin' electricity on the wheels of a streetcar, that's all."

"Couldn't you get off for a few minutes?"

"Who? Me? I couldn't get off to help put out the County Court House if it was a-burnin' up. No sir, I'm a necessary man."

"Never mind, I can get somebody else. I'm a-goin' to put the shenanigan on an old he-catawampus and I thought maybe you'd like to watch me do it."

"The only way to handle them kind is to use electricity. It'll mow 'em down."

"I reckon I'll have to use spizzerinktum. It's nine times as servigerous as electricity. Don't even leave a smell. You ack like you mighty stuck on this electricity pourin'."

"I wouldn't trade it," affirmed College Grove with emphasis, "to be the crowned head o' four different furrin countries. But they's one thing agin it." He lowered his voice to suggest great confidence. "I think it's hanted."

"Hanted!"

"Yes sir, hanted. You can see a mule, can't you? Well, it ain't a hant, but anything that'll pull a streetcar and you can't see it, why, it's a hant. Someways it does all right, but I wouldn't run an electricity streetcar by a graveyard for all the greenbacks I could tote. Whereat you goin'?"

College Grove being an old and tried friend, Mr. Overall explained the occasion and nature of his trip.

"I'd shore like to go. Looks like you got the entitlements on him. Why, look-a here . . ." Memory dawned in his eyes. "I know the very feller to go with you. He stayed with me last night."

"Who did?"

"That ol' scounderl that drives for the Coles. He come in yestidy for some late seed potatoes and got here after the stores done closed, so he stayed with me and got a night's lodgin' for nothin' when the ho-tels would 'a' charged him fo' bits. He's jest about gettin' ready to go for them potatoes now. I reckon you know where I live." Mr. Overall knew.

The invitation to accompany Mr. Overall was readily accepted by the driver. He wouldn't lose much time. Besides he felt the need for a modicum of excitement.

Mr. Dilly sat in his office, and in close counsel with him sat Clem Purvis.

"Look-a there," breathed Mr. Overall. "Beelzebub's a-workin'."

By then Mr. Dilly had seen Mr. Overall and he rose in eager greeting. But Clem Purvis saw not only Mr. Overall but the driver coming right behind him. Mr. Dilly's enthusiastic salutation died on his lips, for he caught the warning which his henchman flashed to him. The look was imperative. Some emergency was on, but Mr. Dilly didn't know what it was nor what to do about it.

"Have cheers, gents," he said lamely. His eyes darted from Mr. Overall to Mr. Purvis and back again. Who was the old gray man who, hat in hand, followed Mr. Overall into the room, whose calm gray eyes missed nothing for which they searched? Mr. Dilly knew that something was wrong but he didn't know what to do about it.

"You ready to go see that property?"

"It's got to be neplussyulter to get my money, Mr. Dillingham."

Mr. Dilly's lips drew into a thin straight line. "You made a mistake. The name's Dilly," he said harshly.

"Why not, why not? They ain't no law agin changin' a name. But it's right funny. Now me, I think Dillingham is purtier'n Dilly any day."

"Listen," said Mr. Dilly with emphasis, "I said the name is Dilly."

"Don't leave yet a while," said the soft-spoken gray-eyed old man to Clem Purvis, who was manifesting signs of discontent. "We might open a keg of nails, or sumpin'."

Clem took one look at the old man's hand moving lovingly toward a bulge in his shirt and sat down without further ado.

"I couldn't place you," Mr. Overall was saying to Mr. Dilly, "until you said that about givin' a bargain to anybody that shook the long green in your face. I heard you say them identical words fourteen years ago down on the market when you was puttin' on a show to sell Lightnin Elixir for Pains and Aches, and jest about ever'body in the crowd got his pocket picked. Kind o' overdone it, I'd say. Raised a lot o' stink and you left town sudden-like."

"He might 'a' been one of them pickpockets out in the crowd," said the driver, gesturing mildly toward Mr. Purvis. He had taken his whip from inside his shirt and was idly flicking it through the open window.

"Could 'a' been," said Mr. Overall. "I don't know of nobody that'd go to much trouble to deny it."

"You git out o' here!" yelled Mr. Dilly.

"There now, Mr. Dillingham, take it easy. And the very next county court day at Clarksville you picked the pockets o' jest about ever'body there and you swindled all the rest. Yes sir, they needed that Elixir to soothe their pains when they found out what'd happened to 'em."

"I saw you handin' out the Elixir down on the market," observed the driver. "You was a-wearin' a beard that looked like a hay field in a good crop year."

"Now to git down to the brass-headed triple-plated tacks. We ain't the sort o' fellers that blab when it ain't good sense to. All this Elixir and pickpocketin' business is water that's run over the bridge and under the dam as far as we keer. Funny nobody ain't caught on afore this but folks is good forgitters. Want to hear how to git us to forgit? 'Cause if we stayed on rememberin' you'd be in the middle of a lot o' bad signs and predicaments."

"You set still," the driver admonished the uneasy Mr. Purvis.

"A thousand dollars ain't any more'n that tract of ground out by the Centennial is worth, though when you priced it to them you must of thought you was still sellin' Elixir and pickin' pockets. Yes sir, you jest take up that pen an' write an agreement to sell that tract to the Centennial for one thousand dollars. And you're gittin' our forgittin' mighty cheap at that."

The driver corroborated Mr. Overall. "Better do your writin' now. We might get so we couldn't forget."

Mr. Dilly did his writing. On the street the driver said, "That mighty nigh makes us pardners in crime, don't it?"

"Don't you worry none. He won't stay here no longer'n he can git packed up. His conscience is troubling him right now. Purty neat way o' gittin' the Phillisteens to depart and go away."

Mr. Overall handed Mr. Dilly's written statement to Mac Dickinson. Mac read it through. "Good God!" said he. He read it through again. "How beautiful is a bad conscience," he said softly.

20

Mrs. Dorris arrived at the Hermitage early. The morning was clothed in a delicate freshness, and the sun, hanging low above the Tulip Grove plantation, gave its brilliance to myriad diamonds of dew.

Mary Dorris, who had the gift of seeing things, always saw General Jackson as she drove between those stately cedars up to the mansion. Time slipped back and it was the autumn of 1837. There the General was and by his side Earl, the artist. The General had in his hand a large sheet of paper, and Earl was pointing at something on the paper and explaining it. The General followed him intently, then nodded his head. She could see that it was the sketch for the planting of the cedar trees that lined the driveway. Then slaves came with young cedars from the near-by glade and began setting them out. General Jackson looked at one of the young cedars, and shook his head.

"No," he said sternly, "dig it up. It's out of line. Move it over eight inches. It would haunt me." He looked at his companion. "I can't abide any lack of order or precision. The Hermitage must never be marred by those who love their ease more than perfection." And Earl smiled his artist's smile and bowed his head in agreement.

The vision passed and it was Bettie Donelson who left the porch and came down the walk.

"Am I late, Bettie?"

"No, early. The men have not come yet."

"The lumber's here, isn't it?"

"Yes, it's here and those are the prettiest palings I ever saw."

"They ought to be. They cost all the money Will Allen Drom-goole made with her concert. I could have got palings for half the price."

"Quite so, but they weren't good enough for the Hermitage, Mary."

"General Jackson set the pattern, Bettie. I wish those men would come on."

Those men were two carpenters in the neighborhood who had performed various chores in carpentry at the Hermitage whenever the Hermitage Association could afford it. On their last trip they had set new posts around the garden and nailed on the stringers. But that left the treasury exhausted, and the Hermitage garden without palings. In the meantime Will Allen Dromgoole's con-cert had yielded money to buy palings that would have met with General Jackson's approval. So on that day the garden fence was to be completed.

An hour later the carpenters had not arrived. The two women did not waste time in waiting. With brush and broom and cleaning rag they made the rounds.

"If they are not here in thirty minutes I'll start putting those palings on myself."

"Who am I to flinch in an emergency?" inquired Bettie Donel-son. "I imagine we can find two hammers, or hatchets, or what-ever they use somewhere about the place."

They worked ahead. The sun rose higher and the day grew warmer.

"All right," said Mary Dorris grimly, "let's build a fence."

They carried the palings from the rick in which the delivery-man had piled them to the posts and stringers that waited. They found two hatchets in the smokehouse. They pooled their in-genuity in locating the first paling. They placed it against the stringers and dropped a weighted string from the paling's top center. When it stood so that the string veered neither to the right nor the left but lay taut along the middle they nailed the paling in place. It was Mary Dorris who solved the problem of spacing. She found a cleanly cut block which the carpenters had sawed from a plank. Its length was the interval she desired be-tween palings. She split it in two and gave her friend the other piece. One end was placed against the paling and a pencil mark traced on the stringer against the other end. This was done on both stringers and the pencil marks used to locate the next paling. From that initial paling Mary Dorris moved east toward the tomb and Bettie Donelson west toward the house. Their care so balanced their awkwardness that a half hour later when they stopped to survey their workmanship they could find no flaw. They nailed ahead. Their efforts were bearing the look of a fence.

"Come here, Mary."

"What is it?"

"This doesn't look right. I think I've done it wrong."

The paling was undeniably slanted. They used the weighted string. Three were found out of plumb.

"I guess I slipped. I suppose I should take them off."

"I don't think General Jackson would want them crooked. I'll help you."

"Perhaps I could help too," said a familiar voice. It was Eugene Lewis. "Duncan told me you were here, but he was slightly evasive in saying what for."

"He didn't know." Mary Dorris told him what had happened.

"I'll not lose faith again. The country is safe. So is the Hermitage. I've been intending to come out for months. Well, well, so some palings have to come out! Did you know, ladies, that I hold the world's championship as straightener of ailing palings? May I remove my coat, please?"

Eugene Lewis's hands were adept and his eyes accurate. Five minutes later the palings were straightened.

"You ladies take that end and I'll go on from here."

The sun rose higher and poured its heat more directly upon the earth. Bettie Donelson measured and held the palings and Mary Dorris nailed them in place.

"Look," she said holding up a hand. "Look at that blister. An honorable wound. Have you a blister yet, Bettie?"

"No, but I'll try."

"Mawnin', ladies," said a voice.

They turned. "Good morning, Uncle Alfred."

The old Negro leaned against a hickory tree. "Sho is a nice fence fo' Gin'ral Jackson."

"Thank you. We could use another hand."

Uncle Alfred straightened and there was rebuke in his glance. "Gin'ral Jackson never asked me to wuk on no fence, ma'am."

"Oh," said Mary Dorris. "Well, as a matter of fact, he never asked me either. Still, I get your point."

"Gin'ral Jackson he had some to do this and some to do that. I was his pussonal man."

Eugene Lewis had stopped work and joined the group. "The General would want the Hermitage fixed up like it used to be, wouldn't he?"

"Gin'ral Jackson? He wouldn't *want* it a-tall. He'd jest natchelly pint his walkin' cane at somebody and say *fix it up,* dat's what he'd do."

"He loved the Hermitage very dearly."

"Loved it! Gin'ral Jackson loved three things—Miz Rachel, the Hermertage, and the Dimmycrat Party. Yes sir, when he was a-leavin' here to go off to Washington to be President he'd go back to Miz Rachel's grave, by hisself. He didn't want nobody to go with him. He'd stan' by de grave mebbe half a hour. Den he'd come back. But before he'd git in de coach he'd stan' dar an' jest look at de house. Den he'd take off his hat like it was a lady. Den he'd climb in an' go off to run the Dimmycrat Party."

Mary Dorris looked at her hand. "What a lovely blister!" she said.

"I have one forming," said Bettie Donelson.

21

A little after that Eugene Lewis told Hunt that the Commissioners of Forrest County had scheduled a new courthouse, and that the owners of some property on Church Street in Nashville were planning a new office and apartment building to be erected as soon as property returned. Hunt spent three days in Forrest County. The commissioners were cordial. They showed him where the building would be placed. They were not able to say when it would be constructed, nor how much money, except in a wide range, they could put into it, nor what style of architecture they preferred. They did give him a sheet naming the agencies to be housed in the courthouse and the approximate space required for each. That was as far as they cared to go at the time. If he wished to submit plans on such skimpy information they would be given consideration. Hunt gathered such essential facts and measurements as he needed and returned to Nashville.

The Nashville owners knew better their situation, but a certain diffidence led Hunt to suspect that other architects had already established themselves in the owners' favor.

Two days before he left for Providence he delivered one set

of plans and mailed the other. Eugene Lewis had studied both plans with interest.

"Too beautiful. What I mean is that only the elect really prefer the beautiful. Maybe your county commissioners belong to the elect, but I doubt it."

He looked again through the plans for the Church Street building. He lifted his eyes from the sheets. "I'm proud of you, boy. This is architecture. I don't see an important defect, but I haven't much idea that the owners will choose your plans. You have traded space for beauty—and the owners can't rent beauty."

He thought for a moment. "Come; my trap is hitched out here. Let's take a little trip."

They drove across the bridge, out Shelby Street, along the road that curved down through the woods to Shelby's Pond, on up the hill on the other side until they came to the place Lewis and Barksdale Reeves had visited not long before. Eugene Lewis pointed. "There is, I think, an ideal site for a home. I saw it a little while ago, and I've wanted you to see it ever since."

They hitched the horse and walked up the rise that swelled gently to a narrow plateau whose eastern and southern sides dropped away to the curving Cumberland a half mile distant. Hunt looked about him saying nothing for minutes. Then he asked in a sort of intent quietness, "Why has no house been built here?"

"That's exactly what I'd like to know. Hunt, I want you to do something. I want you to draw for me some preliminary sketches of a home that would answer the possibilities of the place."

Hunt Justice looked at him in surprise.

"It's all right, Hunt. The place belongs to a friend of mine. Frankly, I want this as a sort of final examination for you. I even brought the paper along for you to use."

Hunt made notes, drew sketches, crossed them out, started others, traced the perspective in all directions. That night and much of the next day, with Neely Barrow sitting at his side, he worked on those sketches. He gave them to Eugene Lewis on the way to the railroad station.

22

Mrs. Felicia Love gave a tea jointly for the Executive Committee of the Centennial and the Regents of the Ladies Hermitage Association. It was on a late afternoon of an April day, soft and brimming with the flavors and fragrance of life. Mrs. Love's home looked out upon the Capitol grounds and upward at the eastern front of the great building. The guests came at five o'clock and presently the entire block of Park Street was filled with carriages, and a long line of guests was moving up the steps and onto the portico. In the dining room Neely Barrow Roane and Mary Bass poured tea, and Nannie Dudley Pilcher, Sammie Keith, Medora McAlister, Roberta Sewell and Idelle Sawrie served those who drifted into the dining room, having run with honor the course of the receiving line.

Mrs. Love fairly tinkled with pleasure as she welcomed each guest. "Ah, my dear, how charming, how unutterably charming you are. . . . My dear lady, you must tell me—confidentially, of course—who your dressmaker is. It's positively a vision. . . . My dear Merrie, my dear Weaver. I'd take you to be bride and groom. Not almost twenty years! Impossible! Unutterly impossible! My dear Nellie Stokes, my dear Walter, you come to see me too, too seldom. How is that charming son? Four, you say? It seems but yesterday that I saw the cherub then but a day old. Mrs. Marks, may I present Mr. and Mrs. Walter Stokes? When the three of you are together what a fraction of Nashville is there!"

The guests came, passed down the line by their hostess and her guests of honor. Then the line dissolved and all melted into the little groups that were sprinkled about in the various rooms. They stood and drank Mrs. Felicia's jasmine tea, and ate her beaten biscuits with ham from Mr. Ridley's farm in Maury County, and talked of many things, of the Hermitage, of the Centennial, of the Civil War, of their grandparents, of the current yield of trivialities. Mrs. Felicia Love made a hurried trip to the dining room to see whether it was integrating itself properly into the occasion. She stooped to say something to Neely Barrow, in whose eyes an impish gleam suddenly danced.

"Mrs. Love, your brooch . . ."

Mrs. Love's hand flew to her throat. "My grandmother's brooch! Where is it? Oh, I know now, I must have been excited. I forgot to put it on. This is terrible. I am not presentable without it." She fluttered away, disappearing up the stairs.

"You should see the Hermitage," Mary Dorris was saying to the group gathered about her. "You wouldn't know the place. Oh, of course you'd know it, but you would be surprised. It is all painted and the fences are all in good order, and there isn't a weed in sight. You must drive out to see it."

"It will be, I honestly believe," Eugene Lewis was saying to his group, "the greatest Exposition ever held in this country. Not as pretentious as some, the one at Chicago, or perhaps the one at Philadelphia, but the most distinguished of all. Take our Parthenon, for instance . . ."

Mrs. Felicia Love came back down the stairs and her grand-mother's brooch was very visible. Just then Dr. Atchison came into the room. Mrs. Love hurried to greet him.

"Why, dear Dr. Atchison, come into the dining room and have some tea. It's poor tea but it is poured by such lovely girls. The ham is from the dear Ridleys' in Maury County."

He drank the tea and ate the ham from the dear Ridleys' with obvious appreciation. "How well you look!"

"Martha says I always look well just before a fatal attack. I miss my daughter. I wish she'd move back to Nashville. You'd think a girl with her breeding would move heaven and earth to get back to Nashville. But she seems perfectly content to remain in Lexington. I can't understand it."

"Perhaps her husband has something to do with it," suggested Dr. Atchison suavely. "They do sometimes, you know."

"Not Martha's husband! If she said, 'Let's move back to Nashville,' he'd follow like a lamb. What else could he do?"

Dr. Atchison smiled and looked about him appreciatively. "There is the inducement of a beautiful home to come to."

"Not here. Not Martha and me under the same roof! It was such a relief when she married and moved away. I wish I could see her every day, but not every hour! But if she'd move back I'd build her the finest house in town. Well, anyhow, one of the fine ones. What is it, Neely Barrow? What are you staring at me that way for? Is something wrong?"

Neely Barrow flushed but she remained serene. "Oh, excuse me, please. I shouldn't have been listening."

Mrs. Love's brow puckered in thought, then her eyes twinkled. "I think I understand, dear Neely Barrow. If one miles and miles away speaks in a whisper of a building it sounds to you like beautiful thunder. Isn't that it?"

"Can you blame me?" inquired Neely Barrow placidly.

"Wait a minute. Do not disturb me. I'm thinking. Something has occurred to me. I have it, I have it, indeed! If Martha ever decides to come back to Nashville I'll build her a house just as I said I would. And, Neely Barrow, I'll have that young prodigy from Boston plan it. That's settled. Wait a minute, let me make sure. Eugene—" she lifted her voice to a neighboring group—"come here, will you? I've been thinking about building a house. And I may do it, too. Do you think this young what's-his-name in Boston . . . ?"

"His name is Hunt Justice, and he's in Providence now," interrupted Neely Barrow calmly.

"Do you think . . . what did you call him, my dear? . . . really could build a nice house, or have you just been doing some friendly exercises in perjury?"

"My endorsement of Hunt would stand at the head of all the truths I've ever told. You wouldn't be interested in building a house, would you, Mrs. Love?"

"I might be. The gods, dear Eugene, are the custodians of the possibility. If Martha should ever return to Nashville to live your young genius has a job. And that's a promise, Neely Barrow."

There were tears behind Neely Barrow's smile.

"Why, my dear Jere Baxter, how do you do. You're even later than dear Dr. Atchison. Of course you know Eugene Lewis. How honored I am to have two great railroad men in my home together!"

No motion was made by either Jere Baxter or Eugene Lewis to shake hands, though on the face of each was an icy smile.

"In case you are interested, Major Lewis, Bart Halloran's track layers have reached the city limits."

"I admire Mr. Halloran very much. I still hope to give him a chance to justify his ability in a larger way."

"What could be larger, say, than placing a railroad around the Capitol? Excuse me, please. I'd like some tea. When greatly fatigued I find it particularly restoring."

He moved on. Eugene Lewis looked after him. His mind was upon that reiteration of the Capitol.

"Dear Jere is so stimulating," said Mrs. Love. "You should have him with your railroad, Eugene."

"No," said Eugene Lewis, "we'd like to keep the track at least."

Mrs. Love looked at him a bit uncertainly. "You men are so amusing, but I never seem to understand you. I never understood dear Mr. Love. When he talked he just mumbled, you know. Why, the night he proposed to me I never understood a word he said.

And I listened, too. I just sat there and watched his eyes, and when I saw a certain look come in them I nodded my head. Come here, Susie Foster. Let me look at you. Those Cockrill features, my dear! I claim they're Nashville's best features."

"We've done mighty well out at the Hermitage despite the panic," Mary Dorris was saying to her group. She glanced inadvertently at her hands. "We do need more money terribly, but I feel that we have not done poorly with what little we've had. The home and the grounds are in excellent condition. We need money badly, a lot of money. I'm very unhappy with all of the furniture and furnishings scattered about. It's an awful risk to run. I can't sleep when I think of General Jackson's beds and chairs and dining table in strange hands and places. I don't blame Mr. and Mrs. Jackson for taking the furniture away when they left. It was their perfect right. It belonged to them. If we had only had some money then! But I'll live to see all of General Jackson's furniture back where it belongs."

"And I'll live to carry the last piece back into the Hermitage," promised Mrs. Bettie Donelson.

"And who but you, bound to the home by long bonds of blood and sentiment, would have quite that right?"

Henry Buttorff was saying to a small group, "Things are better. We'll start up when we get through the presidential election."

"You relieve me, Henry. I was afraid a Republican might be elected."

"One might, and with less damage than you think. I think we'd still start up. I am not at all doubtful about the success of the Centennial. I am just about as excited over it as Eugene Lewis."

Mrs. Love stood at the door as her guests departed. "Dear Professor and Mrs. Wallace, I hear such charming things about your school. It would be so delightful to have you tell me about it. I've always claimed that everyone should be educated. Please come to see me. . . . Dear Dr. McGill, dear Mrs. McGill. Chemistry, isn't it, that you teach, Doctor? All about birds and flowers and things. No. No, how silly! It's how to run a drug store, of course. Goodby. . . . Why, dear Dr. Wilson. I missed you when you came and I haven't had a single chance to speak to you. How are you?"

"In excellent health, Mrs. Love . . . as I assume everybody else is. Could you arrange for some sort of minor epidemic to lend succor to struggling physicians?"

"Perhaps something could be done. Are you fond of measles, Doctor? Well, good-by."

"You have done a thoughtful thing this evening," Eugene Lewis told Mrs. Love. "You have brought together in people's minds— far better than we could do in a dozen mass meetings with speeches —two of Nashville's most artistic impulses."

"Oh, dear Eugene, you are too unutterably generous." She turned to Neely Barrow. "My dear girl, it was you who made my tea such a success. I've watched tea pouring all my life, and I've never, never seen it so beautifully done. It was simply unutterably exquisite."

"Thank you, Mrs. Love. And don't forget about the house when Martha moves back home."

"*When?* You speak as if she is coming back."

"Of course she is. And she ought to be coming pretty soon too, now that Hunt is ready to build her house."

23

Bart Halloran and his track layers brought the tracks of the Central Railroad into town. Back of the city hospital they reached the river. On into the station they hugged its bank. Jere Baxter could not stay away from the clank of their hammers falling upon steel, from the sounds of ballast poured into place, the sounds of the hoarse, excited voices of the trackmen, from the sight of Bart Halloran, powerful, alert, seeing everything; standing bareheaded, hair rumpled by the wind, arms folded, a veritable god of the road-building era. *Clank, clank, clank,* the Central road was coming to Nashville.

Jere Baxter was taken to bed with an illness. He fretted and fumed but Dr. Cullom was inexorable. He told Dr. Cullom that it was imperative for him to go out to where the crew was bringing the road in. Anything could happen out there, anything.

"In that case you will not need me any further. I only treat patients who need my services."

"You don't mean you quit?"

"Exactly. If you're as sick as I think you are you mustn't leave that bed. If you are not, my judgment is so poor that you don't need me."

So Jere Baxter fumed and fretted, but he stayed in bed. In the early afternoon Bart Halloran came.

"We'll have the road into the station by five. Do you want me to pay the men off then? You were to let me know."

"No!" shouted Jere Baxter. "We need them now more than ever."

"Need them?" Bart Halloran was puzzled.

"Yes. Keep on building . . ."

"Keep on building, sir?" Bart was studying his employer for signs of further delirium.

"Right on to Broadway, across it, right on up Front Street to the market."

"Are you serious, sir?"

"Of course I'm serious. It's a spur, of course, but it will enable us to put our freight cars at the back door of half the wholesale houses in town. I'd like to see Eugene Lewis's face when he hears of it. Right on up to the market, Halloran. And if anybody gets in your way use him for a railroad tie."

"But that will mean tearing up the street. Have you a permit, sir?"

"Of course I haven't a permit. I didn't intend to get sick. If I applied for one earlier Eugene Lewis would have found it out. He couldn't stop me, but he could be annoying."

"You mustn't excite yourself, sir."

"If I wish to excite myself, Halloran, who's to stop me? Get that track down. I'll send a message to the city government. I wish I could see Eugene Lewis's face when he hears of it. I had planned to take him word of it myself the moment the track was laid. And who's that doctor to keep me from doing it, too? Put that track down, Halloran. I told him we might decide to build it around the Capitol. What're you staying here for? Lay that track."

"Yes, sir."

At the door Bart Halloran stopped and turned back to the man in bed. "I can't lay that track, sir," he said sadly.

Jere Baxter sat bolt upright in his bed. "Can't lay it?" he yelled. The nurse came back into the room and told him he'd have to be quiet.

"You be quiet yourself," he shouted. He turned to Bart. "Why can't you lay that track? Are you working for Eugene Lewis or for me?"

"I haven't any rails to lay that track with."

"Why haven't you any rails?"

"Only enough were ordered to complete the main line. You asked me to calculate that carefully."

Suddenly Jere Baxter was repentant for his outburst. "So I did," he said. "I didn't want the word of any excess iron to get out. Eugene Lewis might have suspected something."

"Lie back down, Mr. Baxter, please," pleaded the nurse.

"Oh, all right. Let me know, Halloran, the minute you get the track finished. Get those rails. If you have to steal them I'll keep you out of jail."

"I'm a track layer, not an iron manufacturer, and I'm not worth my salt at stealing. We won't have a hundred feet of rails left over. I figured close like you told me to."

"Report to me the minute you finish it. I want it done by sunup tomorrow. Put it down as rough as you please. You can grade it later. Now get out."

It was Bart Halloran's definite intention to finish the track into the station and withdraw from Jere Baxter's employ. He walked south on Cherry Street and east on Broadway with that purpose clearly formed. Bart didn't object to doing the impossible if the materials were at hand, but he was finding it irksome to be ordered to provide both materials and performance for the impossible. Doubtless his state of mind found some reflection in his face as he strode out Broadway.

"I say, old chap, first time I've seen you in moons, and anger depicted all over that Irish mug! What ho, me lad."

"Anytime I see a walking cane holding on to an able-bodied man's hand I know it's Ivo Burns that's being led about."

Ivo shifted the cane to his left hand and shook hands with Bart. "What's the news, Ivo?"

"Maybe there's some, but in one ear and out the other. Mine's a leaky mind, old top. Still, there's a morsel. Hunt Justice is coming back next week to stay, to settle down, what."

"It's time. How long has Hunt been away?"

"Oh, since Grandmama was a lass or thereabouts. Remember us chasing him from the Academy that time? Most amusing."

"I heard he's made good."

Ivo was shocked by the understatement. "Of all the boys you ever beat up, Bart, he's done the best. Positively. You like railroading as well as ever?"

"Better than ever, but not some railroaders."

"Oho, so that explains that mean Irish look. Who was it frowned at you, Bart? Or spoke harshly? Tell Old Ivo the ghastly details. He has become a protector of the weak, a champion of the innocent. You just tell him."

"Grow up, Ivo, grow up," Bart said smiling.

"That's exactly what I may do even yet. Go ahead, relate your troubles to me in full. Am I not Irish, too? Is Pater not a railroad man, too?"

"All right," said Bart amused. "I'm in a hurry; walk with me and I'll tell you."

The story was brief and finished by the time they reached the trackmen, a few dozen rods from the station.

"Too bad! I feel for the Baxter chap. Really! So you can't get the rails—and *pouf* goes a beautiful dream. What a situation. A free country, and not a rail to be had!"

The head tracklayer came up and told Bart that they'd be finished in two hours and asked if there would be any orders following that.

"I'll let you know. It'll be a week before they are ready to begin on that White Creek stretch. There may be some switches before then, I don't know."

"Switches!" Ivo was moved by some sudden and strong emotion. "Switches! Didn't you put down this track, Bart—I mean all the way from Lebanon?"

"Just from Mount Juliet. I worked on the north end before then."

"Ah, what a light! What a light! You'll get to lay your Front Street track. It's your lucky day, Bart, old top."

"What are you talking about?"

"Switches and things. The Pater is a railroad man, too, you know. Oh, simply dotes on it. Can't utter a word on any other subject. Couldn't see even a volcano in action if there's a railroad at the foot of it. Oh, positively deranged!"

"That makes two deranged men in your family," said Bart, his eyes on the trackmen.

"But wait; tarry; remain unconcluded till you have heard me through. It was but last week that Pater and I drove to Lebanon in the family gig. He conversed of railroads until I thought I would succumb. On the way he would stop and find fault with the track you laid—no, it must have been beyond Mount Juliet. But, naturally no one, not even the Pater, could find fault with your track, Bart. . . ."

"Do you ever come to the point—or is there ever a point?"

"A little patience, dear friend. There by the track at Horn Springs all hidden by weeds and rusting betimes were enough rails to build your track, Bart."

"What are you talking about? Where?" yelled Bart.

"Horn Springs; six miles perhaps, with an added furlong or two this side of Lebanon. Put there, doubtless, the Pater said, to build a switch which, as the Pater remarked very blightingly, hadn't ever been built. He was very bitter about it, charging waste, negligence, incompetence, laziness, triflingness, and others too numerous to mention. Of course, Pater belongs to the other railroad, but he was greatly pained . . . Where are you going?"

Bart was running back down the newly laid track to where an engine coupled to a flatcar sat on the tracks, snoring gently in the afternoon sun. The engineman sat at the throttle and he too was snoring gently.

"Hey," yelled Bart, "wake up. We going on a trip."

The engineman snored on. Bart swung upon the step and jerked his arm.

"What is it?" he asked sleepily.

"You got up any steam?"

"No. Enough to take her in maybe."

"We're not going in. We're going back to Lebanon."

"Can't. Got no coal."

"Order some sent."

"Wouldn't get here before tomorrer. What's the hurry?"

"I'll tell you on the way. Get some wood. We can pull it with that."

"You see any wood anywhere?" Bart's haste was nettling the engineman.

"Yes, I see some. Hey, you, get some saws and cut these ties in two-foot lengths."

Four of the trackmen came with saws and cut a dozen ties into short lengths. Bart scraped up from the remnants of a near-by pile of coal enough to restore the fire that languished in the inwards of the engine. Wood was added and presently steam surged in the cylinders. Bart commandeered four of the trackmen for the journey to Horn Springs. He told the others to get Howard Kapp and lay off the track up Front Street. He didn't know where Kapp was. But they were to find him. The engineman looked at his gauge. He nodded his head. Bart Halloran climbed the engine steps. The throttle was eased open in reverse, and emitting great creakings of protest the engine and flatcar started on its trip backward to Horn Springs, twenty-five miles away. Above the creaks and the hissing of the steam jetting from the margins of the cylinder heads Bart heard a laconic voice. "Move up, can't you? I have to have a little room, what."

"You're not going, Ivo?"

"And who is so brash to say I'm not going? Pater is a railroad man. In the blood, and all that. Move over into that cab."

Bart moved over.

Late that afternoon John Thomas drove his best horse in a furious trot out to the Centennial grounds. He hitched his horse on Elliston Place and pushed his way through the crowds until he came to the Administration Building. Luckily Eugene Lewis was in his office.

"Eugene, I think there's trouble up."

"What trouble, John?"

"I drove by the foot of Broad a half hour ago, and some men were using a transit on Front Street. They weren't city men. They were a part of the crew of the Central Railroad. I recognized Howard Kapp."

"Sure of it, John?"

"Sure, Eugene."

Eugene Lewis's mind was milling furiously. "So that's it," he said. "Why, of course. That's where the wholesale houses are. So that's the Capitol he was going to build around. That's the tunnel he was going to run under it!"

"An injunction, I should think, Eugene."

"We'll get an injunction. It is definitely contrary to the welfare of the city for railroads to be run indiscriminately along the streets."

They found Judge Vaughn sometime after dark, and he issued an order effective at six the following morning restraining temporarily the Central Railroad from extending its lines farther into the city in any direction.

"We'll stop them before they start," said Eugene Lewis.

At five he arose, breakfasted meagerly and drove down to Front Street. He first heard the noise as he passed Summer Street. There it was, the unmistakable ring of steel striking upon steel, of men shouting. It was an ominous sound to Eugene Lewis. He knew before he arrived that the injunction bore a date too late.

And then he drove into Front Street and saw that Jere Baxter had beaten him. The wholesale houses were the "Capitol" that Baxter had built his road around. And there stood Bart Halloran, his hands on his hips, his hair tousled a bit by the wind, his eyes alertly upon the men who had worked without ceasing through the night. Eugene Lewis's eyes opened wider. There was Ivo Burns, the son of the General Superintendent of his own railroad. At that moment he was carrying unassisted a railroad tie. Ivo's clothes, of Nashville's best tailoring, were somewhat the worse for the night's wear but there was the true jauntiness of the railroad man in the step that bore the railroad tie to its appointed place.

If there was anger in Eugene Lewis's heart there also was admiration for achievement. He saw that the tracks had cleared the last wholesale house. One more joint of rail and the assignment would be complete. He looked at his watch. It was fifteen minutes of six o'clock. No one of the workmen had seen him, so intent were they upon their work. He saw a deputy from the Sheriff's office drive up and look with surprised eyes upon the scene. The officer got out of his buggy and approached Bart Halloran, handing him a paper. Bart read it, smiled broadly, took out his watch, held it where the officer could see, pointing at some line upon the paper as he did so. The deputy shook his head, stood for a moment in thought, then returned to his buggy and drove away.

A few minutes later Eugene Lewis hitched his horse and walked to where Bart was standing. "I have great admiration for you, Halloran," he said. "How long has Ivo Burns been working for you?"

"Since late yesterday afternoon, sir."

"I must confess to some surprise."

"I wasn't expecting him myself. He just happened along and went to work."

"Look at that." Ivo was bringing another tie with apparently no great output of effort. "Why, it's worth some disappointment to see Ivo carrying that tie. We'll make a railroad man out of him yet."

"He claims he has railroad blood in him already," said Bart dryly. He turned squarely to Eugene Lewis. "I wonder if your railroad could use me."

"Use you? I've tried to use you long before now."

"I wasn't free then."

"Are you now?"

"I will be in a few minutes."

"You're hired. Maybe we can build that Lewisburg stretch now. Besides," he added grimly, "I may want to run our road around the Capitol, or maybe tunnel under it."

24

Nashville Day at the Centennial. A September sun swinging its placid way through a cloudless sky. The rich haze of Indian Summer hanging against the distant hills.

There was a full load waiting for College Grove to start his first trip that morning. He put on a little show for them. He stood at the car steps and with mock ardor harangued his patrons.

"Step right abo'd, ladeeze and gents. All it's a-goin' to cost you is five cents, one-twentieth of a dollar which nowheres else you can't get so much for your spondoolix. Step right abo'd. She's hanted but she'll get you there."

"Haunted?"

"Yes, ma'am, that's what I said, hanted. And the hant appears amid dire groanin's and utterances every trip they's a wicked passenger abo'd. And they's been a right smart o' groanin' lately, too. Step right in, ladeeze 'n' gemmun, the hant is jest about to leave here."

Tittering and giggling a bit, they stepped in, and amid dire groanings the hant left, Centennial-bound.

On his fourth trip out to the grounds College Grove brought the hant to a stop at McLemore Street to take on some passengers who had signaled him. While he waited for them to climb aboard, a familiar voice sounded from the street to his left. "Move over to one side so a gent with real hosses can get by."

"Pull them two cases o' walkin' starvation over. It's agin the city law for country hosses to give out completely right in the way of an e-lec-tric streetcar."

The driver cracked his whip merrily. "I'll move on. It ain't in my mind to converse with nobody without he's got good sense."

He drove away in a sprightly trot. College Grove manipulated his throttle so as to sting fiercely the wheels of the car. It was his intention to overtake the Coles's carriage and pass it with a triumphant clanging of the bell. But he was doomed to frustration. He was bearing down upon his quarry, but at Stonewall Street a man stepped out and held up his hand. College Grove gritted his teeth in anger but shut off the current and braked the car to a stop. The man, unmistakably from the back country, looked back at the sidewalk and called out in tones audible a great deal farther than was necessary, "Come on."

They came on, the mother and six children of graded sizes.

"We was a-aimin' to walk to this world's fair," said the man, apparently with only a slight reduction in the volume used in summoning hogs a half mile away, "but Pauleeny, she give out."

"She give out jest as soon as she heard you comin'," testified the number-one son.

But the mother was disposed to add her weight to the Pauleeny side of the argument. "She didn't give out as soon as you did when you was little like her."

"All abo'd," sharply shouted College Grove who beheld the Cole carriage top the rise at the West End Methodist Church. He could never catch it now. "Effn you want to ride climb on."

"I've heard tell it's dangerous," said the man in a voice that caused passers-by to look hurriedly around.

"Ain't hardly a trip that we don't kill somebody."

At that the older children started to climb aboard.

"Don't you git on there till we git this settled. Mister, what's this ride goin' to set me back?"

"Thirty-five cents. No charge for her," pointing to Pauleeny. "She's a passel-young looks like. All abo'd."

An impatient passenger suggested delicately that she had looked forward to attending the Centennial, but it seemed that that pleasure was about to be denied her.

"All abo'd. All abo'd and put thirty-five cents in that box."

The number-two son dropped a quarter and two nickels into the box. He was anxious to get started so that somebody could get killed.

"Hez," yelled his father, "you hadn't ought 'a' done that. You can't get it out."

"Ever' one o' you owes me a nickel," answered Hez, and he too was audible. "Get on. I want to see that world's fair."

They climbed aboard. "Now you give me a nickel, ever' one of you," ordered Hez.

"I reckon you better pay him," said the father, in chastened tones, handing Hez a nickel. From various places of concealment five other nickels were brought forth to liquidate the indebtedness.

The trip to the Centennial was resumed. The family adjusted

itself in seats, but the father lingered on the front platform. "We left home at four o'clock," he said. "Got a ride in Mr. Little's two-horse wagon. He's a-haulin seed wheat. He let us out at the seed store and we figgered we could walk it but Pauleeny give out."

"Whyn't you carry her?" College Grove was still irked by the loss of an opportunity to prove, particularly under the conditions, the superiority of electricity over horses.

"Carry Pauleeny! She's made plumb out o' lead. Besides, when you carry Pauleeny you always have to look to see which end's up. She's that squirmy. Jest look at her back there. Whether she's settin' in her ma's lap or standin' on her haid I ain't certain."

Hez came out to say in effect that they were becoming a bit restive waiting for a passenger to be killed.

"We kill 'em mostly goin' back, though there's a right good chance at the fur end o' Vanderbilt. Go back and set down but keep your eyes peeled."

The driver was in high spirits. You couldn't beat hosses. Just wait! He threaded the Weaver Cole team in and out among the traffic. In his carriage were Merrie and Weaver Cole, and Neely Barrow and Hunt. There was quality in the horses he drove. There was quality in the folks he carried. The driver's heart, old in years, had never grown old in spirit, and on that day it was even younger.

Hunt Justice had come back to Nashville the afternoon before. He had completed his work in Providence. It was time to come home. Eugene Lewis had written for him to come back. In his opinion, Lewis said, a great deal of building would be done in Nashville in the near future. The Forrest County courthouse had already been awarded to an architect-contractor who lived there. The Church Street building plans would be selected soon. He was not too optimistic but there was a chance. He had met Hunt at the railroad station and of course had driven him to the Centennial first. The other buildings were good, their placement and their lines were pleasing. But Hunt had gasped with artistic excitement when he saw the Parthenon.

"Isn't it magnificent? But, Hunt, I'll tell you something. We had to put it up too cheaply. I tried everything I know but I couldn't get enough money. Colonel Smith planned it well, and Creighton and McWhirter built it well with what they had. It's splendid but it won't last longer than, say, one generation. But

Nashville won't let it be lost. It'll be made permanent. I have that faith. Well, I guess you're tired. I wanted you to see this. Tomorrow's Nashville Day."

They had gone then to Mrs. Elrod's on Oak Street. She sat on the porch knitting while she awaited them. "Hello, Major Lewis, who's the city dude you got with you?"

"Oh, that's no dude," he protested. "It's a statue we're going to put in one of the buildings out at the Centennial. I wonder if you could keep it for me till tomorrow."

"I got a room all fixed for such like. Come right in."

Between volleys of ironic but adoring banter Mrs. Elrod prepared supper, and Hunt from the kitchen doorway watched her.

"If you'll excuse me," he said presently, "I'd like to go for a few minutes down to Mother's grave."

"Go right ahead. Be back in a half hour. And that makes me think. Here's a letter—I guess it's from your daddy—that come yesterday." She paused a moment and added with a touch of delicacy, "Take it with you and read it while you're gone."

Hunt stood at his mother's grave and read the letter from his father. He was very busy at the moment, otherwise he'd have come to Nashville to greet Hunt upon arrival. Ed Crayton had been lucky about contracts, and in a way he was Ed's main dependence. He liked it fine. Of course he didn't ever expect to build any fine houses like the ones Hunt had planned for the Centennial, but his were good enough for railroad warehouses. He was at the moment building one at Monteagle, and the railroad was in a hurry for it. He'd be coming to Nashville before long, just as soon as Ed Crayton could spare him for a day or two, and he'd sure be mighty glad to see Hunt once more. He guessed maybe Hunt had grown so much he'd have to look twice to recognize him. Well, tell Mrs. Elrod howdy for him, and put some nice flowers on Lizzie's grave for them both.

In the margins of the cemetery Hunt saw some goldenrod blooming gloriously. He cut some of it and brought it to the grave. "It's from Papa and me," he said.

The stillness in the cemetery was almost unearthly. No wind stirred in the trees; no little creature rustled the grass and leaves upon the ground; no bird sang. The railroad had almost suddenly become quiet. Hunt remembered how much his mother loved quiet. She must be resting, he thought. He turned and walked away.

Supper was waiting, and he was hungry. Mrs. Elrod had seen his father when he had come to Nashville three or four months before.

"He tickled me a good deal," she said. "He told me about a trade he'd made with the Lord, I reckon. He said when he went to preachin' three straight Sundays, why, the next Saturday night he went fox huntin'. Said it looked like a fair trade to him and he didn't ever expect to break it. Said he'd noticed one thing, the better the preachin', the better the huntin'. Have some more of the chicken and dressin'. Oh yes, the Coles are comin' by in the mornin' to take you to the Fair. They said maybe there would be room for an extry one but they wasn't sure."

Hunt smiled. Eugene Lewis had already told him of that arrangement. "Can't you go, Mrs. Elrod? I'll buy you the biggest ticket they have," he said entering into her spirit of gayety.

"No," she said firmly, "but you can buy me one for the last day. I went the first day and I'd like to go the last, but that's all."

He looked at her. Her face was broad and seamed with work and age but there was the warmth of kindliness in her shrewd little eyes. "Mrs. Elrod, I don't think I've ever told you that I know how good you've been to us. I tell you now, and I thank you. I think one of the luckiest things we ever did was to drive up here that day a long time ago."

"You remember that?"

"Just as well as if it happened today. And all the time we were here there wasn't a week—no, not a day—that you didn't do something nice for us. I remember you got Papa his first job for him."

"Well, he's held it and I ain't so sure but that's more than I expected. He's sure pleased Ed Crayton."

"And when Mama got sick . . ."

"Your mother was a good woman. I tried to do what I could for her." She shifted the topic. "What you aimin' to do now?"

"I want to plan some buildings. I'm in Nashville to stay," he added resolutely.

"Any prospects?"

"I've tried for a building some people are going to put up on Church Street though I doubt if I get it. I've saved up a little money and I can live for a while. Major Lewis will help me if he can."

"Well, he can if anybody can. He is about runnin' the town, looks like. Now let me tell you somethin'. One o' my lucky days was that time you all drove up here to see about a house. People never did fool me much. I always could tell a saint from a scalawag.

The minute I saw you and your mother I knew I wanted you in my house. I don't reckon I'd 'a' rented to your daddy if he'd been by himself, but he turned out all right too. You let me tell you this: they ain't been a day since then I ain't been proud o' you. They is peach cobbler for dessert."

He finished the cobbler. She looked at him with a wise twinkle in her eyes. "I reckon you'll be wantin' to go somewhere, see old friends or somethin'. Well, if I ain't up when you get back they'll be a lamp burnin' in your room."

"Thank you, Mrs. Elrod. Who lives in . . . in our house now?"

"Some folks named Marshall. Good plain people, no trouble hardly at all and pay is prompt. From what I heard I don't guess you'll be wantin' to stay here long, but that room's yours just as long as you want it, and when you do leave you got to come back to see me ever so often. And don't forget, you're buying my ticket for the last day at the big fair."

At the gate he looked back and waved to Mrs. Elrod, and she waved in return. She stood there, sturdy of build, hair rapidly whitening, in her eyes and on her seamed face a look tender and wistful.

He walked along the way that he knew so well. There was something strangely exhilarating about life. It seemed to Hunt that all of his days before had been turned toward this one. Life was drawing to a focus. As if in a dream he heard Neely Barrow saying, "Wait there, Hunt. I wanted to meet you farther away."

Nashville Day at the Centennial, and the grounds deep in happy, excited, bright-eyed humanity. Inside the grounds Neely Barrow and Hunt had separated from the Weaver Coles, but with explicit arrangements to meet for their picnic dinner. Hunt wanted to show Neely Barrow the Parthenon—as if she hadn't seen it before. So they went to it and into the West Room. Only a few of the Centennial's visitors were in the West Room. There was a stone bench against a wall.

"Let's sit here," said Hunt. "I've never thought of this room without thinking of you. This is your room, fine and most beautiful. This was Athena's Chamber, but I think it is much more appropriately your chamber."

"Look," said Neely Barrow. "Ionic columns!"

"Columns for you. There are no more perfect columns in the world."

"Hunt," she said hardly above a whisper, "when we marry, couldn't it be here?"

His eyes, very bright, never left her face. "Yes," he said, "here."

"Hunt, I want it to be soon. This is new and fine. I don't want to wait until it becomes dingy."

"When I have one contract, the first one, then that very day. I can't before."

"I want to marry you, not an architect."

"I want to make sure, Neely Barrow. I must know for certain."

"I know now, but if it takes that to convince you I'll wait."

"I didn't get the Forrest County courthouse. Really, I didn't expect it. I'm not too hopeful about the Church Street building, but there'll be something," he said fiercely, "and when there is—when there is!" He looked about him. "It would have to be here. It is the most beautiful place in the world."

"Isn't that Neely Barrow Roane?" a lady across Athena's Chamber inquired of her companion. "They say she's engaged to a young man in the East who's awful smart. They say he planned this very building we're in right now, and before that the Capitol of the United States or something. I guess that's him. Let's go over and meet them. She teaches my little girl in the Howard School."

Outside the day grew warmer and the crowds thicker. Most of the main buildings were crowded.

In the Commerce Building a bright-eyed girl of twelve came hurrying across the aisle. "Hello, Miss Neely Barrow. Are you going to teach next year?"

"Perhaps so, Elsie. Why?"

"Oh, I thought I'd just like to know." Her speculative eyes were resting on Hunt Justice. "You can't guess where I've been?"

"No, dear. You must tell me."

"Inside Mercury. You know, the statue on this building. I didn't know he's hollow but he is. Mr. Buttorff let me on the roof and I saw he's hollow so I stepped in him." Her eyes again rested upon Hunt. "No, Miss Neely Barrow, I don't suppose you will be back at the Howard School any more."

The soft musical cry of the gondoliers on Lakes Wautauga and Katherine were lifted upon the holiday air. The band was playing "Suwanee River" in the bandstand.

Above the clamor a stentorian voice shook the welkin. "I reckon we'll have to set and rest awhile. Pauleeny's give out agin!"

"The way she's been lookin' at that wild goose two hours," affirmed the number-two son, "don't look give out to me."

"She says she's give out," roared the father.

"That's no wild goose," said the number-one daughter, "that's a swan. I heard a man say so."

The mother rallied to the defense of her last-born. "We haven't been here two hours. We just got here. Besides I think that bird's right purty myself."

"That's no bird. That's a swan. I heard a man say so."

Then a voice spoken through a megaphone smote the air. "Lost—a little girl named Belle Ferguson. Find Belle Ferguson. Return her to her distracted parents in the Administration Building. Six years old, light hair. Find Belle Ferguson."

The word spread. *Find Belle Ferguson.* Everybody began to cast a searching eye for Belle Ferguson.

"Hey, you little girl. What you running for? Come here. Are you Belle Ferguson?"

"Yes, but I don't want to be found."

The man resorted to strategy. "How much ice cream could you eat?"

"A gallon," said Belle Ferguson.

"A little high," said the man, "but I'll make you an offer. You go with me to your father and mother and I'll buy you a pint."

"I'd rather stay lost."

"Don't be a cheap skate," called a spectator. "Do you want the little girl to stay lost?"

The man raised his bid to a quart. Belle Ferguson regarded him speculatively. "All right," she said, "but I may get lost again." She gravely offered her hand to the gentleman and they walked away toward the Administration Building.

Somewhere a clock tolled noon. Eugene Lewis at the desk of the Commissioner General arose. "I'm going to walk about a little. I want to see the crowd."

"Have something to eat with me before you go," said Thomas Fite. "I'm sure I have plenty."

"Food at the moment, Thomas, is not one of my interests.

Thank you." He moved on down the hall. On the steps he met Charles Thurman, basket in hand.

"Eat with me, Eugene. I am sure I have plenty."

"Thank you, Charles. Some other time. I want to see the crowds."

"They are here," said Charles Thurman. "And they are worth seeing. I'll defer my invitation, not withdraw it."

He walked on. Presently a hand tugged at his sleeve. It was Rabbi Lewinthal of the Jewish Synagogue. "We are eating our dinner." He pointed. "It would be an honor if you would come and eat a little with us."

"An honor! Certainly. But exclusively my honor. I accept gratefully!"

"I speak for a small group of Jewish people, and they would not agree with you, Mr. Commissioner General, as to where the honor belongs."

They came to the picnickers gathered around a rough table.

"Oh, but he was good enough to come," said the Rabbi. "Mr. Commissioner General, may I name my dear friends? This is Mrs. Adolph Loventhal. These are Mrs. and Mr. Nathan Cohn. This is Ben Herman and this Morris Werthan, and this gentleman is Joseph Lefkovitz. May we congratulate you, Mr. Commissioner General, upon the remarkable success of our Centennial?"

"I found him," said a voice from behind.

"When I want someone I send Lee Loventhal to find him," said the Rabbi, addressing the group. "If he had been Columbus he would have found America a month sooner." He addressed one, obviously a Catholic priest. "Father O'Neill, you are most welcome." He made the rounds with the priest.

"I know Major Lewis," said the priest. "He is one of our very helpful citizens." He looked about him. "This is almost symbolic," he said.

"Behold how good and how pleasant it is for brethren to dwell together in unity, sayeth the Psalmist. Let us establish our unity. Mrs. Loveman, will you take charge of the food?"

"Major Lewis and I have been friends a long time," said Mrs. Loveman, passing a heaping platter of fried chicken, "but as far as I am concerned that friendship has deepened today. It's that, sir." She looked at the Parthenon. "I've been sitting here for an hour, looking at that building, looking at the people passing it. They not only pass it, but they pass. To pass is our common destiny. We all pass. This is the only Tennessee Centennial that you and I will ever see. We will pass. But the Parthenon! It will not pass because it is one of the noblest ideas of men, and noble ideas do not pass. It was you who thought to put the Parthenon here, was it not?"

"I had something to do with it, but I did not think of it."

"No? Who did, please?"

"A young man named Hunt Justice, who happily returned to Nashville yesterday."

"Oh, isn't he the one who is so interested in Neely Barrow Roane?"

"Yes, a pretty romance. It was he who thought of the Parthenon."

"I sat here and looked at that building and some spirit of chaste beauty entered into me."

"The Parthenon may have been pagan to begin with," said Father O'Neill, "but the Roman Church was quick to recognize its beauty."

Eugene Lewis pointed across the lake. "There is a remarkable building. It has one of the best and most vividly arranged exhibits of all our buildings. It is an eloquent testimonial of the resourcefulness and artistry of the Negroes."

The group looked at the building across the lake, and as they did they heard above the confused sounds of the Centennial a song of unyielding faith.

> "Swing low, sweet chariot,
> Coming for to carry me home."

An exasperated father told his eight-year-old son, "If I ever get you back to Cookeville, you'll stay there."

"Papa, I want to see the Streets of Cairo."

"You're not going to. It's no place for a child."

"It was some children that told me about it. I want to see the Streets of Cairo, Papa."

"I oughtn't to have brought you. I'll not next time."

"If you are not going to bring me next time I must have my way this time. I want to go see the Streets of Cairo."

"A week ago you were sick in bed."

"I think I'm going to have another convulsion. I always start screaming before I have one, don't I, Papa?"

"You just so much as open your mouth and I'll . . ."

"So he's goin' to beat up his little boy, and him sick," observed a bystander in a threatening drawl.

"All right, come on," said the frantic father from Cookeville, and he and his son, most felicitously rescued from the very threshold of a convulsion, walked rapidly toward the Streets of Cairo.

A small girl had observed the episode thoughtfully. "Papa," she said, "I do believe I'm about to have a convulsion."

The father took his daughter's hand. "It isn't necessary, Anna Cooper. I'd like to see the Streets myself."

Harvey Cragon, Sr., was accompanying his young son on a tour of the attractions. They had been interested witnesses of the episode presented by the Cookevillians. "I suppose that you are about to have a convulsion, too," said Harvey Senior, to Harvey Junior. "Well, let's not take any risks."

"I'm not about to have a convulsion, and I don't want to see the Streets of Cairo. I want to go back to the Manufacturers' Building and talk over the telephone."

"All right," said the father weakly. Then he addressed the Centennial *in toto:* "Sometime I'm going to ask somebody to explain something about children to me."

Four young men, arm in arm, clad in suits of a beautiful plaid topped by beautiful brown derby hats, walked up and down the Centennial's Broadway beating merrily with their walking canes the time to "I Was Seeing Nellie Home." At the end of a verse Charley Mitchell would assume a pose and lift his voice well above the hubbub. "My assistants, John Kreig, Charles Johnstone and Paul DeWitt, will now pass among you offering for sale that priceless boon for ailing humanity, The Eureka Corn Salve and Toe Remover. Toes refunded and no questions asked if you are not satisfied."

Eugene Lewis passed by on his way back to the Administration Building. He entered into the spirit of the occasion and addressed the crowd in effect that if anyone there used the remedy and it left his toes on his feet he would have the imposters ejected from the Centennial grounds. He winked broadly at Charley Mitchell and went on his way. Mitchell bowed and stepped back into line; the quartet linked arms and resumed lustily "I Was Seeing Nellie Home."

A great crowd watched Ariel pursue a death-defying stroll along a high wire stretched from the Memphis Building to the Pavilion. The band in the auditorium was playing the Anvil Chorus. The buildings were filled, and in each a perspiring interpreter explained the miracles on exhibit. The air was discordant with the cries of the purveyors of lemonade, of pop in all the prismatic colors, of beef sandwiches with mustard, of dolls that cried, and whistles that shrieked and moaned. A constant flow of visitors passed through the most modern of Pullman cars in the Transportation Building, and just outside on a special flatcar Tyree Rodes was exhibiting the mammoth of all Tennessee saw logs.

Hunt Justice and Neely Barrow Roane walked along the Centennial Avenues, and it seemed to Hunt that everybody knew Neely Barrow.

"Why, Neely Barrow, how do you do? You look so charming."

It was on Neely Barrow's tongue to say, *How do you know, Mrs. Reyer? You haven't looked at anybody but Hunt yet,* but instead she said, "Oh, how lovely, Mrs. Reyer. May I present Hunt Justice?"

A plump young lady, with something of distinction in her face, was passing but suddenly she stopped dead still. "Are you Hunt Justice?" she asked. "Are you?"

"Yes, that is my name."

She looked at him intently. "I don't suppose I have seen you since you left Huntland."

"Huntland?"

"Yes, I'm Elma Moore—at least I was. I'm Mrs. Rutledge now."

"Oh," he said, wide-eyed. "You lived in Mr. Moore's house."

"Born there. All twelve of us were. Do you know, one of the most vivid recollections I have is of you looking at our house."

"That was not well mannered of me."

"Oh, but it was. We have talked about it. Sister Lexie was talking about it the other day. Since you have become famous we think it was a compliment to our house."

"Oh, but Mrs. Rutledge, I'm not famous. Please let me present Neely Barrow Roane."

"We've heard about her, too. News gets around in Huntland. My dear, you must let Hunt bring you to see our house. It was the house that inspired him. At least we love to think it was."

"I'd love to come. Do you like the Centennial?"

"Never was a Moore that didn't like shows and fairs. We always go. When they had the World's Fair in Chicago Sister Annie didn't have the money for the trip right then so she sold a place she owned. We always go. But somehow I like this best of all. Oh, there's Cousin Garland. Sister Mamie sent some word to him by me. You come to see our house—both of you."

The Centennial's official announcer was employing his megaphone again. "Major E. B. Stahlman will deliver an address in the auditorium at half after two. All are invited."

"I'm going," said a man, rising from the ground upon which he half lay. "I'd rather hear the Major speak than anybody except Bob Taylor. When the Major waves a hand I sway."

September can grow warm in Nashville. By noon it was a hot day. By midafternoon, the sun was pouring undiluted heat upon the Centennial and its patrons. The avenues and grounds became almost suddenly a curiously uneven sea on whose shimmering and quivering surface bobbed a thousand gayly colored parasols, blunting the attack of the heat against the ladies. The men took the heat as it came, though it wrought visible damage upon the raiment they wore. High collars were laid low; stiffly glazed cuffs were rendered inert and flabby. High patent-leather shoes were dull and mottled with dust. Shirts lost their matin stiffness and became limp and intimate. The beef-sandwich hawkers made sandwiches with one hand and fought flies with the other. The bright-colored pop flowed in an unending stream down dusty throats. One enterprising young man sold ice water. "All you can drink for two cents." It became restful and refreshing to listen to the splash of oars upon the lakes.

Neely Barrow and Hunt were not easy to find, but Weaver Cole found them. They were standing in front of the Woman's Building and Hunt was explaining the architectural development of the structure from the Hermitage motif.

"Mr. Lewis wants to see you, Hunt. Can you come now?"

Hunt hesitated, his eyes glancing toward Neely Barrow.

"Go on, Hunt," she said. "I'll wait here for you."

"No, he said for you both to come."

Eugene Lewis sat at his desk, but stood when they entered. He motioned them to chairs. "The Church Street building didn't turn out very well, Hunt."

"I am not surprised, sir."

"I told you that they would likely expect the maximum space for rental purposes. They have chosen Will Raymond."

Neely Barrow, unconscious that she did so, placed her hand upon Hunt's arm.

"I have just learned of their decision. Mark Buckner said that their building could not hope to equal yours in looks, but their first interest is income."

A rich half-rueful smile was on Hunt's face. "I'm disappointed, of course. Right now . . ." He broke off, his eyes upon Neely Barrow.

"Somehow the good sense of the situation appeals to me," said Eugene Lewis. "I have never thought that love alone should justify rushing into marriage. Some tests should be set up and passed, some goals reached, or else one of the very precious things becomes too cheap."

"Maybe I'm a mystic but I want a sign of my worthiness."

"I'm that sign," said Neely Barrow.

"No," said Hunt, "you're the reason I must have the sign."

"I," said the Commissioner General, "approve of your waiting for the sign."

"It will take more than a building on Church Street to disturb me," said Neely Barrow. "I, too, will wait for the sign."

"This is the stupidest talk I ever had part in," said Eugene Lewis, "and the first time in my life that stupid talk pleased me. I thought you should know of their decision, Hunt."

"I should. Thank you, sir."

"There'll be other buildings," assured Neely Barrow.

"That makes me think," said Eugene Lewis. "I sent for Barksdale Reeves a while ago and had a talk with him. That talk resulted in this." He drew from his pocket a folded paper. "It is an agreement for you to plan and direct the building of his new home. You remember, Hunt. We spent several hours out there. He wants it built from the sketch you drew. It is to be a very nice home indeed. He wants you to begin on it as soon as possible."

"That will be pretty soon," said Hunt huskily, his eyes upon Neely Barrow.

"Isn't this the sign, Hunt?" Her voice was scarcely above a whisper.

"Yes," he said, "it is *the* sign."

"Then the marriage will be soon?" asked Eugene Lewis.

"Today," said Hunt, his eyes never leaving Neely Barrow's face.

"Not today, Hunt," she said gently. "Today is about over."

"There are certain preparations to be made, legal and otherwise. Tomorrow would be better. Where would you like for it to be, Cherry Hill?"

"In the Parthenon," said Neely Barrow. "We have already decided that."

"Exquisite! The very flower of appropriateness. But a trifle difficult. There's always a crowd there. Let me see. We could close it for an hour, say at six tomorrow evening. Leave the inference it is for repairs or something. Does that suit?"

"Yes," said Neely Barrow.

"Yes," said Hunt.

"All right, I'll attend to it. Of course, of course. Now you two run on away, go see the Centennial, watch the people, observe the exhibitions, witness the amazing variety with which life abounds, sense the excitement it affords. Go see the Parthenon, look at those Ionic columns in the Maiden's Chamber, and come back here before you leave. Now run along. Matters of business impinge upon me."

They left, and Eugene Lewis called Weaver Cole. "What a messenger boy you are, Weaver. Go to the Woman's Building and bring Mary Dorris back with you. I think she'll come willingly. If not, bring her anyhow."

Weaver brought her.

"All right," said Mary Dorris. "I haven't been sent for so imperatively in years. I must be needed. I'm complimented. Weaver told me that if I didn't come willingly and rapidly he'd use a club and carry me on his shoulders. Weaver is very convincing. What is it?"

"Neely Barrow Roane and Hunt Justice just left here."

"Yes?"

"They are to be married tomorrow evening in the Parthenon. No publicity, but I thought you should know. Isn't there some gesture which would add a special fitness to their wedding?"

For ten seconds she said nothing. Then, "Yes, there is. The Hermitage belongs in this. Of course, it does."

"I thought so."

"A breakfast," she said, "tomorrow morning. Of course."

"Precisely my thought."

She straightened up. "Get Bettie Donelson. She's at the Woman's Building."

"Weaver, go to the Woman's Building and bring Mrs. Donelson."

"Preferably alive, I imagine," said Weaver.

"Preferably, but quickly."

So Weaver came presently bringing Mrs. Donelson. They told her the story. She stood listening, her brow puckered in thought. "It looks like a breakfast, Mary."

"Of course, Bettie."

"Well, it'll take work, Mary, but it's a little late for you and me to begin flinching."

"One of our old habits is not to. I can bring my cook."

"I'll bring a girl to help. There's one distressing matter."

"So few, Bettie?"

"A Hermitage breakfast calls for turkey hash. Where could we get a turkey in September?"

"We can get a ham."

"That isn't a Hermitage breakfast. I have it now. I have some hens that think they are turkeys. We will not disillusion them. No, nor the guests either."

"I am most grateful," said Eugene Lewis, "for the invitation to breakfast. Tomorrow will be a slack day here. I can arrange to be present at your breakfast."

"You'll be there. But more as a hired man than a guest. Bettie and I will prepare the breakfast. You will run it. You will see that the guests get there and that they enjoy being there. You will not fail to turn anything and everything to the pleasure of the bride and groom. You will see that everybody says the right word at the right moment. If something starts out to be a *faux pas* you will turn it into a brilliant and unforgettable speech. You will . . ."

"We don't know that Neely Barrow and Hunt will want to come to a breakfast," said Bettie Donelson.

"Oh, yes, they will. I'll guarantee their attendance. Who else should come?"

"I could run the errands," said Weaver Cole. "That ought to entitle Merrie and me to a regular serving of turkey hash."

"No errands," said Eugene Lewis. "You will pay for yours and Merrie's breakfasts by bringing the bride and groom."

"There is more color than I've ever seen in September. The trip out there is perfectly glorious. The Hermitage is coming back into its greatness. Look," she said, holding her hands palms up before

Eugene Lewis's eyes. "Do you know where I got those calluses?"

"At the Hermitage, Mary?"

"Yes, at the Hermitage. Those are honorable scars. It has taken work to start the Hermitage back to its greatness. But it has started back. I love to look at those hands. One who stands near the Hermitage today and sees it with understanding eyes half expects General Jackson, tall, erect, commanding, to come out of the front door, across the porch, out under the cedars, and plunge the tip of his cane into the ground saying, *The Union, sir—it must and shall be preserved.*"

"An eloquent speech, Mrs. Dorris. Who are to be your guests, and at what time will breakfast be served?"

"We can't take more than twenty, can we, Bettie?"

"Fifteen," said Bettie Donelson, "would cause us some strain."

"Make it fifteen. We'll work out the list. Breakfast will be served at nine. And be prompt, or by the Eternal . . ."

Neely Barrow and Hunt walked along the Centennial's main street. It was in their minds to get to the Maiden's Chamber in the Parthenon as soon as possible, but they made slow progress. It seemed to Hunt that everybody knew Neely Barrow. "Keep going," she said in Hunt's ear. "I'll exhibit you later. That's what they want."

"Good evening, Miss Roane. Excuse me, please, but aren't you Hunt Justice? I'm Will Beard from the *Banner*. My paper wants me to interview you. There is really some demand for the story. Will you give me a half hour sometime soon?"

"You write my favorite news, Mr. Beard," said Neely Barrow. "Don't expect the interview for a few days yet." She hesitated a brief moment. "If you wish, come to Athena's Chamber in the Parthenon tomorrow evening at six. Maybe you could then write some more of my favorite news."

The "good afternoons" came thick and fast.

Hunt said, "Let's go back to Mr. Lewis's office. We'll never get to the Parthenon like this."

"I guess we'd better. You see, Hunt, it's the old families just now getting into the receiving line."

Nashville Day at the Centennial! It didn't matter too much if feet ached, if throats were dusty, if clothes were damp and limp. Eyes were still bright, and hearts young and gay. It was more than a state's hundredth birthday. It was its matching of challenges, its rebuke to cynics. It was its affirmation of the joy of living and loving, of talking and helping, of seeing and wondering, of exclaiming, "Why, Neely Barrow, I haven't seen you in ages. My dear, how beautiful you are!"

"Thank you, Mrs. Tigert, so is everything. Good afternoon, Mrs. Lindsey. How delightful to see you, Mrs. Giers. Why, how Hunter has grown!"

Nashville Day at the Centennial! Base Street striking its elbows against those of West End! Lebanon calling happy and excited greetings to Springfield. Tullahoma exchanging pleasant banter with Franklin. Memphis clustered loyally about the great pyramid it had built. Chattanooga playing host in its building! Knoxville Republicans fraternizing with Jackson Democrats. Speech flavored with the opulent softness of Georgia mingled with Kentucky drawl as silken as the downward drift of an autumn leaf. In the Woman's Building and the Parthenon the idiom of the forum and the college; on the streets of Vanity Fair the freer speech of the less inhibited! How wonderful the parades of Nashville's grace and loveliness. The gasps died tardily in the throats of those who saw John Thomas driving a horseless carriage along the Centennial's main street. Then came the Lawrenceburg band, the town's mayor marching proudly in front, playing "Dixie" as though inspired.

Tired feet and dusty throats and happiness in fifteen thousand hearts! Tennessee had finished a century. It was starting another.

25

The home which Andrew Jackson had built and christened and in which he had lived and died sat in its sturdy grace among the maples and catalpas. A double row of cedars, guitar-shaped, bordered the lane up which the General had ridden so proudly to his home. The early morning sun of a September day fell through the leaves and sprinkled splashes of soft quiet silver upon the Hermitage. Everywhere was the lovely sadness of autumn.

The driver sat in the Weaver Cole carriage out by the hitching posts which stood in a deep bay to the left of the carriage house. With old but keen eyes he watched the morning pass. He nodded approvingly at the order about him. Not very long ago the disarray of the place had left him distressed, but now everything was trim and neat. Industry and craftsmanship had defeated decay, turned it back. He nodded his head again. It was most pleasing. Sometimes he dozed but invariably a horsefly came buzzing hungrily, settled and prospected for blood. The horse would stir uneasily, stamping and flinging its tail. The driver's eyes would open slowly, then quickly come to focus upon the gorging horsefly. The hiss of his whip would die upon a sharp crack and a dying horsefly would fall slantingly to the ground. Then he would chuckle and talk a bit to himself.

"Didn't miss. Yes sir, I bin a-killing hossflies nigh onto sixty years, an' I don't miss yet. Yes sir, hossfly, you better stay away from here. I need me a nap." But his eyes instead of closing would stray toward the house. Weaver and Merrie Cole had told him of that wedding breakfast. But his mind was alert and he had pieced most of the details together even before they told him. He knew the Coles so well that they didn't have to tell him things. He just knew.

Let's see now, he'd been working for the Coles more than twenty years. He ought to know them. That made him terribly old. So he skillfully slew a horsefly in defiance of his advancing years. The September sun had grown warmer. The splashes of silver shifted constantly. A little vagrant breeze stirred and some leaves drifted lazily groundward. The hum of voices in the dining room lifted above the lazy sounds of Indian Summer. His right arm moved with sudden precision and the number of available horseflies dwindled by one. The sun mounted higher and the shadows of the trees dwindled. The cry of the plowman walking his autumn furrow in the Tulip Grove fields across the Lebanon Pike was half gay, half plaintive. The driver fitted his voice to an ancient lament of the country churches.

"I'm a pore wayfaring stranger
   And this world is not my home."

The guests at the Hermitage sat and ate their breakfasts, and all were happy and a bit excited. They sat at an improvised table, but the linen and dishes Bettie Donelson had brought from her home, and such was the arrangement that no guest, unless he had knowledge beforehand, would have suspected the crudity which that linen concealed. Felicia Love drew in a deep breath. "Turkey hash," she said in sibilant undertones that carried easily the length of the table. "Where could you get a turkey now?"

"You couldn't, Felicia," answered Bettie Donelson, with a subtle accent upon the *you*, "but to one called, a turkey is not seasonal. It is timeless, my dear, timeless."

They ate "turkey" hash served on waffles, and hot biscuits and blackberry jam. They drank the delectable coffee christened after the city's famous hostelry. They performed the sacred rites of Breakfast at the Hermitage.

Eugene Lewis pushed back his chair and stood. The hum and clatter in the room dwindled into silence.

"I wish to make my best gesture to a gentleman who is not here this morning, and yet except for him we would not be here either. Barksdale Reeves! May the home that he plans to build itself be a happy wedding of old grace and new convenience! May it be the forerunner of a generation of fine homes in a community whose founders committed it to fine homes!"

"When is it to be built?" asked Dr. Fort.

"That depends on when Hunt Justice emerges from his haze."

"Then it will not be built," interrupted Neely Barrow. "I intend for Hunt's haze to remain permanent. He won't emerge."

"I hope this Reeves house isn't going to take all of his time," said Mrs. Felicia Love, querulously. "I want Hunt to start on Martha's house pretty soon. She's coming back next summer to live. She'll stay with me till it is finished, but I hope not too long. She's most distracting to my illnesses. I simply can't be sick decently with her in the house. I want her house built with a haze, Hunt. And I'm no mean judge of the sort of haze that houses ought to be built in."

"Oh, how lovely! I'll guarantee the haze," said Neely Barrow. "Mrs. Love, I see you are wearing your brooch. That's a perfect omen. I'll guarantee Hunt's haze. It's permanent, isn't it, Hunt?"

"At any rate," said Hunt Justice, "you're permanent, Neely Barrow."

"And may I make a gesture?" asked Mary Dorris. "How lovely is a world in which young people may fall in love! But let me get down to my business. My salute to all the fine old homes about the city—to the Capitol, to the Parthenon, to all of them! And especially to the home in which we are gathered, a home which gilds strength and grace with the fine gold of unfading memories."

Outside, the driver was singing something half-sad, half-gay, something etched with a quavering sweetness, something as serene as a mid-September morning, something as radiant with hope as love in the springtime.